SECRETS
of
MALTA

Also by Cecily Blench:

The Long Journey Home

Cecily Blench grew up in Herefordshire and studied at the University of York. She worked for an independent publisher before her debut novel *The Long Journey Home* was published in 2021. She now lives in Bristol and is a freelance writer and editor.

SECRETS
of
MALTA

Cecily Blench

ZAFFRE

First published in the UK in 2024 by
ZAFFRE
An imprint of Bonnier Books UK
4th Floor, Victoria House, Bloomsbury Square, London, England, WC1B 4DA
Owned by Bonnier Books
Sveavägen 56, Stockholm, Sweden

This is a work of fiction. Names, places, events and
incidents are either the products of the author's
imagination or used fictitiously. Any resemblance to
actual persons, living or dead, or actual
events is purely coincidental.

A CIP catalogue record for this book is
available from the British Library.

ISBN: 978-1-80418-178-2

Also available as an ebook and an audiobook

1 3 5 7 9 10 8 6 4 2

Typeset by IDSUK (Data Connection) Ltd
Printed and bound in Great Britain by Clays Ltd, Elcograf S.p.A.

Zaffre is an imprint of Bonnier Books UK
www.bonnierbooks.co.uk

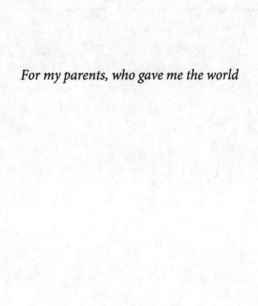

For my parents, who gave me the world

Prologue

London, March 1943

Evening was falling in Whitehall as Dennis Pratchett made his way along the panelled corridor. The lamps had been lit, and the floorboards gleamed in the soft light.

What had seemed to Pratchett to be the hardest winter of the war so far was finally drawing to a close. He felt pale and cold, like a plant kept too long in the dark. Since returning from France with a shrapnel wound three years earlier, he had barely left London and sometimes thought longingly of the world beyond his office, now more distant than ever.

He knocked on Sir Harold's door and waited. Eventually, a voice barked, 'Enter!'

Pratchett went in and saw the old fellow hunched over his cluttered desk. He put down his pen and squinted, wedging his monocle further under a bushy white eyebrow.

'Ah, young Pratchett, isn't it?'

'Yes, Sir Harold. How do you do, sir?'

'Oh, still alive,' said the old man. 'Good heavens, is that the time?'

'Yes, sir, it's nearly six.'

'Been deep in this blasted report,' said Harold. 'One can't complain that we're intercepting so many German communications, but most of them are as dull as ditchwater. This one's about uniform requirements for naval telephonists. Thank God we know how wide their lapels are, that's all I can say.' He gave a hacking laugh. 'What can I do for you, young man?'

'The deputy director thought you ought to see this memo, sir,' said Pratchett, pulling an envelope from his pocket. 'We've received some rather interesting information.'

'Read it to me, if you would,' said Harold, gesturing at the monocle. 'My eyes are tired.'

'Yes, sir. Here it is: *Messages from Berlin indicate knowledge of some of the private proceedings of the Casablanca Conference, particularly the arguments of General Brooke regarding the Italian question. Separate communications over the last few months point heavily to there being a prominent German agent in the Mediterranean. Today we received intelligence from the DSO in Malta that they believe there's a leak in their pipes. Theory: there is a German spy based in or near Malta, possibly inside the intelligence or security services.*'

Harold nodded slowly. 'Any idea who this spy might be?'

'Not yet, sir. The messages about Casablanca referred to buying the information on *der Schwarzmarkt*, or black market, which I thought might be some sort of joke about the source.'

Harold stared at him. 'What did you say?'

'The *Schwarzmarkt*, sir. It's—'

'It is a joke, you're quite right,' said the old man. 'At least, I think so.'

'Sir?'

Harold hauled himself out of his chair and went across to a filing cabinet that stood against the wall. Retrieving a key from his pocket, he knelt down and unlocked the bottom drawer, pulling it open and leafing through the files within, mumbling to himself.

Pratchett waited respectfully. Some people said the old man had lost his touch, but he'd been influential in the establishment of the intelligence service many years ago – a brilliant agent, by all accounts – and the deputy director seemed to trust his hunches.

'Ah, here he is,' said Harold, waving a folder. He clambered up. 'Come and have a look at this.'

The folder was stuffed with closely typed letters, reports, and occasional photographs, but Harold was looking for something in particular. He reached into an envelope pressed between the pages, pulling out a scrap of paper.

'What do you think of this?' He held it out in the palm of his hand.

Pratchett frowned. 'It's a wax seal, sir.'

The wax was a dark blue-black colour, with a scrap of mottled envelope stuck to the back. Pratchett leaned in to look at the image imprinted in the wax. There were sinuous lines, the shape of something coiled, ready to spring, all in the space of half an inch.

'Is it a snake?'

'A snake with a man's head, supposedly,' said Harold, 'although I can't see it myself. It's some sort of damned clever literary reference.'

'Whose seal is it, sir?'

'A successful German spy,' said Harold. 'He operated during the last war, and we heard whispers of him several times during the twenties and thirties. That alone should tell you how successful he was – it's almost unheard of for an agent to operate that long without being caught. Thirty years and we don't even know his real name!'

'What's his code name?'

'Nero,' said Harold. 'Now do you see why I think it's him?'

Pratchett stared. 'It's the Italian for black,' he said at last. 'Black market. *Schwarzmarkt*.'

'Berlin's idea of a joke, I suppose,' said Harold. 'Peculiar sense of humour, Germans. Of course, it might not be him – Nero may be long dead by now. He hasn't been heard of for a few years, to my knowledge.' He pointed a bony finger at Pratchett. 'But we never caught him.'

He thumbed through the folder and pulled out a sheet of paper. 'This is one of the few pieces of evidence linked to Nero, and the only one written in his own hand.'

Pratchett examined the spidery handwriting. It was obviously the last sheet of a longer letter. The first paragraph made reference to shipping movements outside Portsmouth, which meant nothing to him. 'My German's rather rusty. Let's see. *I am* – something – *of service. I shall remain in England and* – messy bit there – *instructions.*' Scribbled under the last line was a snake symbol, like the one on the seal.

'So he spied during the last war,' said Pratchett, looking up. 'But aren't there dozens of men like him?'

'He was one of the best,' said Harold. 'It's as simple as that. Have you heard of Jan Novotný?'

Pratchett frowned, trying to place the name. 'Czech, wasn't he? Assassinated?'

'Czech politician, outspoken against the Germans. Hitler had him killed in 1936. Novotný had a twenty-four-hour guard and was himself a very able fighter. Someone managed to shoot him and get away before the alarm was raised. Rumour had it that the assassin was Nero, which only added to his mystique. That was one of his most high-profile jobs.'

'So he's a German? Or just works for them?'

'We don't know. I always thought he might be English, or at least educated here. During the Great War he almost certainly operated in Britain, as he was leaking intelligence left, right and centre – and it wouldn't have been easy if he sounded like a foreigner.'

Pratchett breathed out heavily. 'So he'd fit in in Malta without any trouble; it's heaving with Englishmen. I wonder what he's doing there – if it is him.'

Harold shrugged. 'He was a spy before he was a killer, and I imagine that's still his main trade. Malta has taken a hell of a battering over the last few years. The place was almost blown to smithereens last year by the Germans and Italians. I wouldn't be surprised to hear that Nero was involved.'

'It's over now, isn't it? The war's moved on.'

'Yes, but what if Nero has his eyes on a bigger prize?' Harold drummed his fingers on the table. 'We're at a critical juncture – the re-invasion of Europe is on the horizon. We can't afford to have a double agent in our midst, especially not one as dangerous as Nero.'

'What do you think we should do, sir?'

Harold frowned. 'Claude won't listen to me.'

'He respects your opinion greatly, sir.'

'Hmm. Tell him I think we should send half a dozen of our best agents to Malta to hunt this fellow down pronto. He'll say he doesn't have the resources, people will grumble, and in the end he'll agree to send someone young and keen out there to have a look and talk to our men on the ground.'

'Who do you think he should send, sir?'

Harold looked him up and down. 'Why don't you go, Pratchett? Look at this dreadful weather. It'll be warm in Malta soon. Lovely place.'

When the young man had left, Sir Harold remained sitting at his desk, staring down at the letter and the wax seal before him.

'Well, well, well,' he said, holding up the seal and peering at it through his monocle. 'Nero's hour has come round at last.' He shook his head, put the folder away and returned to his desk. He scribbled a few notes, frowning and wondering if it was too early for a drink, and then reached for the telephone.

It was answered after three rings. 'Yes?'

'Nero's back.'

Chapter 1

The woman at the corner table was watching the stage with a languid intensity. In one hand she held a drink, and in the other a cigarette holder. She had short dark hair and the pearls around her neck gleamed in the candlelight.

Margarita, singing alone, felt suddenly exposed. It had begun as an ordinary evening. She had performed her main set at the start of the cabaret, and now she had come back to finish off with a few slow, romantic songs. Several couples were dancing, which usually gratified her, but she felt unsettled.

She had been singing at the Phoenix Club in Valletta for nearly a year now, ever since it had reopened after the siege of Malta, and her nervousness in the early days had given way to an unexpected confidence. She could sing, she had always known that, but getting up on stage was another matter. The Phoenix was one of the most exclusive clubs in Valletta, which didn't make it any less nerve-racking.

The war had brought thousands of Allied servicemen to Malta, and at any moment there were hundreds of them on leave, looking for a good time and with money to spend. It helped, she supposed, to blot out the rest of their existence – digging bodies out of flattened houses, rescuing survivors from destroyed ships, defending the island and witnessing their friends die. It was unusual to see a woman come to the club unaccompanied, and those who did rarely went home alone.

Margarita finished the song and began the next, her final performance of the evening. Her eyes moved from table to table and rested again on the dark-haired woman in the corner. She had put her glass down and was sitting bolt upright, her elbows on the table, a small smile lifting the corners of her deep red lips as she watched.

Margarita looked away, fighting desperately to keep her voice steady. She made her way briskly through the song, determined to keep smiling, and ended on a long, high note, blessing her voice for not faltering.

She curtsied deeply as the room erupted in applause and saw the men in the front row stand up to cheer. Flicking her eyes to the corner table, she saw the woman clapping slowly, almost sardonically, her gaze still fixed on Margarita.

Hurrying off the stage, she stumbled to the dressing room and sat down at her mirror, trying to steady her breathing. The Blitz Sisters, a troupe of four British girls, were about to go on stage, tonight wearing matching sailor outfits.

'You were wonderful,' said Angela, adjusting her blue neckerchief. 'They loved you!'

'Thank you,' said Margarita, trying to smile. 'I was a little nervous.' She did not mention that she had almost deserted the stage. That woman! Why was she in the club? Surely she was here to cause trouble! 'Good luck with your set.'

'My husband's in the audience,' said Angela with a wink. 'I'd better make it a good show.'

Margarita stepped out of her silk dress, feeling it catch as she tugged it over her heel. She hung it up and pulled on her blue cotton frock with a sense of relief. Grabbing her handbag, she hurried out into the corridor.

'Ah, Margarita!' Her heart sank as she saw the proprietor striding towards her.

'Hello, Carlo.'

'You were a delight, my dear, as always,' he said, beaming. 'Everyone loved you.'

'You're very kind. I'm just leaving, actually . . .'

'There's someone who wants to speak to you,' he said. Margarita felt her stomach lurch. 'On table six. An English lady.'

'Oh, Carlo, I'm terribly tired. I'm not sure . . .'

'Nonsense, my dear!' he said, propelling her along the corridor. 'You know the rules, Margarita – talking to guests is part of the job.'

'But she's—'

'A woman? So what?' Carlo laughed. 'Perhaps she has exotic tastes. Let her buy you some champagne.'

Hardly likely, thought Margarita. She probably wants to kill me.

They came out into the auditorium. The woman on table six was taking occasional drags on her cigarette and staring at the stage in a rather fixed way, as though lost in thought. It was her – Margarita knew it.

'Go on,' said Carlo, nudging her.

Margarita made her way through the crowd, her heart thumping. As she neared the table, the woman turned to look up at her. She had a piercing stare and, for a moment, Margarita felt as if a spotlight had been trained on her again. She wished she had thought to remove her thick makeup, which felt clownish beside the older woman's subtle glamour.

'Thank you so much for meeting me,' said the woman pleasantly, standing up and extending a hand. 'It's Margarita, isn't it?'

She was forty or so, and good-looking, her dark hair cut in a short, boyish style and her skin tanned, with strong, clear features. Her black silk dress looked expensive. Her voice was low and had the inflections that Margarita knew marked her as a member of the English privileged classes.

'Do you know who I am?' the woman asked after they had shaken hands.

'Yes,' said Margarita, feeling a sense of relief. There. Now there would be no more secrets. 'You must be Mrs Dunn.'

'Call me Vera,' said the woman, sitting back down and gesturing to the chair opposite. 'What will you have?' She beckoned a waiter.

'Oh—' Margarita flailed as she sat down. 'Perhaps a glass of white wine?'

'And I'll have another whisky, please,' said Vera, indicating the empty glass in front of her. 'Talisker, if there's any left.'

The girls on stage began an energetic routine to the 'Beer Barrel Polka', making the men in the audience whoop, while several couples hurried onto the dance floor.

Vera stubbed out her cigarette and heaved a sigh. 'Well, I suppose you're wondering what I'm doing here?'

'Yes,' said Margarita softly.

'I'm not here to make any trouble,' said Vera. 'God knows, that's the last thing I want.' She drummed her fingers on the table. 'Henry is dead.'

Margarita felt her breath catch in her throat. 'What?' She stared blankly at Vera. 'How?'

'That's what I'm trying to find out.'

The drinks arrived and Vera took a sip of whisky. Margarita stared at her wine, feeling unexpected tears starting.

'I'm sorry,' said Vera, sounding surprised. 'I should have been more tactful.' She handed the younger woman a napkin and watched her dab her eyes. 'It must be a shock.'

'It's all right,' said Margarita. She took a sip and sat back in her chair, trying to calm her thudding heart.

'Miss Farrugia – Margarita. May we be candid with one another?'

'Of course,' she murmured.

'Thank you. Let's start again. You had a relationship with my husband Henry last year. That's right, isn't it?'

Margarita nodded numbly.

'And am I right in thinking it's been over for some time?'

'Yes,' said Margarita, surprised at how much she knew.

'Listen,' said Vera, lowering her voice a little, 'I am not interested in salacious details. But I believe my husband has been murdered and I intend to find out the truth.'

'Murdered?' exclaimed Margarita, hushing herself at once. 'Are you sure? What happened to him?'

'Well, you see, I don't know,' said Vera, frowning at her whisky glass. 'His body hasn't been found.'

'Then how—'

'He went missing,' said Vera, 'a few days ago.'

Margarita frowned. 'How did you find me?' she asked abruptly.

'Oh, it wasn't hard,' said Vera with a smile.

'I broke it off months and months ago.'

Vera looked thoughtful. 'Did you know he was married?'

Margarita blushed. 'Not at first, no.'

'I thought as much. When I saw you on that stage – you looked too sweet to be a real *femme fatale*.' Vera laughed softly, but not unkindly.

'What do you think has happened to him?' asked Margarita.

'I suppose he might simply have been kidnapped,' said Vera, 'but if so, he's in great danger.'

'Forgive me for saying this,' said Margarita hesitantly, 'but mightn't he have gone off somewhere with another – another girl?'

'It's possible,' said Vera, 'but I generally knew when Henry was up to something on the side.' She smiled rather bitterly. 'A wife learns to recognise the signs. This wasn't one of those times.'

Margarita was lost for words. 'I'm sorry,' she said at last. 'If it's any – I mean – he was the first . . . I don't make a habit of that sort of thing,' she finished lamely.

Vera shrugged and sipped her whisky. 'I don't blame *you*.' She frowned again. 'Anyway, what I need to know is when you last saw him. You say you broke it off months ago?'

'Yes,' said Margarita. 'In September.' She paused, wondering how much she should tell Vera. It would be easy to say nothing, but a twinge of guilt spurred her on. 'I didn't hear from him again for ages. Until about two weeks ago.'

'What happened?' asked Vera, suddenly alert.

'He was here, in the club,' said Margarita. 'He came for the show and asked me to have a drink with him afterwards. Just a drink.'

She thought back to that evening. She had been surprised to see Henry but relieved, in a way, to know that he was all right. But he hadn't been the same. He was anxious, his hands shaking as he lit a cigarette, glancing over his shoulder.

'Did he say what was wrong?'

'No. He just said he'd received some bad news. I couldn't understand what he meant.' She frowned, trying to remember what Henry had said. 'He asked how I was. I told him I'd just got engaged.'

'Congratulations,' said Vera, raising her glass. 'Nice chap?'

'Very. A submarine captain,' said Margarita distractedly. 'Henry didn't seem to be listening. He finished his drink, ordered another, and then suddenly said he had to go.'

'He didn't say where?'

'No. I think he saw someone across the room – something unsettled him, anyway, and he left. I saw him stop to speak to someone but then he dashed off. It was rather odd.'

'Who did he speak to?'

'A rather tall man – grey hair, heavy features. Dark blue suit. I think I've seen him here before. They didn't speak for long. Perhaps it was an old friend?'

'Perhaps,' said Vera. 'You don't remember anything more about him? Was he English? American?'

'I don't know. I assumed he was Maltese.'

Vera sighed. 'If only I'd been in Valletta.'

'You were away?'

'I'm an archaeologist. I've been back and forth to Egypt for most of the last year, but I arrived in Malta a few weeks ago to set up a dig. I had some foolish idea that being closer to Henry would be good for both of us.' She sighed again. 'Can you remember anything else?'

Margarita thought back. 'He mentioned you,' she said at last.

'Me?' Vera sounded surprised.

'After he said he'd had bad news. He said, "I'm worried about my wife." I thought he meant you were ill or something.'

Vera shook her head. 'I can't imagine what he was concerned about.' She stared at the glass in her hand, then picked it up and drained the last of the whisky.

'Do you think the police can find out what happened?' asked Margarita.

'Possibly,' said Vera. 'But I may have to take this higher.'

Margarita wondered what she meant. She wanted to ask Vera to let her know if she discovered anything, but it seemed like rubbing salt in the wound. Henry's wife probably had no interest in prolonging their acquaintance.

'I must go,' said Vera, wrapping her silk scarf around her neck. 'The concierge at my hotel will be leaving at midnight. He's Swiss and you know what that means: punctuality above all else.' She turned back to Margarita and took her hand. 'It is – truly – a pleasure to meet you, Margarita. I'm sorry the circumstances are so inauspicious.'

Margarita squeezed her hand timidly. 'He told me he was a widower,' she said abruptly. 'I broke it off when I realised he'd lied. I just wanted you to know that I'm not . . .'

'Dear child,' said Vera, her voice catching. 'One's first lover is almost always a disappointment. Forget about it, if you can. You're a sweet girl. Go and marry your captain and live happily ever after, won't you?'

She swept out of the club without looking back and Margarita sank into her seat, feeling utterly drained. She had hoped, after the unpleasantness with Henry, never to have to think about him or her foolish behaviour ever again. But now he was dead. His wife clearly had a steely side and Margarita felt relieved to have avoided its sharp edge tonight. An archaeologist? By comparison, her own life felt small and frivolous.

She finished her glass of wine and stood up, feeling drunk. She hadn't eaten anything since lunchtime. She saw Carlo deep in conversation with a group of men, laughing uproariously, and slipped away.

Chapter 2

Dennis Pratchett arrived in Malta on a warm morning at the end of March. The de Havilland he travelled in did most of the journey during the hours of darkness, to reduce the chances of being shot down by the German and Italian planes that still haunted the Mediterranean, so the first sight he had of Malta was at dawn, on the descent to Ta' Qali airfield.

He had heard it was a dry and barren country, but now, in March, the land looked vibrant, with soft green fields stretching away between crumbling stone walls, under a cloudless sky, almost a paradise after the cold and rain-sodden streets of London.

As they descended, Pratchett began to see ruined buildings and remembered, with a jolt, that until only a few months ago the island had been under heavy bombardment. It was a wonder anything was growing at all. Up close, the country looked battered, frayed around the edges. Even the men who met him on the potholed landing strip looked exhausted.

He had been told to contact Captain Roger Wilson, an intelligence liaison officer who had lived in Malta for ten years, so after a quick wash at his lodgings, he telephoned Wilson, who invited him for tea at his house and to meet his wife. It was charmingly different from the anonymous way of doing things in London. He didn't know the first thing about most of his colleagues' private lives.

Wilson proved to be a mildly eccentric character in his fifties, in shirtsleeves and braces, with a gentle Welsh lilt to his voice. He had a slight build, but his forearms looked powerful, and his sharp eyes clearly missed very little. His wife, taller, with neat grey hair and a smart suit, reminded Pratchett of the fiercely capable aunt who had brought him up.

She gave her husband a tray of tea things to take out to the garden, and they sat talking in the sunshine, Pratchett suddenly feeling very pleased that he had come to Malta.

'You've a lovely home, Mrs Wilson,' he said as he leaned back, looking out across the garden with half-closed eyes. From where they sat, on a hillside above Birkirkara, he could see the distant sprawl of Valletta, and the long, narrow gleam of the sea.

'We're very lucky,' said Mrs Wilson, patting her husband's knee. She put her cup back on the tray. 'Lucky to live here, lucky to do work we both enjoy.'

'Did you say you run a charity?'

'Yes, it's just a small operation,' she said. 'There are so many good causes and we're all struggling for the same resources. But we do what we can.'

She glanced at her husband's watch and stood up, pushing her hair behind her ear. 'I'd better go and get ready for tonight. I'm sure you two will have a lot to talk about.'

'All in good time,' said Wilson, waving a hand vaguely as she went back across the lawn. 'Laura's charity supports the families of dead and wounded sailors and they've been enormously influential.' He sighed. 'It helps to keep busy. Our son, Martin, is a POW in Malaya.'

'I'm sorry to hear that.'

Wilson leaned over and poured more tea, then sat back and looked appraisingly at Pratchett. 'Before we talk about Nero, let's be clear on one thing. Officially, this operation doesn't exist.'

Pratchett nodded. 'That's what I was told in London.'

'Good.' Wilson reflected. 'The DSO here is Major Ede – he's the one who informed London about a possible mole. Apart from him, you and I are the only ones who know that Nero is suspected, and it's going to stay that way. As far as anyone else is concerned, we're working on a routine project to implement better communication between the intelligence and security services and their various departments. All very boring. Got it?'

'Yes,' said Pratchett. 'Where will we be based?'

'For obvious reasons, it was deemed unwise to for us to work at headquarters, so I've taken out a lease on a place in Valletta,' said Wilson. 'Previously a solicitor's office, tucked away but very central. They've already installed a direct phone line and so on.' He gulped at his tea and then set it down. 'I've been given a rundown of what we know about Nero.'

'I've brought copies of a few things,' said Pratchett, pulling out the folder he had cradled carefully all the way from London. 'This is the letter he wrote in 1917, the only sample of his handwriting.'

Wilson put his pipe down and examined the spidery letters, looking admiringly at the quality of the print. 'Very clean.'

'They've got a new machine,' said Pratchett. 'The chap who showed me was very proud of it.' He pushed the file towards Wilson. 'There are some copies of intercepted German messages, that sort of thing, in which Nero is seemingly referred to. Most of them are quite old. It's only this new one, mentioning the *Schwarzmarkt*, that strongly suggests Nero has been reactivated.'

'If, indeed, he ever stopped,' said Wilson, flicking through the papers. 'He turned his hand to assassination during the thirties, I gather, so perhaps he needed a lower profile or was using a different alias.'

'Well, it appears he's back to spying now. We'd better hope that's all he's doing, anyway.'

Wilson nodded and looked up. 'It seems to me that there are two halves of this thing. One is discovering Nero's identity, and the other is looking into the leak in Malta. Of course, if our theories are correct, both will lead us to the same place. But I think it would be wise to tackle them as two distinct avenues.'

'Quite,' said Pratchett.

'I see you've already started looking into Nero the man,' said Wilson thoughtfully, gesturing at the pages of notes on the table, 'so I suggest you focus on that side.'

'I was hoping you'd say that,' said Pratchett with a grin. He looked down at the letter, at Nero's scribbled snake-shaped calling card. 'I'm already fascinated by him.'

'Good,' said Wilson. 'Just don't get drawn in too deeply. In the meantime, I'll look into the Malta side of things. People know me, so they should talk to me. I want to pinpoint where the mole is getting information. We're assuming he works in intelligence or in government, but that doesn't necessarily follow. He's getting access somehow, though.'

'Have you got any leads?'

'Nothing concrete,' said Wilson. 'There are a lot of people up to no good in Malta, but most of them aren't spies. Some of them are just people with pro-Italian sympathies, and there are dozens of smugglers, too.'

'Smugglers?'

'Oh, yes,' said Wilson. 'They bring food and wine from Italy and sell it to the restaurants here.'

Pratchett was rather shocked. 'Doesn't anyone stop them?'

'If that's all they're up to, then we let them get on with it. I like a chunk of decent Parmesan as much as the next man, and Malta's been starving for much of the last few years.'

'I read about the convoys being sunk,' said Pratchett.

Wilson nodded grimly. 'For two years, hardly any supplies got through. To begin with, in 1940, it was just the Italians who bombed the airfields and the ports, but when the *Luftwaffe* joined in the following year, they started attacking everything, including civilian areas. At one point the island was being defended by a handful of rusty Hurricanes held together with packing tape while dozens of Messerschmitts were hammering us day and night.'

Pratchett listened, remembering the Blitz on London, and wondering how people here had coped. It was such a small island, and there was nowhere to run to.

'Most people lived on bare rations for months and months,' said Wilson. 'Thousands of tonnes of food went to the bottom of the Med, and many of those who survived starvation were killed by bombing.'

'What turned the tide?' asked Pratchett.

'Gradually we started to get more Spitfires to Malta,' said Wilson. 'Before that, they were being destroyed before they even arrived. There were other factors, but those combined with the work done by our submarines in destroying German shipping across the Med meant that Marshal Kesselring couldn't afford to continue the siege.' He sighed. 'Anyway. The danger from the air has receded, but now we're at risk on the ground. Where were we?'

'You mentioned smugglers,' said Pratchett.

'Oh, yes. Well, some of the smugglers are our informants – they bring back titbits from Italy. But there are a handful we think may be working with Italian intelligence, so we're keeping an eye on them.'

'Could any of them be working with Nero?'

'It's possible,' reflected Wilson. 'If he's here, then he's almost certainly in contact with the Italians, although the German Abwehr are his employers, or so I understand.'

'Apparently so,' said Pratchett. 'The Abwehr took credit for the assassination of Novotný in Czechoslovakia, and the message mentioning the *Schwarzmarkt* was from an Abwehr station.'

Wilson nodded. 'There's going to be a lot of work to do. Nero could have access to several government departments, and of course there's a lot of sensitive information passing through Malta. There are dozens of people working in security and intelligence in one way or another. Chap called Morton runs our networks in North Africa and he's got several operatives who go back and forth.'

'Could any of them be double agents?'

'No one is above suspicion, sadly,' said Wilson. 'But they're fiercely loyal, from what I understand, and extremely brave.'

He gulped his tea and gestured at the file on the table. 'I'll run you over to Valletta and we can lock this up in the safe. I'll take a look at it tomorrow. Eight thirty suit you to start work?'

In the car on the way back to Valletta, Pratchett looked out at the sparkling sea and decided to go for a swim as soon as possible. By summer, he knew, it would be exhaustingly hot, which would take some getting used to.

If I'm still here, he thought, recalling that he was on a time-limited mission. It was imperative that they caught Nero as quickly as possible, before the retaking of Europe began. But the spy had remained free for thirty years, and somehow he felt sure that it would take longer than a few weeks to track him down.

Chapter 3

So Henry was dead. In the days following Vera's visit, Margarita could hardly believe it. She had hated him passionately after breaking off their affair, feeling miserable and betrayed, until she met Arthur, her submarine captain, and realised that the storm had passed and she was free.

But she had loved him once. Henry Dunn, American, twice her age, a gentle academic with a boyish sense of humour. He was very charming, and he had been kind to her, taking her out for dinner and to the theatre several times before the subject of anything further came up. He was lonely, she knew that, and his little apartment in Sliema was sparsely furnished, matching the widower persona that he had presented that first night at the club.

He was clever, and although even now she felt that he had never *intended* to hurt anyone, he had all the same. His wife was intelligent and beautiful – what had driven him away from her? Was she too cold for him? Was it simply the distance? Or perhaps he was always a cad.

'Weak,' she imagined Vera saying disdainfully.

Margarita was curious about Vera. How could she take his infidelity and death so calmly? She had not seemed at all like a betrayed wife. The whole thing was very strange.

Why was Vera staying in a hotel? That seemed odd in itself, when she presumably lived in Valletta or nearby. She had mentioned a Swiss concierge clocking off at midnight – that narrowed it down to a handful of hotels, as most of them closed much earlier. Allowing her curiosity to win out, Margarita made a list and telephoned two or three until she heard a likely accent.

'Good evening, the Grand Harbour Hotel?'

'Oh – is that Pierre?' Impulsively she put on a Spanish accent, modelled on one of the girls from the club. 'It's Isabella – we met last night?'

'This is not Pierre, madam. I think perhaps you have the wrong hotel.'

'But you are French?'

'Swiss, madam. There are no Frenchmen working here at present. Is there anything I can do for you?'

'No – no, thank you so much. I'll try elsewhere.'

Satisfied, she put down the telephone and stood in the booth, wondering what to do. She now had a good idea of where Vera was staying. Perhaps she could investigate further.

*

The following evening, Margarita stood in the shadows outside the Grand Harbour Hotel, her heart beating painfully fast.

The Grand Harbour was one of the few smart hotels still open after the siege. Most of Malta was surviving on bare rationing, but rumour had it that the dining room still served steaks, fresh vegetables and butter, sourced privately.

It was a cool evening, and a light shower of rain fell as Margarita waited. Should she go in and ask about Vera? To what end? Would it make any difference to know that Vera was who she said she was?

Smartly dressed men and women came and went, descending the steep steps to expensive cars or strolling up into the city towards the bars and restaurants. The immaculate doorman greeted them all, patient and helpful even with the most awkward guests.

After an hour, Margarita was ready to go home, but she lingered, desperately waiting for answers.

At last, she was rewarded. A taxi pulled up and the driver quickly leapt out to open the door. A woman emerged, her jacket slung over her shoulders. Her face was caught in the lamplight as she glanced swiftly around and Margarita saw at once that it was Vera.

She started up the steps towards the hotel and, as she did so, a man got out of the taxi behind her, striding to catch up, a small case in his hand. The young doorman at once swung the door open, greeting them, and they went through, disappearing into the warm light of the foyer.

Margarita gave it a few minutes and then approached the doorman, smiling in what she hoped was a harmless, foolish way.

'Good evening,' she said. 'Was that Gloria Bartolo going in there? The actress?'

'Actress?' he said, glancing back over his shoulder. 'I don't think so, miss.'

'I'm sure it was her!'

'If you mean the woman who just went in, with short hair – she's an English lady called Smith.'

'Oh, how silly of me! I was so excited to see her. I thought the man with her might be famous, too. I was hoping to get an autograph.'

The doorman shook his head. 'No, that's her husband – Mr Smith. She said he'd be arriving today.' He looked curiously at her, smoothing his pale uniform, and obviously feeling he had said too much. 'I'm not supposed to give names out . . .'

'No harm done,' said Margarita, with a smile. 'Thank you for telling me. I'd have felt so silly approaching her and finding I had the wrong person!'

'Good evening,' he said with a nod, and stepped past her to greet another guest.

Margarita walked briskly away, glancing back every so often as she climbed the steep streets towards the city centre, slipping now and then on the wet cobbles. Her heart was still beating wildly but she felt rather triumphant at the success of her little ploy.

It had created more questions than it had answered, however. Why was Vera Dunn staying under the name Smith with a man who was not her husband? It was all too bizarre.

A thought struck Margarita and she paused, glancing into a clothing shop where naked dummies loomed out of the blackness. Henry was dead. Vera was in a hotel with another man. What if she, or they, had killed Henry? He had had an affair, after all, and he was wealthy. Perhaps Vera had wanted him out of the way?

The real question, thought Margarita, as she got into bed an hour later, in her small flat in Floriana, was whether she could prove anything. She closed her eyes, listening to the silence. For two years, she had slept in a bomb shelter almost every night, hearing the carnage above. The worst was over, at least for now. She thought again about Vera. Was it worth looking for answers? Perhaps she should leave well alone . . .

She pulled the blanket over her, glorying in the quiet, and soon fell asleep.

*

'But who is she?' asked the man known as Mr Smith as he poured a drink in Vera's suite and sat down, stretching his legs out with a sigh. He was a few years younger than her, tall with sandy hair and the kind of careless good looks that go largely unnoticed.

'She's one of Henry's girls,' said Vera, throwing her jacket onto a chair. 'I went to see her.'

'Why?'

She shrugged. 'Curiosity. She didn't have much new information, but she's bright and obviously cared about him. Poor little thing. She broke it off when she learned of my existence.'

'Very principled of her,' said Smith, passing her a glass of whisky. He took off his tie and dropped it on the floor.

'Yes, remarkably. I didn't tell her she was one in a long line.'

'But why is she following you now?'

'She's probably suspicious – wouldn't you be? Your former lover's wife turns up out of the blue and tells you he's disappeared. It's a lot to take in. I dropped her a hint about where I was staying, and she clearly followed it up.'

Vera crossed to the window and looked out at the damp night, sipping her whisky. She shivered slightly as the spirit burned her throat, then smiled. 'I think she's got potential.'

'But *what* is she?'

'She works in a nightclub – as a singer,' said Vera, hearing him snort. 'All above board. She's rather good, actually.'

She shook her head, wondering why she had told him about Henry. Smith was, after all, just a colleague. The half-hour in the car together once his boat had docked had been the longest she had spent with him in years. But he had asked after her husband and somehow it was a relief to speak about him to someone she was unlikely to see again after tonight.

Vera turned back to him. 'How does it feel? Getting out?'

He shrugged. 'I'm not needed any more. Tripoli is ours. They'll find a use for me somewhere else – France, perhaps; there's still a great need for agents there. Or perhaps I'll retire.'

'Retire?' said Vera, as if she couldn't comprehend the idea. The years since the war had broken out had been some of the busiest and most fulfilling of her life. The idea of being put out to pasture was disorientating. *What would I do, if not this? Return to archaeology? Try to remember what normal life is like?*

Smith looked at her curiously, lolling back in the armchair. 'What do you want, Vera?'

'Want? I want us to win the war.'

'You must have other wants. Or perhaps needs.' He watched her over the rim of his glass.

Vera laughed. 'I think that's my cue to go to bed.' She picked up a sheaf of papers from the table and turned towards the door.

'I'll get on with my report, then,' said Smith reluctantly. 'Sure you don't want tucking in?'

'Quite sure,' said Vera dryly, downing the last of her whisky. 'Morton's expecting us at eight o'clock sharp. I'll wake you at seven. Good night.'

The bedroom door closed and the lock clicked.

Chapter 4

Syria, 1926

That first journey across the desert was like nothing Vera had ever known. The place was unearthly – an endless flat moonscape punctuated by rolling dunes and craggy rocks. She was disturbed and intoxicated by its wild beauty.

She would never forget those early mornings, when the first light of dawn began to steal across the desert, bathing the ground in a pink glow, the sky a mix of pastels – apricot, lilac, palest rose, baby blue.

They were stiff after sleeping on the sand. Azim made tea on the Primus, and they sat, wrapped in blankets, inhaling the steam and watching the sun rise.

The journey from England had been leisurely. Vera had travelled as far as Istanbul by train with a friend who was going to work as a governess there, and they spent a few delighted days wandering about the city.

The other dig assistants – Matthew, Stanley, and Christian – had come out by ship, and Vera joined them at Haydarpaşa to begin the journey east. Professor Curzon was already in Syria and would meet them in Aleppo.

The train left on time and before long they were travelling along the gleaming coast of the Sea of Marmara. Vera sat with the young men, whom she knew vaguely from Oxford, and listened to their gentle showing off about the digs that they had been on before.

'I found a pagan burial chamber in Orkney when I was sixteen,' said Stanley earnestly, brushing his floppy hair off his forehead. 'Even my father said it would be a good find for a man thrice my age!'

'Wasn't it an accident?' said Matthew slyly. 'Tell them what happened.'

Stanley flushed. 'It's not suitable for present company.'

'Don't let my presence stop you,' said Vera. 'I'm dying to know.'

'He was on a hillside, *answering nature's call*,' said Matthew, mouthing the words, and ignoring the protests of his friend, 'when he fell through the roof of an ancient chamber. Just crashed right through, didn't you, Stan?'

Stanley pointedly refused to answer and folded his arms.

'Oh, come, it can't have been that bad,' said Christian, nudging him. 'Were you stuck there?'

'For a bit,' said Stanley.

'How long?'

'Six hours!' said Matthew, bubbling with laughter. 'And that's not even the worst of it! Shall I tell them the worst?'

'You're insufferable,' said Stanley with a sigh.

'What happened?' asked Vera, as agog as the rest of them.

Matthew glanced at her. 'Cover your ears, Miss Millward.'

'Certainly not.'

'Very well. As he fell through the roof, he broke both wrists and lay there for six hours. When they found him—' Matthew stopped for a breath because he was laughing so much, 'his trousers were unbuttoned and he had to be pulled up to safety in full view of a group of anxious fishwives who'd heard his yells.'

'It isn't funny,' said Stanley, but he could barely make himself heard over the roars of laughter.

'What about you, Miss Millward?' he said coldly once they'd finished. 'What great discoveries have you made?'

'Oh, none at all,' Vera said lightly. 'I'm just interested.'

'Didn't you do rather well in finals?' said Christian.

'I did.'

'Dr Marett told us a woman had got the highest mark of anyone for ten years,' said Matthew. 'That wasn't you, was it?'

'I'm afraid it was.' She smiled and looked out of the window, sensing a mixture of resentment and increased respect. They were crossing a dry, grassy plain. Sheep and goats grazed on either side of the track and, in the distance, she could see mountains rearing up, steep and formidable. They were still in Turkey and she wondered impatiently how long it would take to reach Syria.

'Did Curzon invite you, or did you have to apply like the rest of us?' asked Stanley sourly.

'The latter, of course. I was introduced to him by Dr Hogarth at a dinner and he mentioned that he was looking for assistants for a dig. It all sounded terribly exciting.'

*

In the morning, Vera reached from her top bunk and opened the curtain. The sky was a deep blue already. The elderly Turkish women sharing her compartment offered her tea and sweet pastries, laughing kindly at her attempts to converse with them. Vera sat brushing her long dark hair, drank tea, and watched the landscape jolt past.

Soon after breakfast, they stopped in a narrow mountain pass, where the rocky walls rose up on either side.

'Where are we?' asked Matthew groggily when she bumped into him in the corridor.

'The Cilician Gates!' said Vera, feeling breathless. She stood at an open door and gazed out, trying to drink in this view that for so long had been just a sepia photograph in a book.

The mountains all around were snow-covered, and huge craggy outcrops of rock were ranged alongside the railway line. She felt a lurch of excitement about what lay ahead.

*

After the long journey across Turkey, they crossed the Syrian border and arrived in Aleppo, which seemed rather quiet after the wonders of Istanbul and the Anatolian Plateau. A battered motor car took them to the Baron Hotel, where Professor Curzon had left a message, saying he would meet them for dinner.

After a bath, Vera went for a walk, peering with interest at the ornate carvings on some of the buildings. Flat-roofed houses jostled for space with slender minarets and, in a square, a tall clocktower. It was cool in Aleppo, the onset of winter, and the afternoon sun was low in the sky.

Neatly uniformed gendarmes were patrolling here and there, looking stern, and she swung to avoid them, knowing they would want to escort her back to the hotel.

Following a wider street, she came to a massive stone structure and felt a thrill of recognition: this was the Gate of Victory, built over eight hundred years before and one of the nine gates that guarded the ancient city.

Approaching the Citadel, Vera examined the fort, which stood on a steep slope, the crenellated walls and long ramparts looking much as they must have done centuries before when European crusaders were imprisoned within.

'Alexander the Great was here,' said a soft voice, and she looked round to see an old man pausing beside her. He wore a thick wool coat over his white robe and a knitted scarf was wound tightly around his neck.

'Surely that was much earlier than the fort?' said Vera, gesturing to the squat towers.

He shrugged, unperturbed. 'Before the buildings, yes. Alexander was here twenty-three centuries ago, and he stood upon that hill when he claimed the city.' He spoke in halting but immaculate English.

'Is much of the old city left?'

'It's all here,' he said, pointing to the ground beneath their feet. 'Invaders have come and gone, for thousands of years, but they all end up in the same place.'

'What about the French?' she said teasingly.

He smiled. 'They won't be here for long, either. In the great span of time, their occupation will be as the blink of an eye.'

His face was kind, but there was a strange intensity in the way he looked at her, as if he could read her innermost thoughts.

'You're looking for something,' he said at last. Taken aback, Vera hesitated.

'I suppose I am.'

'Good luck,' he said. 'And be careful.'

'I will,' said Vera, 'but why?'

'You are at a crossroads,' he said simply. 'Choose wisely.'

Vera walked on and found herself passing through the long echoing tunnel of a bazaar. She had forgotten to try speaking Arabic with the man, and was annoyed with herself, but she could not help thinking about what he had said. He was probably just an amateur fortune teller, someone who enjoyed making cryptic predictions to tourists. But he had touched a nerve – she *was* looking for something, after all, she wanted to find treasure or a lost city, something spectacular. Something that would make people sit up and take notice.

'Would you like to look at them more closely?' said a man, and she realised she had been staring at a display of fine silver platters.

'Oh – no, thank you. I am just exploring today,' she replied in Arabic.

He inclined his head. 'You speak my language. Where did you learn it?'

'I've been studying it for four years in England,' said Vera, feeling tongue-tied. 'This is my first chance to practise properly.'

'You will enjoy Syria much more if you can understand,' he said. 'Good luck to you.'

Further on, she came to a display of ancient artefacts – bronze bowls, weapons, carved stone, pieces of armour.

'A ring for you, perhaps, madam?' said the seller, a fat man in a waistcoat and a little felt hat. He, too, wore a warm coat and a pair of leather gloves lay beside him.

'No, but thank you.'

'What brings you to Aleppo?'

'I am an archaeologist,' she told him in Arabic. He looked startled. 'Where are these things from?'

'All found by men who sell them to me,' he said. 'I can assure you it is all done properly. I have certificates.'

'Of course.' She smiled and moved on, searching for a way out of the bazaar.

'Your Arabic sounds excellent, Miss Millward,' said a familiar voice, and she turned to see the Professor. He stood in shirtsleeves, carrying a wooden crate, his black hair ruffled. She felt the heat rise in her face, his gaze seeming to take in every inch of her.

'Professor Curzon!'

'I guessed you might be in the bazaar. I was eavesdropping on your conversation there.'

'I thought the things he was selling might have been stolen,' said Vera as they strolled back towards the hotel.

'They probably are,' said Curzon. 'Every year, things turn up in the bazaar from the digs – not just ours, of course, all of them. We pay well enough, but some men like the thrill of stealing.'

'He said he had certificates, although those are easy enough to forge, I suppose.'

'Exactly.'

Vera felt elated to be alone with the Professor. Ever since first meeting him in Oxford, she had admired him from afar. He was over forty, and though not typically handsome, something about his voice and his muscular physique, not to mention his intellect and obvious ambition, made her pulse race. The feeling was exciting but rather disconcerting.

'Is Mrs Curzon well?' she asked stiltedly, feeling that propriety demanded it.

'I expect she's resting at the hotel,' he said vaguely. 'She doesn't cope very well with the busy streets and so on.'

Then why on earth did she come to Syria, Vera wanted to ask, but instead she made sympathetic noises.

'You did well today,' said the Professor when they reached the hotel. 'I'm glad to see you practising your language skills, and exploring, of course. I like my assistants to have a sense of adventure.'

He smiled and then disappeared, leaving her feeling flushed and pleased by his praise, but a little discomfited too. She was the first woman he had ever selected as an assistant on one of his digs, and she knew that she would have to prove herself.

It took a week to get all that they required together, but at last the truck was loaded with supplies, tools, and building materials. The boys were to ride in the cab of the truck with Laiq, the dig's foreman, and Vera went in the old motor car with the Professor, his wife Dorothy, and Azim, who would be their cook and driver.

At last, they were off.

*

When night fell, Dorothy Curzon chose to sleep in the car, and although Vera was offered a place beside her, she declined. She lay under the stars, rolled in a rug, and listened to the whispering sounds of the desert at night. Ahead of them lay hundreds of miles of emptiness.

All of this, thought Vera, is mine to discover.

She slept deeply and awoke only when she heard Azim clanking around making tea behind the truck as the sky filled with colour.

After a breakfast of porridge, they drove on in the rattling car, Azim stamping ineffectually on the accelerator and muttering under his breath in Arabic. Vera heard only a few phrases, but it sounded as if he was complaining about having to drive such a dreadful car, and why hadn't the Professor bought a new Rolls-Royce when he was obviously so rich?

Curzon, in the passenger seat, spoke to him occasionally, and sometimes pointed things out to his wife and Vera, but most of the time he pored over the maps he had brought with him, pressing them firmly against his knees as the car leapt over bumps in the track.

Dorothy huddled in her corner of the back seat, her eyes closed. She ignored most of her husband's remarks, and instead sat as still as she could, clearly willing the whole ordeal to be over. Vera wondered for the hundredth time why the woman had come and wished uncharitably that she had stayed at home.

Late on the second day, they passed a French military post and drove on to the village of Ithriyia, where they were welcomed by the local sheikh, who owned the land on which they were to dig. The village was surrounded by fields, most of which were bare at this season, the leftover stalks of cut barley being nibbled by goats.

Beyond the village, the land grew wilder again, and dry reddish hills rolled away into the distance. At last, the car stopped, and Curzon pointed to a small hill that looked much like the others.

'This is it.'

Chapter 5

'You seem distracted, Margarita,' said Carlo one night, as she came off stage. He was a kind man, firm at times, and he worked them all hard, but she knew he was trustworthy. Originally from Naples, he had been interned for some months after Italy had joined the war. Once he was freed, and finding his nightclub closed because of the bombing, he had volunteered as an air-raid warden until he was allowed to reopen the Phoenix.

'I'm sorry,' said Margarita. She knew that she had forgotten the lyrics on stage more than once, and that her dancing had been lacklustre. 'I haven't been sleeping well.' She had tried to forget all about Henry, but her mind would not let the matter go, turning it over and over at night. She was curious to know what had happened to him, and what Vera was up to.

'We're all waiting for the bombing to start again,' said Carlo.

'It must be that,' she said, grateful for the excuse.

'We must hope that Malta is spared,' he said wearily. 'If the siege begins again, it will be hard to keep the club running.'

They listened to the band for a few moments. Margarita felt a tug of sadness, without quite knowing what it was for. For Carlo, perhaps, for his business, for all that Malta had lost and would never recover. Some of it was for Henry, she supposed, and took a deep breath. There was no use in thinking about him now.

Carlo patted her shoulder and moved away towards the bar. 'Practise your words, yes?'

In the dressing room, four or five girls sat touching up their makeup and getting changed.

'Oh, thank goodness – Margarita!' Catherine, one of the Blitz Sisters, stood up, wiping lipstick from the corner of her mouth. 'Will you sing in Angela's place tonight?'

'Where is she? Sick?'

Catherine shook her head gloomily. 'No. It's John, her husband – he's been killed.'

Early that morning, somewhere over the limpid blue waters of the Mediterranean, on the approach to Pozzallo, three pilots had been attacked by Italian fighter planes. They were taking photographs of the Sicilian coastline, and it must have seemed, for a few silent hours, that they were the only men in the world. But reality intruded all too soon and the morning was shattered by the rattle of gunfire. Only one of the three had staggered home, his Spitfire and his nerves shredded.

'Will you sing?' asked Catherine.

'Yes, yes, of course,' said Margarita, feeling a lurch of nerves. 'I can't believe it. Poor Angela. Where's her dress?'

Poppy and Flo, the other members of the quartet, appeared. Before long, they were being ushered out under the bright lights, Margarita in a sailor costume that was rather tight and much too short. She did her best to keep up, watching the others out of the corner of her eye to copy their dance moves, but she felt she was doing a poor job of it, and longed for the evening to be over.

She found herself scanning the crowd again, looking for Vera, although there was no reason for her to come back.

There was a man sitting at one of the front tables, part of a large group, who looked familiar. He was tall, with thick features and a grey moustache, and wore a dark blue suit. She realised he was the man she had seen Henry speak to that night, the last time she saw him, as he made his way to the door. The man was smoking a cigar and drinking what looked like brandy from a heavy glass.

'Margarita!' hissed Poppy, and she realised that she had stopped singing for a few bars.

At last, after three or four songs, the set was finished, and they trooped wearily off stage. It was nearly midnight. Margarita changed quickly and hurried through to the bar, which was still heaving.

She scanned around, and her gaze settled on the man in the dark blue suit. He was still talking to his companions, leaning in close, frowning, as one of them spoke in an undertone.

Margarita jumped, feeling a hand on her upper arm. It was Catherine and Poppy. 'We're going to stay for a bit,' said Poppy, shouting over the noise. 'I think we could all do with a drink or two after today – what about you?'

She joined them at the bar, keeping an eye on Blue Suit. 'Have you heard from Angela since it happened?'

'Just a brief message to let us know,' said Catherine, shaking her head. 'I'll go round and see her tomorrow – it's too late to visit now. Poor darling, they'd only been married a year. What a bloody awful thing to happen.'

'How's your chap, Margarita?' asked Poppy, scanning the bottles behind the bar.

'He's on patrol for a couple of weeks,' said Margarita, feeling her insides clench. She was so afraid that something might happen to Arthur, and when his submarine was out on patrol, she could not help imagining everything that might go wrong. What if, like Angela's husband, he went out one day and never came back?

She glanced over and saw that the man in the blue suit was standing up. Was he preparing to leave?

'Actually, I think I'll skip the drink,' she said, seeing the barman turn towards them. 'I've got rather a headache.'

'Perhaps you ought to get some sleep,' said Catherine, looking concerned. 'It's been a long evening.'

The man in the blue suit was heading for the exit. He paused to speak to the girl in the booth, who disappeared for a few moments and returned holding a jacket.

'You're right,' said Margarita, giving them each a brief hug. 'Sorry to rush off.'

'Thank you so much for standing in for Angela.' Poppy smiled wanly.

'Let me know if there's anything I can do to help.' She thought of Angela, white and numb, or sobbing uncontrollably, and felt her heart lurch.

Outside, the man in the blue suit was standing with a few others, still talking intensely, the smoke from their cigars rising up against the navy sky.

Pretending to be rummaging in her bag for something, Margarita paused to listen. They were speaking in Maltese.

'When the shipment comes, we need to be ready,' said Blue Suit. 'I expect you to notify me at once.'

'What about the American?' said one of the other men, so quietly she could barely hear him.

'We'll have to move him.'

One of them glanced at Margarita, and at once she dropped her bag, watching the contents roll out across the pavement.

'Oh, heavens! How clumsy of me!'

The man in the blue suit swung around and watched her scrabbling on the floor with slightly narrowed eyes. Then he turned back and she heard him saying his farewells. The group split up – one or two went back into the club, a few drifted away towards the centre of the city, and Blue Suit and one other walked briskly along Strait Street, then turned onto one of the smaller roads that led downhill towards Marsamxett Harbour.

Margarita hesitated, then followed at a distance. It all seemed rather absurd, now that she was tailing someone through Valletta at midnight. There was no evidence this man had done something wrong; just the fact that she had seen him once with Henry, shortly before he disappeared. Was Henry the American the man had spoken of? Too much to hope for, perhaps.

She kept well back, not wanting to be seen, and followed them through the quiet streets. At last, she saw the two men turn into a side street and paused to let them get a little ahead before hurrying to peer along it. They were gone. The narrow street was a dead end and was completely deserted. They must have gone into one of the buildings, but which one?

Margarita heard the sound of a car nearby and stepped closer to the wall, still trying to see which house it might have been. A hand grabbed her shoulder, and she jumped, turning to find a stocky young man in a dark overcoat.

'Get off me! What do you want?'

'Get in the car, please, miss.' He was English, his face serious.

'What?'

The car she had heard drove slowly up, the headlights dimmed, and the door was flung open.

'Ah,' said another voice. 'The singer.'

'Who are you?' said Margarita, hearing her voice tremble.

'I'll tell you shortly. Please get in.'

'But—'

The man beside her held her shoulder a little tighter, as though he thought she might run away. She looked up at him. He was young, and he looked kind, but appearances could be deceptive. He must be something to do with the man in the blue suit. She was in danger.

Growing tired of her hesitation, the man beside Margarita pushed her gently towards the car, laying a hand on the top of her head to stop it from being bumped on the doorframe. He slammed the door and climbed swiftly into the front.

'Thank you,' said the other man, and she heard the blood roaring in her ears as the car drove away down the cobbled street.

Chapter 6

The black car drove slowly through Valletta. Margarita knew every street intimately, but she felt lost and very afraid.

'I'm sorry to startle you, Miss Farrugia,' said the driver, looking at her in the mirror. 'Roger Wilson. I work for the British government.' He was around her father's age, with grey hair and sharp eyes, and his voice was gentle. 'This is Dennis Pratchett.'

The young man in the passenger seat looked around and smiled at her, holding out a hand. Margarita shook it, feeling dazed. 'I thought I was being kidnapped.'

'No,' said Wilson. 'At least, not by us. You were being followed, though, which is why it seemed wise to bring you in.'

'Followed? By whom?'

'The man you were tailing – do you know who he is?'

'The man in the blue suit? No. I believed—' Margarita hesitated. 'A friend of mine has gone missing. I think the blue suit man may have been involved. Who is he?'

'His name is Matteo,' said Wilson, after a pause. 'He's a smuggler – he buys goods from towns up and down the Italian coast and sells them in Malta for a high price.'

'What did you mean, that I was being followed?'

'Some of Matteo's men were following you, as you were following him. And we were following them – for reasons that are unimportant just now. We made quite a procession.'

Margarita thought about all this. Wilson looked kind, but she was wary of him. Perhaps he was involved in Henry's disappearance. She felt a jolt of alarm, and wondered how on earth she was going to get away from these men.

'Are you the police?'

'Not exactly,' said Wilson evasively. Pratchett, beside him, pulled out an identity card and passed it to her. It told her very little, except that he was a civil servant attached to the Foreign Office. 'But we do have a certain amount of authority here.'

Margarita passed the card back, feeling even more confused. 'This Matteo. If you know he's a smuggler, couldn't you arrest him?'

'We could, although we've bigger fish to fry at the moment. In the meantime, he's very useful – a number of his men pass information to us from their trips to Italy.'

'Was that his headquarters?' she asked, jerking her head back.

'It's one of his places,' said Pratchett. 'He keeps most of his goods in a cave up the coast near Marsascala, or so we believe – boats come in and out at night.'

Margarita looked at Wilson, who was now frowning slightly, his bony face sombre in the half-light as he drove slowly through the city. She got the impression that Pratchett had told her a little too much.

'What do you want with me?' she said at last.

'Firstly, I wanted to warn you off Matteo,' said Wilson, glancing in the mirror. 'Leave him to us. Secondly, you might be able to help us.'

She stared at him. 'Help you?'

'If you're willing, of course – you can say no,' he said, glancing at her in the mirror. 'But I hope you'll do your bit.'

'Are you certain you've got the right person?' said Margarita doubtfully. 'I'm not sure if I can be of any use.'

'You may be surprised,' he said. 'We shan't ask too much of you. But this is a war, and we need as many good people on our side as we can get.'

'I applied to work with the RAF plotters a couple of years ago,' she said, trying not to sound resentful. 'They turned me down. Is that how you found my name?'

'Something like that,' said Wilson. 'You work at the Phoenix Club, don't you?'

'Yes. What is it you want me to do?'

'Just keep your eyes peeled,' said Wilson. 'You're well placed to listen in on conversations at the club – it's a hotbed of illicit activity. Look out for unusual interactions, strangers, rumours.'

'Are you looking for someone in particular?'

'We're interested in everything,' said Wilson, after a pause, and she knew at once that she had put her finger on something. He was hunting a specific person, but he wasn't going to tell her who – at least not yet.

'Will I be in danger?'

'It's possible,' said Wilson gently. 'But we don't think the men following you saw your face this evening, so they shouldn't trouble you. To be sure you're not recognised, don't wear that dress again any time soon. Just keep your eyes and ears open.'

'All right. What about the blue suit man?'

'He may be of interest,' said Wilson, 'but don't go following him again, all right? Just make a note of who he speaks with, who his regular friends are, that sort of thing. Stay away from him. And don't go off alone again.'

She felt the car slowing and noticed with surprise that they were nearing her apartment in Floriana. Somehow she had assumed they were taking her to some secret interrogation cell. How had they discovered her address?

'Here we are, Miss Farrugia,' said Wilson, and the car pulled up beside her building. Pratchett jumped out and came around to open Margarita's door, smiling.

She looked at Wilson, suddenly unsure. 'I can go?'

'Of course. We'll see you safely inside.'

'How do I contact you? If I have information?'

'We'll be in touch,' said Wilson. 'But if you're desperate, telephone this number.' He handed her a business card. 'And please don't tell anyone – anyone at all – about this. Understood?'

Margarita nodded and climbed out of the car, fumbling in her bag for her keys.

'Good night,' called Pratchett, and she waved uncertainly before unlocking the front door. She looked back, but the car didn't seem to be in a hurry to leave, so she closed it and went upstairs.

Once she had the light on, she peered out of the window and saw the car purr slowly off down the street.

Margarita sat on her bed, chewing her lip as she glanced through a letter from her father, hardly able to focus on the words. There were so many questions she ought to have asked. It seemed that she had agreed to work as an informant, and while it was gratifying to think that she might be able to make some small contribution to the war effort, and Wilson and Pratchett had been very friendly, what would they do if she failed them?

Something was nagging at her, and as she finally collapsed into bed at three in the morning, she realised what it was. She had mentioned that she was looking for someone who had gone missing, but she had not mentioned Henry's name, and at no point in their conversation had Wilson asked. Either he thought it was insignificant, or he already knew.

*

The next evening, Margarita opened the door to find her fiancé, Arthur, standing outside, grinning and clutching a bottle of wine.

'Arthur! What are you doing here? I thought you were away for weeks!'

'Engine trouble,' said Arthur, sounding delighted about it, and she flung her arms around his neck. 'We had to turn around. Not much I can do to help while it's being fixed, so I've taken a twelve-hour pass.' He looked suddenly uncertain. 'You don't mind?'

'Of course not!' said Margarita, her stomach fizzing with happiness. 'I'm so glad to see you.' She led him inside and closed the door, then hugged him harder.

'Is everything all right, my darling?' he said, kissing the top of her head.

'It is now.' She took the bottle of wine and ran a sinkful of water to keep it cool. 'Where did you get this?'

'One of the pilots brought back a planeload of booze from Cairo,' said Arthur. 'Don't mention it, will you?'

'Of course not,' she said indignantly. He took her hand and kissed her deeply again, and she felt her stomach flutter. She looked up at him and examined his face – not as pale now as when he had first arrived in Malta from England, his nose dotted with freckles, his blue eyes always carrying a hint of laughter. He was so unlike Henry, and she was grateful for it.

As Margarita prepared supper, she watched Arthur potter around the flat, noting his pleasure at being back on land. Arthur was twenty-five, like her, but sometimes seemed much older. He took the safety of his crew very seriously and was, by all accounts, an excellent captain, but she sensed that he was not made for life on the waves.

'I'll be glad when this is all over,' he said, as if he had read her mind, as he sat in an armchair, his feet up on a stool. 'I'll buy a pair of slippers and a pipe.'

'I could get you some slippers,' she said. 'Why not keep them here?'

'Wait till the war's over,' he said. 'Might be bad luck when I've still got to go to sea.'

She had met him at work, of course, and was taken at once by the serious young English captain who didn't seem at all at home in a nightclub. Arthur had grown up in a small village in Yorkshire and was homesick in the navy, so far away from his family.

'Until I met you,' he told her later that night as they lay in bed, her head resting on his chest.

'We don't have to stay here after the war, though,' she said. 'I'd like to see England when we get married.'

'We'll have a cottage,' he said, 'somewhere pretty. Cumbria, perhaps, or near my parents in Yorkshire. It rains a lot, but the views are beautiful. We could have a little farm. Or we could go to London for a bit, live the city life.'

'What will I do?'

'You could keep singing,' he said, stroking her hair. 'You've got a wonderful voice, Margarita – there must be opportunities in England. There are theatres and concert halls, good ones.'

'I don't know,' she said, listening to an air-raid siren howling somewhere across the city. 'I don't think I'll want to be a singer forever.'

'Work not going well?'

She thought of the club and the men from the government who had recruited her, of Vera, and Henry and the man in the blue suit. It seemed awful not to tell Arthur about any of it, but she had promised, and knew that it must be kept secret. When this is over, she swore silently, I will tell him everything.

'Work's all right,' she said at last. 'Quite busy, though.'

Arthur ran a hand idly over the curve of her naked hip, and she felt desire reawakening as he pulled her to him.

Chapter 7

In a small village on the southern coast of Sicily, a workman stood on a ladder, painting over a sign that had hung there for three generations. Soon the leaping red fish and the name 'Marino's' were obscured by a layer of thick white paint.

'What do you mean, closing?' said Isaac Cardona, as he turned to the proprietor.

'Look, I'm sorry,' said Marino, running a hand through his white hair. 'I know it's bad for you. I have other suppliers, too, and it's going to hit them hard.'

'I've just bought a new boat,' said Cardona. 'Do you have any idea how much motorised boats cost? I paid for it on the basis that my contract with you would continue.'

'I know. I really am sorry.'

'There aren't many other restaurants open.'

'I know. I'll ask around my contacts and give you a reference,' said Marino wearily. 'You're a good, reliable fisherman, Cardona – and a friend. God knows I don't want to hurt your family. I'll pay you up to the end of the month.'

'But why now?'

'My health has been bad for a while,' said Marino evasively. 'You know that. My wife is worried I'll have another heart attack.'

'Come on, Marino. That can't be the only reason.'

The old man sighed and looked around. 'This goes no further, you hear?'

'Of course.'

'My son-in-law was killed a week ago in North Africa.'

'Oh,' said Cardona, feeling deflated. 'I'm sorry.'

Marino inclined his head. 'My daughter is alone and grieving in Palermo with five young children. My wife has already gone to stay with her. We've decided to move there to help with the little ones. I'll get work of some sort in the city.'

Cardona nodded, aware that his own misfortune at the loss of business was nothing compared to Marino's family tragedy. 'Your daughter needs you,' he said at last. 'I am sorry about the restaurant, though – you've built a fine reputation and I hate to see it go to waste.'

Marino shrugged. 'Me too. Maybe in a few years, when the children are older . . . But for now – well, Sicily may be invaded by the Allies in a few months, if the war in Africa is lost. I'm better off without a business tying me down.'

He patted Cardona on the shoulder. 'I appreciate all you've done for the restaurant, and I hope business picks up soon.' He held out a hand. 'Good luck, Cardona.'

'And to your family,' said Cardona, meaning it. He watched the old man hurry back inside, hitching his braces up. Sighing, he walked along the seafront to the jetty. The tide was high and the boats bobbed gently.

Reaching his boat, the *Zafferano*, he sat on a bollard and reached out a hand to stroke the wooden side, warm in the morning sun. He had saved for the deposit on this boat for years, and it was the best fishing vessel now in all of San Leone. But what good was it if there was no one to buy the fish he caught?

'Signor Cardona?'

He glanced around to see a man approaching along the jetty, shading his eyes from the sun. He was older than Cardona, perhaps in his late fifties, with a strong nose and thick black hair, dressed in an elegant suit. He nodded a greeting.

'My apologies for bothering you, Signor Cardona. What a beautiful boat you have. Is it new?' There was something oddly formal in the way he spoke.

Cardona nodded. 'I bought it two months ago.'

'It must be very profitable.'

'It *was*. I've just lost my main customer.' He looked curiously at the man. 'How did you know my name? You're not a local, I don't think.'

'I confess that I overheard some of your conversation with Signor Marino,' said the man. 'And I may have a business proposition for you. My name is Leonardi,' he added, thrusting out a hand.

Cardona shook it. 'A business proposition? Do you have a restaurant?' Suddenly he felt more optimistic.

'Not exactly,' said Leonardi. He looked at his watch. 'I'm late for an appointment. Would you be able to come to my house this afternoon? It's just outside Agrigento. The third left after the Temple of Juno if you're coming from this direction – you'll see a palm tree by the gate. Villa Concordia.'

'I think I know it,' said Cardona. It wasn't far, and the prospect of a new customer was too good to pass up. With luck, he might have something sorted by the end of the day and could reassure his wife Adelina that they were not about to be forced into penury.

'Shall we say three o'clock? I'll be home by then.'

They shook hands again and Cardona watched him hurry back along the jetty.

*

Cardona climbed out of his van and looked around the gravelled yard that lay in front of the Villa Concordia. Along the edge of the house ran a wooden pergola, over which thick grapevines dangled. Large pots planted with lilies and irises were placed on every corner, and looking up, he saw flowers blooming from window boxes and out of cracks in the walls.

He went towards the front door, but heard his name called and saw Leonardi emerging from the side of the house.

'Thank you for coming, Signor Cardona,' he said. 'Let's go round the back – I like to sit on the terrace when it's this sunny. What will you have – beer?'

'If it's not too much trouble,' said Cardona.

They went around the house, passing heavily scented azaleas, and came out onto a rough stone terrace, which overlooked a steeply sloping lawn set among the trees. He could see the glint of the sea a few miles away.

Leonardi disappeared briefly into the house and then returned, gesturing to Cardona to sit on one of the wooden chairs that looked out across the lawn.

'This is a beautiful place,' said Cardona. 'You must have worked hard on the house and garden.'

'I have the previous inhabitant to thank for that,' said Leonardi. 'I'm just renting it for a while. I've been here a couple of months.'

'It must take some upkeep.'

'There's a gardener who comes in part-time, and I've a maid and a cook in the house. Once this place would have had a whole team of staff to look after it. We live in straitened times, sadly.' Cardona listened to Leonardi's voice and wondered where he was from. He could tell the man was not Sicilian, but otherwise his accent was unfamiliar.

A young maid emerged from the house, nodding shyly to Cardona as she did so. She placed two glasses of beer and a bowl of nuts on the table.

'Thank you, signorina,' he said. She hurried back inside.

'She can't hear you,' said Leonardi. 'She's deaf – mostly, anyway. She and the cook seem to have some sort of secret language. Very efficient, though, and that's all I ask. Go ahead,' he said, passing one of the beers.

'Cheers,' said Cardona, and they clinked glasses. He took a gulp, finding the beer ice-cold.

'I'm sorry about the restaurant,' said Leonardi. 'It was one of the best in Sicily, or so I've been told. Do you have other customers for the fish you catch?'

'Yes, a few,' said Cardona. 'I supply several shops and cafés in San Leone and Agrigento. But none of them require the quantity that Marino got through, and of course people are being careful what they spend these days.'

'May I ask where you're from?' said Leonardi. 'You're not Italian, I believe?'

'I'm Maltese,' said Cardona. 'But I've lived in San Leone for ten years.'

'Ah, then I guessed correctly,' said Leonardi with a smile. 'I'm fond of Malta – a delightful country.'

'It's difficult,' said Cardona, thinking of the war.

'Do you ever go back there?'

'Occasionally,' said Cardona. 'I go to see my mother and do some fishing at the same time. Not as often as I would like. I have to be discreet now, of course, since the war began.'

Leonardi nodded. 'I hope my business proposition may be of interest, then.'

'What do you have in mind?'

Leonardi gulped his beer and then leaned forward, his elbows on the table, and lowered his voice.

'My employers have certain business interests in Malta. Naturally, things are rather difficult at present. They have tasked me with finding someone to take occasional passengers and small deliveries to Malta. It would not be more than once or twice a month, generally overnight.'

'Deliveries?' said Cardona cautiously.

Leonardi smiled. 'It's nothing of any great value, but we have to operate quietly due to the – ah – political situation.'

This sounded a lot like smuggling to Cardona. He didn't want to press the point, but it was essential that he knew what he was getting into. 'We are talking about business being done out of sight of the authorities?'

'Something like that,' said Leonardi. 'Discretion is very important. We were using a Maltese fellow for a while, but his situation has ... changed. I'm looking for someone to take his place. I'd rather have someone based in Sicily, out of sight of the British.'

Cardona thought about this. 'All I would have to do is take things, or people, on my boat now and then?' He could barely believe what he was saying. Was he really going to work as a smuggler?

'Exactly. We would pay you a retainer. Tell me, what was the value of your weekly order from Signor Marino?'

Cardona named a sum. 'It varied a little depending on what was available,' he added.

'Understood. Well, I think we could afford to pay you the same each week, whether or not you are needed. How does that sound? And, of course, you are welcome to fish if it's necessary to wait. I'd also be happy to cover any unforeseen costs that arise.'

Cardona glanced out at the lush garden. One day, he would create a garden like that for his children to play in. He imagined the little ones running in and out of the flower beds, sniffing the roses, splashing in the fountain, before remembering the mound of debt he had incurred to buy the *Zafferano*. If he did not take this deal, he would never pay it off.

'It seems like a lot of money for not very much work,' he said. 'Are you sure this makes sense for you?'

'We are willing to pay a premium for a man who is reliable, discreet, and has a fast vessel,' said Leonardi. 'Money is a secondary consideration here.'

'Very well,' said Cardona, although the guilt hummed at the back of his mind. 'I will make my boat available for trips to Malta whenever you need it.'

'That is pleasing to hear,' said Leonardi, and shook his hand. 'I cannot tell you much, as I'm sure you'll understand, but the work we are doing is important. It may even help to hasten the end of the war.'

'That is something I can support, signor,' said Cardona, feeling brighter. Perhaps they were not just common smugglers, after all. Perhaps there was more at stake.

'Are you a political man, Signor Cardona? I imagine your loyalties are rather conflicted while Italy is at war with Malta and her British masters.'

He shook his head. 'I am just a fisherman, signor. Italy is my home, now. All I hope is that in the end Italy and Malta will be at peace again.'

'Agreed,' said Leonardi, clapping him on the shoulder. 'I think we will work together very well.' He frowned. 'I hope you understand that this work may be dangerous. The British are constantly on the alert for vessels travelling between Malta and Sicily.'

'I understand,' said Cardona. 'I will do what I can to be unobtrusive; if questioned, I am a Maltese fisherman. I can give my mother's address if anyone asks.'

'Perfect.'

'Do you have a first trip in mind, signor?'

'I do,' said Leonardi. 'Next Thursday evening. I will come with you this time. There's a small abandoned private jetty just beyond Zingarello. Do you know it?'

'Yes, I think so.'

'I would like you to pick me up there at around five in the evening.'

'Of course.'

'I have a small piece of business to deal with near Marsascala. It shouldn't take more than a couple of hours, and then we can return. Will that cause any problems for you?'

'No,' said Cardona, wondering what he ought to tell Adelina. 'I am often away fishing all night. In fact, I will probably stay out fishing after I bring you home, if you have no objection.'

'Not at all,' said Leonardi. 'The best cover story is one that isn't really a cover.' He smiled. 'When we get to Malta, I'll show you a couple of places where I may ask you to drop things off in future. I shan't be coming often.'

'Very well.'

'Your wife,' said Leonardi, sounding hesitant. 'I'm sure you trust her, but it's important that you tell no one about what you're doing, including your family. Is that understood?'

'Yes, signor,' said Cardona. 'I will tell anyone who asks that I am away fishing. If it becomes known that I have been to Malta – well.' He spread his hands. 'I am Maltese.'

They walked back around the house and crunched across the gravel. 'Oh, and about the money,' said Leonardi. 'I will pay you in cash each Monday. Is that agreeable to you?'

'Of course, signor.'

'I'll have someone drop it off. You're usually out at the jetty around lunchtime, aren't you?'

'Yes. If I'm not there, it can go under the seat of my boat. It will be safe – people are very honest around here.'

'I've noticed that,' said Leonardi. 'It makes a pleasant change from the lying and cheating one encounters elsewhere.' He looked out across the bay, breathing in deeply in the stiff breeze. 'I like it here.'

They shook hands and Cardona drove slowly between the stone pillars. In the mirror, he could see Leonardi wandering back to the house. He paused by the front door and pulled down a rose to sniff, before the van rounded the corner and he was out of sight.

Chapter 8

Arthur left early, after hearing that the engine of his submarine, the *Tenacious*, had been fixed, and Margarita's heart ached. He would be away for a fortnight at least. But it would be hard to keep what she was doing secret from him – perhaps it was for the best that he was out of the way.

He was aware that she had had a lover before him, but she had avoided telling him Henry's age or the fact that he was married. Even Arthur, she thought, might recoil at that, although she knew she would have to tell him one day. He would be even less pleased to hear that she was now investigating Henry's apparent murder.

I'm not really investigating, Margarita told herself. Just ... curious. She liked things to be tidy, and this most certainly was not.

'What about the American?' one of the men outside the Phoenix had asked, and she felt certain they had been talking about Henry.

Roger Wilson had not asked any further about her reasons for tailing Matteo, the man in the blue suit. She supposed she ought to talk to him about Henry at some point, but it was rather an embarrassing story.

She thought about Matteo. Pratchett, Wilson's colleague, had mentioned that he kept smuggled goods at a place along the coast near Marsascala. What if they were keeping Henry there? She could go there by bicycle and have a look. I need the exercise, she thought, knowing it was an excuse.

*

Margarita marched along the low clifftop, following an animal track that she hoped led down to the rocks. She had spent the day exploring the coastline near Marsascala, beyond Triq il-Wiesgħa Tower, and had found a few caves, but they were all empty. Each time she had had to scramble back up to her bicycle, getting hotter and more disillusioned as the day wore on.

Margarita paused for a moment to look out at the sea, which gleamed bluer than ever in the bright spring sunshine. She had forgotten her sunglasses and found herself squinting in the glare from the waves.

The track led downhill, and in the distance, an expanse of flat rocks became visible, just above sea level. Arthur had complained that Malta had no beaches, but Margarita had taken him to one of her favourite swimming spots, where they swam off warm rocks in clear water, watching colourful fish dart beneath their feet, and he had admitted that perhaps this was better.

'Almost as nice as Whitby,' he said, laughing, and she laughed too, although she had no idea where Whitby was or what it was like.

As she clambered down, she could see two people standing on the flat rocks. One of them was wearing a yellow shirt and was much shorter than the other. They were talking, but she was too far away to hear anything.

Clinging onto the dry shrubs that bordered the path, Margarita descended as quickly as she could, grazing her ankles on the rough rocks. The path wound around and she could no longer see the people on the rocks.

At last, the path levelled out and she emerged at the back of what she had begun to think of as the beach, although it was made entirely of rock.

The people she had seen talking were gone, but she could see the taller of them making his way along the rocks. She followed at a distance – and then blinked. He had disappeared. Going closer, she saw that set into the cliffs was a narrow entrance shaped rather like a keyhole. It was dark inside, and she guessed that it led into a wider cavern.

Keeping as close to the cliff as possible, Margarita edged towards the cave, keeping a watch for any movement. Her heart beating fast, she peered gingerly into the tunnel entrance, and saw a rough passage curving back into the hillside. A handmade sign said 'FALLING ROCKS – DO NOT ENTER' in Maltese and English.

Stepping around the sign, she tiptoed along the passage, trying to control her breathing. She came to a cavern and saw piles of large wooden crates, most of them empty. Cigarette butts were scattered on the pebbled floor, which was scuffed by shoe marks. Surely this was where Matteo kept his stolen goods. What else might he be keeping here?

Margarita sniffed, breathing in a damp smell, but there was something else, something familiar, although she could not think what. Then it occurred to her that it was cigar smoke, and she recognised it because Henry had always smoked cigars. She didn't know enough about cigars to know if it was the same brand or if all cigars smelled like that, but it took her back in a moment to the evenings with Henry in his flat.

Suddenly she heard a man's voice, rather muffled, somewhere deeper into the cave system, and an answering voice.

They drew closer, until it sounded as though they were just around the bend, and her nerve broke and she bolted out of the cavern.

Emerging onto the beach, Margarita ran as fast as she could to the path where she had descended, not daring to look back at the cave entrance. Her breath tearing at her throat, her heart pounding, she scrambled upwards, feeling her hair catching on sharp shrubs and tearing the hem of her dress.

At last, she reached the top and made her way back to where she had left her bicycle. She sank down beside it and put her head between her knees, waiting for her breathing to return to normal.

'That was foolish,' said a voice, and Margarita spun around to see Vera sitting on a rock nearby.

'It was you!' she exclaimed, recognising Vera's yellow blouse. 'I saw you talking to one of the smugglers – you're working with Matteo!'

Vera smiled thinly. 'You're clever, Margarita, but in this case you're completely wrong, I'm afraid.'

Margarita stared at her, feeling angry and frustrated. 'I don't believe you. They know something about Henry, and you do too. Perhaps it was you who killed him?' She imagined Vera standing behind Henry on a clifftop and coolly pushing him off, or slipping poison into his bourbon, or stabbing him as he slept. Oh, yes, she was capable of it.

'I didn't kill Henry,' said Vera impatiently. 'Don't you think I would have done it years ago if I was upset about him sleeping with anything that moved?'

Margarita blushed. 'Then what are you doing here? I saw you at the hotel – Mrs Smith, they said you were called.'

'He's a good boy, that doorman,' said Vera. 'So helpful. Did he tell you everything you wanted to know?'

Margarita spluttered and was silent.

'I can't tell you exactly what I'm doing,' said Vera, 'but you can rest assured that it's all for a good cause. The man I was talking to is an informant, part of a smuggling ring.'

'And Henry?'

'Collateral damage, sadly,' said Vera. 'At least, I think so. I haven't got the whole picture yet. When I find out, I'll tell you.'

'Will you?' asked Margarita, surprised.

'Of course,' said Vera. She looked around. 'We ought to leave. Better not to be seen here.'

Wheeling her bicycle, Margarita walked beside Vera, her thoughts a mass of unanswered questions. They followed a narrow farm track between fields, until it passed a stone chapel with a little domed tower. A battered car was parked on the verge.

'This is me,' said Vera. 'I'd offer you a lift but we shouldn't be seen together in the city.'

'I'll be fine cycling,' said Margarita.

'All right.' Vera walked around to the front door and opened it. She looked back at Margarita. 'You ought to leave this alone, Margarita. It isn't safe and I can't protect you if you get involved.'

'Protect me from what?' she asked, frustrated.

'You've stumbled on a dangerous game. Matteo isn't the enemy.'

'Then who is?'

'Pray you never find out,' said Vera, getting into the car. She slammed the door and sped off.

Chapter 9

Syria, 1926

The first week after their arrival was spent setting up the camp at Tell Ithriyia. Two years earlier, Professor Curzon had done a survey of the area, finding evidence of an Assyrian settlement, and had begun mapping out the ruins. Shortly afterwards, Syria had been engulfed by revolution, and he had been forced to delay his return.

The lines of the dig had disappeared under the sand, but Curzon seemed unsurprised and began to organise things with furious energy. On the second day, a procession of men arrived to sign up as labourers, and Curzon oversaw their enlistment as his foreman, Laiq, made the necessary arrangements.

'They don't look very enthusiastic,' observed Vera, standing beside the Professor as a straggling line of men approached Laiq, who sat behind a tea chest serving as a table.

'They were rather suspicious about the whole business,' he said. 'They usually trade in goods and food. "What use is money to us?" they said when I came last time.'

'But you talked them into it?'

'I pointed out that they could use the money to buy more goods, or save it for their children.'

'They are foolish country men!' muttered Laiq, shaking his head.

'Enough, Laiq,' said Curzon. 'I'm sure we seem just as foolish to them.'

Laiq pressed his lips together and said nothing, writing carefully in the ledger as the next man approached the chest.

'Are there enough?' asked Vera.

'Not yet. More will come when they see the digging start and see that the others are being paid handsomely for their finds.'

Next to enlist was a boy of about twelve, wearing a tunic that was much too big for him. He had large intelligent eyes and corrected Laiq's spelling of his village name on the ledger, which made the man scowl. The boy laughed and caught Vera's eye, looking away quickly and then glancing back when he saw that she was smiling too.

'You can go, Mohammed,' said Laiq, sounding disgruntled, and waved his hand. The boy bowed deeply and then ran off, his bare feet dancing across the dry ground.

Their camp was based for now around a large tent, divided into rooms, with smaller tents for sleeping off to one side, well away from the dig site.

'Will you come and tell us where you want things in the main tent?' said Vera. 'The boys have started arranging the workroom, but you ought to see it first.'

Curzon appraised her for a moment. '*You* can do it,' he said at last. 'You know what we need and how we're planning to work. I leave it in your hands.'

Surprised but gratified, Vera marched back to the tent, taking off her hat and feeling the sweat on her forehead. It felt warmer here than it had in Aleppo, despite the lateness of the year, and the midday sun was hot. She saw Dorothy Curzon sitting just inside her tent, reading a book, but she did not look up.

Stanley and Matthew were unpacking boxes of equipment and laying it out on folding tables.

'Hello, Vera,' said Matthew eagerly. 'Any news on how we're to set things up?'

She surveyed the large tent, which was split into rooms with hanging walls. 'We'll keep this room for cleaning, as it's near to the door – it'll be easy to bring water in. That room at the back should be for storing what we find when it's clean. And we'll make a darkroom eventually, although that will have to wait until the brick workroom is built.'

'We ought to have somewhere we can lock,' said Stanley, wiping his hands on a handkerchief. 'In case we find anything valuable.'

'We'll have the workroom built soon enough,' pointed out Matthew, heaving another box onto the table. 'I saw Azim unpacking tubs of whitewash, and the bricks are arriving tomorrow.'

'Over there, we ought to have a temporary workroom,' said Vera. 'With as many tables as we can get our hands on.'

'Who put you in charge?' asked Stanley grumpily.

'Who do you think?'

He shook his head. 'I should have known.'

Vera turned sharply to look at him. 'What do you mean by that?'

'Oh, nothing . . .'

'I'm here because I'm qualified to be here. Perhaps if you showed an ounce of initiative, you might be in the Professor's favour, too.'

'Vera, he didn't—'

'Never mind.' She grabbed a case of cleaning supplies and hauled it through to the next room, her face flushed with fury.

*

Before long, the dig was up and running. The first bricks of the workroom had already been laid, and it would not be long before it was in use. Vera was pleased that they would keep sleeping in tents – there was something thrilling about going to sleep under canvas and waking to see light creeping through the thin walls.

She went out to the dig site early each morning with the others. They took the car if there was much to carry, and otherwise walked the half mile to the site, following a path worn by car tyres and footprints, seeing the mound around which the dig was based rising before them.

Many of the workmen came from villages a long way away, starting their walk by starlight, and arrived just as the sun was breaking over the horizon.

'How do they do it?' asked Christian on the first day, as he set up his camera to begin documenting the dig. 'When they don't have watches or clocks?'

'One of the mysteries of the East,' said the Professor, watching them with pride. 'They are told to get here at sunrise, so sunrise is when they get here.'

The men began work at around seven, then stopped for breakfast at nine before continuing. They worked in gangs, one or two of them brandishing pickaxes to break the surface and churn it up, followed by men with spades who shovelled the earth into baskets, and then the younger boys of the gang carried the earth away to a dumping area.

At each stage, the labourer in question was searching carefully through the earth, looking for any solid item amongst the mass of dirt. Often they found fragments of pottery, which were pleasing but not exciting, and only occasionally did they find something truly important, like a bead from a necklace or an ancient pendant. Now and then the call went up that gold had been found, and everyone crowded round to have a look.

It was usually the men with spades who found things, but Vera often saw Mohammed, the boy who had enrolled on the first day, combing through his basket of earth before he dumped it. She smiled, hoping that his dedication would be rewarded. The older men often bullied the boys into handing over their finds, and she silently urged Mohammed to find something that he could claim as his own.

Day by day, the dig burrowed down into the mound. They were still at the top layer, which was mostly Roman, but the Professor believed that below it were layers stretching back to the Neolithic period.

'Do you really think we'll get back that far?' asked Vera, feeling a rush of excitement.

'It depends on our rate of progress,' replied the Professor, putting a hand to his brow as he surveyed the work. 'I think we'll get there within a month or so. Who knows what we'll find?'

'Dr Hogarth said this might be the lost city of Washukanni,' said Vera. 'Do you think that's possible?'

Curzon glanced at her and laughed. 'One can only dream. People have been saying they're close to finding Washukanni for years. I'm happy to take this place on its own terms. If we find a lost city, then so much the better.'

She nodded. 'Is it true the Germans found this place first?'

'Oh, yes. Oppenheim was nosing around this area twenty years ago,' said Curzon. 'I don't think he's been back since the war. But there are other German digs around, I gather, and a few Americans. The French authorities will give anyone a permit as long as they pay.'

Vera looked out at the dig before them. It was just a series of trenches and a few pits, at the moment, but she was sure that something was waiting to be found. What if it really was

Washukanni? How thrilling it would be to be part of the team that found it. She imagined the press, the publicity, the triumph with which they would return to Britain. She would be the most famous woman archaeologist since the heyday of Gertrude Bell, who had died in Baghdad just a few months earlier.

She looked up to see Curzon watching her, his dark eyes inscrutable, and felt a tingle run down her back.

*

They celebrated the end of the first week's digging with a huge stew, made by Azim in the tent serving as a kitchen. He managed to produce surprisingly good food with limited resources, although, after seeing him tenderising a slab of meat with his bare hands, Vera had resolved not to think about where the food had been before it arrived in front of her.

'What meat did he say was in the stew?' asked Dorothy Curzon, picking at it distastefully. 'It looks rather odd. Ralph—' But her husband was engaged in animated conversation with Laiq.

'I'll ask him,' said Vera, and spoke to Azim in Arabic, although she knew he could perfectly well understand English. He was sitting on his haunches, a little way back from the group, and leaned forward when she spoke.

'It's dog,' replied Azim solemnly, with a bow. 'You don't like it?'

Vera glanced down at her bowl and felt queasy. 'You're joking, aren't you?'

'Of course I'm joking,' he said, rolling his eyes. 'It's mutton. Very old, stringy mutton, but that's not my fault. Shall I tell Mrs Professor that it's dog? It might liven her up a bit.'

'Absolutely not,' said Vera.

'She's fussy, isn't she? She doesn't like it here. She thinks we're savages. And she's not interested in archaeology.' He looked disdainful.

'I'm sure that's not true,' said Vera stiffly. 'She'll be all right when she's adjusted a bit.' Speaking in Arabic was becoming easier, and she was pleased to find that he understood her accent.

Azim watched her slyly, his head on one side. 'You don't like her either, do you?' He looked at Mrs Curzon, who was prodding at the stew in her bowl, frowning. 'And she certainly doesn't like you.'

'That's enough, Azim.'

'Probably because her husband does – a little too much, eh?' He winked and began gathering people's empty dishes.

Vera turned back to Mrs Curzon, feeling hot and bothered.

'Well? What is it? I don't think there's any real meat in it at all. Heaven knows what they eat in this ghastly place—' She broke off suddenly, looking tearful, and Vera felt sorry for her.

'It's mutton,' she said soothingly.

Chapter 10

'Que voulez-vous, madame?'

'Un café, s'il vous plaît.'

'Êtes-vous française?' the waiter asked.

'Non. Italienne.'

'Ah.' He bowed and hurried away, pushing through the beaded curtain that led into the kitchen.

Vera turned her attention to the street outside, where children were playing cricket with a plank and a homemade ball. An imam in a white robe walked slowly by and glanced in at the window of the café. Vera pulled the scarf further over her hair. It wouldn't do to draw attention.

She had arrived in Tunis from Malta the day before and had taken a room at a modest hotel off the Rue du Pacha. Her papers showed her to be the widow of an Italian merchant, in Tunis to wind up her late husband's business affairs and have his possessions shipped back to Milan.

Axis troops had occupied Tunisia for nearly five months. Italian and German soldiers were on every corner, but she had encountered no trouble except for the occasional wolf whistle from a man young enough to be her son. Presumably the local girls, chaperoned and demurely dressed, were off-limits. Vera laughed to think of her nylon-clad calves and high-necked blouse inciting unbridled passion.

The waiter brought her coffee and she sipped from the tiny cup. The ceiling fan pushed the warm air around. Vera listened to the ticking of the clock. It was five minutes past five and her contact was late. He had never been late before.

At a quarter past five, a young Tunisian slipped noiselessly into the seat opposite.

'You are waiting for Emilio?' he asked in Italian.

'I am just enjoying my coffee,' said Vera cautiously. 'Is there something you want?'

'Emilio sent me,' he said, looking touchingly sincere. 'My name is Ahmed. He said you would be here at five. You are Flavia?'

'I am not in the business of giving my name to strange men.'

Ahmed nodded. 'Of course. I understand. Emilio was unable to come today because of a burst water pipe. He will have to spend some time mopping up.'

Vera maintained a look of polite disinterest, but inside she was raging. A burst pipe meant that Emilio's cover was blown, or close to being blown. Ahmed was watching her anxiously.

'I'm sorry to hear that,' she said at last.

'He said he would try to meet you tomorrow instead,' said Ahmed. 'In the meantime, he thought you might like to have this painting that he found among Aunt Carlotta's belongings.'

He placed the flat brown parcel on the table. 'Emilio is going to have another rummage in the attic in the morning. If he finds anything you might like, he will bring it tomorrow. He thinks there is a rather valuable painting.'

Ahmed looked out of the window and stood up. 'I must go. Emilio will hope to see you tomorrow at the museum, but he understands that you may have to leave the city if the weather does not improve. He suggests an umbrella.'

He was only a boy, eighteen or so, and Vera wondered if he knew what he was caught up in. She nodded to him and sipped her coffee as he hurriedly left the café.

*

Back at the hotel, Vera opened the parcel. Inside was an unremarkable watercolour of a simple Italian street scene – Sorrento, she thought, seeing the lemon trees.

Gently she removed it from its frame and laid it face down on the bed. The backboard was overlaid with thick cream paper. She peeled up one edge and pulled out the narrow sheaf of papers concealed therein. Most of the documents were typed sheets, written in Italian, and seemed to be old production reports from a handbag factory.

Vera rummaged in her bag for a bottle of scent. Holding up one page at random, she lightly sprayed the corner with the perfume, then waved the paper around to dry. After a moment, handwriting began to show up, very faint between the typed lines.

The few words that were revealed were adequate confirmation that Emilio had managed to get hold of the documents he had promised. She had hoped for photographs, but they were harder to smuggle out, and he must have spent many nights laboriously copying out the secret military reports that his master, an Italian general, kept in a safe.

Vera memorised the words that had been exposed, then tore off that corner of the page and burned it. She placed the rest of the documents back in the frame and pasted the paper to the backboard, then wrapped up the parcel and laid it flat at the bottom of her suitcase.

She wondered what had happened to Emilio and how much danger she was in. Ought she to leave straight away? She had the first batch of information that Emilio had promised, and the longer she stayed, the more likely it was that he – and she – would be caught.

But Ahmed had mentioned another document, something valuable, and she was reluctant to leave without it. The war in

North Africa was at a critical stage. What if she brought back to Malta something that made a real difference? It could change the course of the war. Vera felt a familiar frisson of fear and ambition, and knew it was a dangerous combination.

*

Emilio had advised an umbrella. That meant she should have an escape plan prepared. She remembered sitting with him at their first meeting, when the Axis were in the ascendancy and he was desperate to do something, anything, to check it.

They had hammered out the rules of engagement. They would always meet two hours before the agreed time. If he finished a letter or wireless transmission with 'Distinti saluti' then he was being controlled by an enemy and she should disregard anything therein. If his communications failed to include a specific word, then he was captured or dead. And so on.

In the morning, Vera took a cab to the harbour and had her suitcase taken on board the boat that had brought her. The captain, a Tunisian trader, asked no questions, and she – and ultimately the British government – was paying him enough to do as she asked.

'We may need to leave a little earlier than planned,' she said. 'Something has come up.'

He nodded, locking the door of the cabin and passing her the key. 'I will finish my business by midday. After that, I will go straight to the departure point.'

Vera paid off the cab and walked slowly through the city. The second official meeting point was at the museum, and if Emilio was being controlled by the enemy, that was where he would lead them. The real rendezvous was in the Christian cemetery. She wasn't due there until one o'clock, so she repaired to a nearby French restaurant and ate a passable soufflé, followed by coffee.

At last, it was time to go. Vera made her way to the grave of Giacomo Ruocco, which was worn and crumbling. She wondered if any of his real relatives ever came to visit. She had stopped to buy a bunch of wildflowers from an old man, and now knelt to lay them on Giacomo's grave.

Dry grass was growing around the stone, and she took her time weeding it, remembering her mother weeding the garden of their home in Devon. It was the first and last house in England she had shared with her parents, after their return in 1914 from her father's diplomatic postings abroad. What had happened to that garden? The house had been sold by the end of her first year at Oxford, and she imagined someone else weeding it, or else letting it all go, and the resulting wilderness.

'I'm glad to see you, Flavia,' said the man as he knelt beside her. He had brought a bouquet of lilies and laid them down.

'Emilio. I wasn't sure if you'd make it.'

He looked quite different from the last time she had seen him. He had worked for General Russo for many years, but the stress of his double life was starting to show on him, and he looked tense and exhausted. His eyes, bracketed by deep lines, were as kind as she remembered.

'They are not following me – I'm sure of it. I took every precaution.'

'Who are they?' she asked, pulling a clump of moss off the gravestone.

'There's a man, he's the General's private secretary. He started a few months ago and he seemed a lot more alert than the old one. He saw me coming out of the General's office one evening. I had a good cover story, but he's been very interested in my doings ever since.'

'What happened yesterday?' asked Vera.

'He wanted to speak with me. He started talking about loyalty, about how important it was for the General to have men around him that he could trust.' Emilio frowned and swiped his arm across his forehead. 'It seemed he was trying to trip me into a confession.'

'What did you do?'

'I played it cool. I reiterated my loyalty to the General and said I hoped he would tell me if there was ever something about my conduct that worried him. Then I left. I thought he might be watching me or knew that I had a meeting planned.'

'Is that why you sent Ahmed?' asked Vera. 'How much does he know?'

'Oh, nothing,' said Emilio. He looked around the cemetery. 'He does errands for me. He's just a boy. I have reason to believe that he is sympathetic to the Allies – it's a sort of unspoken thing between us. But he doesn't know who you are or what our business is. I told him you were my cousin.'

Vera looked seriously at him. 'What are you going to do?'

He breathed out heavily. 'I can't run away – they know where to find my family. I'll give it a week or two and see what happens. If he's watching me closely, I will just have to stop. If it seems that all is well, I will send you a message.'

There was a third option, which they both knew was the most likely. That sometime soon, Emilio would be hauled before his employer and accused of spying. Vera wondered if they had any evidence. If they had read his messages, he was already a dead man.

'You'll have to be twice as careful.'

'I know.' He smiled wanly and reached into his pocket. 'Before I forget.' He brought out a tiny rectangular parcel, no bigger than a novel, and placed it gently in her hands.

Vera slid it into her handbag. 'The money will be sent as usual,' she said.

'Thank you,' he said. 'You know I'm not doing this for the money. But my children . . .'

'I know.'

'How are things on your side?' he said. 'I often wonder if the information I pass you is of any use.'

'It is of great value,' said Vera. 'I don't always know myself what it leads to. But every additional piece of intelligence is crucial and will help us to win the war.'

He nodded. She understood that feeling, a desperate wish to know that all the sacrifices had been worth it.

'Arnim is losing ground,' he said at last. 'They say that the British will take Tunis soon. I suppose at that stage I won't be needed any more.'

'None of us can take victory for granted,' said Vera. 'But you should give some thought to what you'll do if the city falls. I may be able to arrange something.'

Emilio stood up and looked around the cemetery, pausing as he saw a lone mourner standing at a grave a hundred yards away. Other people were strolling along the paths between the graves, but the man stood silently, looking down at the slab before him.

'I recognise that man,' said Emilio quietly. 'I've seen him somewhere before.'

'Keep still.'

He turned back towards her, and Vera could see that he was alarmed.

'You ought to leave,' he said. 'Get out of the city, as quickly as you can.'

'What about you?' she asked in the same low murmur, as though they were discussing flower arrangements for Uncle Giacomo's memorial.

'I'll send you a message if I can. Look out for the password. If it's not there, then it's not me.'

'Understood.'

Vera looked at him and felt a pang of sadness. Here was a man who had risked everything, and now it seemed likely that it would all come crashing down around him. If he was caught, he would probably be executed for selling information to the Allies.

'If I don't see you again,' said Emilio, with a flicker of a smile, 'good luck. To you and to our mutual friends. I don't regret any of it.'

'Thank you,' she said, and gripped his hand tightly. Then she turned and walked away between the graves, feeling the hot sun on the back of her head, not daring to look back. She was aware that the lone man had moved, but she could not see where he was.

Vera headed for the gate that led out of the cemetery, clutching her bag tightly. The package was all that mattered. If she could get the parcels of information back to Malta, then it would all have been worth it. As for Emilio . . . she would have to harden her heart and assume the worst. He knew the risks, she thought, but it was little consolation.

A group of black-clad mourners stood near the main entrance. Vera heard them speaking in French and slipped between them.

'Madame?'

Someone was converging on her from the left – a different man to the one Emilio had recognised in the cemetery.

'Stop,' he said in English, and she looked up at him. He was a small dark man, probably Italian, she thought, wearing a smart suit and gleaming leather shoes.

'My employer would like to speak with you,' he said, his voice ingratiating.

'I'm sorry, my English is poor,' she said in Italian. There was no reason to blow her own cover. She had arrived as a widow from Milan and she would leave as one. 'What is it you want? I am in a hurry.'

He shrugged, switching to Italian. 'My employer has asked me to bring you to see him. He believes he may have an offer that will interest you.'

Vera laughed. 'Do women usually fall for that line?'

'Ah, you misunderstand me.'

'I don't think so,' she said, and her voice was cold. 'Please do not bother me further. I have an appointment to keep with my late husband's lawyers.'

She noticed a pair of gendarmes nearby. He saw her eyes flicker towards them. They were talking quietly, but it would be an easy matter for her to bring them running.

'I am leaving now,' she said, turning. 'Please go away.'

'My employer was so eager to see you,' said the man, spreading his hands.

'Who is your employer?'

'You will find out if you come with me.'

'Absolutely not.' She marched away, leaving him standing on the hot cobbles outside the cemetery.

'He tells such stories of your time in Syria together,' the man called after her, switching to English again. 'Don't you want to see an old friend?'

Vera felt her stomach lurch. For a moment, she wanted to stop, to go back and demand answers, but she forced herself to keep moving. She had a job to do. She flagged down a taxi and had it take her to a lawyer's office. There she conducted a small piece of business and left by a different exit, slipping into another car that took her briskly out of the city and along the coast.

At last, they came to a bend in the road, shaded by scrubby trees, where the car dropped her off and departed. Vera followed a rough path down through olive groves to a rocky cove, where the boat was waiting offshore.

She waved her handkerchief, and before long, the captain brought it in to the rickety jetty. Vera looked back at the surrounding countryside. There was no one to be seen, and she was confident she had not been followed.

They set off at once, the boat's motor puttering gently as they moved out into open sea. They would be in Malta by midnight. She sat at the back of the boat, watching the wake rippling and glimmering in the afternoon light. Who on earth was looking for her? Someone she had known in Syria, many years ago. Perhaps it was just the enemy playing games. But she knew, with a fiery certainty, that it was not a game. Someone from those years had found her.

Chapter 11

Syria, 1926

Vera put down the basket and wiped muddy hands on her apron. She pushed back her damp hair with her forearm and looked out over the site, which was quiet. Most of the men were resting in the shade of a few rough canvas tents, their faces covered by a fold of cloth as they slept.

The blue sky shimmered over the abandoned tools and the outline of the settlement that had begun to take shape. Two figures were walking between the pits. She could see that one was Professor Curzon, but the other was unfamiliar.

Across the expanse, she heard the Professor's laugh echoing, and felt a vague stab of envy that this stranger could amuse him so easily. She saw them turn to look in her direction, and at once she picked up her basket and made her way down the hill, out of sight.

Matthew was kneeling on a tarpaulin, arranging pottery fragments, his breathing shallow with concentration.

'Who's the man with Professor Curzon?' she asked.

He looked up. 'Oh – that's the German chap, Schuster. He's some sort of antiquities expert, apparently. They were at Oxford together. He arrived this morning, after you left camp.'

'What's he doing here?'

'Come to participate for a week or two, by the sound of it. Heading for Aleppo and fancied popping by when he heard we were making progress.'

Matthew sat up and winced, flexing his shoulders. 'Look, Vera. I've got almost all the pieces. It was split into about thirty fragments, and we've found all but a handful of the smallest.'

Vera knelt beside him and peered at the pieces of pottery, which he had carefully numbered with chalk.

'It's not very elegant,' he said quickly. 'Probably just a peasant vessel. Good practice, though.'

'I rather like it,' she said, and pictured the sturdy little pot being used in someone's home a thousand years ago. 'The everyday things are just as valuable for expanding our knowledge of the period. What do you think it was used for?'

'Perhaps olive oil,' he said, pointing at one of the fragments. 'Or wine. It's a much darker colour inside. It could just be due to the passing of time, of course.'

'You've done well,' said Vera with a smile.

He was a nice fellow – they all were, really, even Stanley, who was gradually warming up to her. Sometimes she loathed the boyishness, the silly jokes, the times when they didn't take it seriously. They had no idea how lucky they were. Vera would always have to work twice as hard to get the same opportunities, and while she understood that that was how the world worked, she didn't have to like it. But they had accepted her into their little group as something approaching an equal, for which she was grateful.

'Vera!'

She turned to see the Professor and his friend picking their way down the path. 'There's someone I'd like you to meet. This is my oldest friend, Dr Karl Schuster. Karl, this is Miss Vera Millward.'

'Ah, you're the clever young lady I hear so much about,' said Schuster, taking her hand and bowing deeply. 'My friend Ralph here is very impressed by you. I am glad to make your acquaintance at last.'

'I'm pleased to meet you, too,' said Vera, although she felt flustered. Schuster was tall and slender with dark hair and sharp eyes that seemed to be sizing her up. He must have been in his forties, like the Professor, but he had a youthful charm. His accent was barely perceptible, but it did not change the fact that he was a German and that only a few years ago he had been the enemy. It was astonishing that he and Curzon had managed to remain such good friends.

'Karl will be staying for a couple of weeks,' said the Professor. 'He's based in Damascus, runs the museum there. He's very interested in the Neo-Assyrian period.'

'I hear you have found an ancient city,' said Schuster. 'How exciting!'

'Well, it's early days,' said Vera. 'So far it's just the foundations of what we believe were houses and possibly a temple. But we have high hopes.' She smiled, wondering how much the Professor had told him.

'I gather several cuneiform tablets have been discovered,' said Schuster, looking at the Professor. 'I would very much like to see those, if I may.'

'Of course. We've a couple of hours' work to get through before sunset, and then we'll head back for dinner. I'll show you to my office in the new building, too, if you need somewhere to work quietly. All right?'

'Perfect,' said Schuster. Vera caught his eye, and for a moment felt disconcerted – there was something steely there, something hard. Then he beamed, and the feeling was gone.

*

Vera sat in the newly whitewashed workroom, slowly rolling a clay cylinder across a wax tablet. She held her breath and watched the markings appear clearly on the wax. It was like magic, every time.

There was a gentle knock at the door. Looking up, she saw Karl Schuster hovering in the doorway.

'Miss Millward.'

'Good afternoon, Dr Schuster.'

'You are well?' he asked, looking at the wax in front of her. 'Ah, very nicely done. A beautiful example.'

She smiled and waited for him to speak.

'I wondered if you would like to join me for a ride tomorrow morning,' said Schuster after a moment. 'It's very pleasant when the sun is just rising. I would like to hear your theories about the temple here. It's an area of great interest to me.'

'Oh . . .' She was taken aback but rather pleased. 'Well, I'm not yet an expert, Dr Schuster. But I'd be glad to come and enjoy the sunrise.'

'You are comfortable on a horse?'

'Oh, yes,' said Vera.

'That's wonderful. I'll see you in the morning.' He bowed again and withdrew.

*

The horse assigned to Vera was a spectacular mare that had been loaned to the Professor for the season by the local sheikh. She was strong-willed but gentle, and Vera felt wonderfully happy as she galloped across the steppe, seeing the sun rise over a stand of cypress trees in the distance.

'You're a skilful rider, Miss Millward,' called Schuster, who was riding a horse he had hired in the village. 'Did you have horses as a child?'

'No, we lived abroad,' said Vera. 'But my grandmother kept a whole stable at her home in Wiltshire. I used to ride them when we came back for holidays.'

'Ah, those English country houses,' said Schuster nostalgically. 'I remember visiting friends' homes when I was at Oxford. Hunting, parties, boating on the lake. I spent five glorious years in England. What a time I had!'

'Have you ever been back?' Vera patted her horse's neck and slowed a little.

He shrugged. 'Occasionally. I stayed in touch with Ralph and a few other friends. There were some difficult years during the war, of course, but afterwards things largely went back to normal.'

'Of course.' Vera hesitated. She wondered if Schuster had been conscripted to fight against his English friends. Perhaps he preferred to forget.

'I came to Arabia just after the war, in fact it was to visit Ralph on one of his first digs. He introduced me to many people and I ended up taking a job in Damascus.'

'Was Dorothy with him?' asked Vera. She didn't know why she'd asked; she preferred not to think about Curzon's wife at all.

'No,' said Schuster thoughtfully. 'She is not fond of the East, I think. I wonder what made her come this time?'

Vera shrugged and turned to look at the view. The far-off horizon was shimmering slightly, heralding the start of another warm day. She reached up and pulled her sun hat further down over her forehead.

'Where did you live, if not England?' he asked. 'When you were a child.'

'My father was a diplomat, so we moved around. We were in Vienna until the war. I was fourteen when we left.'

'Ah! Sprechen sie noch deutsch?'

'Sehr schlecht, I'm afraid,' said Vera. 'I've had little opportunity to use it.'

'You haven't been back?'

'Never.'

'You should,' said Schuster, after a pause. 'Austria is as beautiful as ever. I spend most of my time in Arabia, these days, but Europe will always be where my heart is. I keep an apartment in Munich and I go often to Innsbruck to walk in the Alps.'

They rode on, and Vera thought back to the years in Vienna, the trips to the mountains, and then the rushed departure. She had never wanted to return; at first, it seemed unlikely that she would be welcome after the war, and then her parents had died, and the happy years there were blotted out. It was easier to keep the place preserved in her memory, as a perfect sunny interlude in which the sky was always blue, the air was clean, and she had been happy.

'I am very interested in religion, Miss Millward. Tell me your ideas about this temple – Ralph mentioned something about a goddess,' said Schuster, pointing back at the tell, which loomed behind them. All around, the desert glowed with that unearthly morning light.

'It's just a theory,' said Vera. 'We've found several little statuettes of a female shape, a symbol of fertility or motherhood or something along those lines. You know the sort, I'm sure.'

'Ah, yes. They are – rather sensuous, if I may say?'

'Yes. I've read about other digs where they found shrines with single statuettes that were dedicated to a mother goddess, and it occurred to me that having found so many, we might discover a whole temple devoted to her here.'

Schuster nodded enthusiastically. 'You know, in my museum in Damascus, we have some of these little goddess figures. We have nothing on the scale you're thinking of. If you're right, Miss Millward, there could be a remarkable prize hidden under there.'

They both gazed back at the tell, now flooded in the soft morning light. It was quiet, and all that could be heard was the breeze whistling across the sand.

Chapter 12

Arriving home late from an evening working at the club, Margarita threw her coat and bag onto a chair and peered into the cupboards.

During the worst months of the Axis attacks on Malta, when food had been hard to come by, she had lived on the rations provided by the Victory Kitchen where she worked at the time, ladling out food to other desperate people. She had supplemented her diet with vegetables that her father sent from his farm on Gozo whenever he could spare them. Things had greatly improved since the siege had been broken, but never again would she take food for granted.

Margarita found two eggs and added chopped onion and herbs to make an omelette. As it was cooking, she made a rough dough and hammered it with her fists to make two flat discs. When the omelette was cooked, she threw one slab of dough into the pan and turned up the heat to make a flatbread. This she drizzled with more oil and rubbed half a tomato over it, eating the mushy tomato when she was done.

She took the meal to the chair on the balcony and sat looking out over the darkened city. In the distance, she could see lights in the harbour. As always, the ships made her think of Arthur. Where was he? Somewhere far away, perhaps deep below the surface. Her stomach clenched at the thought and she turned back to her meal, trying not to think about the danger he could be in.

Putting her plate down on the floor, she stretched. As she did so, there came a sound from the front room. Quickly she stood, listening intently, but all was quiet, and she sat down again.

'You shouldn't leave your door unlocked,' said a voice. Margarita whipped around, her heart thumping, and saw Vera standing in the sitting room, holding a small suitcase.

'Vera!'

'Sorry, Margarita,' said Vera, looking penitent. 'I didn't mean to alarm you.'

'You could have knocked!' said Margarita, knowing she sounded more hysterical than was necessary. She took a deep breath. 'What on earth are you doing here?'

'I didn't want to alert your neighbours by knocking so late,' said Vera, now pulling off her shoes. 'Is there somewhere I can put these to dry?' She was wearing a plain skirt and blouse, and Margarita saw that her clothes were clinging to her.

'Put them on this newspaper,' said Margarita. 'Have you been swimming fully dressed?'

'In a way,' said Vera.

'Do you want something to change into?'

She shook her head. 'I'm nearly dry, actually. I had to walk a couple of miles, so my clothes got a good airing.'

'Come and sit down,' said Margarita, pulling another chair from the kitchen onto the balcony. She was desperate to know what Vera had been doing but restrained herself. 'Are you hungry? Thirsty?'

Vera shook her head. 'I'll find something later.'

'Well, I'll get you some water, at least,' said Margarita. In the kitchen, she filled a glass and looked around. She knew Vera wouldn't admit to being hungry. Quickly she turned on the gas again and cooked the other flatbread. She put it on a plate with a tomato, an apple, and a lump of sheep's cheese that she had been saving.

She took it out to where Vera sat on the balcony, the lamp beside her turned down low. She was watching the street but looked up when Margarita appeared.

'You didn't need to,' said Vera, taking the plate, but she tore off a piece of bread and chewed it steadily, closing her eyes for a moment.

'How long is it since you've eaten?' said Margarita, sitting back down beside her.

'I can't remember,' said Vera. 'I had a handful of almonds on the boat.'

'The boat? Where were you coming from?'

'Tunisia,' said Vera.

'Really?' Margarita blinked, and something fell into place. 'Are you a spy?'

'Of sorts,' said Vera. 'It's not nearly as exciting as you might imagine.'

'What were you doing there?' asked Margarita. 'I shan't tell anyone, I promise.' She was aware of Vera observing her closely.

'There are several people in Tunis who provide information to British intelligence,' said Vera at last. 'I had a meeting with a contact, but something went wrong and I had to leave earlier than planned.'

'How did you end up in the water?'

'The captain of the boat that brought me back got spooked. There were lights on the rocks – he thought the police might be waiting. He didn't want to go any closer until morning, so I had to swim to shore.'

'You swam to shore in the dark with a suitcase?' said Margarita, awed. 'Wasn't that terribly dangerous?'

Vera shrugged. 'It wasn't deep, and the sea's very calm tonight. Had to hold my case over my head and I scraped my leg, but that was all.' She lifted her skirt and looked critically at the livid graze on her knee. 'I see you've been swimming too,' she said, nodding to Margarita's bathing suit, which was drying on the balcony.

'There's a lovely spot just below the gun battery in Valletta where the water is beautifully clear. I went there this afternoon.'

'I know the place, I think,' said Vera. 'My house is in Senglea, right at the end of the peninsula, so I can see it across the harbour.'

Margarita felt a jolt of surprise. Henry had never taken her to a house in Senglea. They had always gone to a flat in Sliema, which she had assumed to be his home. It occurred to her now, with another wave of humiliation, that he must have kept a separate property in which to conduct his affairs. The place had been tastefully furnished but lacking in any personal touches – very few clothes, no ornaments on the mantlepiece, no photographs. What a fool she had been.

'From your captain?' asked Vera, nodding to a letter lying opened on the table.

Margarita shook her head. 'My father,' she said. 'He lives on Gozo with my stepmother, Livia.'

'Do you get on with her?'

'I do now,' said Margarita after a pause. 'I was awful to her when I was a child – my mother had died and I suppose I was angry. But Livia was always kind to me, always patient. She's Italian so she was interned when the war started. When she was released, my father insisted they hasten their plan to retire to Gozo, so that's where they are now. She sends me recipes.' Margarita thought about it, recalling Livia's sweet laugh and warm hugs. 'I love her, I suppose, although I've never told her that.'

'You should,' said Vera simply.

Margarita nodded. 'What about *your* family?' she asked timidly.

Vera picked up the apple from her plate and took a bite. 'My parents are both dead.'

'I'm sorry. How old were you?'

'Nineteen, nearly twenty,' said Vera. She was silent for a while, staring at her plate. 'My father was a diplomat. We lived all over the place – I was born in Tangiers and later we lived in Italy, France, Austria. We spent the war in Devon, a lovely part of England.'

She put down the apple. 'They died in a car accident a year or so after the end of the war. It was winter, very icy.'

'How awful,' said Margarita. 'Where were you?'

'I'd just started at Oxford,' said Vera. 'Various aunts and uncles tried to get me to come and live with them, but I couldn't give it up. After the funeral I went back to Oxford and worked hard. I worked and worked, in those years – hardly did anything else.'

'Were you lonely?'

Vera looked thoughtful. 'Do you know, I've rarely been lonely. The work was everything to me. I wanted to see the world.'

'And did you?'

'Oh, yes. My first dig was in Syria and then I went to Egypt, China, Peru – all over.'

Margarita listened in wonder. 'You travelled alone? I think I'd be afraid to do that.'

'You get used to it,' said Vera. 'I used to be terribly nervous when I was a little girl – scared of my own shadow.'

'Really?' said Margarita with a smile. 'I can't imagine that.'

'Well, it's true.'

'How did you get over it?'

Vera leaned forward. 'Someone gave me some good advice. When I was about ten, we were visiting London and my parents took me to some diplomatic shindig. Lots of lords and ladies, politicians, that sort of thing – dinner, dancing and candlelight. I hid from the festivities, peering out at the crowds.'

Margarita listened, picturing the little girl and the crowd of British aristocrats, a shimmering mix of silk and chandeliers, music and the tinkle of cutlery.

'I retreated to a side room and bumped into a boy, a few years older than me, who was hiding from the party just as I was. He was a naval cadet and looked very uncomfortable in his uniform. He was just as shy as me but his father was terribly important and very strict, so he had to do what was expected of him. We ended up talking for hours. "I'd give anything to have your life instead of mine," he said. "Embrace your freedom. Be brave!" It was like a light coming on in my mind. I kept thinking of him and how hard it must be to live a life entirely in the service of others. I realised how lucky I was, and that I could do anything if I was determined enough.'

Vera was staring out into the darkness. She seemed suddenly to rouse herself. 'Sorry, Margarita, I've been droning on. You must be tired. I ought to get going.'

'Not yet,' said Margarita. 'You haven't told me why you came to my flat.'

'I was being followed by someone,' said Vera. 'Probably just police, but I didn't want to risk it. There are Axis spies everywhere, even in Malta. I threw them off once I reached Floriana and thought I'd better get off the street.'

'How do you know where I live?'

Vera merely blinked at her and scraped up the last of the sheep's cheese on her fingertip. 'I'm sorry to turn up unannounced. I'll be off soon.'

'I know a safe way out,' said Margarita.

*

They went cautiously down the stairs. At each landing, Vera paused and listened, but there was no sound other than their own breathing, and she gestured again for Margarita to lead the way.

At the bottom, Margarita opened the cellar door and felt around for the light switch, but nothing happened.

'Bulb must have blown,' said Vera. 'Not to worry. I've got a light.'

She went a little way down the stairs into the cellar and Margarita saw the pale beam of a torch, which was immediately shaded by Vera's hand.

They went carefully down into the blackness, holding tight to the railing. The stairs were uneven.

'How did you find this place?' said Vera in the darkness ahead.

'During the bombing,' said Margarita quietly. 'It was very heavy one night, and I was afraid to run along the street to get to the shelter. So I came down here – watch out at the bottom, there's lots of broken furniture. The impact of one of the bombs knocked over a cabinet in the left-hand corner. There's a door bolted from this side. I moved the cabinet back over it.'

Vera reached the bottom and shone the torch across the mass of junk that filled the room. 'Quite a collection. Does your landlord come down here?'

'I don't think so. His sons throw old chairs and things in but no one else seems to know about the door.'

'I see the cabinet,' said Vera, wending her way through the chaos. 'Where does the tunnel come out?'

'It joins up with the main railway tunnel if you go far enough in that direction. There were hundreds of people down there last year, sheltering from the bombing, but it's probably empty now. What if the main doors are locked?'

'That's all right,' said Vera, and together they shuffled the cabinet a foot or so away from the door. She slid back the heavy bolt. 'I know my way around the tunnel network under Valletta, I've used it before. There are various ways I can get out into the city.' She looked back at Margarita. 'You must bolt this behind me – all right? Be careful going back up without a torch.'

Vera opened the wooden door and a rush of cooler air came through, slightly stale. She stepped cautiously into the tunnel beyond, and the torch picked up the low-hanging cobwebs. 'I'll be off, then. Thank you, Margarita. I won't forget it.'

'What if someone catches you?' said Margarita anxiously.

'They won't,' said Vera. 'I promise. Now, lock the door and go to bed.'

Margarita pushed the heavy door closed, and suddenly she was in darkness. She felt for the bolt and slid it home, then stood, listening carefully, but she could hear nothing except her own heartbeat. Vera had already gone.

Chapter 13

The next day, Margarita climbed onto a stool in her kitchen and reached for the top shelf. She lifted down a dusty jug and peered inside, her heart leaping with a mixture of relief and disappointment.

Upturning the jug on the table, she watched as the spare keys to Henry Dunn's flat slid out, along with a piece of string, a button, and quite a lot of dust. There were two keys, one large and one small, on a plain steel hoop.

Henry had given them to her one night after a few too many bourbons. He had arrived at the flat, later than agreed, to find her sitting on the doorstep as darkness fell.

'I don't like to think of you waiting around outside for me,' he said, and he pressed a set of keys into her palm. 'It isn't safe. If I'm not here when you arrive, you can let yourself in.'

'This is Malta,' Margarita had replied, laughing, as they went upstairs. 'I know this country. I'm sure it's safe.'

'There are a lot of soldiers around,' said Henry, frowning. 'It's best to be careful.'

'All right,' she said, to humour him, and put them away in her bag.

'Just don't go in my office,' he said, gesturing to the door that he always kept closed. 'There are exam papers and so on.'

'Of course.'

It was not until weeks after their affair had ended that Margarita found the keys at the bottom of her handbag. By that time she had no wish to see Henry ever again, so until she could think of how to get them back to him, she put them in the jug and forgot about them.

Hearing Vera speak of her house in Senglea had reminded Margarita that she still had the keys. She had assumed that Henry's flat would already have been searched – by Vera, and perhaps by the police. But what if no one else knew it existed? If it was, as she guessed, just a place that he used for assignations, then he would probably have kept it secret, perhaps even rented it under an assumed name.

Margarita stared around her own flat. Before meeting Henry, she had shared a drab apartment in the suburbs with three other girls. The place had a hole in the sitting-room wall from bomb damage. When Henry discovered where she lived, he had found her a new one-bedroom flat in Floriana owned by a friend of a friend, who apparently didn't need the money and charged an astonishingly low rent.

Margarita had wondered if she would be expected to give the flat up once she was no longer with Henry, but a letter from the owner had arrived once the initial six months had passed, renewing her contract on the same terms, so that was that.

She drummed her fingers on the table and picked the keys up again. Did she dare to go to Henry's flat? Perhaps she ought to go to the police, but what would she tell them? That she wanted them to search a flat belonging to her married former lover? They would laugh at her.

Feeling her cheeks burning, she stood and slipped the keys into her pocket.

*

Margarita took a bus to the waterfront at Sliema and marched briskly uphill. She passed a number of familiar apartment blocks and carried on, her feet remembering the walk she had done many times. Less than a year ago, she thought incredulously. It seemed much longer.

Several of the buildings still had scaffolding on, and one or two had been left in ruins, more than a year after the bombing. There was no money for rebuilding and landlords were reluctant to repair when the Italian and German planes could return at any time to finish the job.

She spotted an ornate iron balcony and knew that she was close. Some things had changed: on a corner she saw a huge tub of flowers blooming, a hopeful gesture that made her feel strangely emotional.

Reaching a familiar door, Margarita stopped suddenly. This was it, the place where she had come so many times with Henry. At the time, their short relationship had been deeply meaningful to her. Now she understood that a man in his fifties, married or otherwise, would never see a girl half his age as anything but a pleasant distraction. Arthur, in contrast, truly loved her. How much had changed, and – despite her fears for Henry's safety – how relieved she was now that it had.

She stepped up to the front door, which had a new hanging basket outside, and hesitated. There was a landlady on the premises, she recalled, although they had never met.

Margarita slipped the large key into the lock and opened the door quietly, listening carefully. A wireless was on in the downstairs flat. She closed the door quietly behind her and stood for a moment in the hallway, breathing in the familiar smell, before crossing to the stairs and making her way up, her footsteps as light as she could make them.

Henry's flat was on the third floor. On the landing, she paused. Then she heard a sound from one of the neighbouring apartments and let herself in quickly, closing the door before anyone saw her.

More than half a year had passed since she had last been in the flat, but it looked hardly changed. A hallway led into a large sitting room, lined with bookcases, with a drinks trolley in the corner. The décor was simple, modern, with expensive wallpaper and carpets.

Four doors led off the sitting room: a modest bathroom, a kitchen she had never seen him use except to put things in the imported refrigerator, a sun-filled bedroom, and Henry's office.

The doors all stood open except the last. For a moment, Margarita had the strong feeling that Henry had just nipped into the other room, and stood stock-still, half expecting him to appear and ask her what on earth she was doing here.

But no one was in. She could see the bed, neatly made up in unfamiliar sheets, and the kitchen was clean. She went through and opened the refrigerator, but it was completely empty except for a bottle of champagne which, when she touched it, was room temperature. The fridge had been switched off. By whom?

In the bathroom, a single toothbrush stood in a glass. The only other items were a folded flannel on a shelf, a safety razor and a bar of soap. Henry's flat had always been minimalist and she had assumed that was just his style. Now she knew it wasn't his real home, it all made sense. In Senglea was a house that held the rest of his belongings. Margarita pictured his suits hanging in a wardrobe beside Vera's silk dresses, their shoes lined up together, his watch on the dressing table beside her pearls.

She tried the door of his office and was unsurprised to find it locked. She went into the bedroom and looked around.

She had seen Henry locking his office; he had carried the key into the bedroom.

It was in the first place she looked, the bottom drawer of his bedside cabinet. Before picking it up, Margarita observed the thin layer of dust that had accumulated on the paper that lined the drawer. The dust was scuffed, and the key itself was clean when she picked it up. She frowned, wondering when Henry had last been here. Or had someone else been in the flat?

Her body tense, she listened to the silence. The clock in the sitting room used to tick loudly, she remembered, but it had obviously not been wound, and now stood silent.

Shaking her head, Margarita hurried to the office and unlocked it. It looked just as she had imagined: a tidy desk, the shelf above it laden with books about archaeology and history. Her eye was caught by a stone figure, mounted on a wooden base: a little fat lady, her feet tiny and her bottom enormous, seemingly pirouetting.

There was little of interest on the desk, but in the top drawer she found a leather-bound journal. The first few pages were empty, then Henry's messy handwriting began to fill the space – notes about a book he was reading, a list of lecture titles, deadlines for articles due in.

Margarita turned the page, unsure what she was looking for.

Jan Novotný. (Princeton, 1895 – Whig Club.) Died Prague, 1936. Locked room – armed guard. Nazi connection – Nero killed him. (This was underlined.) *How did he get in? Jan told bodyguards he was heading for bed – they checked an hour later and he was shot dead. No sound, no sight.*

There was a space, and then the writing started again.

Novotný was decorated in 1918. British connection? Able fighter – self-defence.

There were other scribblings like this, notes on times and places, names.

Walter Sommer – 1934/5 – Lake Geneva. Found Feb 35 but thought to have died months before. Journalist – anti-Nazi. Nero in Switzerland? Contact Hans.

That name again. Margarita frowned, feeling anxious perspiration forming under her arms. It sounded as though Henry was involved in something serious. He was looking for someone, a person known as Nero, and he wasn't just anyone – he was a killer.

None of it made any sense. She flicked through the notes. Now and then, intrusions from Henry's day-to-day life were visible – a scribbled note about a dinner at the university, a brief shopping list, a reminder to pay the water bill. No sign of me, thought Margarita gloomily, wondering if she should be relieved or dismayed that she had apparently made so little impact upon his life. His wife appeared occasionally – *Check time of Vera's arrival Cairo* – but even she seemed oddly absent, as though his focus was elsewhere.

The last page of the notes held a roughly drawn map, with an arrow pointing between two circles. Henry had labelled the lower circle 'Prague'. The top one, which he had written in capitals and circled several times, said 'BISKUPIN'. Underneath this, written diagonally in a different ink as though he had noted it down later, were the words: *Meet M tonight 7p.m.*

M for Margarita? Or M for Matteo, the smuggler in the blue suit?

There was a voice in the corridor outside and Margarita leapt up, her heart hammering. She shoved the journal back into the drawer, afraid that she would be mistaken for a thief. Grabbing her bag, she stood still, listening, but heard nothing.

A door clicked somewhere along the corridor and she peered out. She could hear voices nearby, but no one was in sight. Margarita shook her head. Suddenly she could not bear to spend another moment in this awful, empty flat. She darted out, locked the door, and ran down the stairs without looking back.

Chapter 14

Margarita barely slept that night. She could not stop thinking about what she had seen, and she wished she had brought the journal home with her as evidence that she had not imagined the whole thing.

After a restless night, she went to the nearest public telephone and placed a call to the number that Roger Wilson had given her.

He answered straight away. 'Yes?'

'This is Margarita Farrugia,' she said. 'Is that Mr Wilson? We met—'

'Hello, Margarita,' said Wilson, sounding surprised. 'Everything all right?'

'I need to speak to you,' she said.

'Is it about the matter we discussed? Have you seen something significant?'

'Sort of,' she said. 'It's . . . connected.'

'All right,' he said, and it was hard to tell if he was annoyed at her for wasting his time or interested that she might have a lead. 'I'm busy for the next few hours – can you meet me at the Cathedral at around two? By the main door.'

'Yes, of course.'

'Good. See you then.'

*

Wilson was sitting on the steps in shirtsleeves when she arrived, looking off into the distance. He saw her hovering and stood up, dusting down his trousers.

'It's probably best if we go to the office,' he said, after greeting her. 'If you've no objection? It isn't far.'

Margarita shook her head, although she knew her father would disapprove of her going to a strange man's office. Wilson gestured and she followed him through a warren of small streets, turning off onto Archbishop Street, a steep cobbled lane with a view, at the end, of the rich blue water of the harbour.

Under a faded sign for a solicitor's firm, Wilson unlocked an unmarked door. Inside was an empty office, with doors leading off towards the back of the building. He gestured to a seat in front of a bare desk. She sat down, feeling as nervous as she had when going to the dentist as a child.

'What is it? You've seen something at the club?'

Where to start, thought Margarita. There was nothing for it. 'Last year, I had a relationship with a man called Henry Dunn.' Almost imperceptibly, Wilson's eyebrows rose. Did that mean he knew who Henry was?

Her cheeks pink, she told him about her affair with Henry, about learning that he had disappeared, going to his flat the day before, and about the journal she had seen. Wilson listened carefully, saying nothing as he made notes.

'So I believe that Henry was looking for someone, this man Nero,' she finished. 'He sounds dangerous – Henry thought he had killed people. And now Henry has disappeared. What if this Nero has kidnapped him? Or . . .' She hesitated.

'Or killed him?' said Wilson, watching her.

Margarita nodded. 'It's possible, isn't it?'

'Yes, it's possible.'

'Do you know who this Nero is?' She waited as the silence grew.

'No,' said Wilson at last. 'I'd like to find out, though.'

'You've heard of him?'

'Oh, yes.'

Margarita breathed out heavily. She had hoped to find that it was nothing, some flight of fantasy of Henry's, but Wilson's reaction suggested that it was just as serious as she had first thought.

'What were you doing on the beach near Triq il-Wiesgħa Tower?' said Wilson.

She blinked. 'Have you been following me?'

'No. You were spotted there.'

Margarita shook her head. 'I thought he might have taken Henry. One of his men mentioned an American, that night when I followed him. I heard people in the cave—'

'I don't want you doing any more private investigations,' said Wilson. 'It isn't safe.' Vera had said the same thing, she remembered, and wondered what they knew that she didn't. Then it occurred to her that Wilson must know Vera, if they both worked for British intelligence. Perhaps it was she who had told him about Margarita going to the cave, in which case she had probably already told him about Margarita's affair with Henry. She flushed again at the thought.

Wilson looked at the scribbled notes he had made as she spoke. 'I'll need the keys to Henry's flat.'

She pulled them out of her bag and he slipped them into his pocket.

'Is Nero a spy?' said Margarita.

Wilson sighed. 'I don't know much more than you do.'

'But you're looking for him. Is he in Malta, do you think?'

Wilson said nothing. The telephone rang shrilly in the silence and he picked up the receiver.

'Yes?'

Someone spoke at the other end.

'At the cave? Good heavens.' There was a pause. 'All right,' said Wilson. 'I'll be with you shortly.' He banged down the receiver and put his notes in a drawer, which he locked.

'The cave?' said Margarita eagerly. 'Have they searched it? Has Matteo got Henry?'

Wilson shook his head and reached for his jacket. 'Matteo's dead.'

Chapter 15

Henry Dunn's flat looked like any other place used by a married man in which to meet his mistress. Roger Wilson prowled through the rooms, looking for anything that seemed out of place. He was acquainted with Vera Dunn, but he had never met her husband.

'The journal isn't here,' called Pratchett. Wilson went through to Henry's office, where Pratchett was on his knees, rummaging in a drawer. He looked perplexed.

'It must be,' said Wilson, looking at Henry's desk, which stood with its drawers wide open, the contents in disarray. 'Margarita said it was in the top drawer. She was only here a couple of days ago. Look again.'

Without complaint, Pratchett did so, leafing through the faded handwritten essays, the typed reports and the books that filled Henry's office. He shook out each of the books on the shelves, hoping that something would fall out, and peered on hands and knees under the desk in case it was on the floor.

He sat back on his haunches and peered around the room. 'Margarita must have been mistaken. Or she was lying – how do you know we can trust her?'

'I don't,' said Wilson with a shrug. 'But I don't see what reason she'd have to lie. Why would she draw our attention to a non-existent notebook?'

'Hmm,' said Pratchett. He stood up. 'Well, if it was here two days ago and it's gone now, someone must have taken it.'

Wilson sighed. 'We should have come before. This Matteo business has been a distraction.'

The death of the smuggler Matteo looked very much like an accident. He had been found crushed beneath a pile of rocks just inside the cave where he had kept stolen goods. The cave itself, once they cleared a way in, had been emptied. The young man who had worked as an informant for the British was gone – either dead or escaped – and there was no expectation that he would reappear. Matteo's known associates had all professed to know nothing about his death, and although they had his lieutenant in custody, he was saying nothing.

Wilson suspected that Matteo had been working with Italian intelligence and presumably the lieutenant had been promised a reward if he stayed quiet. They would probably be able to jail him on a smuggling offence, but treason would be hard to pin on him. He guessed that the man was banking on the Axis winning the war. When they arrived to 'liberate' Malta, he would be well rewarded for his silence.

He thought again about the journal Margarita had described and pulled out his notes. 'We'll need to have this place turned over. In the meantime, we can do our own research. Margarita recalled a few things she'd seen in the journal, including the names Jan Novotný and Walter Sommer.'

'It doesn't tell us much,' said Pratchett, looking over his shoulder.

'It tells us that Henry was looking for Nero too,' said Wilson. He pointed. 'We knew already that Nero was implicated in Jan Novotný's death. I looked him up this morning and it seems that Henry was at Princeton with Novotný, as his notes suggest.'

'So that was why he was invested,' said Pratchett. 'He was looking for his friend's killer.'

'But this name,' went on Wilson, tapping the paper, 'Walter Sommer. I don't recall ever hearing him connected with Nero before. According to the archives, he was a journalist, found floating in Lake Geneva in 1935. It was ruled to be an accident, but he was a strident anti-Nazi. Hitler might have ordered his death, too. Sounds like Henry thought Nero was the killer.'

'And someone doesn't want us to find out about it if they've taken the journal,' said Pratchett. He sighed and leaned back against the wall. There was a crunch, and a small painting fell to the floor.

Wincing, he turned and picked it up. A painting of a Greek village, with white houses against a blue sky, the glass in front of it now a spiderweb of cracks.

'What's that?' said Wilson, staring at the back of the frame.

Pratchett turned it over. Tucked into the back was a photograph, very small and faded. It showed three people – two men and a woman in a white dress, sitting on a low wall, with a hill rising up behind them. Both men wore old-fashioned suits, and one wore a straw boater.

Pulling the photograph out, Wilson turned it over and caught his breath. Scribbled on the back, in messy handwriting, were the words: *Nero, 1926?*

They both stared at the note for a moment and then Wilson flipped it back over, his hands fumbling slightly. Leaning in close, they peered at the image.

One of the men was clearly talking to the woman – his mouth was open and he was looking intently at her, while she listened, laughing, or so it seemed. They were not interested in the picture being taken, consumed only with one another.

The other man was staring directly at the photographer, his eyes piercing even in the blotched photo. He wore a thin smile but it did not reach his eyes.

'Do you think it's real?' said Pratchett. 'Could one of them really be Nero? The handwriting is Henry's, by the look of it – it's the same as all the notes in that drawer.'

'I don't know,' said Wilson uneasily. 'A photograph of the fellow we're looking for just happens to appear, after thirty years of no one knowing what he looks like? And what are the chances it was behind that painting?'

He peered at the wall and saw a small hole. 'The hook was loose.'

Pratchett frowned. 'What does that tell us?'

'Probably nothing,' said Wilson, stooping to pick up the small picture hook. 'I wonder if someone loosened it.'

'To what end?'

Wilson shrugged. 'I don't know.'

'Henry must have heard something,' said Pratchett, looking down at the photograph, 'or connected an old acquaintance with Nero. It's got to be him.'

'Perhaps,' said Wilson. 'But let's be cautious. It's a pretty old picture, and it's tiny.'

'I'll get it enlarged,' said Pratchett. 'That'll give us somewhere to start.' He put the smashed frame down on the desk and looked up at the faded patch of wall it had hung against. 'Nero – or someone working for him – must have found the journal and taken it, but they didn't find this.'

'Or it was left deliberately,' said Wilson. 'To muddy the waters.'

'By whom? Nero?'

Wilson shrugged. 'That's what we need to find out.'

Chapter 16

The combined headquarters of the Allied armed forces in the Mediterranean was based in a series of tunnels that had been blasted out of the rock far under Valletta. Not far away were the offices used by the security and intelligence services, equally anonymous and equally difficult to enter, hidden behind heavy doors and iron gates.

Vera walked along an echoing passage, listening to distant thuds, and knocked on a door. She had made her report on her trip to Tunis to her commanding officer the week before, and she knew that today's summons was probably connected.

'Bad news, I'm afraid,' said Major Morton briskly, waving Vera to a seat. 'We've intercepted a transmission to Berlin that claims a spy has been captured in Tunis.'

'Oh, God,' said Vera, closing her eyes. 'It's Emilio, isn't it? Chaffinch, I mean.'

'We don't know that yet.'

'It's bound to be,' she said heavily. 'He hasn't been seen by our sources since I returned. I've been trying to find out if he's left General Russo's employ, but no one seems to know.'

'Looks like we were right to keep Chaffinch separate from the other Tunis networks,' said Morton. 'Otherwise we'd be looking at the loss of multiple agents.'

'His position was very precarious,' said Vera, 'and he knew what he was signing up for. All the same . . .'

'I know it's hard,' said Morton, watching her with something like sympathy. 'When you get to know a source like that. I gather he had a family.'

'Yes, near Siena. Two children.'

'They'll be taken care of,' said Morton. 'His wife's allowance will continue until he's either confirmed or assumed dead, at which point she'll get a lump sum.'

'Have you heard anything further about the General's private secretary?'

'Nothing yet.'

'I suppose Emilio must have slipped up somewhere,' said Vera. 'Or perhaps this fellow was already on the lookout for a leak. Either way, he's the one behind all of this.'

'But you don't think he's the fellow who accosted you at the cemetery?'

'No. He said his employer wanted to meet me.'

'And he didn't say why, or who the employer was.'

Vera shook her head and tried to remember exactly what the man had said. *He tells such stories of your time in Syria together.* She had not divulged that part of the conversation to Morton or anyone else. It was a private matter. Soon the feelers she had sent out would yield information and she could track down the man who was looking for her and find out what he wanted. Then, if it was relevant, she would tell Morton.

'I'm told the Eighth Army captured Enfidaville last night,' said Morton. 'Things are developing fast over there. They hope to take Tunis within a month, although I suppose it'll be too late for poor old Chaffinch.'

A few more weeks, thought Vera bleakly. Then he would have been safe.

*

A plane droned low overhead as Vera drove across the island. She glanced up, trying to see the markings on the fuselage, but the sun was in her eyes. She looked back at the arid road ahead of her, lined on both sides by prickly pear trees. There was a dot in the distance and, as she drew closer, she saw that it was an old man driving a cart. She slowed to pass him, and saw that he was asleep, nodding over the reins as the donkey trotted along obediently.

The road wound downhill until the sea was visible before her, calm and sparkling blue. She turned off at last onto a rutted track and bumped slowly along for another mile until she reached the dig site.

Vera climbed out and looked around. Nearby was the tent that she was using as an office and workroom. In the distance, several more were pitched on the field that they were excavating. Mr Muscat, the farmer who owned the land, had been baffled to hear that his fields were of archaeological interest, but was canny enough to negotiate a decent rent.

'Will it be another Ħaġar Qim?' he had asked eagerly.

'Probably not,' Vera replied. 'We'll of course be open about anything we find, but I wouldn't get your hopes up.'

True to her word, she had shown him around the site and he had stared blankly at the ridges and furrows that marked out the temple they were investigating.

'It's not much, is it?'

'Not to look at, no,' said Vera. 'But from an academic perspective, it's fascinating. My colleagues here and overseas are very interested in what we've found – it's teaching us more and more about how people worshipped in Neolithic times.'

Muscat looked hopeful. 'Have you found any treasure?'

She took him to the largest tent, where ornaments and fragments of pots were arranged on trestle tables.

'These must be worth something,' he said, looking around. 'Have you found any gold?'

'Not yet.'

*

Vera could see a figure hunched over a wheelbarrow in the distance and recognised Marcel, one of the university students working on the dig with her. There were four or five who came sporadically, fitting the work around their studies. She did not have the funding to employ anyone full time and it suited her to work alone.

She sometimes wondered what it would be like to devote all her attention to archaeology; in the last few years, it had often been neglected in favour of her work for the intelligence service. Her career, which had been punctuated by success for many years, had stagnated of late, thanks to the war. I'm doing something far more important, thought Vera. But what would happen when it was all over?

Marcel had seen her and was crunching over, his curly hair windswept. 'Afternoon, Dr Dunn!' he called.

'Hello, Marcel. How are things?'

'Haven't found anything new. I've been sorting pot fragments.'

He followed her into the tent, stopping to wipe his boots on a patch of scrubby greenery before ducking through the entrance.

'This arrived at the university for you yesterday,' said Marcel. He pointed to a box that lay on Vera's desk, neatly wrapped in brown paper with a printed pattern.

She leaned over to look at the label, on which her name and the address of the university were typed.

'Thanks for bringing it.'

After watching him pick up his trowel and crunch away across the yard, Vera looked again at the parcel and felt her pulse quicken. Reaching for her camera, she photographed the box from all angles, then ripped open the packaging, which she noted had small birds – storks, perhaps – printed in diagonal stripes across the paper.

The small plywood crate was nailed shut. Lifting a screw-driver, she levered it open impatiently. Inside the crate was a carved jewellery box, made of a hard dark wood that she guessed was teak. She lifted the lid and breathed in sharply.

Inside, on a bed of soft black velvet, lay a tiny gold statue of a woman, polished and gleaming. Without touching it, Vera lifted the box close to her face and examined it from every angle. She looked at the rounded stomach, the delicate pointed feet, and the hands cupping the voluptuous breasts.

'That's beautiful,' said a voice, and she realised that Marcel had returned. 'Sorry, I forgot my tape measure. Didn't mean to make you jump.'

'It's all right.' She put the box down.

'It's not from Malta, is it?' he asked, looking curiously at the statue, his round glasses slipping down his nose.

'No,' she said. 'It's . . . just a gift.'

'How extraordinary. I wonder where it came from?'

'Syria,' said Vera. 'I was there when it was found, back in the twenties. My first dig.'

'Oh. Who sent it?'

'I don't know.'

She knew that Marcel was deeply curious and felt guilty that she couldn't tell him anything, but she must not let him be drawn into the web of secrets in which she was enmeshed. As far as he was concerned, she was an archaeologist, and that was all.

'I think it must be from a man I once knew,' she went on.

His expression cleared. 'Oh! An old – er – boyfriend?'

'Something like that.'

'Anyone I've heard of?' he asked eagerly.

'A lady never tells,' said Vera.

Marcel blushed slightly and nodded. 'Of course. I'd better be getting on.' He cast one more curious look at the statue, but she knew he was less interested now that he believed it to be a love token.

When he was gone, she lifted up the square cushion of black velvet and placed it on her desk, the little lady still reclining peacefully in the centre.

Underneath was a neatly folded slip of thick cream paper. On it was a handwritten sentence: *A souvenir from Syria.*

She had last seen the gold statue seventeen years before, and seeing it again here in Malta felt very strange – like seeing someone you knew was dead walk past you in the street. Vera knew she could protect herself, and she wasn't afraid of her mysterious correspondent, but she was alarmed that her cover as an agent might be in jeopardy, especially if it was connected to Henry's disappearance. She had spent years compartmentalising her life; now it seemed that someone who had known the student Vera had connected her with the spy.

Chapter 17

Syria, 1926

'I don't trust him,' said Matthew at sundown, seeing Schuster once again exploring the dig site a few days after his arrival.

The men had finished work and were now on their weary way back to their villages. The little boy Mo, as always, had been the last to leave, after diligently sweeping the paths and collecting stray tools.

'Schuster? Why not?' asked Vera, dumping the last of the trowels into a wheelbarrow.

'I think he's up to something. It seems odd that he's spending so much time poking his nose into our dig. He asks so many questions.'

Vera shrugged. 'He's just interested, I suppose.' But she recalled the hard look that she had seen in Schuster's eye and wondered why she was defending him. She didn't trust him either.

'Perhaps he's thinking of taking some of the things we've found for his museum.'

'The Professor wouldn't allow that, surely?' said Vera.

They watched Schuster making his way methodically around the site, pausing to look at the digging work. He pulled out a notebook at one point and scribbled something before returning it to his pocket.

'You have admit that looks rather suspect,' said Matthew.

They walked back to the main camp, Matthew pushing the barrow. The other boys were in the workroom, hunched over trestle tables.

'Evening,' said Stanley, as they entered. 'Want to see something pretty? You'll like this, Vera.'

They clustered behind him and peered over his shoulder. On the table was a shallow basin of muddy water, in which his hands were submerged. He drew them out carefully, holding in his palm something small and round. The water dripped away from it, and he held it up to the lamp.

'Oh,' said Vera, feeling a jolt of delight. 'How beautiful!'

It was a tiny figurine, slightly battered, from centuries under the earth, but the shape of it was unmistakably female: a little fat-bellied woman, hands cupping her enormous breasts, her legs and tiny feet pressed together.

'Solid gold,' said Stanley. He brushed away the loose mud with his fingers and the figure gleamed.

'Another of your little ladies,' said Christian, looking over from his camera, which he had taken apart and was cleaning carefully. 'And the first one made out of gold. She's rather charming.'

'May I?' asked Vera.

'Of course.'

She stretched out her hand and felt the weight of the figure drop onto her palm. Slowly she drew it up to eye level and marvelled at the care that had gone into making it. She felt drawn to it, hypnotised by the woman's unblinking stare, her self-confidence, her poise. She exuded – what? Power, that was it.

'It seems you may be on to something, Vera,' came a voice, and she saw the Professor at her side. She had no idea how long she had been staring at the figure. 'There's definitely a theme here,' he added, and smiled at her. 'Well done.' She felt her heart jump.

'Stanley found it,' she said quickly, and carefully passed it back.

Stanley shook his head. 'One of the workmen dug it up. I think it was Mohammed who spotted it first, actually, but Farid took over and wouldn't let him near it, poor little chap.'

'Mo is always very observant. We ought to reward him,' said Vera. 'This could be worth a fortune.'

'I'll make sure of it,' said the Professor. He looked around the workroom, his eyes alighting on the shelves full of artefacts that they had found and carefully cleaned or restored.

'Vera, I want you to take over direction of the site for a few days,' he said suddenly. 'I've promised Karl that I'll go with him to visit one or two places of interest and meet up with some old friends. I'll leave you in charge.'

After a moment's surprised silence, Vera glanced around at the boys. 'Are you sure?'

'Of course,' he said. 'I'm sure the gentlemen will support you in any way they can. Won't you?'

'Certainly,' said Stanley, although he sounded irritated.

'Of course we will,' said Matthew, and he smiled at her. Christian nodded, then disappeared into the darkroom next door.

'What about the workmen?' said Vera. 'They won't listen to a woman.'

'Just pass any instructions through Laiq,' said the Professor. He glanced at Matthew. 'If there's any hint of trouble – and I'm certain there won't be – ride to the French encampment. And as a last resort, there is a pistol in the safe, for emergencies only.'

'Where will you be going?' asked Matthew.

'Oh, here and there,' he replied vaguely. 'Karl has the details. There's a town near the Turkish border where he wants to buy something for his museum.'

When he was gone, Matthew breathed out heavily. 'Schuster's definitely involved in something strange.'

Vera rolled her eyes. 'He's odd, I agree, but he's an expert in antiquities. It goes with the territory.'

'What do you think, Stanley? Don't you think he's a bad egg?'

Stanley stood and took the little gold figure over to the safe where they kept the most valuable things. After placing it carefully inside and locking it again, he returned.

'He's a German,' he said abruptly. 'That's all I need to know about him.'

*

At dinner that night, Vera sat between the Professor and Schuster. The latter was as courteous as ever, but Stanley's comment had given her pause. She knew he had lost people in the war – who hadn't? – so he was not well disposed towards the Germans, but perhaps he was right not to like Schuster. There was something unknowable about the man, something cold and hidden, even behind his smile.

All evening, she could feel the Professor's attention on her, like the heat from a fire. He had always been friendly, but now she sensed his attraction, and it felt exciting and dangerous at the same time.

At one point, she caught Dorothy's eye and knew that she noticed it too. The look was angry, unhappy, and for a moment she felt sorry for the woman, but it soon passed. She did not seem supportive of what her husband was doing, nor did she show any excitement about the discoveries they were making. Was it any wonder that he was drawn to someone who did?

Late that night, walking back to her tent after a bath, Vera heard the sounds of a muted argument and paused, her heart thudding. She knew it was the Professor and his wife.

'Can't you see what this is doing to me?' came Dorothy's voice. 'He's not a good man. Can't you say no, this time?'

'There's nothing I can do about it. Be patient, please.'

'I can't!'

'Then you know what to do.'

There was silence. Vera withdrew, disturbed, and returned to her tent, wishing that she had not stopped to listen.

Chapter 18

Vera walked briskly along the seafront in Gżira, looking out at Manoel Island and the naval base that was visible a short distance across the water. Margarita was engaged to a submarine captain, she recalled. She wondered where he was now and whether he would come home. The tide was turning in North Africa, but the war was far from over. For some reason she felt protective of Margarita – God knows why, she thought wryly, as Henry's face flitted through her mind.

She turned away from the seafront and made her way through the backstreets, pausing at an anonymous office, where she was admitted after a brief knock. The young man closed the door after her and bustled around his desk, ruddy-faced and with floppy hair.

'Thanks for telephoning,' said Vera. 'Am I to understand you've made some headway with my parcel?' She could see the packaging that the parcel had arrived in, smoothed out flat on a table with a microscope and a magnifying glass nearby.

'I believe so,' said Forde, buzzing with enthusiasm.

'All right,' said Vera. 'Talk me through it.'

'Well,' he said, 'to start with, you were right that it didn't come from Europe.'

'Oh?'

'I'm fairly sure it came from Egypt.'

'Interesting. How did you find out?'

'I did some analysis of the packaging and the stains found thereon. One of them was an American brand of instant coffee called Washington that's mostly used by troops in North Africa – I've seen it for sale on the black market here in one or two places, but it's not widely consumed.'

He pointed to some small marks on the wrapping paper. 'I also found traces of seawater on the paper, cigarette ash, and a slightly bleached corner where it seems to have lain in the sun. My hypothesis is that it was brought in on a troop ship calling at Valletta. I suspect it was brought here in someone's luggage as there are no postal marks. The sender probably paid a sailor to bring it with him. This is all conjecture, you understand.'

'Of course,' said Vera. 'Please continue.'

'Anyway, the ship could have come from anywhere, but the coffee made me think it had come from Alexandria, as Egypt is where the biggest concentration of American troops is at the moment. Tripoli is another possibility, or perhaps Port Said. My feeling, though, is that the parcel probably originated in Cairo, as it's the most likely source of that kind of paper. Storks are a popular symbol in Egyptian mythology, and the quality – and therefore price – suggests it came from somewhere frequented by Westerners. It looks like the sort of thing used by upmarket jewellers and so on, or it might have been bought at a fancy stationery shop.'

'That's very useful. Thank you.'

'Want me to do any further investigating?' asked Forde eagerly. 'I've a pal in Cairo I could ask to go and make some enquiries.'

Vera shook her head. 'You've done plenty. I'll take it from here.'

She folded up the sheets of paper with their bird print and slipped them into her handbag. She had learned enough about the parcel's provenance.

The question now, she thought, as she walked back towards the ferry a little later, was who had sent it. It was someone she had known in Syria, that much was clear. For a moment, a face loomed in her mind, but she blotted it out at once. That was impossible.

*

Morton was sitting at his desk, frowning down at the documents in front of him. He looked up with a weary smile.

Vera sat down. 'Anything more on Chaffinch?'

'No. I think we have to assume the worst.'

She nodded soberly. 'Has anyone been in touch with his wife?'

'At the moment we can't risk it – we've got someone in Siena but he doesn't want to put her in danger by going to her house, the area is crawling with soldiers looking for Allied spies. It may have to wait for some time, I'm afraid.'

Vera sighed. 'Poor Emilio. He was dreaming of Tuscany. They have a little farm, apparently, overlooking the sea.'

'It must have been hard to leave.'

'He didn't have much choice. And he felt he was doing something important.'

'Quite.'

There was a pause and then Vera asked, 'You didn't bring me in to talk about Chaffinch, then?'

'No. Something else. A new lead – but it's connected to him in some way.'

Vera was intrigued. 'Go on.'

'Cairo have been in touch to tell us about a possible German agent in the city who wants to talk,' said Morton.

'And? Won't they deal with it?'

'The man asked for you.'

'For me?' said Vera, surprised. 'A German agent in Cairo?'

'He's a moneylender or some such, an Egyptian. Claims to be employed by Rommel's lot, but he has some prior connection with Chaffinch. He presumably heard on the grapevine that Chaffinch had been blown, so his request was to meet with Chaffinch's British case officer.'

Vera nodded, feeling relieved. 'He doesn't know my name, then?'

'It seems not. But he was adamant that he wanted to speak to the person Chaffinch had worked with – no one else.'

'I see.'

'We're ironing out the details,' said Morton. 'He had several conditions regarding where, when, etcetera. The main question is: will you go?'

'Of course I'll go,' said Vera, and she sat up straighter. 'I imagine there'll be a risk, but isn't there always?' Already she could feel her heart pounding faster, along with a heady surge of adrenaline.

'Cairo are going to be running as many checks as possible, but they can't guarantee anything.'

'Seems a bit pointless,' said Vera. 'He's told them he works for the Germans, so anything incriminating they turn up will just reinforce that. Why does he want to come over to us?'

'That's what you need to find out,' said Morton, shrugging. 'Probably money. It's possible he's nurturing a long-standing affection for the British, but that seems increasingly unlikely.'

'When do you want me to go?'

'Probably on Friday,' said Morton. 'Where is yet to be decided, but it'll probably be somewhere central. We've insisted that the safety of our agent is paramount.'

'I can handle myself,' said Vera.

'I know,' he replied. 'But we don't want any cock-ups. This needs to be as clean as possible.'

Vera nodded. She was thinking of Cairo and how easy it would be to disappear there, even under the noses of the Allied forces who swarmed through the city. She had no doubt that her employers would do what they could to keep her safe, but in the end, it would be down to her.

She could see Morton observing her closely. 'Don't take any risks,' he said at last. 'Find out what this fellow has for us and what he wants. If he seems legitimate, we'll take him on for a trial period.'

Vera nodded. 'Understood.'

'Should be able to get you a lift there. We'll go over the arrangements tomorrow.'

She stood, already thinking of her plan of action. 'I believe there's an archaeology conference starting in Cairo on Saturday at the university,' she said. 'I received an invitation months ago, but I didn't think I'd make it. Shall I wire to say I'll be there after all?'

'Good idea,' said Morton, nodding. 'Keep it all above board, as if you were there for the conference. Prepare a story about why you deemed it important to get to it – a new discovery in Malta, perhaps?'

'I'll think of something,' she said. 'Leave it with me.'

*

After hesitating on the threshold, Vera entered the house in Senglea she and Henry had owned together. She had never been there for more than a week or two at a time, and it did not feel like home – not then, and certainly not now.

After Henry's disappearance, she had searched the house carefully for information, but she had found nothing of interest. She much preferred staying in hotels, which were pleasantly anonymous. She suspected that Henry too had rarely slept there when she was away, presumably spending his nights with the mistress of the moment.

It was a beautiful house, right at the end of the narrow peninsula Senglea was based on, with high-ceilinged rooms and a view over the harbour. The house next door had been all but destroyed by a bomb, but hers was unharmed apart from one smashed window. She prowled through the deserted rooms, thinking about Cairo and the parcel and who could be looking for her.

Eventually, she would have to sell the house, if Henry was dead. She wondered again if there was anything she had missed, anything she ought to have done differently. The informant she had spoken to near the cave at Triq il-Wiesgħa had confirmed that Matteo had been keeping him prisoner, but he did not know where Henry had been moved to, whether he was still alive, or who had ordered Matteo to kidnap him in the first place. Vera knew, deep down, that her husband's disappearance was connected to her work, and thinking about it for too long brought a hot flush of guilt. It was easier not to think of him at all. They had purposely crafted a marriage in which they spent long periods apart, living their own lives, so it was possible to pretend that he had simply gone away and push him out of her mind.

Vera turned her attention to the matter of the person who had sent the parcel, her 'old friend', as the man in Tunis had put it. She was tempted to let it lie, but she was sure he wouldn't stop, not now that he had gone to such trouble to make contact.

It was up to her to get ahead of him, to find out for certain who he was and what he wanted.

She sat down at the dining table to draft a telegram. It seemed absurd to be writing in search of someone she had not seen for seventeen years, but it was the only way she could think of to gain the information she sought.

She had a friend at the university in Aleppo, an academic called Elizabeth she had met on a dig in Jordan some years before. Keeping her message as brief as possible, she asked Elizabeth if she knew anything of the whereabouts of Laiq Khalil, the foreman who had worked for Curzon on their dig all those years ago. He had been good at his job, and she guessed he might now be working for one of Elizabeth's colleagues. She added the address of her usual hotel in Cairo in case a reply was swift in coming.

The last days at Tell Ithriyia had been something of a blur. Vera remembered being summoned to Aleppo to speak to the police, and suddenly they were not allowed to go back to the dig site and were being sent home. She recalled the clacking of the train that had taken her back towards Europe, and the mingled feelings of fear and elation at what the future held.

She had no idea what had become of Laiq since they had left the dig, but it seemed essential to make contact. She would have to question him carefully to see what he knew. Perhaps he would have information that might help to identify the person who was looking for her.

Chapter 19

Vera jerked awake as the wheels of the plane touched down on the runway. She felt it shake as they raced along, bumping over ruts, and then at last the plane began to slow.

Pulling herself up, she peered out of the window. For a moment, nothing could be seen in the half-light except bare earth. Then the plane turned, and suddenly she could see red seeping across the sky, and the outlines of tall buildings: sunrise over Cairo.

The two army officers who had given her a lift were sitting calmly, each holding his bag on his knees, as the plane slowed and finally came to a halt. They had chatted with her for the first hour or so of the journey, but the noise of the engine had made conversation a struggle.

The door swung open and Vera felt the hot rush of the *khamaseen*, the desert wind, which came laden with sand and dust and a hint of danger. She never thought of the desert without remembering Syria, the site of her first dig, and the place that more than anywhere else had made her who she was.

'After you, ma'am,' said one of the officers, and they stood back to let her off first. The nearest man held out an arm and she took it briefly as she alighted from the plane.

A young blonde driver, neatly dressed in khaki, saluted. She stood beside a smart black car. 'Ma'am. Captain. Lieutenant. May I take your bags?' She was English, well-groomed, one of the many middle-class girls from the shires who had found a purpose in the war, possibly for the first time in her life.

Vera climbed into the proffered front seat and looked with interest at the driver as the men settled themselves in the back. 'I don't think we've met.'

'Lieutenant Jean Berry, ma'am. ATS.' She started the engine, swinging the car around and rattling across the airstrip.

'Vera Dunn. Been here long?'

'Nearly three years now, ma'am.' She waved to a soldier standing guard at the entrance, and then they were off, bumping along a rutted road. In the distance, Vera could see the outline of the city, gleaming as the sun rose.

'What do you think of Cairo?'

'I love it,' said Jean simply. 'The heat took some getting used to, but it's been such fun.'

'What's the nightlife like now?' said Vera. 'Last time I was here, there were some wonderful parties.'

'Oh, the parties are terrific,' said Jean. She looked in the mirror, but the two officers were talking and weren't listening. 'Whenever we have leave, we dash off somewhere thrilling. But, of course, I take my work very seriously,' she said, as if conscious that she might have said too much.

Vera laughed. 'God, what I'd give to be your age again.'

'I wouldn't have guessed you were much older,' said Jean.

'That's very sweet of you,' said Vera. 'Sadly, the years pass all too fast.'

'Well, let me know if you want a night out,' said Jean, then checked herself. 'Sorry. I'm sure you're on important business.'

'That's kind of you,' said Vera, amused. 'I'm staying at the Continental. I expect I'll be rather busy, but an invitation is always appreciated.'

*

Vera waved as the car pulled away outside the Continental and allowed the porter to take her bag. She was pleased to note that most of the staff looked familiar.

'Ah, Mrs Dunn, nice to see you again,' said the young Greek at reception. 'Here for work?'

'Yes,' said Vera, placing her passport on the counter. 'I'm attending a conference at the university.'

'Shall I have some breakfast sent up?'

'That would be wonderful.'

She unpacked in the bedroom while a waiter laid out her breakfast on the balcony. She waited for him to leave, then sat at the wicker table and applied herself to the toast, eggs and coffee, looking out across the roofs as she did so.

She could see the heat shimmering over the city. It gave the place an exciting, buzzing atmosphere. Cairo was a place where things *happened*. She felt optimistic that she would find what she was looking for here.

After breakfast, Vera took a bath and then slept for a couple of hours under the slowly rotating ceiling fan. She had left Valletta late last night, and her sleep on the plane had been unsettled.

She dressed quickly in a light linen dress, finished the outfit with a large hat and a pair of sunglasses, and went out into the city, feeling her forearms already burning under the merciless sun.

The Continental was close to the river, and she walked along it for a while. There were servicemen and women everywhere, sitting in groups by the river, going in and out of shops, standing guard at the entrance to government buildings.

Now and then she saw a young couple, off duty, strolling hand in hand near the water, or rushing along together looking preoccupied. She supposed that they were on their way to a hotel to take advantage of their few hours away from work, and who could blame them? Until recently, Cairo had been at constant risk of attack from Axis forces. Nothing does more to stimulate one's sex drive than a war, she reflected, seeing a giggling girl scamper past, her paramour a few yards behind.

Vera took a taxi to Giza. Her first port of call was the university, where she attended a lecture and then participated in a short seminar on the Neolithic culture of the Nile Valley, making sure to speak to several acquaintances and have her photograph taken with a group of other attendees.

That duty done, she begged heat exhaustion and slipped away, walking briskly out into Giza. She glanced at the scrap of paper in her pocket, walked for a little longer, then turned down a side street. The storefronts she passed were mostly small curiosity shops, with the occasional large wholesaler of furniture or antiques sprinkled between them. She called in at one or two but found nothing to suggest her parcel had anything to do with them.

At last, she came to a shop with a freshly painted frontage. The name on the sign was written in curling Arabic, and underneath in smaller letters it said in English: *Masri Antiquities. Buy and Sell.* A bell tinkled as she went in.

Inside, it was cool and quiet. The heavy door shut slowly behind her and she looked around in the gloom. Vases, statues and mannequins wearing heavy jewellery were arranged haphazardly, with occasional coloured glass oil lamps casting a strange flickering glow across the shop.

'Good afternoon.'

An elderly man had appeared behind the counter. He wore a white robe and carried a brass vessel, which his beard was long enough to brush, in his hands.

'How can I help you?' he asked, putting the vase on the counter.

'You have some beautiful things for sale.'

'Thank you.'

'Do you wrap items in pretty paper if they are intended as a gift?'

'Yes, madam.' He gestured to a stack of wrapping paper sheets on the counter, and Vera peered at them. They were mostly floral patterns, printed on thin tissue. There was a thicker brown paper like the one she had received, but instead of blue storks, it had a pattern of green crocodiles.

'I'm looking for a particular paper. It has a print of little blue storks on it, rather like this one. Do you know it?'

He observed her impassively for a moment. 'We only have these patterns.'

'Have you ever had one with storks?'

'I do not recall, madam.'

'Do you sell gold?' she said, switching to a different tack.

'Indeed, madam.' He hobbled over to a glass cabinet and flicked a switch, so that a light came on inside. She went closer and examined the contents. Most of it was jewellery, but there were one or two tiny statues, lying on black velvet, that bore a passing resemblance to the figure she had been sent, although the style was quite different.

'Where are these from?' Vera asked.

'Nubia,' he said, gesturing to one. 'Palestine, Aswan, Baghdad.'

'Any from Syria?'

He glanced at the range and shook his head. 'Sometimes. Not today.'

'If I wanted to get in touch with someone who had sent me an item bought in your shop, how would I go about it?'

The old man shrugged. 'Wait for him to find you.'

He shuffled back behind the counter and began rummaging in the drawers underneath it, then disappeared into the back room.

Vera waited a few moments, but he did not reappear. She thought it quite possible that the parcel had come from this shop – it was impossible to tell if the proprietor knew something or was just being awkward – but she was reluctant to be heavy-handed. It might not have come from Cairo at all. She might have it all wrong.

Sighing, she pulled open the door and went out, remembering that another of the shops on the list she had made was somewhere in this area. She would go there and see if she could glean any information.

In the shop behind her, the old man poked his head out of the office and watched through the glass as Vera disappeared along the street. He pursed his lips and called for the boy who was dozing in the back room.

'Come here! I need you to take a message.'

Chapter 20

At Miġra l-Ferħa, on Malta's western coast, tall cliffs loomed over the brooding Mediterranean. Before the war it had been a popular place to watch the sunset.

For a long stretch of coast, there was no way down to the sea; only the occasional narrow ravine sliced into the cliffs. It was in one of these that a local fisherman, paddling his boat at the base of the escarpment, saw the body of a man floating face down, his clothing snagged on a rock.

Looking uneasily up at the cliff, which now seemed more sheer than ever, the fisherman wondered what to do. He supposed the man was a pilot who had been shot down, but whether he was an enemy or an ally was impossible to tell.

He weighed up his options; a long row back to his village, a call to the police, and then probably another journey back with them in a motor launch to show them the ravine. By that time, the tide might rise and wash the body back out. This plan at least had the merit of taking the problem out of his hands. He stared at the black waterlogged shape. It was tempting.

But he was a man with a conscience, and he knew that he could not leave the corpse to the waves. The dead man probably had a wife and children. He would take the body back to the village and hand it over to the police.

Sculling nearer, conscious of the strong swell that was pushing his boat towards the cliffs, he leaned out with an oar and prodded the body, trying to shift it from the rocks where it was caught.

It came loose suddenly and began to drift past his boat. Leaning over the side, the fisherman grabbed the dead man's shoulder, took a deep breath, and flipped him over.

He was surprised to find that the body was in good condition; the face was bruised but otherwise undamaged, the eyes mercifully closed. What was even more surprising was the fact that this was clearly not an airman or even a mariner. He was older, perhaps sixty, and he wore a suit of good quality.

He was not Maltese, surmised the fisherman. His colouring and his clothing weren't right. He thought that the man was probably English, perhaps one of the men who worked for the government, or a senior soldier out of uniform.

With an effort, he pulled the body over the side of the boat, handling it as carefully as possible, although the waterlogged clothing made it heavy. At one point, he took hold of the cold white hand and was startled by how soft it was. At last, the body lay facing upwards in the boat, the man's arms lying neatly by his sides, water puddling under him.

The fisherman looked at him for a while longer, then pulled out his mackintosh and carefully arranged it over the face and as much of the body as it would cover.

Then he lifted the oars and rowed slowly towards home.

*

Please come to the office as soon as possible, said the telegram from Roger Wilson. That was it, although Margarita read it again in case she had missed something.

Could it be about Henry? They had been to his flat, after all, they must have got the journal. Perhaps, at last, they had found him – being kept prisoner in another cave, maybe, or far away in New York with a girlfriend. She could almost laugh at the idea, now, although she felt a pang for Vera.

Abandoning her housework, Margarita hurried out and caught a bus into Valletta. It was early afternoon and the sun was hot as she walked briskly through the city to the office in Archbishop Street.

Dennis Pratchett answered the door, looking grave, and she felt her heart plummet. He led her through to an inner office where Wilson sat at a broad desk. He closed the notebook he was scribbling in and looked sombrely at her.

'What is it?' she said.

'I'm afraid there's bad news. They've found a body in the ravine at Miġra I-Ferħa,' said Wilson slowly. 'The police believe it's Henry Dunn.'

Margarita put a hand to her chest and felt her heart thudding. Outwardly she felt numb and was surprised at the numbness. After all, she had loved him once.

'I see.' She dropped into a chair. 'Was he murdered?'

'We don't know yet.'

She nodded. 'Does Vera know he's been found?'

'We've sent her a message,' said Wilson. 'She's away on business.'

'Do you think that this Nero might have killed him?'

Wilson said nothing, but his frown told her it was possible.

'The journal – he was looking for Nero, investigating him,' said Margarita. 'Nero must have found him first.'

She saw Wilson catch Pratchett's eye. 'We don't have the journal,' he said at last. 'It was gone.'

'Gone?' Margarita stared at him. 'But it was there, I left it in the top drawer. It was there!'

'Not by the time we arrived,' said Pratchett, perching on the desk nearby.

'I didn't take it,' said Margarita, her eyes wide. 'I swear. I thought someone was coming, so I left it as I found it.'

'Well, that's as may be,' said Wilson. 'But it was gone when we got there. It seems that someone went there after you and took it away.'

Margarita felt her skin crawl at the thought. Someone – someone dangerous, perhaps Nero himself – had been into the same rooms, had stood beside the bed where she and Henry had made love, had opened the desk, prowled through the kitchen . . .

'Margarita,' said Wilson, making her jump and drawing her out of her horrified reverie. 'Can you remember the town name you saw written in the journal? You said there were two, attached to a diagram – Prague and somewhere else.'

'No,' she said, shaking her head. Then she frowned. 'Biskupin? Does that mean anything to you?'

'Biskupin,' said Wilson, writing it down. 'It's in Poland, I believe. That's something, anyway.'

Frowning as she tried to remember, Margarita's eyes fell on a photograph pinned above Pratchett's messy desk. It was large and rather blurred, but it looked somehow familiar. Three people sat on a wall, including a woman in a long white dress. Beside it was a scrap of paper with a drawing on it – a snake forming a circle, its face oddly human.

The telephone rang again, making her jump, and Wilson snatched it up. 'Yes? All right, thank you. We'll meet you there.'

He put the phone down. 'They want someone to identify Henry.'

'Someone?' said Margarita, with dread.

'I won't make you do it,' said Wilson, seeing her hesitation. 'Vera will be back in a couple of days. It can wait. In the meantime—'

'I'll come,' said Margarita, although she was already having second thoughts.

'Sure?' said Wilson.

'Yes.'

He led the way out of the office. As Margarita passed Pratchett's desk, she saw another smaller copy of the photograph he had pinned up, half-hidden under the mess of papers on his desk. Hardly knowing what she was doing, but sure she had seen it somewhere before, she picked it up and slid it quickly into her bag.

Pratchett turned back to look at her and frowned. Her heart felt as though it might leap out of her chest, but he looked sympathetic, and spoke in a low voice. 'You oughtn't to feel obliged, you know. You don't have to see him.'

Margarita swallowed and shook her head. Henry. Of course. 'I sort of – want to see him. Does that sound odd? Everything to do with Henry has been so confusing and distressing that I'd like to find some sort of . . . closure.'

Pratchett shrugged. 'Not odd at all.'

'Where is he?'

'They're taking him to the mortuary,' said Wilson, looking back. 'We'll meet them there.'

Chapter 21

Margarita paused in the doorway and looked into the room, suddenly feeling calm. The figure on the marble slab, covered in a white sheet, could have been anyone, but she knew without a doubt that it was Henry Dunn.

Once they were all gathered around the body, the mortuary assistant gently pulled the sheet down. Feeling as though she was far away, Margarita looked carefully at the face of the man she had once loved.

He looked very old, somehow, and she was relieved to see that his eyes were closed. They said he had been found in the water – his skin had an unpleasant clammy appearance – but he was undamaged, except for a dull bruise across the left side of his face. She felt unmoved, although she guessed that the shock would hit her later. It was him, all right, but this was not the flirtatious academic who had made love to her as air-raid sirens howled. This was just a shell.

'Well?' asked Wilson gruffly. 'Is it him?'

'Take all the time you need,' said Pratchett.

'It's definitely him,' she said quickly, looking around. 'Do I need to do anything else?'

'That's all,' said the assistant, covering Henry's face again. Margarita felt a swell of relief. That was that.

'What happened to him?' she said at last.

The assistant looked at Wilson, who shrugged.

'We can't be sure yet, but his neck was broken, and he'd hit his head somewhere along the way. We think he probably fell over the cliff.'

'Or was pushed,' said Pratchett, 'surely.'

'It's certainly a possibility,' said the assistant. 'We'll make a report on preliminary findings and then pass him up the chain.'

Wilson nodded, staring at the body. 'All right, you can go, Margarita,' he said briskly. 'Would you like a lift home?'

'I'd rather walk, I think, but thank you. Will you find out who killed him?' said Margarita as she left the room.

'Yes,' said Wilson grimly. 'Eventually.'

*

Floriana was quiet as Margarita walked home. Here and there, she saw old men sitting in the shade and groups of children playing, but the streets were empty of traffic. A plane droned far overhead and somewhere she could hear music trilling from a window.

She turned onto her street and saw someone sitting on the pavement outside her flat. Margarita squinted, then felt her heart leap.

'Arthur!'

He jumped up and spun her around. 'I'm back!' His whole face had lit up on seeing her, and she thought once again how lucky she was.

'Is this new?' asked Arthur, brushing the checked cotton dress she was wearing.

'Sort of – a hand-on from Catherine at work.'

'You look beautiful,' he said, kissing her. 'But you always do.'

Inside, she poured lemonade and they sat holding hands, grinning at one another, then both tried to speak at once.

'You go first,' said Arthur.

Where to start? Margarita swallowed and tried to find the words.

'What is it?' said Arthur, looking anxious. 'Is everything all right?'

Margarita took a deep breath. 'I have to tell you something. I had to go to the mortuary today to identify a body.'

Arthur's eyes widened, and she rushed on, telling him the whole story of her relationship with Henry, about Vera, and about the men from British intelligence. The only thing she did not mention was the name Nero, although it was hard not to talk about him when he occupied her thoughts constantly, whoever he was.

Arthur listened quietly. At some point, he let go of her hand and she felt crushed. Perhaps telling him was a mistake. When she had finished, he sat silently, chewing his lip.

'Arthur? Say something!'

He breathed out heavily. 'Sorry. It's just . . . a lot to take in.'

'I know.'

'Why didn't you tell me before?' His voice was gentle.

'About . . .'

'All of it!' he said, pushing his hair back. 'We're supposed to be getting married, Margarita. How can we do that if you don't trust me?'

'I was so embarrassed,' she said quietly. 'About Henry. When I found out that he had a wife . . .' She shuddered, recalling that awful day. 'I didn't want you to think badly of me.'

Arthur sat beside her again and took her hands. 'I could never do that.'

Margarita wiped the tears that had gathered. 'What were you going to tell me?'

'Oh.' He frowned, then sighed heavily. 'I'm being posted to Alexandria. Leaving tomorrow. We'll be based there from now on.'

She looked up. 'Permanently?'

'Well, as permanent as anything is in wartime,' he said. 'I'm sorry, I know it's going to be difficult. I'll write to you – we're not allowed to say much, so you may have to read between the lines. And of course I'll come back as often as I can on leave.'

'You will?'

'Of course!' he said.

'Even after . . .'

Arthur pulled her to him and she felt the beat of his heart against hers. 'I love you, Margarita,' he said into her hair. 'Just don't keep me in the dark from now on, all right?'

As she stood to make him a drink, Margarita felt the crinkle of paper in her pocket and withdrew the photograph she had snatched from Pratchett's desk. She looked blankly at the writing on the back for a moment, wondering why on earth she had taken it. It's not my job to find Nero, she thought, and dropped it into the wastepaper basket.

*

That evening, as they walked into the city, Margarita could tell that Arthur was preoccupied. She squeezed his hand, and he looked across at her, immediately banishing the glum look on his face.

'Sorry, just thinking.' He smiled, stroking her hand with his calloused thumb.

'About what?' she asked, hoping it was anything but Henry.

'Tomorrow,' he said. 'Leaving again. All of it.' Arthur shook his head. 'I just feel so helpless. I'm fed up with following orders, of my life not being my own. It makes me want to shout and yell, or else drink myself silly.'

'I wondered why you suggested going out tonight,' said Margarita teasingly, and he laughed.

'Don't worry, I shan't embarrass myself – or you.' He shook his head again. 'It's just the usual pre-departure gloom. I'll feel better tomorrow.'

They found a group of Arthur's fellow officers drinking in a bar near the harbour, and a little later Margarita was pleased to see Catherine and Poppy from the Phoenix Club. Catherine was with her boyfriend, an army officer, but Poppy quickly got talking to one of Arthur's colleagues and they were soon dancing together.

'He's a good chap,' said Arthur reassuringly as they watched the pair twirl across the floor. 'He won't mess her about.'

'I should hope not!' said Margarita, laughing. She leaned back in her seat, feeling a swell of something like happiness as she listened to the conversation of friends around her and watched the dancers move to and fro. It was easy to forget sometimes, when the sirens were howling, about real life – about the simple pleasures there were to be found in good company and good music.

Arthur held a hand out and she scrambled up, feeling his strong arms around her waist, her feet automatically recalling the steps to the dance. She liked dancing, she remembered. She had been so preoccupied recently; perhaps she had lost sight of what mattered.

'All right?' Arthur was looking down at her, as perceptive as ever. He gently ran his thumb down the slight frown line between her eyes. 'Are you still thinking about Henry?'

'Sort of,' said Margarita, feeling guilty. 'But I want to forget, I really do.'

'Take all the time you need,' said Arthur, kissing her fore-head. 'You've had a shock.' He was quiet for a moment. 'You didn't do anything wrong, you know.'

No, I didn't, thought Margarita. She had spent so long feeling ashamed of her affair with Henry that she'd almost forgotten she'd been deceived. He was too old for her, that was clear, and she would never make that mistake again, but she had behaved as honourably as she knew how.

She looked up at Arthur's handsome, honest face and felt relieved that he was so different from Henry – and far away from the world of secrets and lies that Vera seemed to inhabit. Despite the events of the morning, she could feel a lightness, as though the worry and the hurt were draining away. She was young, she was loved, and there was music and laughter all around. Margarita remembered that there was a letter from her stepmother waiting at home, and she resolved to answer it as soon as possible, to express her love, her gratitude. If nothing else, Vera had been right about that.

'The past doesn't matter,' said Arthur, as if he had read her mind, and he kissed her. 'Let's talk about the future.'

Chapter 22
Syria, 1926

The Professor and Schuster departed one morning on the first of their trips, taking the old motor car. Dorothy Curzon took most of her meals in her tent and only occasionally emerged to go for a ride or to read in the shade. Vera went out early to the dig site each day with the boys, returning when the shadows began to lengthen.

In the evenings, they spent another hour or two in the work-room, cataloguing the day's finds and doing small cleaning and mending projects, eager to impress the Professor when he returned.

'I think it looks rather good,' said Matthew, surveying the shelves, now laden with shards of pottery, lumps of carved stone, small statues, bowls, tablets and axe heads. 'Looks like a proper dig now.'

'We haven't found a real treasure trove yet, though,' said Vera, frowning critically at the pendant in her hand. 'These are all very well, but I want to find something extraordinary.'

He shrugged. 'I like the humble things – the houses and the pots and the furniture. That's history.'

'I want to *make* history,' said Vera, then laughed. 'Perhaps I'll have to wait until I have a dig of my own.'

'This is good experience,' said Matthew seriously. 'With Professor Curzon on our side, we'll be set up for success and interesting jobs in the future. Think of it as an investment.'

He watched her tidying up her workspace in the lamplight, humming slightly, her white shirt rolled up to the elbows and smudges of mud on her nose.

'Vera . . .'

'Hmm?'

He smiled and shook his head. 'Nothing. Some other time. Shall we go and see if supper's ready?'

Outside the arched doorway, they sat side by side and pulled on their boots. Suddenly, Vera yelped and kicked off the boot she had just put on.

'Vera? What is it?'

'There was something in there. I've been stung. Scorpion, I think.'

Wincing, she pulled the thick stocking off her foot and saw a red blotch on the heel. Matthew peered at it.

'We'd better get you to Mrs Curzon, she's got the medical box.'

'No – I'll be fine.'

'Don't be silly, Vera. Here, grab my arm. Want me to carry you?'

'Certainly not.'

Leaning heavily on Matthew, she hopped awkwardly through the camp, feeling her heart racing. They found Dorothy Curzon in her tent, and though she looked alarmed at first, she quickly sprang into action, bathing the wound and pressing it gently while elevating Vera's foot on a stool.

'We've no ice, I'm afraid,' she said. 'That's the best thing. Matthew, will you run to the cool cellar and get a cold bottle of something? Wine, beer, anything will do, the coldest you can find.'

He dashed away and in silence Dorothy pressed a wet cloth to the wound. Vera bit her lip, relieved and resentful at the same time.

'Thank you,' she said at last. 'I'm grateful for your help.'

Dorothy looked at her, her head slightly on one side.

'You're in charge now,' she said, her tone measured. 'Ralph would never forgive me if something happened to you. You're his favourite student – this year.'

Vera flinched at the meaning inherent in her words; for a moment they stared at one another, full of mistrust.

'Be careful,' said Dorothy at last. They looked up to see Matthew hurrying towards them, brandishing a bottle of beer that had been buried deep in the sand.

*

The next afternoon, Vera returned to base, walking slowly on her bandaged foot. She felt tired and suspected that the scorpion's venom was still in her veins. She had taken several aspirin, but the pain flared up again each time she walked, and all her muscles ached.

'Why not have a rest day?' Matthew had said worriedly that morning, but she was determined not to show weakness.

Walking through the camp, she noticed that one of the biggest tents was empty, the cotton flaps tied neatly back and the inside billowing white and clean. She frowned and hurried on to the main building.

'Where is Mrs Curzon?' she asked Azim, who was busy cooking in their new brick-built kitchen, a filthy apron around his waist.

'Home.'

'She's gone home?'

He nodded. 'A car came to collect her. Alep first, then back to England.'

Vera felt relief wash over her, and something like guilt with it. She wondered again why Dorothy had come out here at all.

Was she keeping an eye on her husband? Or was there something else? She had clearly mistrusted Schuster too. What did she know about him?

*

As her foot began to heal, Vera felt her enthusiasm for the dig renewed. Progress was slow, but they were finding new evidence every day of the settlement that had once stood here.

She made her way to the main pit, where a group of six men and two boys were working. They noticed her approach and saluted vaguely before redoubling their efforts.

'Good afternoon,' she said in Arabic. 'Anything interesting today?'

'Nothing,' said Farid, their leader, after a pause. 'Only the little pot this morning.' He gestured to a chipped clay vessel that lay on a sack in the shade a dozen yards away.

She wandered over to look at it, and saw the smallest boy, Mohammed, come over with a bucket of earth, which he started to sift onto a heap nearby.

'Madame?'

She looked up and smiled at him. He was small, his face round and childlike, although he had told her he was nearly thirteen. His long robe was too big for him, and he had hitched it up with a belt.

'What is it, Mo?'

'Perhaps we might dig here next.'

'Here?' she said, looking around. 'Why?'

'The ground feels different,' he said.

'Different how?'

'I don't know,' he said, frowning. 'It just feels different when you walk on it.' He put down the bucket and brushed his hands together, then jumped up and down, flexing his bare toes in the dust. 'I don't know how to explain it.'

'Show me,' said Vera, following him. 'Shall I jump here?'

'Yes,' he said, 'and then try over there.'

'Mohammed, get back to work,' said Farid, appearing behind him. 'You shouldn't be talking to the lady.'

'It's all right,' said Vera. 'He's showing me something. I'll send him back in a few minutes.'

Farid nodded, but shot an angry look at Mo and departed.

'Here?' said Vera.

'Yes.'

She jumped up and down a few times, feeling rather foolish. 'Perhaps I should take my boots off.' She was conscious of the scorpion sting, which had only recently healed, but Mohammed's suggestion had piqued her interest. She unlaced her boots, removed her socks, leaving the bandage in place, and jumped again.

'And now here,' said Mohammed, pointing to a place a few yards away. Vera jumped there and frowned.

'You feel it?' he said.

'Perhaps.'

'Try again.'

She went back and forth, no longer caring what anyone thought, and jumped again in a few places.

'You see?' said Mohammed. 'It's different.'

She jumped once more in the first place he had shown her, and looked up at him, astonishment dawning. 'It feels hollow,' she said at last.

'Do you think there is something underneath?' said Mohammed eagerly.

'Perhaps. How on earth did you notice the difference?'

He shrugged. 'I walk a long way every day. I am used to feeling the ground under my feet.'

Vera called Laiq, who was sitting in the shade some distance away, and he ambled over, looking unenthusiastic. He frowned at Mo, who had forgotten his buckets of earth altogether and was now kneeling with his ear to the ground as he knocked it gently with his fist.

'Shouldn't you be working?'

'He's working with me,' said Vera. 'We need the men to start digging over here.'

Laiq raised his eyebrows. 'What have you found?'

'Nothing yet, but the ground feels hollow. Mo and I are going to mark out a new section. Please instruct Farid's team to come and dig over here – as soon as possible.'

He hesitated, then shrugged. 'As you say.'

*

By the next day, they had removed a huge amount of earth from the area that Mo had suggested, although nothing of interest had been found except for a few beads.

Vera brushed the dirt off the beads and looked carefully at them. 'Where were they? Perhaps you should focus on that area.'

Farid hesitated, glancing at Laiq, but he was talking to someone else. Vera internally rolled her eyes and waited.

'Very well,' said Farid at last, and she could have cheered as she watched him move over to the place that she had indicated.

She knew that it would not help to hover over them, so she went back to the open-sided tent where Matthew and Stanley were having a picnic lunch. As soon as she saw the sliced figs and crumbly white cheese, she realised she was ravenous.

'Do you want a chair?' said Matthew, looking around.

'No, this is fine,' said Vera, sitting beside him on the rug. She bit into a fig, feeling the sweetness on her tongue.

'Cheese?' Stanley held out the plate, then passed a hunk of Azim's coarse homemade flatbread.

'Looks as though they're making good progress,' said Matthew, nodding towards the dig as he poured lemonade. 'Nothing yet?'

'Just a few beads,' said Vera. 'But it's early days.' She held a hand over her brow and watched the men. Farid and two others were out of sight in the pit, digging hard, and she saw Mo and the other boy carrying away buckets of earth.

'Clever of you to notice that the ground felt hollow,' said Matthew.

'It was Mohammed, actually,' said Vera. 'And we haven't found a cavity yet. We may be barking up the wrong tree entirely.'

There was a shout, and she looked around to see Mo running towards her, cradling his bucket, while two of the men behind called for him to return.

'What is it?'

Panting, he reached her and held out the bucket. Inside were several large clods of earth that he had been splitting apart with a trowel. But one of them was not a clod at all; instead, the trowel had scraped away an inch or so of mud, and underneath it was something that gleamed.

He held out the trowel, but she shook her head. 'Let's do it together.'

They knelt down, and placing the bucket between them, Mo prodded gently at the earth where the metal was visible. Another chunk of mud fell away, and Vera could see what was unmistakably a carved eye.

She reached out and ran her finger gently over the surface. It was cool to the touch. Bronze, she thought.

'Is it a statue?' said Mo anxiously.

Vera put down the trowel and lowered both hands into the bucket. Feeling the dry mud disintegrate under her fingers, she began to scrape away at the lump of earth until the bronze was visible on all sides. She saw a flash of gold and her heart leapt. Once upon a time, the statue had been thinly coated in gold and now fragments remained here and there across the surface like paint splashes.

'Yes, it's a statue,' she said at last. 'It's a head. Look, here's the face.'

Mo stared wonderingly at it, then said, 'Water,' and trotted away.

'What a find,' said someone behind her, and she jumped. She had almost forgotten that the boys were nearby.

Matthew knelt beside her and looked at the head she was cradling. 'What's it made of?'

'Bronze, I think,' said Vera. 'But coated with gold. Dash it, where's my handkerchief?'

'Here,' said Matthew, after rooting in his pockets. 'It was clean this morning.'

Vera rubbed gently at the earth that covered the statue, seeing more of it fall away. She could see now that it was the head of a woman, about six inches long from neck to scalp. Instead of hair, a headdress had been cast, the detail of the beads clearly visible.

Mo returned with a bucket of water and between them they cleaned the head carefully. He was gentle with it, and she saw the delight on his face as he ran his fingers gently over the gold.

He looked back at the dig, where the other men were still working. 'Do you think we will find more, Miss Vera?'

'I'm sure of it,' she said, shading her eyes as she smiled at him. 'I've been hoping and hoping we'll find some sort of treasure chamber or temple. I think this is it.'

'Mohammed!' called Farid. 'Back to work.' The boy smiled resignedly and loped away.

Chapter 23

The message waiting for Vera at the Cairo Continental was worded starkly: *Please telephone Morton at once.* She knew it was bad news, and with little surprise she heard that Henry's body had been found in the sea. She felt a rush of anger and a strange powerlessness that she had not felt for a long time. Henry might have slipped and fallen, of course, but she knew without a doubt that he had not – someone had killed him. Then came the guilt, like a punch to the gut, for they had almost certainly done it because of her.

Poor Henry, she thought. He had no idea what he was getting into when he married me. Perhaps I ought not to have accepted his proposal. But she had accepted it, for better or worse, and for several reasons: he was kind, he wanted the same sort of marriage she did – one with complete freedom – and he understood her in a way that only one man ever had before. And look how that ended, she thought glumly.

Vera brushed off Morton's suggestion that they might postpone the meeting with the German informant.

'Don't be ridiculous,' she said. 'Henry wouldn't want me to stop working. If I don't go, I shall just sit about the place and get hopelessly drunk.'

'That's our Vera,' said Morton, but he let it go, and it did not occur to her to be offended until after she had replaced the receiver and left the booth.

The meeting was set for seven o'clock and she slept for an hour before washing and changing into a demure outfit. The linen suit was bulky and drab, but she looked exactly what she was supposed to be – a middle-aged bluestocking.

She walked briskly through the streets to the restaurant. Inside, she could see people of all nationalities dining.

'Good evening, madam,' said the young maître d'. 'Table for one?'

'Two, please. I'm meeting someone.'

'Of course. Perhaps you'd like to wait at the bar until he arrives. What would you like to drink?'

'Whisky, please.'

'Alas, the whisky is finished tonight, madam. A cocktail, perhaps?'

'All right,' said Vera, seating herself on a tall stool. 'Nothing too sweet.'

A waiter brought her a fizzing concoction and she tasted it, feeling the sting of fresh lime juice. 'Delicious. Thank you.'

She wondered, not for the first time, if this informant, Tariq, really wanted to offer up secrets to the Allies. He was almost certainly a double agent. But he had known Emilio in Tunis. Perhaps he could be of use.

Eventually, she saw a man enter and speak to the maître d'. She watched him carefully: he was young, tall, with dark hair carelessly tousled over his brow. Presumably he was Egyptian, although he might have been from anywhere in Arabia. He was attractive, in a way, but his mouth was thin and she instinctively felt that he would be arrogant. Pinned to the lapel of his smart suit was the identifier she had been told to look for – a golden Eye of Horus.

'Good evening,' said the man, and he held out a hand. 'I am Tariq. I hope you weren't waiting long?'

'Only a few minutes,' said Vera.

He smiled slightly as he caught her examining him. 'I am not what you expected?'

'I expected nothing in particular,' said Vera. 'I'm Juliet. Shall we sit down?'

'Another drink?'

'Perhaps some coffee.'

'A good idea. I do not drink alcohol.' Tariq spoke briefly to the waiter and turned to look at her as they sat down. 'Ah, yes, I heard that you understood Arabic.'

'Heard from whom?'

He smiled again. 'We have a mutual friend. So . . . I am Tariq and you are Juliet. It's strange, isn't it, that we are about to work closely together and yet we cannot use each other's real names?'

'What makes you think it's not my real name?'

He laughed. 'I know you're not a fool.'

Tariq sat back as the waiter approached with coffee, placing the cups carefully between them. Vera observed him over her cup, trying to read his expression. His eyes, she thought, were kind, but there was something about his mouth that she did not trust at all. He reminded her strongly of someone, but she could not think who. Then it came to her – Curzon, of course. He too had had a hard, arrogant mouth, and although she had found it attractive once, it now spoke to her of betrayal.

'Well, Tariq, what do you think you can offer us?'

He drank slowly and looked thoughtful. 'I am a moneylender – among other activities. It is for this reason that I was recruited by our friends in the desert two years ago. I see many people, I do a great deal of business. I am well placed to hear things.'

'Which you feed back to them.'

'Yes, but I have no loyalty to them – I find them uncivilised. I often gather information that would be detrimental to them, and it has been on my mind for some time that I might find a buyer for it.'

Vera sipped her coffee unhurriedly. She could hear the conversations of the cooks in the kitchen, and here and there the murmured chat of other customers. The waiter passed, carrying a tray laden with food, and she smelled the sharp tang of vinegar, followed by garlic, coriander, and the scent of fresh bread.

'Our mutual friend,' she said. 'What is your connection with him?'

'I sometimes do business in Tunis,' he said. 'We crossed paths there. He was very discreet, but I am a good detective. I realised he must be passing information to the British.'

'Was it you who betrayed him?' she asked, remembering Emilio's haggard expression, his certainty that he had been discovered.

'Absolutely not,' said Tariq, looking offended. 'I am not a – what do you say? A rat. I have no love for the Germans or the Italians.'

'Do you know what has happened to him?'

Tariq shook his head. 'Only vague rumours. I heard on the grapevine recently that he had been caught, but not what happened after that. I imagine my assumption is the same as yours.'

Vera nodded, feeling depressed. Somehow, she had hoped to hear that Emilio was alive. But no – they had almost certainly tortured him and then killed him.

'I'm sorry,' added Tariq.

'That's the job,' said Vera, although she struggled to believe it sometimes.

Tariq put his head on one side. 'It's a strange job for an English lady archaeologist to be doing. How did you end up here?'

Vera put her cup down. 'I don't recall saying I was an archaeologist.'

'I told you I was a good detective,' said Tariq, shrugging. 'You cannot blame me for doing a little research. After all, that's why you're in Cairo, isn't it? Officially?'

'There's a conference at the university.'

'So I have learned.'

'You seem to know a lot,' said Vera.

'It's my business,' he said. 'I began as a trader, but over the years I have learned that secrets are the most valuable commodity there is. I can walk down the street unnoticed in any country of the Levant, under the eyes of whatever power happens to be occupying it.'

Vera pictured him moving quietly through busy streets, or serving in a restaurant, or driving a taxi, anonymous and unmemorable. As a moneylender and smuggler, his work would take him everywhere. He was, in many ways, the perfect source.

'What insurance can you provide?' said Vera.

'Insurance?'

'How do we know that you're really working for us and not just feeding back information to our enemies?'

'You don't know,' said Tariq smoothly. 'There is nothing I can tell you that will make you trust me. But I can see which way the wind is blowing, and the Allies are making gains. I would rather be part of that success than Rommel's failure. I am prepared to risk a lot in order to contribute – and, of course, to earn some money.'

Vera questioned him as closely as possible, but he was cagey about his life and his business.

'Were you born in Cairo?'

'No,' he said, gesturing with his hand to the south. 'Far from here.'

'Do you have family here?'

'No,' he said, understanding the question. 'No wife, no children, no vulnerabilities.'

She need make him no promises; she had been sent to listen and to assess his suitability as a source. At last, she noted down his requests regarding money and promised to pass them on.

'When will you be back in Cairo?' said Tariq eagerly. 'Soon?'

'I don't know.'

'I will only speak with you,' he warned. 'I cannot risk my communications being intercepted.'

'What if your associates hear that you have met with me?' said Vera.

He shrugged. 'I'll tell them I've learned of a possible leak in British intelligence. But there's no reason they should find out.'

She nodded slowly. 'Is there anything else you wish to tell me? Anything I should take back to my colleagues?'

He was silent for a moment, watching her carefully. 'Does the name Nero mean anything to you?'

'Nero, like the emperor? Why do you ask?'

He shrugged. 'It's nothing. Just a rumour. I'm curious.'

'I can't help, I'm afraid.' She drained her cup and looked at her watch. 'I must go.'

Tariq nodded. 'You'll be in touch soon?'

'Yes. Someone will.'

'I will speak only to you about important matters.'

She hesitated. 'Very well. It was a pleasure to meet you, Tariq.' It wasn't true, she didn't like him much at all, but her job was to flatter him and see if he would be a useful source.

He took her hand and stared into her eyes for a moment. Again, she felt a sense of familiarity, but not a pleasant one; she knew that it was because he reminded her of Curzon, although in background the two men could not have been more different. She also sensed something negative emanating from him – was it disappointment? Anger?

She left the restaurant first, leaving Tariq, at his insistence, to pay for the drinks. The narrow streets were still busy, shops and restaurants glowing gently on all sides. Groups of servicemen laughed loudly as they swaggered down the middle of the road, calling out to veiled Egyptian girls who flitted past in pairs.

The warm night air smelled of sewage and flowers, one never quite managing to extinguish the other. Cairo was a dirty place, but it was not so far to the desert. These days it was home to hundreds of thousands of troops. But armies could only hope to cover a tiny area, and the lone and level sands stretched for thousands of untouched miles in all directions, under a clear navy sky.

Vera saw the bright lights of the Continental in the distance and walked faster, passing couples who were ambling slowly along, hand in hand, and the groups of elderly Egyptian men who watched them impassively.

A tall man in a dinner jacket was smoking outside the hotel, his profile so familiar that her breath caught in her throat – it couldn't be him! She hurried to cross the road and a car appeared from the darkness, its headlights turned off, driving straight at her.

Chapter 24

Vera blinked, lying in the road, and saw the car tearing off down the dark street. She closed her eyes, feeling dazed. When she opened them, two or three people were kneeling over her, looking concerned, and the concierge from the hotel was rushing down the steps.

'Madam – don't move, please. I will fetch a doctor.'

'I'm all right,' she said, carefully lifting a hand to her head to check for damage. 'It barely touched me.' She sat up and one of the men put his hand on her shoulder to support her.

He wore a dinner jacket and she looked closely at him. He was in his twenties, with thick blond hair, quite different from the man she thought she had seen. 'Was there another man outside the hotel with you? Wearing a jacket like that?'

He looked startled. 'I don't think so. Look, why don't you lie down again?'

'I'm staying in the hotel,' said Vera. 'I'll be fine once I've got to my room.'

The main place that hurt was her right hip and thigh, where the car had caught her, and she knew that she would have a huge bruise and some stiffness tomorrow. But she had protected her head as she fell and otherwise felt undamaged. She looked again at the man in the dinner jacket, feeling frustrated. In the half-light he had looked so familiar. But of course it wasn't him, it couldn't have been him.

She stood up slowly and allowed the concierge to take her arm and lead her inside. Walking wasn't painful, and she felt remarkably lucky. She wondered vaguely who had tried to run her down but pushed the thought away. That was a problem for tomorrow. Tonight, she needed a drink.

'Oh, I thought I might see you!'

Vera turned to see a girl waving at her. She wore a long silver evening gown and elbow-length gloves, and it took Vera a moment to realise that it was Jean Berry, the driver who had collected her from the airfield the day before. It seemed a long time ago.

'Hello,' said Jean. She took a closer look. 'Are you all right? You look shaken up.'

'I'm fine,' said Vera. 'I just had a silly fall outside, but I'm quite all right now. You look terrific. Having a nice evening?'

'Lovely, thanks. Those are my pals over there at the bar. We've been up on the roof having a dance. Apparently there's a party over on the river, so we thought we might look in. Like to come?'

'Wouldn't miss it,' said Vera. 'Have I got time to dress?'

'Oh, yes,' said Jean. 'We'll be down here having a drink.' She smiled then went to join her friends at the bar and Vera went up to her room.

She took off her clothes and examined the damage. The first signs of a huge bruise were already blooming on her thigh and she prodded it gingerly. A few drinks would help to numb the pain.

Luckily she had brought an evening gown, a narrow black dress in silk crepe, with long sleeves and heavy gold embroidery.

'What a glorious dress!' said Jean, when Vera arrived at the bar and ordered a whisky and soda. 'You didn't get that in Cairo.'

'It's Schiaparelli,' said Vera, smoothing the silk. 'A gift from my husband Henry, last time he was in New York. My *late* husband,' she added.

'Oh, I'm so sorry,' said Jean, passing her drink.

'Best not to dwell on these things, I find, or one gets very downcast,' said Vera, and she took a long drink. 'I'm here to have a good time. Won't you introduce me to your friends?'

They were charming girls, all British except Cleo, a glamorous Egyptian, said to be a cousin of King Farouk. They were all employed by the ATS and taking advantage of a rare night off.

'What brings you to Cairo?' said Molly, as they mingled near the bar. Jean looked anxiously at Vera, but she smiled.

'I'm an archaeologist. I'm here to attend a conference.'

'How exciting! Have you dug up anything interesting recently?'

'One or two things,' said Vera. 'Shall I get another round of drinks?'

It was nearly midnight by the time they wove along the waterside to the party that was being held aboard a moored steamer. Vera had drunk enough by now to dull the pain, and she even found herself dancing, feeling no more than a twinge from her hip. Her partners were mostly aristocratic Englishmen, although she danced once with an Egyptian prince, half her age and smoothly handsome.

'You are a very beautiful woman, Mrs Dunn,' he said, leaning in confidentially and pulling her a little closer. 'Perhaps you'd like to come for a cruise on my boat one day – I have a beautiful felucca, newly painted, the fastest on the Nile.'

She smiled up at him. 'I'd love to, but I'm afraid I'm leaving Cairo tomorrow.'

'Perhaps the next time you are here?' he said, and spun her away from him, pulling her back in with a flourish. 'We will go out and drift along the river one afternoon and drink champagne and eat figs and listen to the water lapping.'

Vera could imagine the scene and what came next. 'That does sound lovely. Shouldn't you be out with a girl of your own age, though?'

He shrugged, his hands caressing her waist. 'I am not interested in girls. I am interested in women. I have found that they are much more passionate – even Englishwomen.'

She danced with a few others, although her mind was not fully present. The matter of Tariq was simple enough to deal with – she would return to Malta and tell her superiors that he might be useful but that they should proceed with caution. She did not altogether trust him, and thought it quite likely that he would double-cross the British for his own gain. He was young and power-hungry; she knew what that was like and knew it was dangerous.

The other matter was more worrying. Someone from her past was playing a strange game, and she was afraid that he might endanger the work she was doing. What did he want? She thought of the car that had driven straight at her. It might have been an accident, but she had worked in intelligence long enough to know that few things were truly accidental. Someone had tried to kill her and they would probably try again. She carried a gun everywhere, but she could not shoot a car, nor would she be able to do much if a knife was thrust into her back in the street.

The young prince asked her for another dance, but Vera made her apologies. Before long, she saw him dancing with a woman who really was old enough to be his mother and kissing her hand. Vera smiled and pushed through the crowds, emerging on the deck.

She walked a little way along the promenade and sat on a bollard, looking at the water, where the reflections of the strings of lights gleamed. A warm desert wind was blowing along the river and it made her ache with longing. Her time in Syria had ended abruptly, cut short by drama and tragedy, but she would never forget those first few weeks in the desert, beneath an extraordinary sky, when the world seemed suffused with possibility.

'Are you feeling all right?' said a voice, and she looked around to see Jean, who was holding out a lit cigarette. 'Smoke?'

'Thanks,' said Vera, taking it. She pulled heavily on the cigarette and sighed, looking up at the girl. 'Had a nice evening?'

'Oh, not bad,' said Jean. 'It's always the same people, you know . . . once you've been to one party, you've been to them all.'

'Yes, I know.'

'Has your trip been successful?'

'I'm not sure yet,' said Vera thoughtfully.

Jean moved sideways to look at the river, the silk of her dress billowing in the breeze. Her profile was silhouetted against the water and moonlight gleamed on her pale neck. Vera smiled and stubbed out the cigarette.

Chapter 25

Dennis Pratchett sat hunched at his messy desk, moving pieces of paper between piles and muttering to himself. Occasionally one slipped onto the floor or disappeared into the dusty darkness beneath the desk and he sighed heavily.

He was trying to put together everything that was known about Nero into some sort of order. He had spent the last few weeks gathering information, communicating daily with archivists in several countries to dig up anything that might be connected with Nero. Stacks of notes, reports and fragments of longer documents had materialised, most of them quite useless. There were a number that looked promising, but working through them and trying to discover the man's identity was another matter. It was dispiriting; he had expected the hunt for a master spy to involve more action and less paperwork.

News had come through early that morning of an intercepted German message regarding British submarine movements off Libya. The information seemed to have come directly from a secure communique sent to Malta by Allied forces in North Africa. Major Ede was convinced that Nero was behind it and had ordered Wilson to ramp up his investigation into the potential mole.

'If there is a mole, he probably already knows we're after him,' Wilson had said irritably before leaving for a meeting. 'If Ede got his way, I'd have gathered all the staff into a room and demanded to know which of them was a traitor. He likes to go in guns blazing.'

'What do you want me to do?' said Pratchett, keen to get away from his desk.

'Find out who Nero is,' said Wilson. 'We don't know that he's the mole, but someone working for him almost certainly is. Either way, finding his identity will be a step towards catching him.'

But it was easier said than done, and Pratchett occasionally had flashes of panic at the scope of the task before him. If he found Nero, he'd be lauded and set for life in his career. If he didn't, and Nero remained at liberty, he would have failed, and his future in the intelligence service would be in doubt. Not to mention the damage that could be caused if the spy continued his work – the planned re-invasion of Europe might be jeopardised. Nero was only one man, but he was extremely dangerous, and the course of the war could hang in the balance.

Pratchett lifted up the letter that Nero had written in 1917 to his masters in Berlin. It was the oldest piece of evidence they had. The same year – he picked up a typewritten page – the British had decoded messages sent from a German agent inside Britain. They couldn't be certain that it was Nero, but most of the German agents in Britain had been rounded up in one swoop soon after the start of the war. Any that avoided the net and slipped away must have been good – very good.

The messages had come from someone who knew the country well and understood it. He had a clear grasp of British geography and understood the differences in attitudes between those who lived in London and those who lived outside it. The content of the messages was dull, mostly about shipping, but it was the subtext that Pratchett was interested in.

The spy of 1917 had been in Britain for some time and had probably arrived before the war; once war was on the cards, a more careful approach was taken to new arrivals in the country, and it seemed unlikely that a spy would have slipped through.

If their theories about Nero's age now were correct, he would have been under twenty when he arrived in Britain, possibly a student. Pratchett made a note to request a list of foreign students who had studied in Britain before the first war. If Nero was among them, that would explain his ability to pass himself off as an Englishman.

He turned to the next piece of paper, a letter dated November 1926 that had turned up in the archives after a search for the synonymous terms *Schwarzmarkt* and *Schwarzer Markt*, an idea he had been rather proud of. A translation had been clipped to the back:

> *My good friend,*
> *I must thank you for arranging the gift as I requested. Our old friend has done fine work in securing it on the black market! Lucky that its arrival in Switzerland coincided with you being there, after all the delays.*
> *I will write separately to N. with my thanks.*
> *With best regards,*
> *H. H.*

The letter was thought to have been sent to one of Heinrich Himmler's lieutenants. At the time, Himmler had been the Nazi Party's deputy propaganda chief, one of many ambitious subordinates. Now, he was one of the Führer's closest advisers. If the letter referred to Nero, it seemed he had connections at the very top of the Nazi hierarchy.

Switzerland might be a profitable line of enquiry, thought Pratchett. He would make some telephone calls. London might be able to exert some pressure on the Swiss to get to the bottom of it – Switzerland was officially neutral, but her people had no love for Hitler.

If they could trace the mysterious gift that had been sent to Himmler via Switzerland in 1926, it might eventually lead them to Nero, the shadowy figure who operated on the 'black market', always out of sight.

Pratchett stared, for what must be the hundredth time, at the enlarged copy of the photograph they had found in Henry's flat. He looked around vaguely for the original, wanting to see the writing on the back, but it was lost in the chaos of his desk. No matter – the scribbled text had been short and to the point. *Nero, 1926?*

He looked down at the Himmler letter. What was Nero doing all that time? Between the wars, when Germany had been theoretically at peace with her neighbours, what jobs had been sent his way?

For twenty years, the Germans had not been the enemy. They had been friends, even, recovering like everyone else from the chaos and destruction of the Great War. At times, the British had even shared intelligence with Germany, and vice versa – unthinkable now.

'We were more concerned about Russia,' Wilson had said. 'I cut my teeth infiltrating various Red groups in Britain, as did many of my cohort. We assumed that the next war, if there was one, would be against the Bolsheviks.'

'Weren't we spying on Germany, too?'

'Oh, yes,' said Wilson. 'All countries spy on each other, even allies. It's quite likely that Nero continued working for Germany in the twenties, feeding back information from Britain or Russia or elsewhere in the world. He was implicated in at least one assassination, as you know, so perhaps he developed a sideline. He kept his hand in, anyway. Perhaps he guessed he might be needed again, and he knew he was the best.' He laughed grimly. 'We could do with someone like that on our side.'

'What about Snowdrop?'

Wilson had snorted. 'A fairy tale.'

Snowdrop was a legendary British spy within the Nazi high command, whom Pratchett had been told about during his first week in intelligence. It was a silly name, he thought, but the man himself was far from silly. Whispers of his existence had swirled around the intelligence agencies for years. His British case officer was rumoured to be someone at the top. It was a reassuring thought – that there might be someone inside the Nazi state working against them.

He must be very brave, thought Pratchett, feeling a chill as he recalled what the Nazis were known to do to traitors. He looked back at the heap of information on his desk. Even Snowdrop wouldn't be much use if Nero was allowed to go free. He gritted his teeth and started to organise the evidence. They *had* to find him.

Chapter 26

Syria, 1926

Like flowers blooming overnight in the desert, a mass of tents had sprung up beside the river. They were Kurds, said Laiq, nomads, on their way north with their animals for the winter. Half a dozen women from the camp came to call on Vera and she sat with them in her tent, serving coffee and admiring their brightly coloured gowns and tinkling golden jewellery.

They told her about their husbands and children and were surprised to hear that she possessed neither. Vera, who had expected them to marvel at her independence, found instead that she was an object of pity.

'Perhaps you can marry this Professor of yours,' said Gulda, their leader. 'He is tall and handsome, they say.'

Vera, laughing to cover her embarrassment, explained that the Professor was married to another woman, who had gone back to England. This was not considered an obstacle; Gulda's husband had three wives and she was good friends with the other two.

A little later, they left, with warm embraces and instructions not to delay any longer in finding a husband. 'You don't have to like him!' said Gulda with a wink.

Vera watched them stream back towards their camp, their beautiful gowns vivid against the scrubby ground. She found herself envying them. The life they lived out here in the desert was hard, certainly, and they had little say in who they married, but she saw their healthy, handsome faces, their jewels, and the wide blue sky beneath which they lived, and felt they were more free than she had ever been.

*

When the Professor returned from his trip with Schuster a few days later, he said nothing about his wife's absence. Vera watched him carefully, but he did not seem either disappointed or relieved that she had gone away.

Instead, he congratulated Vera on the discovery of the bronze head and gave a shilling to Mohammed for finding it.

'Don't let anyone else see it,' she heard him say, before ruffling the boy's hair, and she saw Mo nod earnestly, tucking the coin into his robes before he trotted away.

'I have a great deal of work to do,' said Schuster. 'My book deadline is approaching and I have been off gallivanting!'

'Use my office,' said Curzon. 'I prefer to work outside. Make yourself at home, Karl.'

Curzon got stuck back into work quickly, rolling up his sleeves and joining the boys and Vera on the dig. That afternoon, he appeared as she was going through a collection of pottery fragments the men had found in the new location, turning them over and grouping them by colour and pattern.

'Beautiful,' said the Professor, glancing over.

'Aren't they?'

'I'm very pleased with what we've found so far.'

'You are?' said Vera eagerly. 'How does it compare to other years?'

'It's hard to draw a direct comparison as the sites vary so much,' he said. 'But, all things being equal, I'd say this is one of the most successful digs I've been in charge of. This new area looks very promising.' Vera felt a swell of pride that he saw such potential in the spot she had selected. She wanted, more than anything else, to impress him.

'You don't mind having only students? I know you usually have another expert on the team.'

He shrugged. 'Each has its benefits. Three years ago I ran a joint dig with a chap from Cambridge and we couldn't stand each other. He'd been working in Iraq for thirty years and had very fixed ideas. A brilliant fellow, but a bore. This year, I'm surrounded by youth and beauty.'

Vera flushed and looked down at the pottery. He was attracted to her, that much was clear. But what if he was just playing games, she wondered, feeling her hands clench. He was a brilliant archaeologist, which was what had drawn her to him in the first place, but she knew very little about his life beyond that. Perhaps he was used to flirting with unattached young women. Perhaps it meant nothing.

'I've had a telegram from my wife,' the Professor said abruptly. 'She's in Istanbul, staying with friends. She'll be back in England in a week or so.'

'I'm glad to hear she's well,' said Vera stiffly, wondering why he was telling her.

'She's never liked it out here,' he said. 'A pity, really, when it's so important to me.' He sighed. 'If I could give any advice to my earlier self, I'd say don't marry young.'

Vera said nothing. Picking up a damp cloth, she wiped the surface of the largest fragment of pottery, and saw the blue colour come to life.

'What do you think about this bronze head?' said Curzon, gesturing back towards the camp. 'A one-off?'

'No,' said Vera, putting down the cloth and turning to him. 'I think we may have found something really extraordinary. Perhaps we're on the site of a palace. There could be more treasure waiting to be found, perhaps the temple I've been hoping for, who knows?'

'Who knows, indeed,' said the Professor. He was listening to her intently, his dark eyes fixed on hers.

'I did a few drawings yesterday and asked the men to dig in the most likely area. They seem to be obeying me now.'

'They respect you,' said the Professor. 'As they should.'

There was a shout from the pit, followed by a loud discussion. Vera saw Laiq looking down, then he turned and strode over to where they were kneeling.

'Professor Curzon,' he said, inclining his head. 'Miss Millward. The men say they have found a wall and a tiled floor. You should see this.'

'After you,' said the Professor to Vera, gesturing. She leapt up and walked briskly to where the men were waiting, forcing herself not to run.

'What have you found?' she said in Arabic to the man in charge, who had emerged from the pit and was standing at the top of the ladder.

'The floor of a room,' he said, pointing. 'There is the edge of a slab, and the wall beyond.'

She peered down into the pit, which was supported on all sides by wooden scaffolding. It was hard to see much from this distance in the dim light, but when she clambered down the ladder she could see the corner of a stone slab emerging from the dirt.

They started digging again. Vera stayed close this time, watching carefully as the layout of a room came slowly into view. Four men were now down in the pit, widening it carefully, and shovelling up great piles of earth.

After several hours, they called her down again, and showed her what they had found. A raised platform, with grooves in the top, and shallow stone steps leading up to it.

'Professor!' she called, climbing back up the ladder, and he came at once. He did not look into the pit but at her, and she felt her stomach lurch.

'What is it, Vera? What have you found?'

'I think it might be a throne room,' she said, fighting to keep her voice level. 'A platform, steps, grooves where a throne could have stood, just as Dr Woolley described at Carchemish. It's all there.'

For a moment, she thought he was going to embrace her – she saw the movement of his arms before he thought better of it – but the look of admiration in his eyes was enough.

'Well done,' he said simply.

Vera watched the men work, feeling a rising sense of exhilaration. She had found a throne room! Who knew what treasure might be within? The colour was high in her cheeks and she could feel her hair escaping from its scarf.

'What do you want, Vera?' asked the Professor.

'What do you mean?'

'Money? Glory? Fame?'

For a moment she didn't answer and focused on the work before her. Then she said, 'Everything.' She looked up at him. 'I want everything.'

Chapter 27

Vera looked eagerly down at the coastline as the plane banked, seeing the verdant countryside gradually become dryer as they moved further inland. The desert, shimmering under a heat haze, was punctuated by stands of trees, low scrub, and glistening rivers. She felt a swell of excitement. She was back in Syria at last.

Vera had woken in her room at the Cairo Continental to find Jean Berry dressing swiftly, throwing her long gown back on and quickly brushing her tangled blonde hair.

'I'm due at work in an hour,' she said, casting around for her shoes. 'I'd better run home and get changed.'

Vera watched Jean fastening her heels, her long legs bare. 'This was fun.' She threw over a pair of stockings that had been tangled in the bedclothes.

'Thanks for a terrific night,' said Jean, tucking them into her bag as she moved towards the door. She hesitated. 'Look me up next time you're in Cairo, won't you?'

'Of course I will,' said Vera, leaning back against the pillows.

Jean laughed. 'I'm sure you say that to all the girls.' She blew a kiss and left. Vera got out of bed and winced as she saw the huge bruise that had developed all down one side of her body, the result of the car's impact the night before. She took a long soak in the bath before making her way downstairs.

'Ah, Mrs Dunn – there is another telegram for you,' said the concierge.

Oh, God, thought Vera. What is it this time?

But it was from her friend Elizabeth at the university in Aleppo:

VERA. LAIQ KHALIL NOT IN ALEPPO. RETIRED TO
DAMASCUS YEARS AGO. HE WAS IN JAIL HERE BEFORE
THAT. WILL SEEK FURTHER INFO. LETTER TO FOLLOW.
BEST REGARDS ELIZABETH.

In jail? It did not take long to pull a few strings and soon, after showing her face once more at the university, Vera was at the airfield, waiting for a flight to Damascus. It would have to be a brief visit; she was due back in Malta shortly. But she could not let this opportunity pass – she had to speak with Laiq and see if he could shed any light on who was looking for her.

*

A few hours later, in a small house in a suburb of Damascus, Vera watched the woman pouring tea, her hand steady. On her wrist was a narrow silver bangle, but her clothing was unadorned, and she wore the loose black gown of a widow.

'I'm very sorry for your loss,' said Vera at last. A few well-placed enquiries had led her to the home of Laiq Khalil. His wife had answered the door, looking frail and weary, and had told Vera that he was dead.

'I am getting used to being alone,' said Mrs Khalil with a sad smile. She paused. 'Your Arabic is good.'

'I studied it in England some years ago,' said Vera. 'I'm afraid I don't often have the chance to use it these days.'

She looked towards the window, where green and yellow panes of glass were casting pools of colour onto the floor, elongated in the evening sunlight.

'Laiq died in 1938,' said Mrs Khalil, passing her a cup. 'Why do you want to know about him?'

'I'm trying to trace an old friend who was working on one of his digs in the twenties,' said Vera. 'I thought Laiq might be able to help. I'm sorry to have disturbed you for nothing.'

'Laiq worked on a dozen digs in northern Syria – we lived in Aleppo in those days. They were all run by Europeans. The last was in 1926.'

Vera desperately wanted to ask what had happened after that, but she restrained herself and waited. She had not told the woman that she once knew Laiq.

'There was an accident,' said Mrs Khalil after a long pause. 'At the dig site, a place called Tell Ithriyia. Laiq was arrested almost immediately.'

'Why?' said Vera, startled. It had not occurred to her that Laiq's imprisonment was related to the dig at Tell Ithriyia, or the tragedy that had ended it. 'Why was he arrested?'

'They said he had been negligent,' said Mrs Khalil in a low voice, swilling the tea gently in her cup. She looked up. 'It was a lie! Laiq was always very conscientious. One of the pits collapsed and it was suggested that Laiq and the other men had been doing illegal excavations – trying to steal treasure – that had weakened the structures. It happens, of course, but he would never have done something like that.'

'I'm sure you're right,' said Vera. She knew all too well that Laiq had been honest, and that he had had nothing to do with the accident. 'What happened?'

'Several men were killed, including one of the Englishmen. The French brought Laiq and several other men to Aleppo. They were charged with negligence and endangerment. I suppose it was because the English archaeologists were wealthy and well-known – the authorities needed to set an example.'

Vera chewed her lip. 'Was there an inquest?'

Mrs Khalil shrugged. 'If there was, it was kept secret. We were told that the bodies were recovered, but no one saw them.'

'How many of the men were jailed?'

'Seven,' said Mrs Khalil. 'It was a dreadful time. Laiq was freed in 1932 because of his heart condition, but the rest were not freed until later – 1935, I think.'

'What happened to the British?' said Vera cautiously. She was sailing close to the wind, she knew that, but she wanted to get a clear picture of what had happened after her departure.

'They left quickly,' said Mrs Khalil, looking angry. 'They did not stay around to argue on behalf of Laiq and the rest. No! They were gone from Syria in a matter of days. At Laiq's instruction, I sent a letter to England, to Oxford University, but we never heard back. No one cared.'

The guilt that Vera had felt ever since hearing that Laiq had been jailed now rose and threatened to choke her. She took a deep breath. She wanted, more than anything, to tell the woman who she was, and to accept her blame and her anger, but it could not be done – not now. One day, she thought, when all of this is over, I'll come back and put things right.

*

The sun was setting when she emerged from Mrs Khalil's house. She passed a pair of Indian soldiers, who stood on a corner, talking quietly – remnants of the force that had retaken the city from the Vichy regime two years earlier.

'Evening, ma'am,' said one of them, looking curiously at her. 'Are you lost?'

'Just exploring,' said Vera. She paused. 'I thought the French were in charge of Damascus now.'

'They are,' said the other soldier, pointing along the street. 'If you go that way, you will see many Free French soldiers. We're almost the last British left. We'll be going home soon.'

'Into another battle,' said the other wryly.

'I'm sorry,' said Vera. 'I hope you can return to your families.'

But she knew that they would not. They would return to India to help drive the Japanese out of Burma, and there was a high chance they would die out there in the jungle. Just like Laiq Khalil, they were sacrifices to the ambitions of arrogant white men.

And I am complicit, thought Vera. She remembered those days on the dig in Syria, how the workmen had done her bidding. They had obeyed her because they had no choice, and seven of them had been jailed for something that was not their fault.

As she emerged onto one of the broad thoroughfares of the city, Vera looked around, feeling as though someone was watching her, but there was no one to be seen except the men selling carpets, the street sweepers, the cart drivers.

A movement caught her eye, and she saw someone walking away through an archway. He was gone before she could register the sight, but she hastened after him. Reaching the archway, she went through, and saw his back retreating once again down a narrow alleyway.

'Hello?' she called after him, and then, 'Excusez-moi, monsieur?'

He did not respond, and Vera ran after him, but when she reached the alley, he was nowhere to be seen. There were turnings to the left and the right; taking a gamble, she ran along the right-hand passage.

'Madame?' A wizened old man looked up from his doorstep with concern. 'As-tu besoin d'aide?'

'Non, merci,' she said, slowing down as she saw a dead end. She sighed. 'Avez-vous vu un homme? Un européen?'

He shook his head. 'Non, madame.'

Chapter 28

Syria, 1926

Vera watched the car pull out of the yard and rattle away along the bumpy road. She was disappointed that the Professor was leaving again so soon, but relieved that Schuster had gone with him. He had seemed very interested in the throne room they had found, standing beside the pit and scribbling extensive notes, which he said was a diary. He spent much of the rest of the time holed up in Curzon's office, apparently working on his book and dispatching copious letters whenever the post boy arrived from the village.

She made her way to the workroom. Matthew was already there, frowning over the fragmented pieces of some ornament. He looked up and smiled.

'Good morning. Sleep well?'

'Very,' said Vera, although it was a lie. She had tossed and turned for hours. How could she tell Matthew that she had lain awake thinking of the Professor, knowing that he was alone in his tent not far away? That she had had to resist the urge to get up in the darkness and go to him and feel his arms around her? She felt the blood rise in her cheeks and sat down quickly.

'I wonder where they're going this time,' said Matthew. 'Curzon and Schuster, I mean.'

'Visiting old friends, apparently,' said Vera, picking up the tablet she had come across the day before. 'Somewhere on the way to Aleppo.'

Matthew nodded. 'It all seems very odd. I thought this dig meant everything to the Professor, but he seems a lot more interested in whatever he's up to with Schuster.'

She shrugged. 'I'm rather hoping that we'll find something spectacular while he's away. That would show him.'

'Show him what?'

'That we're decent archaeologists,' said Vera, but she knew it was more than that. She wanted to impress Curzon – no, to dazzle him. She wanted him in the palm of her hand. It would not be enough just to seduce him – that was easy. She wanted to triumph over him.

'I hope Schuster stays away,' said Matthew. He picked up a soft brush and delicately began dusting the grooves imprinted on his little statue. 'I saw him measuring the bronze head you found, but when I asked him about it later, he pretended not to know what I was talking about.'

Vera nodded gloomily. 'He's been sketching things too, including the little golden nude. He shut his notebook when I went past, but I'm sure he was drawing it. What do you think he wants?'

Matthew shrugged. 'All these letters he keeps sending to Damascus and Aleppo and Istanbul ... I've seen some of the addresses – I think they must be men who deal in antiquities. I think Schuster's been telling them about the things we've found, like the bronze head.'

'To what purpose?'

'Perhaps he wants to sell it.'

'But he can't!' she said, staring. 'It won't be for sale, not now and not ever.'

'Perhaps the Professor's in league with him.'

'Do you really think that?'

Matthew breathed out sharply. 'No. I think Curzon's genuine. He's internationally renowned, I don't think he'd throw away his reputation like that.'

'And he doesn't need the money,' said Vera. She looked pensive. 'I wonder if he trusts Schuster?'

'They've been friends for donkey's years,' said Matthew. 'Schuster plays the dusty old museum curator act and Curzon laps it up. He'd never believe Schuster was capable of stealing.'

Vera stared at the tablet in her hand, which had been quite forgotten. 'I don't see what we can do.'

'Just keep an eye out, I suppose,' said Matthew. 'Probably nothing to be done just now, but when they come back we'll have to be extra vigilant. Perhaps we can catch Schuster in the act. Or he'll leave and we'll be rid of him.'

*

In the afternoon, Vera went to the dig site, eager to see if the throne room had been revealed any further, but her usual team were elsewhere, busy reinforcing the wooden supports that lined the pit on all sides, so she stifled her impatience.

Mo appeared at the end of the day, wiping his hands, and bowed briefly to her before pointing to the throne room.

'We look again tomorrow?' he said in English.

'I hope so,' Vera replied, 'but there may not be much more to find.'

He shook his head. 'There is more. I'm sure of it.'

'I trust your instinct,' said Vera, smiling. 'You've been right before. Perhaps we will find something else. What do you think it will be?'

He paused, clearly picturing the treasures that might be waiting for them, then grinned at her. 'Gold,' he said at last. 'Lots of gold.'

Vera waved as he scampered away, but she felt a stab of doubt. What if Matthew was right? What if Schuster was trying to steal from the dig? She had longed and longed to find something extraordinary, but now she almost hoped that they would uncover nothing but dirt.

At dusk, she walked slowly through the camp, turning it all over in her mind. Perhaps they were wrong. All Schuster had really done was show an interest – taking measurements wasn't inherently suspicious. She knew how angry Curzon would be if they accused his old friend of lying and stealing. For that reason alone she wished they could forget the whole thing. She wanted Curzon's approval, not to make him despise her.

Vera stood still, feeling indecisive for the first time in her life. Oh, dash it all, she thought, ashamed of her timidity, and turned around, hurrying back towards the main building, where Schuster had been working in the office. She could hear voices in the distance and knew that the boys must be having a drink before dinner was served.

She went first to the workroom and lit a candle, then to the office door. It was locked. She had not expected otherwise. Her thoughts went to the pistol in the safe, but she shook her head. Pulling out a hairpin, she jiggled it in the lock. For a moment, nothing happened, and she thought with relief that she might have to call the search off. Then there was a rusty click and she turned the handle.

Vera held the candle aloft. Schuster's desk was a mess, and she felt relieved. He was clearly an academic, not a master criminal.

She sat at the desk and hurriedly flicked through the papers, looking for something – anything – that would explain what Schuster wanted with the discovered artefacts. There were letters, lists of antiquities, maps, drawings, but all of it was clearly related to his work.

She went through the drawers; they were full of wads of paper, books, broken pen nibs – all the detritus of academic life.

The bottom drawer had nothing but a copy of Herr Schuster's own massive tome, a book on Assyrian art of which he was very proud. She closed the drawer.

Then a thought occurred, and she opened the drawer again and reached in to lift up the book. Underneath was a lining made of an old piece of wallpaper; she lifted that too and stared down.

Underneath it, flattened at the bottom of the drawer, was an envelope. There was no address on the front. By the weight of it, it contained a long letter, and it had been sealed with a thick blob of black wax. Imprinted in the wax was a writhing snake.

Vera held it up to the light and tried to peer under the flap, but it had been carefully closed and she had no wish to make her presence known.

Looking back into the drawer, she saw another folded piece of paper – a letter. Picking it up, Vera saw at once that it was written in German. She smoothed out the paper, which was crumpled and water-stained. At the top, someone had scribbled a symbol which was clearly meant to resemble the snake seal on the envelope. Under the drawing was the first line of the letter: *Für NERO . . .*

It had been a long time since Vera had spoken German with any regularity, and she recalled brushing off Schuster's enquiry about her fluency; she hadn't wanted to embarrass herself in front of a native speaker. She frowned at the words on the page, trying to make sense of them. The letter seemed to be from someone in authority, an employer, thanking Schuster for his reports and requesting further details. It made reference to the expansion of a radio surveillance programme and asked him to meet a contact in Ankara on his way back to Europe in order to collect some documents. The contact was employed at the British Embassy.

Vera stared at the paper, feeling her heart racing. What on earth was Schuster involved in?

The letter stopped mid-sentence, and any following pages were missing. Vera's eyes were drawn back to a line above, which began *Das Vaterland* . . .

Well, she thought, there's no mistaking that. *The Fatherland thanks you for your service.* She read the words once more and then replaced the letter and the envelope carefully in the drawer.

She had hoped to find proof that Schuster was stealing from the dig, but instead a more alarming conviction had gripped her: he was a spy.

*

What on earth is a German spy doing in Syria, Vera wondered later, as she sat near the fire, listening to the boys laughing as they finished off the scrawny chicken that Azim had roasted for supper.

After finding the letter, she had gone through the rest of the papers again, hoping to find something that backed it up, but there was nothing, nothing except the envelope, tantalisingly sealed with wax and completely inaccessible.

'You're quiet, Vera,' said Stanley, offering her a basket of apricots and sliced melon. 'Everything all right?'

'Fine,' she said, trying to smile. 'Just tired. Did you find anything else this afternoon?'

'A couple of decent tablets and a few other bits and pieces,' he said. 'Chris, show Vera the beads you found.'

'Oh, yes,' said Christian, feeling in his pocket. 'These turned up just when the men were laying down tools.' He opened a folded handkerchief, and Vera saw a cluster of large beads, some turquoise and some gold.

'How lovely. Was it a necklace, do you think?'

'That's my guess,' he said, touching the beads gently. 'They were all lying close together – I suppose the cord must have perished. I hoped there might be some sort of pendant too, but no joy yet.'

'Keep looking tomorrow,' said Matthew, craning over his shoulder. 'You might find the rest of it.'

And what else will we find, thought Vera, as she bit down on a slice of melon, feeling the juice on her chin. Schuster would be away for another day or two. Perhaps they ought to take a closer look at the throne room before he returned. But he wasn't just a thief, he was a spy. Nero. The name was intriguing. What was he really doing out here in the desert?

Chapter 29

'Cheers,' said George Borg, gulping at his beer. 'It's jolly good to see you, Dennis.' He winced and put the glass down, rubbing at his right arm. 'This damn shoulder.'

'You're injured?' said Pratchett, speaking over the music. George, an old school friend, had been in Malta with the RAF for over a year. He had been in the air cadets at school, Pratchett recalled, and he was not surprised to find that George was now a flying ace.

'Took a bullet on a reconnaissance mission,' said George. 'I was lucky to make it back alive.'

'What happened?'

George sighed heavily. 'Three of us from 683 Squadron were taking photographs of Italian defences in Sicily. This was back in April. All very hush-hush, carefully planned. We should have been there and back in a couple of hours.'

'But they saw you coming?'

'They didn't see us,' George said slowly, after another swig. 'They *knew* we were coming.'

Pratchett put down his glass. 'They knew?'

'I don't know how,' said George. 'The whole thing had been planned inside out, our comms chaps had broadcast misleading information on frequencies we know they listen to, we'd done everything right. But as soon as we were within sight of the coastline, four Italian Macchi C.202s appeared and started firing. My pal John O'Brien went down at once, no time to bail out. Must have been killed instantly. Then Fitz – Larry Fitzwilliam, the third pilot – was hit, but he managed to parachute out.'

'He survived?'

'We don't know,' said George. 'If he did, the Italians are holding him prisoner.' He breathed out heavily. 'Anyway, I got home, although my Spit had been hit too – she's a tough little plane. No idea how I managed to land. Now I'm off active service for a couple of months.'

Pratchett shook his head, impressed and astonished. 'Do you really think the Italians knew you were coming?'

George considered, lifting his beer with both hands and gulping it. 'Well, it could have been a lucky guess,' he said at last. 'But it felt very much like an ambush. As I was turning tail, I saw a boat coming out from the coast, heading straight for where Fitz had gone down. It seemed they'd thought of everything.'

'Would he have been able to tell them much?'

George grimaced. 'Enough to make it worth their while. He's a brave lad – only nineteen – but I don't know if he'd be able to withstand heavy treatment.'

Pratchett was silent as he took a long drink. Perhaps someone had warned the Italians they were coming. Could Nero have been involved? This was the sort of information he had leaked in the Great War. They had assumed that he was now interested in more important matters – conferences, troop movements, intelligence that could influence the course of the war – but surely he would not be above leaking information like this if he came across it?

Pratchett fought his way to the bar for more drinks. The barbershop singers on the stage were coming to the end of their set and he found himself hoping that Margarita would be on next. George had suggested the Phoenix Club, and he couldn't say he was sorry to be there.

'It's not the first time it's happened,' said George when he was seated again. 'Other pilots have reported being ambushed in a similar way, as though the Italians have insider information. Perhaps there's a mole in HQ.' He laughed. 'Anyway, that's your area, isn't it? Didn't you say you're in intelligence these days?'

Pratchett smiled. 'I'm not involved in anything that exciting, I'm afraid. I'm in Malta to help make communications between departments more efficient – all rather dull. I don't get to do anything very heroic.' The truth of the statement stung.

'Well, heroism's not all it's cracked up to be,' said George seriously. 'I lost two friends on that mission alone. My wife is desperate for me to get a desk job.'

'Will you?'

George shook his head. 'If they let me fly again, then I'll fly. But if I survive this war, as soon as it's over I'll hang up my goggles for good.' He drank half of his beer in one, then looked at Pratchett's glass. 'You'll have another?'

*

'Who's the pilot?' said Flo, peering through the door into the main room of the club. 'He's rather handsome, isn't he? Do you know, I recognise him. I think he's in the same squadron that Angela's husband was in, he's been here before.'

Margarita looked where she was pointing. She had noticed Pratchett in the audience when she was on stage, and although he was deep in conversation with the dark-haired pilot at his table, and getting through pints at a rate that was almost impressive, she could tell he was listening to her singing.

'I know the other chap,' she said without thinking.

'Oh, really?' said Flo. 'I told Lois I'd walk home with her, but next time you must introduce me to his pilot friend. It's something about the uniform – makes me feel quite weak at the knees!'

Laughing, Margarita went into the auditorium and had a drink with Poppy and her boyfriend, who were sitting at the bar. She had almost decided to go home when she saw the pilot stand up and shake Pratchett's hand before weaving his way unsteadily towards the door.

Pratchett gulped at his beer then looked around, smiling as he caught Margarita's eye. He raised a hand and waved, and she went over to him.

'Great show, Margarita,' said Pratchett, his voice slightly slurred. 'You were terrific. Can I get you a drink?'

'Nothing for me. Are you here on – er – business?' she asked, perching opposite.

Pratchett shook his head. 'I was meeting an old schoolfriend. He's just left, got an early start.'

'I saw him,' said Margarita. 'My friend Flo was rather taken with his uniform.'

She thought longingly of Arthur, now stationed in Alexandria, and remembered how smart he had looked the night she first met him, his buttons gleaming in the lamplight and his eyes full of laughter.

Pratchett chuckled. 'George has no shortage of admirers, lucky chap, but he's got a wife back home he's devoted to.' He took another drink and looked around at the crowds. 'Quite a place, this. Is it always this busy?'

Margarita shook her head. 'Only at weekends. I prefer it when it's quieter – I get nervous when there are this many people watching.'

'Have you always been a singer?'

'Not professionally – I only started here last year. But I've always loved singing as a hobby.'

'Well, you seem like a natural,' said Pratchett, and he downed the rest of his beer. 'Bloody good show, I thought.'

'What about you?' said Margarita. 'Did you always know you wanted to work as a—' She hesitated, for she wasn't really sure what he was. A spy?

'Oh, no,' said Pratchett, placing his glass back on the table with a thump. 'I was going to teach English. I taught in Portugal for a couple of years after university. Then the war started and I went to France but got sent home with an injury after a few months. Then . . . well, this.'

'Are your parents pleased that you're not fighting anymore?'

'They're dead, actually. Spanish flu. I was brought up by my aunt.'

'Oh, I'm sorry,' said Margarita. She recalled that Vera was also an orphan, and wondered if it was common among intelligence operatives. Less to lose, she thought, feeling a surge of gratitude that her father and stepmother were alive and safe.

'It's quite all right,' said Pratchett. 'I never knew them. My aunt and uncle have always been very kind to me. They're pleased I'm doing this. Not that they know what "this" is, of course. They just know I work for the intelligence service.'

'What do people in intelligence actually *do*?' she asked, lowering her voice.

Pratchett looked downcast. 'It's probably a lot less exciting than you imagine. There's a lot of paperwork involved. I've been given one main task and that's what occupies most of my time.'

'Finding—'

'Yes.' The name Nero hung between them, dangerous and obscure.

'I hope you do,' said Margarita with feeling. 'I keep waking up in the night, imagining he's in my flat. It's horrible.' The bad dreams had started as soon as Arthur had gone away. Often they featured a body that she thought was Henry's, only to turn it over and find it was Arthur's, floating white and blank-eyed in the water. A dark figure she knew was Nero was prowling nearby, waiting for her.

'There's no reason he should want to harm you,' said Pratchett, laying a clumsy hand on hers. 'Even if he's as dangerous as we think he is. You shouldn't ever have been involved.'

She remembered the photograph she had stolen and felt a flush of shame. 'What do you think he wants?' she said abruptly, withdrawing her arm. 'What's he doing here?'

Pratchett chewed his lip. 'There are a lot of valuable secrets passing through Malta. We think he's sending information to the Germans.'

'About what?'

'Politics, RAF operations, submarine movements . . .'

'Submarines?' She felt her heart jolt in her chest.

'I shouldn't have said anything.'

'My fiancé, Arthur, is a submarine captain.'

'Oh, I see,' said Pratchett, and a frown crossed his face. 'Brave chaps, all of them.' He sighed heavily.

Margarita leaned forward, knowing that she was taking advantage of his drunken state. 'How much damage can he do? Is he putting them in danger?'

'Oh, yes,' said Pratchett, sounding gloomy. 'Great events are afoot. He might just ruin everything.'

'What events?'

'I don't know much myself,' said Pratchett, pushing his floppy hair out of his eyes. 'But the retaking of Europe is in the offing. This is all confidential, you understand. The Allies have been feeding information to the Germans that they're planning to invade Greece or Sardinia or various other places.' He seemed to take a boyish pleasure in knowing so much and Margarita realised that he was showing off for her. Poor Dennis, she thought. He's going to kick himself when he's sobered up. Lucky for him I'm not a spy.

'But where is the real invasion going to take place?'

Pratchett opened his mouth, then seemed to stop himself. 'That's even more secret. All that matters is that a massive web of false intelligence has been created.'

'And you think Nero knows about this.'

'If he's as deeply embedded as we think, then yes,' said Pratchett. 'If he works in an official capacity, in government perhaps, he'll have had access to documents, secret transmissions, telephone calls, confidential reports of meetings.'

'But if he knows,' said Margarita slowly, 'then why hasn't he told the Germans?'

'Perhaps he has,' said Pratchett. 'But we've heard no indication that the secret is out, no mass movements of troops to the real location. So either Hitler is playing us at our own game and pretending to be oblivious, or . . .'

'Or Nero hasn't told them.'

He nodded. 'Why, we can't possibly know. But one thing we do know is that he loves power – he enjoys being able to control the fates of lesser men. My guess is that he's kept back this crucial piece of information as some sort of insurance. Perhaps he'll reveal it at a time when it will have maximum impact.'

She thought about this. 'So many lives will be at risk.'

'Yes,' said Pratchett, and he suddenly sounded sober. 'I'm afraid so.'

On the way home, Margarita thought again about what she had learned. It was too late not to feel invested. Arthur was in danger. Nero had already killed her former lover, and now he was ready to sacrifice her fiancé on the altar of his traitorous ambitions. It was personal.

Chapter 30

Wilson sat in a small office, leafing through paperwork, deep in the warren of rooms and passages that had been bored out of the rock far below Valletta. It was uncomfortably warm and he pulled at his collar, feeling the sweat trickling down the back of his neck.

He was investigating two recent incidents that might be linked to Nero: the Italian attack on a reconnaissance mission over Sicily that Pratchett's friend, Flight Lieutenant Borg, had been involved in, and a recently intercepted German message about British submarine movements.

The details of the first event were in a folder beside him. He pulled out a photograph of a clean-cut young man in a pilot's uniform, grinning toothily at the camera as he leaned against the side of a small plane, an airfield visible behind him.

The plane was an older model but the man beside it, John O'Brien, looked proud, delighted to be serving his country, his cheery wave and broad grin belying the fact that he would never come home. The Italians had been forewarned about his arrival and had shot him down, along with his colleague Larry Fitzwilliam, presumed dead or captured.

The second, more recent, incident had followed a similar pattern. The Germans had known the whereabouts of two submarines on related classified missions long before they were in radar range. Fortunately, a message indicating as much had been intercepted, and one of the subs had got away. The other hadn't received the warning in time and had been torpedoed, with no survivors, a few miles south of Corfu.

Advance information about the subs' routes had been sent in an encrypted message from the base at Alexandria to Malta HQ. Either the Germans had broken the code that had been used, or someone in Malta or Egypt had access to high-level messages – or both.

The Sicily reconnaissance mission had been planned here at Lascaris, and only a few people, working within these walls, would have known it was happening. Even fewer would have known enough details to leak it. Wilson was loath to think that one of them might be a traitor, but he knew that he would have to examine all avenues. There had been a series of similar disasters over the last few months and he couldn't rule anyone out.

Before him were the records of visitors to the operations room in question, all carefully signed in and out, which he had been scouring for any anomalies. The Sicily mission had taken place on the seventh of April. He flicked to the end of March, then turned over the page, reading every name that was listed. None of them jumped out at him. April the first, the second, the third, the fifth. He stopped and looked back, but it was clear: the record for the fourth of April was missing.

Wilson stiffened, hearing a thud somewhere in the distance that seemed to reverberate through the stone, followed by another and another – guns being fired at a plane overhead. On the way to Lascaris that morning, he had heard sirens, and saw that several streets in the city centre were roped off. Another bomb had been dropped, it appeared, and every disaster now seemed to bear the mark of Nero.

*

Wilson made his way wearily up the steps that led from the bunkers of Lascaris, which were at sea level, to the city above.

He paused at the top of the last flight of steps, feeling old, and noted a spire of smoke coming from the harbour.

He returned to the office in Archbishop Street, preoccupied by the series of calamities that seemed to fill his waking hours. At night, he lay awake worrying about his son in Malaya and sometimes it all seemed too much to bear. After decades working for the intelligence and security services in one role and another, he had started to wonder if he had had enough.

'Hello,' said Pratchett. 'Hot out there, isn't it? Find anything useful?'

'Possibly,' said Wilson. He told Pratchett about the missing visitor sheet. 'It might just be an administrative mistake. I asked the secretary and she was very put out – she said they have visitors every day. She was going through her filing cabinet when I left, so it may turn up.'

'What if it doesn't?' said Pratchett. 'Do you think someone took it?'

'It's one theory,' said Wilson. 'I don't know, though. It seems pretty unlikely that Nero – or someone working for him – would have put his own name in the visitors' book. But then why take it?'

'Look at this,' said Pratchett, waving a long spool of paper. 'It's the list of names I requested from London – just arrived. European students who studied in Britain in the years before the Great War.'

'That'll take you a while.'

'There aren't many Germans by the look of it,' said Pratchett, already scanning the sheet.

'We don't know he's German,' Wilson reminded him.

'It seems most plausible—'

'Yes, but don't limit yourself,' said Wilson. 'We need to be thorough.'

Feeling drained, he sat down at his desk and tried to muster his thoughts. He recalled the picture of John O'Brien, beaming and unaware, and felt a surge of anger, coupled with a desire to find the man who had caused his death. O'Brien had been the same age as his son Martin. He could not give up – not yet.

*

Pratchett read through the list of names one by one, unsure of what he was looking for. It occurred to him now and then that he might be on a wild goose chase. He had no real evidence that Nero had studied in Britain, and he could not use up too many resources on a hunch.

Still, it was a start, and of the various avenues of investigation they had opened, this was the one he felt most drawn to. The intercepted messages from Nero in the Great War had hinted of a man who knew the country well; who had walked its streets, drunk in its pubs.

Pratchett had begun to draw a picture of a man in his mind, now at least fifty, who had once been a rebellious student and had gone on to become a master spy. He had studied in England and taken all that it had to offer – perhaps he had even loved it, once.

But then the Great War had come and he had unquestioningly offered his services to the Fatherland. The information he had absorbed as a student had suddenly become useful. Had he felt a twinge of remorse as he betrayed the friends he had made, the landlords who had pulled him pints, the girls he had flirted with? At first, perhaps. But years had passed in which Nero had grown in confidence and the England of his youth must have seemed very far away.

By now, thought Pratchett, he had probably forgotten what he had so loved about the place. As he sent information gleaned from British intelligence to aid his Nazi masters, did he ever think of those years? The advent of the second war must have been a boon to such an accomplished spy, offering almost unlimited opportunities to gain favour and increase his standing in Berlin. As he sent Englishmen to their deaths, did he push aside the memories? Or had he simply transformed himself into someone else with a new identity, new allegiances?

Pratchett started as the telephone beside him rang. He picked it up and waited as the line crackled and the operator connected them, and then he heard a distant voice, as though the caller was standing in a deep well, rather than an office in London.

'Pratchett? This is Sandford. I've got some information for you.'

'Thanks for getting back to me so soon,' said Pratchett.

He heard the creak of a chair as Sandford leaned forward. 'The matter in Switzerland you asked me to look into – the parcel sent to old Heinrich. I suppose you can't give me a clue as to what this is about?'

'I'm afraid not,' said Pratchett.

Sandford chuckled. 'Correct answer. Well, I've got a name for you. Our friends in the OSS were most helpful.'

'Go on.'

The call ended a few minutes later and Pratchett turned back to his desk, picking up the list of students again and holding his breath. There was no sign of the one he was looking for as he scanned onwards through the pages and he felt a stab of uncertainty. Perhaps he had been wrong, after all. It was in the very nature of the man to be unknowable; he was shadowy, instantly forgotten, capable of putting on many faces. They would never find him.

And then his finger alighted on a name, halfway down the page, and he stared, feeling his heart racing.

'I've got him!' he whispered.

'What's that?'

Pratchett jumped to see Wilson standing in the doorway with a pile of folders. He had almost forgotten the other man was in the office.

'There's a match,' said Pratchett, feeling breathless. 'Look.'

He pointed at one of the papers. Wilson came over and peered closely at it.

'Karl Schuster.'

'He's a German from Augsburg, Bavaria,' said Pratchett. 'He studied in Oxford from 1907 to 1912. He was the source of this parcel sent to Himmler in the twenties, according to our friends in Switzerland.'

'Where was it sent from?'

'Istanbul,' said Pratchett. 'But they're going to see if they can trace it any further as it may not have originated there.'

'It's not much to go on,' said Wilson. 'Schuster might just be a dealer or a postal agent or something.'

'I know,' said Pratchett. 'But it's a start. I'll see if we can get a photograph.'

He chewed his lip, trying not to get ahead of himself, but it was irresistible. Schuster was the man they were looking for, he was sure of it. He saw Schuster at Oxford: quiet, clever, soaking it all up. Soon they would know what he looked like – and then they would find him.

Chapter 31

Syria, 1926

Vera tried not to think about the letter she had found in Schuster's desk. There was nothing to be gained by dwelling on it. She would have to wait for the Professor to return and perhaps she could take her suspicions to him. Until then, she would focus on the throne room that was being excavated.

'What do you want the men to do?' asked Laiq, watching Vera walking slowly across the tiled floor at the bottom of the deep pit. She stopped to run her hand over the wall, on which life-sized figures were carved in low relief. 'The Professor said there was nothing else in here.'

'Well, there may not be,' said Vera reluctantly. The carvings were beautiful, and a remarkable discovery, but they were not the treasure she had longed for.

'Still an impressive find, though,' said Laiq, gesturing to the steps and the platform where a throne had almost certainly once stood. 'He's pleased with it. Although I suppose he wishes he'd found it himself.'

Vera looked up. 'Why do you say that?'

Laiq shrugged, looking uncomfortable. 'Well, you're . . .'

'Inexperienced?' said Vera sharply. 'A woman?'

'The world is how it is,' said Laiq, holding his hands out. 'He's a man. My wife says that men have egos where women have brains.'

'I think I'd like your wife,' said Vera with a smile.

'Anyway, it isn't my place,' said Laiq, and he bowed briefly. 'I will pass on your instructions to the men once you decide what you want them to do.'

Mohammed climbed down the ladder and waved, squatting to look at the carvings they had uncovered. Laiq frowned at him but said nothing. Vera walked across the floor, tilting her head now and then. She had noticed, when the dirt came out, that the tiles were uneven. Leaning down, she prodded the raised corner of one tile, and felt it give slightly.

She knelt beside it and peered at the gap between the tiles. At one end, they were pushed close together, the stone touching, but the gap grew wider, and at the other end there was a half-inch space between them, filled with tightly compacted earth.

'It looks as though they've been taken up and put back at some point,' she said, squinting.

'Same here,' said Mo, pointing near the entrance. 'This is uneven.'

'Surely they wouldn't have been laid like this,' said Vera. 'Not in a palace. They can't have been taken up recently, though.'

'It must have happened before they were buried under the earth,' said Mo.

Vera looked around the room. She tried to imagine what this chamber had been like thousands of years ago when it was first built. She pictured the ornate carvings, the guards standing by the door, the golden statues, the mighty throne, and on it, a queen.

'Laiq, tell the men to lift the tiles.'

He summoned a group of workmen and at once they began to lever up the tiles.

'Carefully, carefully!' said Laiq, frowning. Before long, one of the men was able to slip his fingers under the edge of a tile. He and one of the others lifted it gently and deposited it a few feet away.

Soon they had cleared an area six feet square and Vera stopped them. Stepping gently to the edge of the tiles, she surveyed the layer of dirt that had been revealed beneath, then knelt, brushing it with the palm of her hand.

'What's underneath?' said Matthew from behind her and she jumped. She was so caught up in the discovery that she had not noticed him arrive.

'Bricks,' she said, clearing a wider patch.

'Does that mean . . .?'

She looked up at the surrounding men, all of whom were watching intently. 'I think there's a chamber here,' she said at last. A whisper ran through the workmen, and she was pleased to see that even they looked intrigued.

'What now?' said Matthew, kneeling down beside her. He ran a hand gently over the bricks. Vera imagined them being made by hand and laid out to dry in the sun, a thousand years or more ago. She looked at him and raised her eyebrows.

'You think we should take up the bricks, too?' said Matthew.

'Of course. It's the only way to know what's underneath.'

'What if it's just more earth and dust?'

She shrugged. 'Well, that's archaeology. Nine times out of ten that's all we find. But we've got to keep trying.'

He smiled. 'It's a shame the Professor isn't here. He likes these moments of truth.'

Vera was glad Curzon wasn't there. If her hunch was wrong, then she would rather he did not witness her failure. Stanley and Christian had arrived too and she hoped that her idea came to something, as the audience was growing.

'Are they to take the bricks up?' said Laiq impatiently. 'Everyone wants to see what's underneath.'

'Don't get too excited,' said Vera. She looked around. 'But yes. Take up the bricks. Tell them to cover their faces, it's going to get dusty.'

She stood back and watched the men go to work, after tying strips of cotton over their mouths to protect them from the dust. The bricks had been carefully cemented together, although much of it had begun to crumble.

There were three layers of brick, then long slabs of limestone, and then one of the workmen exclaimed, although she could not understand his words from beneath his mask, and she saw dust begin to billow up.

'What did he say?'

'He says there is a hollow space between the slabs,' said Laiq. 'He's going to try reaching down to see how far it goes.'

'Be careful,' she called in Arabic. 'We don't know how well the floor is supported.'

The man lay full length and reached his arm gingerly into the hole, until only his shoulder was visible.

'There's nothing under there,' said Laiq. 'It's too deep for him to reach.'

They fetched a long pole and lowered it down.

'Carefully,' said Vera, suddenly realising how tense she was. 'Very carefully.'

'They've reached something about six feet down but it's not solid,' said Laiq. 'Probably more earth or dust. Then ...' He listened to the murmurs of the men by the hole and nodded. 'All right. Now they've got to solid ground.'

Pulling her scarf over her mouth, Vera picked up her torch. 'Ask them to move back. I'm going to have a look and I don't know if the floor will bear all of our weight.'

'Be careful, Vera,' said Matthew.

'I will,' she said, and knelt down, lowering herself carefully onto her front.

Inch by inch, she shuffled her body across the tiles. The ground felt solid and it had lasted this long, but she had no wish to test it.

Vera leaned over the hole and shone the torch down into the space below. For a moment she could see nothing amid the circling dust, caught in the beam of the torch, but then she began to make out indistinct shapes, coated thickly in the dirt of centuries.

'What is it?' said Christian.

'There's something down there,' she said, trying not to give away her excitement by the tremor in her voice. This was the moment she had dreamed of, and she could not quite believe it had finally arrived. 'Objects – statues, perhaps, or furniture. It's all covered in dust and fallen earth.'

Vera heard talking break out among the workmen. She peered down again. The dust had settled slightly and the shapes were clearer. She flashed the torch around again, trying to see more. And then – as if to reassure her that she was on the right track – she saw the glint of gold. It was there for only a second, but it was enough.

She turned and looked back at the men, who were waiting for her verdict. 'I think this is it,' she said breathlessly. 'I think we've found it.'

There would be no going down into the chamber that day, or probably the next, but she had seen gold. Vera remembered the visions of piled treasure, of newspaper headlines, of a sparkling career ahead, that had dominated her dreams in the months before she came to Syria, and she felt for a moment completely invincible.

At last, the sun went down and they tidied up the dig site. Laiq deputed six of the most trustworthy men to guard the pit and said that he would stay with them.

'One of us ought to stay, too,' said Matthew. 'Not that I don't trust those fellows, but . . .'

'I'll stay,' said Stanley resolutely. 'If you'll take a shift later.'

'You ought to have the pistol, just in case. I'll fetch it for you now and then swap places with you in a few hours, how about that?'

'All right,' said Stanley. 'Vera, go and celebrate. You deserve it.'

Blinking in the low evening light, she and Matthew walked back to camp. She felt elated – more than elated. She had been proved right.

'Whose motor is that?' said Matthew, putting a hand over his brow. She could see a car parked near the camp. 'Can Curzon and Schuster be back already?'

As they approached, Vera saw a huddle of workmen, all talking loudly. They were gesturing towards the dig site, and as Vera approached, she saw that in the middle of the group was Professor Curzon.

He was listening intently to all that they said. At last, someone noticed her, and the Professor looked up. His eyes caught hers, and she felt her stomach swoop in the intensity of his gaze.

*

The celebratory meal went on into the night. Once all the workmen had been fed, and portions taken to the men guarding the pit, not much remained of Azim's roasted sheep. The Professor brought out bottles of champagne, and the boys revealed brandy and gin that they had cradled all the way from Istanbul.

There were fireworks – Vera wondered vaguely who on earth had brought fireworks into the desert, but soon she was sighing with the rest of them as golden sparks shot up into the night sky.

And the music – where had the music come from? An old gramophone crackled away near the fire. She remembered dancing with little Mohammed before he scampered home, then with Matthew and Christian, and at last with the Professor, who caressed her face for a moment with his warm hand. Over his shoulder, she saw Karl Schuster watching, a sardonic smile on his face, as he lifted his glass.

Then she was dancing again with Matthew, his cheeks ruddy in the firelight. 'Congratulations, Vera,' he said, his hands light on her waist. 'I'm delighted for you.'

'It was a team effort,' she said.

'It's going to be thrilling when we get back to England,' he said. 'I expect it'll be in the paper.'

She smiled. 'We'll be busy. There are reports to write, lots of work to be done.'

'Vera,' said Matthew, gazing at her. 'You're extraordinary, you know.'

'You're very charming.'

'You know how much I admire you, don't you?'

She leaned in and kissed his cheek. 'Yes,' she whispered. His face grew pinker and he whirled her around with more energy than ever, her long white dress billowing out in the evening breeze.

'I'd better go and take over from Stanley,' he said at last, and she knew he was regretting having volunteered.

'See you tomorrow,' said Vera, trying not to laugh at his acute frustration. He kissed her hand and disappeared into the night.

*

Later, in her tent and preparing for bed, Vera heard someone pull back the outer flap, and stood, her heart pounding. He ducked and came into the tent, eyeing her silk nightgown with an expression hard to read.

'Expecting someone?' asked the Professor. His waistcoat was gone, and his white shirt was unbuttoned at the neck, the line of his suntan visible.

'Yes.'

'Anyone I know?'

She reached for him, the champagne making her bold.

'Vera,' he said, his voice low, almost a whisper. She kissed his neck and felt his hands roaming. 'I oughtn't to have come,' he said, but he didn't sound much as though he meant it.

'Well,' she said, biting his lip gently as she pressed against him, hearing him groan, 'we can stop if you want.'

Taking hold of the hem of her nightdress, he pulled it up and over her head in one movement, his eyes drinking her in.

'Come here,' he said, and she began to unbutton his shirt. Hearing the sound of carousing outside, they paused. The lamp flickered, throwing shadows on the walls.

The Professor pulled Vera to him and blew out the lamp.

Chapter 32

Margarita stood on the corner of Strait Street, looking past the police cordons at the chaos beyond. Just before dawn, only a few hours after she had left the Phoenix Club, a low-flying German plane had evaded detection and dropped a bomb that had crashed through the roof of the club. It had miraculously failed to explode, but the roof was almost destroyed.

Someone hurried past and she caught his arm. 'Carlo?'

The club owner looked as though he hadn't slept, and his hair and clothes were covered with dust. He looked at her, dazed. 'Margarita. You heard?'

'Is everyone all right?'

'Yes, yes,' he said distractedly. 'No one is hurt. The cleaners usually come in at around the time the bomb was dropped, but they were running late, thank God.'

Margarita felt a wave of relief and stared at the shattered club. 'What's going to happen?'

'I don't know,' said Carlo, shaking his head. 'There's quite a lot of damage, and the bomb could still go off. They're going to try to defuse it. It's lying in the middle of the dance floor at the moment – four hundred pounds, they say.'

Numerous fire engines were visible along the street, as well as half a dozen police officers, all milling around. As they watched, a van rolled to a stop near the entrance. Three soldiers of the Royal Engineers emerged and began to unload equipment.

'I need to go,' said Carlo, then glanced back at her. 'There won't be any work for some time, Margarita. I'm sorry. We'll be closed for the foreseeable future. I'll write to everyone as soon as possible with more information and sort out payment for your last shifts.'

'I understand,' said Margarita, although she could feel a gnawing anxiety setting in. No work meant no money. How was she to pay the rent? Her father would help her if she asked, she knew, but he had little enough as it was, trying to run a farm on Gozo. She had money saved, but it would not last more than a few weeks.

She watched Carlo hurry towards the club, stopping to speak to one of the police officers. He was gesturing up at the Phoenix and she wondered gloomily if he had insurance.

Forgetting the errands she had come out for, Margarita wandered home, feeling disorientated. For a year, she had been doing something she loved, being paid to sing, and suddenly it was all gone. She resolved to make a list of the other clubs in Valletta, but many of them were still closed and there was not enough work around. In the short term she would have to find something else.

She bought a newspaper and began to circle the positions advertised, gritting her teeth at the thought of waitressing again. Perhaps she could learn to type . . .

Margarita wondered if the bomb had anything to do with Nero. She had heard nothing further from Wilson or Pratchett. Wilson had told her to get in touch if she heard anything in the club. No chance of that now, she thought, imagining the bomb lying on the dance floor, four hundred pounds of gleaming destruction.

*

A photograph arrived from London. Someone at the University of Oxford had scoured the archives to find a picture of Karl

Schuster, the young German who had studied there between 1907 and 1912.

Pratchett picked it up with trembling hands. It was a photograph of the 1911 winning Boat Race team, captioned with the names of the rowers. And there he was: second from last, before A. S. Garton (Magdalen), came K. Schuster (Corpus Christi).

Pratchett looked at the row of young men who stood in front of their boat, several of them holding up oars, all of them clearly delighted. Schuster, second from last, was a thin, dark-haired boy. He had a small, rather smug smile and was looking directly at the photographer. Pratchett took down the enlarged copy of the photograph they had found in Henry's study and compared them. Despite the fifteen years that had passed between the two photographs being taken, it was clear that the man who sat on the wall, a little apart from his companions, was Karl Schuster. He had the same piercing gaze and satisfied smile, as if he knew something that he wasn't sharing.

Pratchett reached for the notes he had made after speaking to Sandford in London. The parcel dispatched for Heinrich Himmler from Istanbul in 1926, apparently sourced by Nero, had been sent by Karl Schuster. Karl Schuster appeared in a photograph that Henry was sure contained Nero. Schuster *had* to be Nero. Pratchett sat back, feeling dazed.

He didn't have much on Schuster yet, except that he had been a museum curator in Damascus at around the time the photograph was taken. Himmler was reportedly obsessed with ancient history and discovering the origins of the Aryan race. If Schuster was Nero, it made perfect sense that he had been in touch with Himmler. Perhaps that was what Nero had been doing during his 'missing years' between the wars: helping Himmler to pursue his absurd anthropological theories.

'Of course, I'll pass you over,' said Wilson behind him, and Pratchett started. He hadn't even noticed the telephone ringing.

'It's your aunt,' said Wilson, covering the receiver. Pratchett felt his heart plummet. He had given the number to Aunt Emma to use only in cases of emergency.

*

Margarita sat on the floor, surrounded by a heap of scrunched-up letters and pages torn from newspapers. Her legs ached after walking for miles through Valletta, looking out for positions advertised and calling in unsolicited to anywhere that looked hopeful. She had had vague promises that the manager would be in touch – he never was – and that they might be looking for new staff in the autumn. What use is autumn, Margarita wanted to snap.

She heard the post arrive downstairs and stood up, wincing as the blood rushed back into her feet. After hobbling down the stairs, she picked up the letters that were for her and returned to her flat. The first was from her father. He was concerned to hear that she was out of a job and enclosed a postal order for £5, offering to send more if she needed it.

Margarita felt her eyes fill with tears. She resolved not to cash it unless she was truly desperate. Livia, her stepmother, had scribbled a note at the end of the letter that they were keen to see her and perhaps she might come for a visit? Not yet, thought Margarita, stuffing the postal order into a drawer. She missed them, but going on holiday when she needed to find a new job would only push her problems a little further down the road.

Tearing open the other letter, she blinked to see that it was from the estate manager at Verdala Palace, a Mr Grech, thanking her for her application for the position of house-maid and inviting her to an interview. Margarita had no recollection of applying for the position, but she had written so many letters that they all blurred into one. Perhaps it had come through an agency. The word 'housemaid' gave her pause, as it sounded like hard work for little money, but the salary listed was higher than the average servant's wage.

Verdala Palace, she knew, was the summer residence of the governor, and the letter noted that the position in the first instance was only for three months. Presumably the governor and his family lived somewhere else the rest of the year.

Margarita looked up the Palace on a map. It was quite far from Valletta, almost on the other side of the island, but she could get there by bicycle in an hour or so. She sighed. Working as a maid, even in a palace, would be something of a comedown after performing in a silk dress under the bright lights of the Phoenix Club. But it would be a change to be out in the countryside and not have to work at night – and she simply couldn't afford to be picky. She quickly wrote a reply, confirming that she would come to the interview.

Chapter 33

Approaching Verdala Palace by bicycle along a hot road lined with prickly pears, Margarita saw the towers of the Palace appear behind the trees and felt a jolt of nervous apprehension. A young guard, unarmed, let her in through the main gate and directed her up the long drive to the trade entrance, where the housekeeper was waiting for her.

The interview was brisk. Mrs Lastra, a no-nonsense but kindly woman, asked her about her work at the Victory Kitchen, appeared unfazed to know that she had been employed until recently in a nightclub, and set her a few small tasks including laying a dinner table correctly, polishing silver, and folding linen. Margarita passed these tests easily, blessing her stepmother for the housekeeping lessons she had endured as a girl. Then Mrs Lastra introduced her to some of the other staff, including a friendly housemaid of her own age called Daniela, and showed her around the Palace.

'Lord Gort and his family are away until tomorrow,' she said, as they emerged into the front entrance hall. 'You won't spend much time above stairs, but you ought to know your way around.'

The main banqueting room was huge, the arched ceiling painted with colourful frescoes, faded but dramatic in the dim lighting. Suits of armour stood here and there, sinister in their stillness. Next, they went upstairs, following a broad stone staircase that circled lazily up.

'Shallow steps,' said Mrs Lastra, pointing, 'so be careful if you're carrying things. We use a dumb waiter for food going to the dining room, to avoid accidents.'

On the second floor, they made a brisk tour of the studies, libraries and bedrooms that surrounded a huge central reception room with space for dozens of guests. Mrs Lastra opened the shutters to show the view over the gardens, which were green and lush even at this baking time of year.

They returned to the main landing. 'Is there another floor?' asked Margarita, thinking of the great height of the building and the towers that stood at each corner.

Mrs Lastra shook her head and pointed to a narrow door guarded by another suit of armour. 'That staircase goes up to the roof. There's nothing up there.' She looked around the hallway, running a finger over one of the light fittings and gazing critically at the result. 'The other housemaids haven't been dusting properly – because of the ghost, no doubt.'

'The ghost?' said Margarita, trying not to sound alarmed.

'It isn't real,' said Mrs Lastra sharply. 'Just a myth – for centuries people have said this place is haunted. Well, I've worked here for thirty years and I've never seen one.' She looked narrowly at Margarita. 'You're not one of these silly girls too, are you?'

'No,' said Margarita quickly. 'Of course not.'

'Good. I need someone sensible who'll work hard and doesn't faint with shyness if someone from the governor's household speaks to her. Can you manage that? Your English seems good enough.'

An hour later, Margarita had been offered the job. The pay was decent, and the hours were not onerous, although there would be some weekend work. She thought longingly of the Phoenix, the music and the tinkle of glasses, and pushed it from her mind.

*

Taking advantage of her last day of freedom, Margarita cycled to an unfamiliar part of the coast and lay baking on the rocks, listening to the crunching of pebbles being nudged by the waves nearby. Her eyes were closed, but through her eyelids she could feel the vivid blue of the sky.

She had written to Arthur to tell him about the job. He would be pleased, she knew – he loved to hear her sing, but he could see how tired the late nights made her and worried about her getting home safely. He would be relieved that she had found something straightforward and respectable, as would her father.

Margarita turned over, brushing shards of stone from her skin, and remembered she had brought Arthur's latest letter with her. She pulled it out and scanned through it. He was still in Egypt, it seemed. *Yesterday I met a lion with a broken nose*, she read, frowning before she remembered what Arthur had said about writing to her in code. *Resisted the temptation to climb on its back for a ride – the reputation of the Navy is shaky enough already!* She pictured him standing solemnly beside the Sphinx in his white uniform, squinting against the fierce desert sun.

Suddenly she sat up and reached back along the thread of thoughts that swirled past. She thought again of the scene she had imagined and, in a flash, she remembered the photograph she had taken from Pratchett's desk.

Margarita closed her eyes, trying to recall it. Three people sat on a wall, two men with a woman between them. One of the men, sitting away from the others, had been looking at the camera. She thought again about the woman, the long dark hair, the white dress, the straw hat that cast a shadow across her face.

She remembered the day she had ended things with Henry. When she arrived at the club, Catherine had hesitantly confided some gossip she'd heard: that Henry was married. Her sister had been invited to a party at the university and had seen him there with his wife. She didn't want to give credence to a rumour, but she thought Margarita ought to be told.

'He can't be,' said Margarita blankly. 'He's with me . . .'

She thought anxiously of the many times she had gone with him to his flat. He lived alone and there was no woman's touch to be seen. It couldn't be true!

She did her set that night as usual, trying not to think about it. It was a mistake. Everything would be all right.

But then Henry had come into the club and looked at her on the stage, smiling proudly, and she knew at once that it was true. He was thirty years older than her. He had never told her much about his life – he said it was all very boring and that he mostly just worked. Now she knew why.

After the show, Margarita was tempted to leave, but she knew Henry was waiting for her. She went through to the bar, which was busy as always, and saw him at a table, smiling up at the waitress. He wasn't trying to flirt, but there was something about him that women liked. He was boyish, despite being over fifty, and his glasses slipped down his nose in an endearing manner. Of course he had a wife!

He saw her coming and smiled brightly, asking what she wanted to drink, calling to the waitress to bring champagne before he saw her expression.

Margarita didn't want to say anything, but she knew it was over, and so she told him, hoping against hope that he would laugh and say it was all a mistake. But he stammered and dissembled, and she knew it was true. In angry tears she got up to leave and he told her to wait, that he would just pay the bill and he'd come with her, and she had knocked his wallet out of his hand.

Money and scraps of paper scattered across the floor, among them several small photographs, including one of a young woman in a white dress, riding a camel.

'Is that your wife?' said Margarita coldly, pointing at the photograph. Henry scrabbled around, picking things up, and swiped the picture before she could take it. But she had seen it clearly, and she saw his shoulders droop. He knew there was no way out of this.

'She looks young,' said Margarita, feeling strangely unemotional. 'Don't you ever go for women your own age?'

'That was taken years ago.'

'Let me see.'

She prised it from his grasp and gazed at the woman in the picture. Long dark hair splayed over her pale dress, and a white lace parasol hung at her side. She was laughing at the photographer, her whole face alight with life and happiness.

Chapter 34

The woman in the photograph Margarita had taken from Pratchett's desk was Vera. Sitting at her kitchen table, Margarita stared intently at her. There she sat on the wall, listening to one of the men speak, her head tilted and her mouth curved in a smile. She was even younger in this picture, and it must have been taken before she met Henry. It wasn't the same dress, but the style was similar, and her hair was long and thick, her skin pale.

Now that she knew it was Vera, Margarita could see the older woman in the girl's face. Vera's face had slimmed with age, she was more tanned by the sun, and she had cut her hair short. She was no longer the innocent young woman who had laughed from atop a camel, but somehow she had become more beautiful.

The picture was crumpled from the wastepaper bin, and Margarita smoothed it out again as she turned it over and gazed at the scribbled words: *Nero, 1926?*

The man on Vera's left, the one she was listening to so intently, wore a wide-brimmed straw hat, and had a handsome, laughing face. The other man was sitting a little further away, and he was looking directly at the camera. He had dark hair and rather piercing eyes.

It could have been taken anywhere, but the ground looked dry and the pale clothing suggested hot weather.

My first dig was in Syria . . .

Vera had been on a dig in Syria in the twenties and had been photographed beside a man who was almost certainly Nero.

Grabbing the photograph, Margarita stood up, scraping back her chair, and hurried out again.

*

Margarita hammered on the door of Wilson's office and looked up at the building. The floors above were taken up by flats, and she could hear a child singing. Did the residents of the flats know what the office below them was being used for? That the manhunt of the century was taking place beneath their feet?

Of course not, she thought. The place looked every bit what it was supposed to be: a down-at-heel solicitor's firm. Wilson and Pratchett both had the sort of forgettable faces that were presumably an enormous asset for intelligence agents. She thought about Vera and wondered how on earth she was able to operate successfully with her striking looks.

No one answered. They were probably off doing much more important things than hearing her breathless theories about a photograph. But it wasn't just any photograph – it was one that Henry had believed contained Nero, enough to write his theory on the back.

Vera must know Nero, thought Margarita. Or at least his real identity. Perhaps she doesn't know he's a spy. But she must know! She began to feel her head aching with all the possibilities.

She hesitated, hoping against hope that Wilson or Pratchett would appear. But the door stayed closed. She turned away and hurried down the steep steps that led towards the water, which gleamed, bright blue, at the end of the street.

Vera had said that her house was on the far tip of Senglea point, which lay across the harbour from Valletta. Margarita took a boat to Senglea, trying not to show her impatience as the old boatman rowed her across. It was late in the day but the hot sun still beat down on her bare arms and she peered up at the high promontory as they approached.

At last, she climbed out onto the jetty and strode uphill, trying to get her bearings. The old city of Senglea narrowed to a point, jutting out above the water. Panting slightly in the heat, Margarita made her way up the steep cobbled streets until she was almost at the end of the peninsula. She could see sandbags and fencing ahead and realised it must be the gun battery. During the first years of the war, as bombs were dropped all over the city, she had often heard the loud report of guns firing from this point, and once she had watched as an Italian plane plummeted into the harbour, trailing smoke.

There were five houses that could be said to be at the end of the point. One was a bombed-out shell. From another, Margarita heard the wailing of a child. Another had ugly curtains, which she could not imagine Vera tolerating. The smartest house, and certainly the one with the best view towards Valletta, had vivid blue shutters, a glorious profusion of bougainvillea growing outside the door, and a dolphin-shaped doorbell on a long chain.

Before she could change her mind, Margarita pulled the bell, and heard it jangle inside. After a minute, she heard footsteps and the door was flung open.

'Margarita,' said Vera, sounding surprised. 'Are you all right?' She was wearing a white shirt that emphasised her suntan and suddenly the young woman who had gone to Syria in 1926 was evident, although she was looking quizzically at Margarita.

'I'm fine,' said Margarita. 'I need to show you something.'

She followed Vera into the cool hallway, looking around at the shining marble floors and the stairs that wound out of sight. The place seemed deathly quiet, like a museum.

'I don't spend much time here,' said Vera, as if she had read Margarita's mind. 'Come on up.'

She led the way up two flights of stairs and out onto a flat roof with a stone balustrade, where two reclining chairs were placed under a sun umbrella. Margarita looked out at the harbour and caught her breath. This had to be one of the best views in the three cities, perhaps in all of Malta. Boats plied back and forth across the harbour. It was nearly sunset and the water gleamed, almost unbearably bright.

'Drink?' said Vera, pointing to the glass of whisky on the table and the decanter beside it.

Margarita shook her head and fumbled in her pocket. 'Look,' she said, and laid the photograph on the table between them. Vera stepped closer, leaning to look at it.

'That's you, isn't it?' Margarita pointed to the woman sitting on the wall.

'Yes,' said Vera, sounding shocked. 'Where did you get this?'

'I borrowed it,' said Margarita evasively.

Vera turned it over and became very still, her eyes fixed on the words on the back: *Nero, 1926?*

'That's Henry's writing,' she said at last, sitting down heavily. She looked back at the photograph, her eyes going from one man to the other.

'I think they found it in Henry's office,' said Margarita. She was expecting Vera to ask who 'they' were, but she seemed not to be listening as she stared intently at the picture.

'He is back, then,' said Vera.

'Nero?'

'I didn't want to believe it.'

'How did you know?' said Margarita. 'Has he contacted you?'

Vera frowned and looked down at her hands. 'Someone has,' she said at last. 'I received an anonymous parcel.'

Margarita stared at her. 'What do you mean? A gift?'

'Or a threat,' said Vera.

'I don't understand.'

'Someone is looking for me,' said Vera. 'Someone from . . . long ago.' She seemed calmer now, her mind obviously far away.

She looked up sharply, as though surprised to see that Margarita was still there. 'I've got to go,' she said, standing up.

'But . . .'

'Please, Margarita. This is important. I'm going to deal with it.'

'You knew Nero,' said Margarita quietly. 'Didn't you?'

Vera stood very still, then her shoulders dropped. 'I knew him a long time ago,' she said, her voice almost inaudible over the gentle hum of the sea. 'I'm sure he's someone very different now.'

Margarita picked up the photograph. 'Please tell me – who are they?'

Vera returned to the table, looking down sadly at the faded faces, as though trying to reconcile the girl she had been with the woman she had become.

She sighed heavily and pointed an elegant finger at the man who sat slightly apart. 'That's Karl Schuster,' she said. 'He was a German museum curator.'

'That's Nero?'

'No,' said Vera. '*That's* Nero.' She pointed at the other man, talking as the girl beside him listened breathlessly. She looked bitterly down at him.

'Who is he?'

'His name was Ralph Curzon,' said Vera, her voice cracking. 'He was my professor.'

Chapter 35

Syria, 1926

Vera dressed slowly in her tent. She was very aware of her body, for the first time in a long while, and noted the flushed skin and the dilated pupils when she looked in a mirror.

The Professor had been everything she had hoped for – thoughtful, considerate, and practised in pleasing a woman. If anything, he was too gentle at first: she wanted him to be rough with her, and it wasn't difficult to persuade him.

He had left long before it grew light, putting on his clothes before kissing her hard and disappearing. She was left with a sense of triumph and a little disappointment that the night was over so soon.

Reluctantly, she scrubbed the traces of him off her skin, although she could still smell his cologne, and wondered if anyone else would notice.

At breakfast, it seemed that everyone must guess what had happened. The Professor sat some distance from her, tucking into his porridge and chatting animatedly to Schuster and Laiq. He looked unruffled, but Vera felt as though a flashing beacon was attached to her forehead. Her skin was pink and her hands trembled slightly as she poured yoghurt from a bowl.

'Are you all right, Miss Millward?' asked Schuster, seeing her spoon clink against the porcelain.

'Just a headache,' said Vera, tightening her grip and forcing herself to look calmly at him. 'I think we all had rather too much to drink last night.'

'I feel awful,' said Stanley in a low voice. He was slumped against a tent pole. He had returned from guarding the throne room and had immediately joined the party. 'I don't think that was real brandy at all. More like some sort of Turkish moonshine.'

'The older you get, the better you'll handle it,' said Curzon, and Vera jumped as she heard his deep voice.

Schuster laughed, passing his old friend a glass of fruit juice and sipping at his own. 'The voice of experience.'

'You can't be hungover, Vera,' said Matthew. 'You had less to drink than any of us. I only saw you drink a glass or two of champagne all evening.'

'Miss Millward has her reputation to think of,' said Curzon. 'She's very sensible not to overindulge. Perhaps we could all learn from her good example.'

He bowed his head slightly and Vera flushed, impressed and irritated in equal measure by his audacity. She knew he was teasing, but his words seemed to contain the hint of a threat. Her reputation had never been in doubt. She saw no reason why Curzon would want to ruin her good name, and of course he was married – he had his own reputation to maintain.

She glanced over at Matthew and saw him look between her and the Professor with a slight frown. She supposed he had noticed the strange energy crackling between them. Perhaps he had guessed what had happened, but he said nothing and returned to the bread and apricots he had been picking at.

Vera felt a pang of guilt. Matthew was her favourite of the three, and if Curzon had not existed, she might have taken him to her bed instead. But it could not be undone.

*

After breakfast, Vera made her way out of the camp. She was hoping to speak to the Professor. It was time to do what she had not had the courage to do before: to warn him about Schuster.

She found Curzon in the yard where Schuster's motor car was parked, putting a small case onto the back seat.

'Are you leaving?'

'I'm going with Karl into Aleppo,' said Curzon. 'He's got a meeting there. I'm going to report the discovery of the throne room to the consul.' He looked at her curiously and she felt herself blush again. He looked clammy, she noticed, and wondered if he too was hungover.

'Professor, may I speak with you?'

'Ralph, I'd like to get going—' Schuster appeared. 'So sorry, Miss Millward. I interrupted you.'

'Not at all,' said Vera, with a forced smile. She hesitated, hoping that Schuster would take the hint, but he seemed in no hurry to leave.

'I just wanted to ask you about – our storage system,' she said at last, looking back at Curzon.

'Can it wait?' He gestured to Schuster. 'Karl is concerned that he won't make his appointment.'

I bet he is, she thought, but shrugged. 'Of course. It's nothing significant.'

'Do whatever you need to,' said Curzon, looking intently at her. 'I'll trust your judgement. I should be back on Wednesday.'

'Of course.'

Vera forced a smile and then hurried away. She brushed her teeth over the basin in her tent, trying to think about anything but Curzon.

A little later, she found Stanley and Matthew in the workroom.

'I'm going out to the dig site,' she said. 'Is Christian on guard there?'

'Yes. Laiq's out there too.'

'Any idea where the Professor is?' said Stanley. 'I wanted to ask him about these tablets.'

'He's gone to Aleppo,' she said, surprised. 'With Schuster.'

'Oh,' said Stanley. 'I didn't notice him in the car as it went past. I thought he must have changed his mind.' He shrugged. 'Perhaps he was sitting in the back.'

Matthew said nothing and Vera thought she detected a hint of resentment – or jealousy – from his bowed head.

'I'm sure he went to Aleppo,' she said, but she felt uneasy. Why would Schuster have left without Curzon? She recalled how sweaty and pale he had looked.

'Schuster's cleared out the office,' added Stanley, gesturing to the open doorway, and she looked in, surprised to see that the room was empty of his clutter. 'Perhaps he's leaving us soon.'

Vera walked briskly back through the camp. She peered into the kitchen, but Azim was lying asleep next to the stove and there was no one else around.

Passing between the tents, Vera kept her eyes open. She stepped into her own tent and picked up a towel so that she could say she was heading for the bath house if challenged.

Where was the Professor? He had looked unwell. He might have discovered what Schuster was up to – perhaps, like Vera, he had become suspicious of Schuster's activities. He would be horrified to find out that his old friend was a spy. Schuster had cleared out the office; could it be that he had left for good after doing . . . what?

She remembered Schuster passing Curzon a glass of juice that morning. The Professor might be lying dead in his tent.

Vera shook her head fiercely – *of course he isn't* – but she could not get rid of the nagging feeling that she had missed something.

On silent feet, she approached Curzon's tent, her heart thudding, the camp dozing in the warm morning. An ibis flew overhead, its long neck outstretched, its plaintive cry echoing as it receded into the distance.

Vera stepped inside, pushing back the rough canvas flaps. The inner layer was slightly transparent, and her stomach jolted as she saw the shape of a man in front of her. Then she breathed out heavily, realising that it was headless: a suit hanging up.

She pushed through the inner flaps and found herself in Curzon's tent. It was empty.

Her eyes went first to his bed, but it was neatly made, the white sheets folded carefully back in the way she imagined he had learned at boarding school.

On the table beside his bed was a stack of books and a few letters. Nearby was a washstand, where his comb and shaving kit stood beside the basin. Vera moved closer to the bed, and saw that the letter on the top of the pile was written in a woman's hand: *Darling Ralph . . .*

It felt strangely intimate, even after last night, to be in Curzon's bedroom – to see the dent in his pillow where his head had rested. His suit hung beside her and she supposed that in the drawer were his undergarments. There was a faint smell of sandalwood and pepper lingering in the air, the scent of his skin as it had pressed against hers.

Vera moved over to the basin and touched the shaving brush, which was soft and worn. A thick silver ring lay in a little wooden tray and she imagined him taking it off before washing. He had not been wearing his wedding ring when he came to her tent.

She lifted the ring up, feeling its weight in her hand. It wasn't a wedding ring, she realised. It was too thick, and there was an engraved pattern set into the silver.

The symbol was a snake, a writhing snake making a circle, and as Vera looked closer, she saw that it had the face of a man. Everything seemed to pause and she felt as though she was hovering somewhere yards above, looking down, as a rushing wind threatened to unbalance her.

She had seen the symbol before, on the envelope and the letter she had found in the study. Why on earth would Curzon have the ring that sealed the letters from the German spy Nero? Perhaps Schuster had planted it here?

But Vera knew, with a sinking feeling, that there was only one explanation: Professor Ralph Curzon was Nero.

Chapter 36

Vera drove across the island, too fast, her mind full of the photograph Margarita had shown her, flicking through images like a film reel. Curzon, Curzon and Schuster, Schuster and Vera, Vera and Curzon, Vera and Nero. Three figures, frozen in time.

She recalled that painful day in Curzon's tent, after he had spent the night in her bed, the shock and disappointment she had felt. She had created, she realised, an idealised image of the Professor, and in a moment it had crumbled to dust in her hands.

I will never do such a thing again, she had vowed then, and she never had. No man could compete with Curzon, and she would not allow herself to be swept away. She had made herself powerless, weak, and that was foolish. It could not happen again.

Margarita had recognised her in the photograph from 1926. She was an intelligent girl. Vera wondered who else had seen it. They had failed to recognise her, but Margarita had, a girl who sang in a nightclub. Perhaps because they were both women. Perhaps because of Henry. Perhaps because they had more in common than either wanted to believe.

She thought again of the gold statue her pursuer had sent her. She was unsettled at the thought of him. Why, if he knew where she was, was he staying elsewhere? Then the thought followed: perhaps he's not elsewhere. Perhaps he's here.

It was nearly dark, and the outskirts of the city slowly gave way to countryside, increasingly dry and dusty at this season. Stubbly fields were enclosed by meandering stone walls, and occasionally the spiky silhouette of a prickly pear tree was visible in the half-light.

She passed through another small town, and then a village, and then she was driving on a rough track through deserted farmland, blasted like a moonscape. Now and then, a square chapel was visible in the distance, and on a hill a few miles away she could see the distinctive domed profile of Mdina Cathedral, miraculously untouched during the bombing of Malta.

Vera bumped along the track that led to her dig. None of the students would be here at this hour. At the bottom of the hill, she came to a halt, abandoning the car outside the tents, then got out and stood still for a moment. The air was warm, the gentle breezes carrying with them dust and the scent of wild thyme. She glanced at her watch then pulled out her torch and pushed her way into the main tent.

She quickly flashed the torch around, reassuring herself that everything was as she had left it. The students had been working here, she knew, but they would not touch her things. She went to the drawer and pulled out the little wooden box that the statue had come in. She opened it, holding the torch high, and saw the figure lounging back on her velvet cushion.

Vera frowned. Which way had the statue been facing? She thought she recalled placing the woman on her left side, but now she was on her right. Unnerved, she glanced around the tent, moving the torch slowly so that the light illuminated each corner. Nothing looked out of place.

She looked back down at the statue. Vera was not used to doubting herself, and it was an unfamiliar and unwelcome feeling. Pursing her lips, she decided to worry about it later, and lifted out the cushion and the statue, placing them carefully on the table. There was nothing underneath, just the plain wood of the box, and she shook her head, frustrated. She picked up the note that had come in the box – *A souvenir from Syria* – and turned it over, before discarding it.

After putting everything back where it had been, Vera sat at her desk and leafed through the pile of letters that one of the students had brought from the university. One was an invitation to contribute to an academic journal. Once upon a time, offers like this had come in regularly, but now they were rare. She put it aside, knowing in her heart that she did not have the time to dedicate to writing articles, and wondered when the invitations would cease altogether.

She paused, seeing a handwritten letter in the stack. Elizabeth, she thought – this must be the letter she had promised from Aleppo. She ripped it open and saw instead a brief note on plain white notepaper. It was unsigned, and simply said: *Looking forward to seeing you soon.*

Vera felt her heart leap into her throat. She turned the paper over, but there was nothing written on the back. She looked back at the handwriting. The same hand had written the note that came with the statue. Had she seen it somewhere else, long ago?

Picking up the envelope, Vera saw that there were no postal marks. It was addressed to her at the university, but it had not arrived there by mail. Someone had hand-delivered it. She stared, feeling the hair rise at the back of her neck. The tent flapped, making her jump, and then she heard the sound of gravel crunching outside.

Vera flicked the torch off at once and sat completely still, feeling her heart pounding. She breathed in and out, straining to hear the sound again. She heard another crunch, but it was further away.

She made her way slowly to the doorway and stepped out into the balmy night, allowing her eyes to adjust to the darkness. There was nothing to be seen, and no sound except the gentle whispering of the breeze.

Walking slowly, so as not to make any noise, she approached her car, and was reaching for the door handle when she heard the crunch again behind her, closer now.

Vera whirled around. A man was visible in the half-light.

'Vera,' he said, and she recognised his voice at once. 'It's me.'

Chapter 37

A mile or so off shore, Cardona's boat bobbed gently. It was dark, but he could see distant lights on the Maltese mainland.

The sea all around was calm and he could hear nothing except the lapping of the waves. He had been fishing for several hours since dropping Leonardi off in the late afternoon. Most of the journeys he had undertaken to Malta in the last few weeks had been alone, carrying small packages, which he much preferred to the trips where his employer accompanied him. The man was always affable, always charming, but Cardona could not bring himself to trust him.

'Wait until ten o'clock,' Leonardi had said, 'and then get as close as you can to St Mark's Tower. You know it?'

'Of course.'

'Bring the boat in quietly and keep a dim light burning. There's an RAF facility nearby on Qawra Point. They shouldn't bother you as long as you behave like a fisherman.'

Behave like a fisherman, thought Cardona. Well, that was easy enough. He fished in the darkness, hearing the gentle murmur of the sea, until it was time to go.

He lit his lamp and dimmed it as instructed, putting it in the bow of the boat, and made his way unhurriedly towards the coast. At last he saw the square outline of St Mark's Tower against the sky, standing alone on a rocky promontory.

Cardona brought the *Zafferano* in gently and switched off the engine once he was close to the rocks. With the help of an oar, he brought it closer to shore, until at last, with a soft bump, he could go no further. Leonardi had told him not to anchor; he would not have to wait long.

He checked his watch. One minute to ten. Suddenly he saw movement and realised that two people were walking across the rough rocks towards him. He tensed – he had not expected Leonardi to have company.

Their faces became visible in the light of his lamp, and he saw Leonardi, tall and dark, his face lined, surrounded by black hair.

With him was a woman, much younger, wearing wide trousers and a white shirt as though she had come straight from working in an office. She looked pale and tired and said nothing as Leonardi raised a hand in greeting.

'Thank you for waiting, my friend.'

'It's no problem,' said Cardona, although he was unnerved by the woman's presence.

Leonardi stood back to let the woman go ahead of him, holding out a hand to help her. She looked down at it for a moment, her lips tight, before taking it and stepping onto the boat.

Cardona saw that she was not as young as he had first supposed. She was rather beautiful in the dim light, although her expression was strained. She looked worried, and her short dark hair was tousled. She nodded to him and made her way round to sit in the bow.

Leonardi followed her onto the boat and stood for a moment, watching as Cardona pushed off from the rocks with an oar.

'Any problems?'

'Nothing,' said Cardona. 'Everything has been quiet.'

He put the oar away, blew out the lamp, and then started the engine, which sounded shatteringly loud in the quiet night. Soon they were moving north, and the lights of mainland Malta were slipping away.

Leonardi looked back for a few minutes, then followed the woman to the front of the boat, out of sight.

They passed a group of tiny islands and Cardona saw the great statue of St Paul silhouetted against the starry sky. Then he blinked, for a light was moving somewhere near the islands, faint but unmistakable.

It was almost certainly another fishing boat, Cardona knew, but he felt uneasy and adjusted his course. Glancing back, he saw the light bobbing. It was hard to gauge how far away it was. He shook his head and focused on steering.

He could hear his passengers talking faintly up front. The woman had raised her voice slightly and he guessed she was angry.

After a mile or so he looked back and saw that the light had not receded. Was this other boat following him? It might just be a coincidence, but he was worried.

Cardona stepped out of the wheelhouse. He heard the woman's voice again. 'Don't be absurd! They know already.'

Resisting the urge to keep listening, he said, 'Signor?'

Leonardi stood up sharply. 'Everything all right?'

'I can see a light. I think we're being followed.'

Leonardi followed Cardona around the edge of the cabin and looked in the direction he was pointing, frowning as he saw the distant glow.

'Fishing boat?'

'It could be. But it's coming this way. I don't see how they can see us, though, without lights onboard.'

'They may have radar.'

Leonardi stared into the blackness. Cardona could see his face only dimly in the moonlight, but the man's expression made him shiver. There was something ruthless about it – a hard, calculating look. Cardona felt, not for the first time, that he was involved in something much deeper than he could understand.

'How much faster can you go?' said Leonardi.

'About twenty-five knots on calm water,' said Cardona. 'We're doing sixteen at the moment. Shall I speed up?'

'Not yet,' said Leonardi. 'If they think we're a fishing boat, going too fast will blow our cover. Just be ready to speed up if they lose interest.'

'Understood.'

Leonardi's words just increased the tension that gripped Cardona. *What am I doing?* With a jolt, it occurred to him that he was helping a strange man to evade the authorities and putting himself at great risk. Surely smugglers ought to be taking something to Malta, or else bringing something back. But Leonardi and his companion carried nothing – at least nothing that could be seen.

Leonardi went back to the bow and Cardona retreated into the wheelhouse. He gripped the wheel tightly, glancing back now and then at the bobbing light.

Eventually he looked back and it was gone. Had they dimmed it? Or had the boat stopped following? He stared into the blackness for a minute or more. Suddenly a light flashed – once, twice, three times, and it seemed much closer than before.

The flashing stopped, and he saw no more lights. After fifteen minutes, when he was sure that they were no longer being followed, he sped up.

At last, they rounded the edge of Gozo and began to travel north. Cardona started to relax. He could no longer hear his passengers talking and even the bombers seemed to be taking the night off. Ahead was nothing but calm black ocean, under a starry sky, all the way to Sicily, and home.

Chapter 38

Pratchett sat in the silent bedroom, listening to the slow, even breathing of the man who slept before him. He watched his chest rise and fall and saw the fluttering of his moustache. The clock on the wall ticked loudly, measuring out what remained of his uncle's life.

He had arrived in London from Malta in the early hours. After a brief sleep he had come down to Kent where Emma, his aunt, met him at the station and cried the tears she had been unable to share over the telephone. He held her tightly. She was the only mother he had ever known and he felt his chest tighten to see her in such distress.

Uncle Andrew had been ill for some years, but he had never been bedbound. Now he had had a stroke and had not been properly conscious for two days.

'I don't think he knows you're here,' Emma said sadly, seeing Pratchett sitting patiently at the bedside, but he was quite content to stay. It seemed the least he could do. He had seen so little of them over the last few years, except for the months after he had been wounded in France, when they had cared for him again as if he was still a little boy.

It was remarkable to think that less than twenty-four hours ago he had been in Malta, in a warm city by the sea, investigating a ruthless spy.

He had promised Wilson that he would go to Oxford as soon as he could be spared, to see what he could dig up on Karl Schuster. To pass the time, he pulled out his notebook and flicked through it, reading the notes he had made. He recalled the photograph of Schuster, a grinning boy on the winning rowing team, and wondered yet again what had happened to him.

Aunt Emma called him to come down for lunch and they ate soup and bread and talked of his cousin, Brian, who had been in North Africa for over a year with the Eighth Army.

'He's already bored with Tunisia,' said Emma. 'He says he liked Egypt much better – better food, friendlier people.'

Brian's letters to Dennis were more candid than those to his parents. He was depressed, he said, and could see his best years passing him by. He was longing to come home and to get married to Lucy, a clever girl now serving as a meteorologist with the WRNS, but that could be years away.

'I suppose the Tunisians have been occupied for ages,' said Pratchett. 'Not surprising that morale is low.'

Emma nodded and took a spoonful of soup. 'At least he's safe there, now that the Germans have withdrawn. We're just glad he's alive.'

As she said it, her eyes flicked upwards towards the bedroom where her husband lay unconscious. How utterly unfair it was, thought Pratchett, that Brian might survive the war only to lose his father. Andrew was only fifty-five, but he too had come through a war, and his health had never recovered.

'I don't suppose Brian will be in Tunisia for long. They're already being prepared for a new front,' said Emma with a sigh. 'Andrew thought – thinks – that it will be Greece. Or perhaps they won't have to go anywhere yet. Perhaps he'll be safe for a while longer.'

Pratchett nodded, but he wished he could tell her what he knew: that Italy was where the next stage of the war in Europe would unfold, and Brian was certain to be caught up in it.

After lunch, he placed a call to Malta.

Wilson sounded strained, and what he had to say was startling. 'It seems that Karl Schuster may not be the man we're looking for. See what you can dig up on a chap called Ralph Curzon.'

'What?' said Pratchett, feeling disorientated. 'Who is Curzon?'

'The woman in the photograph we found in Henry Dunn's study is his wife, Vera,' said Wilson. 'The man sitting beside her is Ralph Curzon. Apparently, she knew him back in the twenties and found evidence that he was a German spy with the code-name Nero.'

'Mrs Dunn told you this?'

'Margarita came to see me this morning,' said Wilson. 'She recognised Vera in the photograph.'

'But what does Vera say?' said Pratchett, frowning as he tried to take all of this in.

'She's gone missing,' said Wilson. 'Her car was found abandoned on the outskirts of Naxxar. Her neighbour saw her leave the house last evening, but no one's seen her since.'

Pratchett breathed out heavily. 'And she knows Nero's identity . . .'

'Exactly,' said Wilson, sounding grim. 'She may turn up. But the signs aren't promising. I think she's gone somewhere with him, willingly or unwillingly.'

Pratchett nodded, listening to Emma's feet padding about upstairs, and wondered where Vera could possibly be. Malta was a small island. Surely she wouldn't be difficult to find.

'What do you want me to do?' he asked, sensing all the work he had done crumbling away.

'Carry on as you were,' said Wilson. 'I don't think we can discount Schuster altogether yet. His name was on that parcel sent to Himmler, after all – which, incidentally, seems to have been dispatched from Aleppo before it went to Istanbul and then Switzerland. Find out all you can about Schuster *and* about this Curzon.'

*

The following morning, Pratchett took the train back to London. His uncle's condition had not changed, and it seemed pointless to wait around. Emma had urged him to go. He promised to come back to Kent before he left the country, whatever happened, and hugged her again. Upstairs, Andrew slumbered, his breathing shallow. His aunt and uncle had barely changed since Pratchett was a boy and now he felt unsettled, adrift, as though everything he loved and relied on was slipping away.

In a drab office off an unfashionable side street in London, a typed sheet of paper was waiting for him. It was a translation of a recent German newspaper article about a museum curator in Berlin who had been given an award.

> *Dr Schuster spent many years in the Middle East, latterly as curator at the National Museum in Damascus. He returned to Germany in 1929 and joined the Pergamon in 1930. He played a key role in the reconstruction of the Ishtar Gate and in developing the Vorderasiatisches collection.*

Pinned to the translation was a copy of the original article, which included a grainy photograph of a man leaning heavily on a cane. Peering at it, Pratchett tried to see the man who had sat with Vera and Curzon on the wall all those years ago, and who had as a boy helped Oxford to win the Boat Race. His face was plump and fleshy, but it was him. He was smiling proudly as he held up a medal.

An infected wound on his ankle led to Dr Schuster losing the use of his right leg shortly before he arrived at the museum, but he has never allowed it to hold him back. He is a beloved colleague and friend.

Pratchett looked narrowly at the picture, trying to think of a way that Schuster could still be the man they were looking for. He might have exchanged places with someone else or be directing other operatives from his comfortable position in Berlin. He made a note to investigate further, but he could feel his certainty melting away like ice in the sun.

Chapter 39

In an office at Lascaris, Mrs Gordon was waiting with a sheaf of papers laid out on the table in front of her.

'Any joy?' said Wilson, sitting down. Through a glass panel, he could see several young women moving wooden chips around a plotting table and scribbling on a blackboard. In the gallery above them, two men in uniform prowled back and forth, occasionally calling down an order.

'There were a handful of unknown vessels spotted on the night in question,' said Mrs Gordon, pulling out a map and smoothing it between them. 'We've already identified most of them and the majority were traced coming back in. But you're looking for one that didn't?'

'Yes, in theory.'

'There was a larger boat out near St Mark's Tower that didn't respond when signalled.' She pointed with a pencil. 'The station at Qawra Point picked it up on radar but they thought it was probably a fisherman who'd drifted off course.'

'And it didn't come back?'

'Not that we can see. Not that night or since.'

'Do you have a description of the type of boat?'

'The estimated size and so on are recorded here,' she said, passing him a report. 'Once it started moving again, it was going very fast for a fishing boat, so they think it was one of the newer models with a powerful engine. Does that fit what you're after?'

'I don't know what I'm after,' said Wilson. 'Someone we're interested in seems to have left the island that night. They could have gone some other way, but the simplest solution is that they were picked up by motorboat and taken away, probably to Italy.'

'Well, this is your most likely suspect,' said Mrs Gordon, tapping the map again. 'They were going north when last seen.' She looked at him curiously. 'I suppose this isn't a run-of-the-mill smuggler?'

'Probably not,' said Wilson.

'What do you want to do with this fellow, then, if he comes back?'

'Bring him in.'

Wilson returned to the office, thinking about Ralph Curzon. He had ordered a search of the files, and the results should soon be sent through. If the man was Nero, it seemed unlikely that he used his real name in his dealings, but even the best spies slipped up sometimes. Vera's word alone wasn't enough to go on. They would have to find evidence that conclusively proved he was Nero. More importantly, they would have to find him.

*

Pratchett sat on a hard chair, listening to the occasional thuds that echoed in the bowels of the British Museum. The museum was even quieter than usual, the crowds that normally thronged the galleries nowhere to be seen. Most of the museum's treasures had been spirited away at the outbreak of war to be stored underground, and most of the staff had joined up.

Pratchett remembered visiting with Uncle Andrew as a child and looking with awe at the Egyptian artefacts and mummies. What a thrill it had been, although he had woken up that night, convinced that a mummy was in his room. He shivered, recalling the feeling of dread.

Footsteps hurried along the passage and a white-haired man in tweed appeared.

'Mr Makepeace? I'm Dennis Pratchett.'

The man shook his hand briskly. 'I gather you're asking about Ralph Curzon.'

'That's right. Anything you've got on him. All I know is that he was a professor at Oxford some years ago. I'm heading there later.'

'He was Professor of Arabian and Oriental Studies, or something along those lines. We should have copies of his funding applications,' said Makepeace, gesturing vaguely at a huge bank of filing cabinets. 'I can dig them out.'

'Those would be very useful.' Pratchett paused, wondering if the man knew Curzon personally. 'I don't suppose you know anything of where he is now? He isn't listed as part of the current faculty, but we'd like to get hold of him.'

Makepeace blinked. 'But Curzon's dead.'

'What?' Pratchett stared at him, feeling his breath catch in his throat. 'When did he die?'

The old man screwed up his face. 'Let me see. I remember hearing the news . . . Yes, it was the day of my older daughter's wedding. What year was that?'

He went to the filing cabinet and rummaged around, muttering to himself as Pratchett stood impatiently, questions multiplying. It couldn't be Curzon, after all. Had Vera got it wrong? Had Wilson? Were they on the wrong track altogether?

'Ah!'

Makepeace stood up, brandishing a sheaf of yellowing paper. He put it down on the desk and flicked through. 'This is the funding application for his last dig. I seem to recall he died on the dig, or perhaps on the way back. Sad business.'

'Where and when was this dig?' said Pratchett urgently.

'Syria,' said Makepeace, running a finger along the typewritten text before him. He looked up. 'In 1926.'

Chapter 40

Walking through Oxford's sunlit quadrangles, Pratchett paused for a moment and watched two young men playing tennis. They were only five or six years younger than him, but to his eyes they looked like boys, their faces pink and spotty. One wore thick spectacles and the other had a pronounced limp, which perhaps explained why they were here and not away fighting. He wondered if they were relieved or embarrassed to be left behind.

His own university years had not been entirely happy ones. He had been bright but lazy, and a tendency to leave things until the last minute had given him a poor reputation with his professors. He had enjoyed the social side of university but had spent too long moping after a girl who wasn't interested and writing sad poetry.

In his final year, she rejected him once and for all, and from somewhere he found the impetus to work hard, achieving results that were as much a surprise to him as they were to his tutors. He had taken some time out to travel and work as an English teacher in Portugal, improving his language skills and considering what he might do next, only to be brought home by the outbreak of war.

After being invalided home from Dunkirk, he spent a few weeks in hospital and had gone to recuperate at his aunt and uncle's home. A month after that, he was invited to lunch by a friend of a friend and asked if he'd like to work for the government. Expecting an interview for a civil service post, he had arrived to find a group of men twice his age, who had something rather more secret in mind.

'Good afternoon,' he said now, as soon as the gates of Oriel College opened and the porter appeared. 'I'm here to see Professor Barton.'

'Is he expecting you, sir?'

'Yes. The name's Dennis Pratchett.'

He showed the man his card. The porter studied it briefly.

'Very good, sir. Through the door directly across the quad, turn left along the corridor and then right. You'll see Professor Barton's study on your right, next to the bust of Julius Caesar.'

'Thank you.'

Pratchett crossed the quad, then made his way briskly along the corridor and knocked at the door. He saw Caesar staring sardonically at him, as though he was about to order him back to his rooms.

'Come in!'

Professor Barton was sitting in a huge armchair. His thin hair was white and his eyes were sunken on each side of an extraordinarily beaky nose.

'Thank you for seeing me, Professor.'

'It breaks up the day,' said Barton, laying down the book he had been reading on his skinny knees. 'Not often I have a visit from someone of intelligence.' He laughed, wheezing slightly. 'Just a feeble joke. What can I do for you?'

Pratchett sat down. 'I'm here to ask you about someone who used to be a colleague of yours – Ralph Curzon.'

He saw the old man's eyebrows leap up. 'Curzon? Good gracious.'

'You remember him, sir?'

'Of course I remember him,' said Barton. 'Why on earth are you interested in Curzon?'

'His name came up in relation to a case we're looking into at the moment,' said Pratchett carefully.

'You know he died in the twenties?' said Barton. He reached for the cold cup of tea beside him. 'Terrible tragedy. He had a great deal of potential. When he was appointed, he was one of our youngest professors.'

'What do you know about his death?'

Barton shrugged. 'Negligence. It happens. He was on a dig in Turkey – no, Syria, wasn't it? The native workmen hadn't followed safety procedures and he was killed when one of the pits collapsed. Dreadful situation.'

'Were you friends with Curzon?'

'I suppose I was,' Barton said ruminatively. 'He was a lot younger than me, of course, and he was married, so we moved in different circles. But at college we got on well. He used to come in to see me here and we'd drink sherry, argue over the finer points of Assyrian theology, that sort of thing . . .'

He looked around the room, and Pratchett felt the hairs on his arms stand up as he imagined Curzon sitting in this very chair. Could he really be the German agent they were looking for? It was possible, of course, but there was also the inconvenient fact that he was dead.

'I always thought that dig was doomed,' said Barton. He stood and shuffled across to a tray holding a bottle of sherry. He slopped some into two small glasses and brought one over to Pratchett, who took it, wondering if it was the same sherry Barton had drunk with Curzon.

'Thank you. Er – what do you mean, sir? When you say it was doomed?'

'Well, I wasn't expecting him to die,' said Barton, settling himself back in the armchair. 'But he'd had trouble getting the permits he wanted, then there was a revolution in Syria, and even after that there were all sorts of problems with funding, location, you name it.'

Pratchett nodded and sipped the sherry.

'And there was the girl, of course.'

'What girl?' said Pratchett, trying to sound calm.

'Curzon took three or four assistants with him each season. They were generally recent graduates, young men interested in a career in archaeology. That year, he selected a *woman*.'

'Do you remember her name?'

The old man frowned. 'Miss Millward. She was a languages graduate originally, I believe, before enrolling on the Diploma in Anthropology under Robert Marett. I told Curzon he shouldn't take her.'

'Why didn't you think she should go?'

The old man looked astonished. 'A woman, Pratchett! A young woman, unchaperoned, on a dig in the desert with a team of young men and hordes of native workmen. Not to mention the fact that there were dozens of other candidates who deserved that place.'

'Wasn't she qualified, then?' said Pratchett.

Barton sniffed. 'Academically she was – in fact, she was one of the best in her year, if I remember rightly. But these sorts of opportunities are meant for ambitious young men who want careers. Young women want to get married.'

From the little Pratchett knew of Vera Dunn, she was cleverer than all the men she'd ever worked with put together, but he listened, saying nothing.

'Anyway, I was right,' said Barton, shifting in his chair. 'The dig was a disaster. They'd only been there a few weeks when Curzon was killed.'

'What happened to the dig?'

'The French authorities took it over,' said Barton. 'They worked on it for four or five years, I believe – uncovered a throne room that was one of the best examples of its kind, and a very impressive temple, too.'

'Didn't anyone from Curzon's team want to be involved?' said Pratchett.

Barton looked thoughtful. 'I don't know. I never heard that any of them went back there.'

'I suppose the loss of their professor must have been distressing.'

'Oh, yes,' said Barton. 'I saw one of the boys, Stanley something, a few times. He was subdued. He told me they wrapped up the camp very quickly after that and came home.'

Pratchett nodded. 'Did you see Miss Millward again?'

'No, never. I heard of her occasionally – she became quite a reputable archaeologist, I believe.' Barton looked irritated at her success. 'No idea where she is now.'

Pratchett looked down at his notes. 'What about Curzon?' he said at last. 'Presumably there was a funeral?'

'Just a memorial service,' said Barton, who had creaked over to the tray again and was now pouring himself another sherry. 'Drink?'

'Oh, no – thank you.'

'The memorial was ages after his death,' said Barton. 'There was some sort of holdup with the authorities in Syria releasing his body. Anyway, in the end there was no casket at the service. It was very moving, nonetheless.'

Pratchett breathed out heavily. 'No casket?'

'No. I suppose he may have been buried out there, in the end. There may not have been much left to bury.'

'Quite,' said Pratchett. Although he was reluctant to believe it was Curzon they were looking for, as yet there was no real proof the man had died in the desert in 1926.

'You've been very helpful, Professor,' said Pratchett. 'If I might take a little more of your time . . .?'

'I've nowhere to be!' said the old man. His nose was pink and he seemed to be enjoying himself. 'What else do you want to ask?'

'I'd like to know a bit more about Curzon himself,' said Pratchett. 'His background, what he did in the Great War, and so on.'

'Well, he fought,' said Barton, 'as they all did. He was wounded and came home fairly quickly. Spent a couple of years in London.'

'What about before the war? What did he study as an undergraduate?'

'History of art, I believe,' said Barton, his forehead wrinkling with the effort of thinking back. 'I seem to recall he'd spent a year in Florence at one point – he spoke Italian well. But he soon became more interested in what you might call "proper" history, and of course archaeology. He was appointed professor soon after the war. You know his mother was German?'

'No, I didn't.'

'She'd lived in England for a long time, so I doubt there were any divided loyalties there. He was a cousin of Lord Curzon on his father's side – good British stock. But he was fond of Germany. He went on annual walking holidays in the Black Forest after the war. He'd be rolling in his grave to see what Germany's become.'

'I expect so,' said Pratchett politely. He was thinking of what it might mean for their search if Curzon really was still alive. An

Englishman who spoke both German and Italian and had managed to fool the world into believing he was dead for years. By now, he could be anyone.

Barton sat back in his chair, grunting slightly, and closed his eyes. 'A dreadful business,' he said ruminatively. 'Curzon was clever, ambitious – brilliant, really. I always thought he'd go far.'

You have no idea, thought Pratchett.

Chapter 41

Cardona puffed as he pedalled along the road, watching the dust flying up from his tyres. He was heading uphill, sweating heavily in the afternoon heat, his shirtsleeves rolled up and his cap set low over his brow.

He had been mending his nets on the dock when a boy brought a note from Leonardi, summoning him to the house in the hills. For a moment, Cardona wanted to ignore the message, to pretend he had not received it, but he knew that Leonardi must have another job for him, and he could not afford to turn it down, although he was starting to dread the work.

Adelina had gone off in the van that morning, taking the children to visit her parents along the coast at Sciacca, so he had had to go by bicycle. It was much too hot to be cycling in the middle of the day.

The scrubby trees at the side of the road provided very little protection, but he could see a deeper stand of trees a little further on and pushed the pedals hard until he reached the shade. Then he stopped, wiped his brow, took a swig of water from the bottle in his knapsack and pedalled on more slowly. He felt his wallet slipping from his pocket and pushed it back in.

Further on, the pillars of the Valley of the Temples rose before him. He remembered taking the children around the temple complex and watching them run excitedly back and forth, laughing hysterically at the naked statues.

Cardona frowned as he cycled past. He had heard that the temples were closed to visitors, but he could see a woman standing at the foot of the steps that led up to the Temple of Juno. She was peering up at it, a hand over her brow, her hair gleaming golden in the sun.

'You know,' Adelina had said as they watched the three children playing, 'this temple is dedicated to Juno.'

'Yes?'

She nudged him with her hip. 'The goddess of fertility. Perhaps we should say a prayer.'

'All right,' said Cardona, teasing her, and put his hands together. 'Goddess Juno, I beg of you to send us no more children ... the ones we have already are awful creatures.'

She laughed. 'Very well, I'll do it myself.' He watched her close her eyes, then he turned away to supervise the children, who were running amok among the columns.

Later, as they were getting ready for bed, he said, 'I suppose you don't need my involvement if Mother Juno is looking after things. Perhaps I'll just go straight to sleep.' He kissed Adelina's shoulder.

She laughed huskily and pushed him back onto the bed. 'It can't hurt ... just to be on the safe side.' Their fourth child was born the following year.

Cardona chuckled as he remembered all this, wiping the sweat from his brow as the temple disappeared behind the curve of the hillside. He heard an engine and pulled the bicycle in to the side of the road, feeling it rock in the wind as a car roared past.

He recognised the car as one of Leonardi's: a bright blue open-top Alfa Romeo, in perfect condition. He could see a blonde head behind the wheel. Perhaps she was one of Leonardi's many girlfriends; according to gossip in Agrigento, he had an endlessly rotating cast of visitors at his beautiful house.

The road led steeply uphill again, until at last he turned off onto a winding track between the trees and he could hear nothing but birdsong and his own breathing.

Passing between the stone pillars at the entrance to Leonardi's property, he was not surprised to see the blue car parked in the yard. He dismounted and leaned the bicycle against a tree.

Cardona smoothed his hair and wiped some of the sweat from his face. He crunched across the gravel and rang the doorbell. After a few moments, the maid opened it and led him into the house.

'Signor Leonardi . . .' said the girl, gesturing to the door of his study. Her voice was unclear, and he recalled that she was deaf. He smiled and she hurried away.

Cardona tapped on the door. 'One moment,' said a voice from within, then it swung open.

'Come in, come in,' said Leonardi, shaking his hand. 'Thank you for coming, Signor Cardona.'

He thought Leonardi must be over fifty, but he was always full of energy. He was dressed stylishly, his silk shirt and leather shoes gleaming, his hair slicked back. Cardona remembered the dark-haired woman who had come with him from Malta to Sicily on their last voyage and wondered what had become of her.

'Have a seat,' said Leonardi, gesturing to the armchairs nearby. 'Are you thirsty? Shall I call for coffee or lemonade? Or beer?'

'No, thank you, signor,' said Cardona, shaking his head. 'I'm fine.' He wanted to get this over as quickly as possible.

'Your family are well?' said Leonardi.

'Very well, thank you,' he said. 'Enjoying the good weather.'

'Of course.' Leonardi smiled. 'Plenty of time on the beach, no doubt.'

'Oh, yes.' Cardona waited.

'I expect you know why I've asked you to come,' said Leonardi. 'I need you to travel to Malta in a few days' time.'

'Certainly, signor. What date do you have in mind?'

'It will be the night of the nineteenth of June. Saturday. Please come to the jetty at Zingarello at six that evening. You'll be given further instructions then.'

'Not a problem. Thank you, signor.' Cardona noticed that Leonardi had not mentioned if he would be coming along this time, but he knew better than to ask. 'I'd better be getting back.'

They shook hands again and Cardona thought what a pleasant man Leonardi was, friendly and charismatic. If it weren't for the fact that he was almost certainly passing information about Malta to the Italians, or perhaps the Germans, he might have liked the man, or at least respected him. But I'm colluding too, he thought, and felt a cloud of guilt. At least Leonardi believes in something. I'm just doing it for the money.

He went along the corridor to where the front door stood open and looked back to see that Leonardi's office door had already closed. Going down the front steps, he saw the maid going along the side of the house, brandishing a watering can.

Cardona grabbed his bicycle and wheeled it between the stone pillars at the top of the drive, then climbed on and rode slowly along the shaded track.

Suddenly aware of a lightness at his hip, he laid a hand on his pocket and realised that his wallet had gone. Sighing, he dismounted and walked slowly back, peering into the dust at the side of the road. It was nowhere to be seen and soon he was back at the gateposts. He put the bicycle back under the tree and scanned the ground all around for the wallet. Nothing. He crunched back across the gravel, looking for the maid. The front door was still wide open, but she was nowhere to be seen. She had probably gone around the back of the house to continue her watering.

With a sinking feeling, Cardona realised that he must have dropped the wallet in Leonardi's office. He stepped through the front door into the cool of the hallway, hoping to see a servant so that he could ask them to look for it. But all was quiet.

He padded along the hallway and turned the corner. Leonardi's study door was closed. He approached, intending to knock, when he heard a voice from within, muffled but audible.

'His death will send a message,' said Leonardi. 'A powerful message that we have people everywhere and that no one is safe.'

Another male voice replied from further into the room, but it was indistinct, and was followed by a woman's voice. He guessed it was the blonde woman whose car was still parked outside.

Her voice became clearer, as though she had moved towards the door. 'It won't be easy. He'll be very well protected, even in Malta.'

'Nero will take care of it,' said one of the men, his voice low and amused. 'We have until Saturday to iron out the details.'

'And your fisherman is to be trusted?' asked the woman.

'He'll keep his mouth shut,' said Leonardi. 'He has a young family.' He left the sentence hanging in the air.

Cardona had heard enough and fled back along the corridor. He ran across the gravel, keeping his eyes open for the maid, but there was no one around. Reaching his bicycle, he leapt astride it and pedalled out of the yard and along the track.

Before long, he was flying downhill. The wind was cooling his sweaty skin, and his heartbeat was beginning to slow. He should not have gone back for the wallet. It was better to live in ignorance and take the money that Leonardi was offering. He wished there was a way to unhear what he had heard.

They were going to kill someone. Surely that was what it meant? *He'll be very well protected, even in Malta . . . His death will send a message.* The journey Cardona was to make to Malta on Saturday night must be to take the assassins there.

Who in Malta would they want to kill? Since the war began, Malta had attained a strategic importance far exceeding her size, but he could think of no one who might be a worthwhile target for assassination, except for the governor. But perhaps he had it all wrong. Perhaps Leonardi and his people were not spies at all, but arms dealers, drug runners, smugglers of another kind . . .

Cardona sighed. He wished he had never got involved. But he had no choice – he needed the money, and surely Leonardi would not be content to let him go back to his life, knowing what he knew? And who was this Nero? Another accomplice? Or even Leonardi himself?

He would stick to the plan, he decided, as he came out onto the road that led towards the coast. He would have to take them to Malta as agreed. And then? Then they would kill someone. Was he really going to stand by and let that happen? The Axis had retreated in North Africa, he had heard, but there was nothing to say they might not regroup and win the war. He imagined his mother and her English friends in Malta being rounded up by men in jackboots and felt a chill as he sped downhill in the afternoon heat.

Chapter 42

Syria, 1926

Curzon did not return to the dig for several days, which gave Vera time to think. She behaved normally with the boys as they went about their work, and tried hard to pretend that nothing was afoot. She could not rid her mind of the image of Curzon's silver ring, engraved with a snake and the symbol of his betrayal.

The workmen were still busy excavating the chamber under the throne room and the pit grew wider and deeper every day. It was over thirty feet deep in places, with scaffolding to support the walls, and numerous side tunnels were being dug out.

Now and then, an object – bronze statues, clay vases, decaying fragments of wooden chests – would be brought out to be cleaned and catalogued before being locked away, but most of the treasures within were inaccessible as yet, buried under centuries of soil.

'Curzon's taking a lot longer than I expected,' said Matthew one day as they watched the workmen tidying the site in the late afternoon. 'Didn't he say he was reporting our find to the authorities?'

'There must be a delay,' said Vera. 'I'm sure it's nothing to worry about.' But she *was* worried – about what Curzon was up to, and what would happen to the treasures they were finding.

'I don't like having all this priceless stuff lying about with only a couple of us to guard it,' he said. 'The sooner he comes back with some more men, the better.'

'I think our men are trustworthy,' said Vera, thinking of little Mo, who was proving to have a knack for finding the most interesting items. He could have gone far, she thought, if he had not had the misfortune to be born in a poor Syrian village. As it was, the most he could hope for would be to become a foreman one day, like Laiq.

Matthew smiled. 'I think so too. But rumours get around. It only takes one of our fellows to be a bit indiscreet in his village and suddenly we might find a gang of men turning up out of the desert to steal from us – or worse.'

Vera felt a jolt of anxiety and knew he was right. It would not be difficult for a group of desperate people to overthrow an Englishman with a gun and a few local labourers. The prize was too great. She felt angry again at Curzon – he was a spy and a cheat, but he had also left them vulnerable. She trusted Matthew, Christian and Stanley, and even Laiq and Azim and the rest of the workmen, but they would not be able to protect her if the worst were to happen. Only she could do that.

She stared at the revolver that hung at Matthew's side. 'Will you teach me to shoot?' she said.

He looked surprised. 'Why?'

'I want to be able to defend myself.'

'Vera, I'm sure that won't be necessary.' He frowned and then touched her arm briefly. 'I'll look after you, I promise.'

'I know,' she said, and felt suddenly affectionate towards him. 'And I'm grateful. But it's important to me that I can protect myself if I have to. I'm not a complete beginner.'

Vera helped Matthew to carry some crates out of the camp into the desert to use as targets. He draped some old rice sacks over them to make them more visible.

'Where did you learn to shoot?' she asked.

'My father,' he said. 'Obsessed with hunting. He made all of us boys learn.'

'I started learning as a child when we lived in Austria, but my lessons stopped when we returned to England.'

She took the revolver and felt the weight of it in her hands. She remembered the day in Vienna when a young man, the son of one of her father's embassy colleagues, had shown her how to hold it. He had pulled her woollen hat tightly down over her ears and had given her his sunglasses to cover her eyes. A few months later, war had broken out and the family had had to flee to England – her father seemingly caught unawares by the turmoil that had been unfolding under his nose, which had led to his dismissal, after decades of diplomatic service.

Twelve years had passed, but instinctively she remembered how to hold the gun, pointed carefully at the ground, and how to check if it was loaded.

'Here,' said Matthew. 'It's going to have quite a recoil. Make sure you're standing firmly, feet a little way apart for balance.'

She copied his pose, then handed him the gun, which he aimed at the crates, twenty yards or so away. He sensed her watching and glanced around, looking sheepish. 'I'm not terribly good. I'm not sure I'll be able to teach you much.'

He turned back towards the crates and she watched him readying himself, his knees slightly bent and his right foot a few inches in front of his left. She noted his position, the right arm straight in front of him, the left slightly bent.

Matthew fired. Vera had been expecting the noise and only jumped slightly. She saw his body absorb the recoil and the way he rocked gently on his feet while retaining his balance.

'A bit out of practice,' said Matthew, frowning at the target, but she saw that he had hit the green sack, which had shifted position on impact.

'Well done!'

'You try,' said Matthew, handing over the revolver. 'Aim for that black square, just under the orange writing. You see it?'

It felt quite natural to be holding a gun. She thought she might tremble, but in fact her limbs felt solid, and she was ready. Vera focused on the sack. She knew she could hit it. She sensed Matthew nearby, could almost hear his heartbeat, and listened to the other faint sounds of the desert – the clang of a spade, the soft scrape of a broom along the ground, the distant hum of the wind.

Her finger tightened on the trigger and she thought of the Professor. If he was really working for the Germans, he was dangerous. Perhaps he had been spying for them all along, betraying his countrymen. Surely he would kill her if he knew that she had discovered who he was. She had seen him shoot a polecat through the head from a hundred yards away just outside the camp, with Schuster egging him on. He was quite capable of doing the same to her, she was certain.

She wondered if she ought to confide in Matthew, but something held her back. She was afraid that events might spiral out of her control. Knowing this secret of Curzon's gave her power. There had to be a way to make the secret work for her – to extract something from Curzon, to make him give her what she wanted. But what did she want?

Vera fired. She staggered back, her shoulder feeling as though a horse had kicked her, and her ears ringing, but she kept her balance, and blinked hard to see a tear in the fabric of the sack, just a few inches from the black square she was aiming for.

'Very good!' said Matthew. 'Really, Vera, that's excellent. Has it really been such a long time?'

'Years and years,' said Vera. 'I want to do better, though. Shall we try another round?'

They kept practising until the sun had set and they could barely see the crates. Vera's aim improved, but she knew there was a long way to go and vowed to take up lessons, privately if necessary, when she returned to Oxford. The world was a dangerous place, and it was vital that she be able to protect herself if she was truly to live an adventurous life.

She took one last shot, almost carelessly, in the half-dark, and Matthew crunched over to pick up the sack. He brought it back and showed it to her. She peered at the black square, just two inches across. It now had a perfect bullet hole in the middle.

Chapter 43

Pratchett walked past the Palace Theatre, which was advertising a new show. 'Open once again!' said a sign, and he saw that the windows on the balcony above the front door were still boarded up, presumably as a precaution against further bombing raids.

After a year's absence, London looked stronger, somehow – more defiant. In the early years of the war, he had walked through the streets and seen a city still reeling from the damage that had been caused.

The posters on the front of the theatre were promoting a show involving a row of energetic chorus girls and a lone singer in a long dress looking soulfully out over a microphone. She had wavy dark hair and reminded Pratchett of Margarita. He wondered what she was doing back in Malta. She was in too deep, now, and he felt guilty that they had allowed her to become involved at all in the hunt for Nero.

'Come in, Pratchett,' said Sandford, a man of around his own age, once he reached the office. Sandford stood alone in a cramped room, looking for a moment as though he couldn't remember why he was there.

'How's the Med?'

'Hot just now,' said Pratchett.

'You'll be glad to go back, I bet,' said Sandford, rummaging around in the messy piles on his desk.

'Oh, yes,' said Pratchett, but Margarita was at the forefront of his mind as he said it. The work and the search for Nero was interesting, and he liked Malta anyway, but somehow knowing she was there made the prospect all the more appealing.

'You requested a handwriting analysis,' said Sandford.

Pratchett's heart leapt. 'And?'

'See for yourself.'

He passed across an envelope and Pratchett pulled out three samples that had been clipped to sturdier card. There was a short report folded along with the samples.

The first letter from Professor Ralph Curzon, which Mr Makepeace had dug up from his archives at the British Museum, had been written in 1924 as part of a funding application. The second was a letter that Professor Barton had handed over, a rather dull personal letter written in 1925 about a theory Curzon was working on relating to some minor theological point.

In both letters, Curzon's handwriting was strong and confident, written with a thick nib – the first in black ink and the second in dark green. His note to Barton had been written quickly, it seemed, while the funding application was carefully constructed and the writing rather neater. At the end of both, he had signed off with a flourish.

The letter that Nero had written to his German masters near the end of the Great War was written with a different, thinner nib, and the style was rather more hesitant, but despite the unfamiliar German words, the handwriting was almost identical to that in the letters from Curzon.

'They're by the same man,' said Pratchett, waving the three letters, looking up at Sandford for confirmation. 'Aren't they?'

'So it seems,' he said, pointing at the report. Pratchett picked it up and scanned it.

'*Ninety-five per cent certainty . . . minor differences contiguous with the age and experience of the man in question . . .* Of course, he would have been years older, people's handwriting matures with them ... *It seems clear that the 1917 letter was written by a man for whom German was not his first language ... We can say with confidence that these three samples were written by the same man.*'

Pratchett sat down heavily and thought over the implications of this. Curzon was Nero – the evidence was in front of him. The question, he thought, was how on earth Curzon had managed to convince the world he was dead in 1926. More importantly, where the hell was he now?

Chapter 44

Adelina wiped down the kitchen table and reached for the broom that stood in the corner. She and the children had had crusty rolls for breakfast and the crumbs were scattered in a ring around the table. She swept them up and threw them out of the front door for the birds, putting a hand over her brow as she watched a magpie arguing with the tiny sparrows. San Leone was quiet and there was no movement to be seen except the gentle shifting of the sea.

As she shut the door, she heard a car engine somewhere nearby. For once, the house was calm – she had sent the older children away to the beach, and the baby was sleeping upstairs. Deciding to make stuffed sardines for supper, she took a head of garlic and peeled the cloves before crushing them one by one.

There was a light tap on the door. Sighing, she wiped her hands on her apron and went to open it.

A blonde woman stood outside. She had sunglasses propped on her head and her thick hair was cut stylishly. She wore an expensive-looking suit, and Adelina could smell perfume.

'Good morning,' she said. 'Can I help you?'

The woman smiled. 'Good morning. It's Signora Cardona, yes?' She spoke Italian with a slight accent, and Adelina couldn't place it.

'Yes. What can I do for you?'

'My name is Frau Weber. I am visiting friends nearby.' She reached into her pocket and pulled out a leather wallet. 'I think perhaps this belongs to your husband? His name is printed inside.'

'Oh!' Adelina reached for it, but the woman didn't seem in a hurry to hand it over.

'Such good quality,' she said. 'You Sicilians have wonderful craftsmen among you.'

'It was a gift,' said Adelina. She remembered what Isaac had said about the work he was doing for the man who lived at the Villa Concordia. He had refrained from giving her too many details, but she felt at a disadvantage. She had the feeling that this woman was connected – she was a foreigner, after all, a German, if her name was anything to go by.

At last, Frau Weber placed the wallet in her hand and she gripped it tightly. 'I found it on the road,' the woman said, gesturing vaguely towards Agrigento. 'I expect your husband must have dropped it.'

'Probably. He keeps it in his trouser pocket – I'm always telling him it's not safe.'

'What does he do, your husband?' asked Frau Weber with a smile.

'He's a fisherman,' Adelina said reluctantly.

'Is that where he is now? Out fishing?'

'No, I think he's working on his boat this morning,' she said, pointing towards the jetty a mile or so away. 'Repairs and so on.'

'I've been thinking about finding someone to take friends out for boat trips,' said Frau Weber. 'Does your husband ever take passengers?'

'Never,' said Adelina, feeling her heart pounding. She knew the woman must be checking up on Isaac, seeing how much he had told his wife. 'He's just a fisherman, I'm afraid, signora.'

'Ah, well, no matter,' said Frau Weber, smiling again. 'I must get going.' She held out a hand. 'It was a pleasure to meet you.'

'And you,' said Adelina, shaking it, although nothing could be further from the truth. She knelt and pulled out a few weeds that were sprouting around the doorstep, making sure to keep half an eye on Frau Weber. She saw the woman climb briskly into a blue car, and it pulled away, heading towards Agrigento.

*

'What did she look like?' asked Cardona later. He was washing his hands at the sink and watching the children running around the garden.

'She was blonde,' said Adelina. 'Very fashionable. She said her name was Frau Weber.'

'German?'

'Yes, I think so.'

Cardona paused. He had often wondered if Leonardi was really Italian. His accent occasionally had a twang of something else. Could he possibly be German? There was also something about the way he dressed, always the embodiment of a stylish Italian from the big city, that was almost too perfect, as if he was playing a role.

Adelina was watching him. 'Do you think she's something to do with . . . your arrangement?'

'I don't know,' he said, worried. He recalled the blonde who had overtaken him on the road towards Leonardi's house. 'What kind of car was it?'

'Bright blue.'

'An Alfa Romeo?'

'I don't know,' said Adelina, shrugging. 'It was an open-top sports car, quite expensive, I should think.'

He sighed. 'It sounds like a car I saw yesterday. Where did she say she found the wallet?'

'On the road. She wasn't specific.'

Cardona frowned. He felt sure that he had dropped the wallet in Leonardi's office. It had still been in his pocket shortly before he arrived at the house and had not been soon after he departed. Assuming it was the same woman, she must have found it in Leonardi's house. Why had she lied? And why had she come at all? She could have left it somewhere for him anonymously, or given it to Leonardi to return to him.

'I think she was checking up on us,' said Adelina, lifting the lid off the dish that she had just taken from the oven. A delicious savoury smell wafted over, and he saw the chunky rolled sardines that he had pulled from the sea early that very morning.

'Checking up?'

'To see if you had told me anything about your work for this man. I didn't rise to it, of course.'

'Well, that's something,' he said, kissing her cheek. 'I've given them no reason to doubt me.'

As he set the table, he wondered if Frau Weber knew he had come back for the wallet and had overheard the conversation in the office. It seemed unlikely, unless she could see through doors. He was sure that no one had seen him return. All the same, it seemed odd that she would turn up at his house now, after he had worked for Leonardi for months without any problems.

'What is a German woman doing here, anyway?' said Adelina. 'She said she was visiting friends. What friends would a Nazi have in Sicily? Or are all fascists friends now?'

'Not all Germans are Nazis,' said Cardona, but immediately he felt a pang of guilt. Leonardi was in league with the Nazis, he was convinced of that now, and the woman surely was too.

Perhaps she had come from Germany to check up on Leonardi's operation. Once again, he wondered who they were planning to kill. Was he really going to help them go through with it? He remembered the other woman he had brought from Malta, her dark hair in disarray, her face pale in the moonlight.

'Do you think they'll hurt us?' said Adelina quietly, not looking at him. 'Suppose your – friends – decide they don't trust you anymore?'

He sighed heavily. 'I wish I'd never got involved.'

'Is there anything you can do?'

'Not yet,' said Cardona, but his mind was busy.

Chapter 45

Pratchett returned to Kent with a heavy heart. Uncle Andrew was still alive, but he was fading. The doctor had told Aunt Emma that he was unlikely to wake.

He walked in the garden with his aunt as she pointed out all the new things she had planted. There were neat rows of beans and courgettes, tomatoes in a little greenhouse, and enormous sunflowers towering over the garden.

The sweet peas were coming out, a huge mass of them, hurling themselves over a trellis. Pratchett watched Emma picking a bunch of them to take up to Andrew's room, tying the stems together with a piece of string.

He looked towards the window of the bedroom where his uncle lay. The curtains were closed. His gaze fell on the garden next door, where a woman sat on a hard chair outside the back door, staring at them. He recognised her and waved, but she looked away.

'Poor Mrs Porter,' said Emma quietly, seeing her neighbour. 'Did I tell you her son was killed? Jimmy, who you used to play with.'

'Yes, I heard,' said Pratchett. 'No details, though.'

'His plane went down on the way to India,' said Emma, kneeling to pull out a weed from the paving slabs that formed a path up the garden. Pratchett knelt to help her, feeling a closeness that he hadn't felt for a long time.

'Enemy action?'

'His mother didn't seem to know,' she said. 'Poor dear. She looks so lost when I see her now. We used to chat often, swap cuttings across the fence and so on, but now, whenever she's in the garden, she just sits and stares.' She sighed. 'His father says he was shot down in combat. But I think that's just a hope, really. He doesn't want to believe it was an accident, that the boy died for nothing.'

'Either way, it's not for nothing,' said Pratchett with feeling.

'We went to the memorial service a couple of weeks ago,' said his aunt. 'They never recovered his body, so it wasn't like a normal funeral. I got the impression that made it much worse for his parents. They had no real evidence that Jimmy was dead.'

'Didn't his CO write to them?'

'Oh, yes,' said Emma. 'He's definitely dead. But it's how it *feels*. Mrs Porter said after the service that she kept imagining he'd just walk through the door one day and say it was all a mistake.'

Pratchett stared at her. Of course, there wasn't always a body – it was common in wartime but not unknown in other situations. There had been a memorial service for Curzon. It would have been easy enough for him to fake his own death – bribe the authorities in Syria, perhaps, or substitute a body for his own. Then he could have slipped away and forged a new identity. But what of his wife? She must know one way or another if he was dead.

'She said she wouldn't believe it until she saw his body,' said Emma, and he realised his aunt was still talking about Mrs Porter. 'Until then, she'll always have hope.'

*

Pratchett recognised Matthew Townsend from the photograph one of the tutors in Oxford had dug out for him. In the picture, taken soon after his arrival at university, he had been a callow boy of eighteen. Now he was middle-aged, in a scruffy tweed suit, with the slightly harassed air of the professor he had always been destined to become, as he opened the door to his office near Westminster.

'I don't have much time,' said Matthew apologetically, looking at his watch, as he piled folders onto his desk. 'This is a very busy period for me, I'm afraid. Exams and so on.'

'I just want to know anything you can tell me about Professor Ralph Curzon,' said Pratchett, taking the proffered seat.

Matthew blinked. 'Curzon? Good lord.'

'You were on his last dig, weren't you?'

'Yes, but it was a long time ago.'

'What happened the day he died?'

Matthew sat down and pushed his greying hair off his temple.

'I was still in my tent,' he said at last. 'It was early. I remember one of the workmen came running into camp, saying there had been an accident and that someone had been killed. We all leapt into the truck and drove over and found that the walls of the pit had collapsed. Apparently Curzon was on the scaffolding and two workmen had been down below when it all caved in.'

'What about Vera Millward – where was she?'

'Vera? She was sitting on the ground, white and shaking. She couldn't tell us anything. She just kept saying, "He's dead, he's dead."'

'What happened next? Did you see the bodies?'

'No. I took Vera back to camp and then Stanley and Christian drove to the village to summon the police. I sat with Vera, as I was worried about her, but she was very calm once she'd stopped shaking. I saw her crying once or twice, but that was to be expected, what with—' He hesitated.

'She was fond of Curzon?' said Pratchett.

'He was a flirt,' said Matthew, his lip curling. 'He liked the attention – encouraged it. He was known as a womaniser.'

'Didn't he have a wife?'

'Yes, Dorothy. She was there at the start of the dig but she left and went back to England – must have been a couple of weeks before it all fell apart.'

'What happened afterwards? After the accident?'

Matthew sighed and frowned, trying to remember. 'The French authorities swarmed over the site and took charge of everything. We were all young, you see, and our professor had just been killed. We did as we were told. We were given half an hour or so to pack overnight bags and things and then we were taken to Aleppo.'

'What happened in Aleppo?'

'We were all interviewed, made to give statements and so on. We were still expecting to go back to the camp. But then we were told that they had brought all of our personal belongings in a truck and that tickets would be booked for us to leave Syria as quickly as possible.'

Pratchett scribbled this down. 'Why do you think they were so desperate to send you all home?'

Matthew shrugged. 'I think they were embarrassed that an eminent professor had died on their patch. They may also have wanted to get their hands on the treasure room we'd found – well, Vera found. There was a truckload of artefacts – I wonder what happened to those?'

'Did you see Curzon's body?'

'No. I assume the French took care of all that. I remember being told that an ambulance was on its way there, although it would have been too late to save any of them.'

'I gather the French took over the dig,' said Pratchett. 'I wonder why Vera didn't go back to work on it with them? Given that it was her find.'

Matthew looked thoughtful. 'At the time, I assumed she was too distressed about Curzon's death. She published a paper the following year, based on notes she'd made in Syria, but as far as I know, she never asked to go back there. Or perhaps the authorities rejected her request.'

'Did you see much of her after that?'

Matthew shrugged. 'Not really. We bumped into one another at conferences over the years. The third time, she was with her husband, an American chap. I gathered she was in Greece with him before the war. I don't know where she is now.'

'What happened to the other assistants who were with you in Syria?' asked Pratchett.

'Stanley Green died about ten years ago – leukaemia. Sad business. And Christian Palmer went to South Africa.'

Pratchett asked a few more questions about Curzon, but he was wary of revealing too much. He didn't want anyone to know that they thought Curzon could still be alive.

'One more thing,' he said at last. 'Curzon's wife, Dorothy – what became of her?'

Matthew frowned. 'Someone told me she'd emigrated – Australia, I think. Or New Zealand, perhaps? I never saw her again after the memorial service.'

'Thank you, Professor, you've been helpful.'

'It's quite all right,' said Matthew. He hesitated. 'I suppose you can't tell me what any of this is about? Is it anything to do with Vera?'

'I can't elaborate,' said Pratchett apologetically. 'We're looking into something that might be connected to Curzon. It may all come to nothing, of course.'

'I see,' said Matthew, although he still looked confused. 'Well, good luck with – whatever it is.'

*

After leaving the office, Pratchett made a few phone calls. He confirmed that Dorothy Curzon had indeed gone to Australia a year or two after her husband's apparent death. Briefly, he considered a theory that Curzon had gone there to join her – perhaps they had both created new identities – but dismissed it almost immediately. What would Nero find to occupy him in Australia? As far as they knew, he had been active in Europe and the Middle East during the twenties and thirties.

Dorothy must have gone to Australia alone, then. It was important that they get in touch with her and see what she had to say about her husband – whether she ever suspected he was a spy, and what she believed about his death.

'Add it to the list,' said Wilson wearily when they spoke on the telephone. 'I've just had the results of a search I requested. Curzon's name cropped up a couple of times in case notes during the thirties – in Paris in 1931 and in New York in 1937. In the latter case, a hotel register was signed by an English couple calling themselves Mr and Mrs R. Curzon – they were under observation as potential foreign agents. I'm looking into whether anyone of his description has cropped up recently – his name alone isn't enough, there must be dozens of Curzons.'

Soon after dark, Pratchett was driven out to Croydon to await his plane. In the past, he had watched enviously as agents left, bags in hand, on their way to some secretive mission. Now he was the one departing into the night.

They took off punctually at ten o'clock. For a few minutes, they circled back towards London, and he looked at the darkened city with little regret. Then they were off, on the way to the first refuelling stop at Gibraltar. He was impatient to be back in Malta – to see the turquoise Mediterranean, the sun coming up over the airfield, and the dew of early morning steaming on the quiet streets of Valletta.

Chapter 46

Standing under the high stone walls of Verdala Palace, Margarita knocked nervously at the trade entrance. There was a pause and she glanced over her shoulder. The guard who had let her in through the gate had returned to his spot in the shade, and no one else seemed to be around.

The door swung open and she blinked at the white-aproned figure within, recognising Daniela, the housemaid she had met on the day of her interview.

'Hello! Come on in. I told Mrs Lastra I'd look after you.'

'How long have you worked here?' Margarita asked as they made their way towards the kitchens.

'Oh, a year or so,' said Daniela. 'I was looking after my sister's children before that, but I couldn't stand it anymore, so here I am. Anything's better than cleaning up after three toddlers. How did you end up here?'

Margarita explained about the Phoenix Club and the bomb that had fallen. It was a common story in Malta, and she knew she was lucky to be alive.

She changed into her uniform and spent most of the day in the scullery, washing the endless dishes that seemed to emerge from the kitchen. The governor had returned and was holding a dinner party that night. The other members of staff were all friendly enough, and Mrs Lastra, who appeared occasionally, kept a close eye on everything that was going on.

Later, Margarita was asked to prepare the dinner table out on the terrace, where strings of lanterns were being hung in the trees by the gardener's boy. She took her time, making sure the heavy white cloth was perfectly even, as she knew Mrs Lastra would inspect her work. She was almost sorry that she had not been asked to work into the evening – it must be a magical scene once the sun went down and the lanterns began to twinkle. She imagined the clink of silver and music drifting onto the terrace, and lots of wealthy people in their finery.

She wondered if Vera knew the governor and concluded that she probably did – she seemed to know everyone. She wished now that she had not gone to see Vera. She ought to have waited until Wilson could be found. Surely it could not be a coincidence that Vera had disappeared so soon after their confrontation?

The day after going to Vera's house, she had been relieved to find that Wilson opened the door in Archbishop Street at once. He asked her in and listened carefully as she told him all about Vera and the photograph and Vera's revelation that Nero was a man called Ralph Curzon. Later, he sent a note to tell her that Vera could not be found and to let him know at once if she got in touch. Unlikely, thought Margarita. Vera had seemed shocked and rather displeased to see the photograph of her younger self, and it had clearly provoked her into doing something impulsive, although no one seemed to know what.

'Have you heard about the ghost?' said Daniela later, as they were making up one of the guest bedrooms.

'Mrs Lastra said it was a myth,' said Margarita, plumping up a pillow.

'I've seen her,' said Daniela dramatically as she polished the mirror over the dressing table. 'The Blue Lady.'

'Where?'

'In the Grand Master's bedroom,' said Daniela. 'I'll show you.' She led the way through to the largest of the bedrooms, where a huge wooden bed, empty of bedclothes, dominated the room, underneath an ornately painted ceiling. 'No one's using this at the moment.'

'Where was this ghost?' said Margarita, trying to sound sceptical.

'There,' said Daniela, pointing towards the fireplace. Beside it was a clock with a bronze cherub perched on the top. 'I was passing the open door, and it was almost dark; I saw her walking across the room in a long blue dress.'

Margarita shivered. Pull yourself together, she thought, recalling that she had been hired on the basis of her promise not to be a 'silly girl'.

'Surely she can't really have been a ghost.'

'When I looked back, she was gone,' said Daniela. 'If she wasn't a ghost, where did she go?'

'She might have left the room.'

'There's no other way out except the secret staircase,' said Daniela, pointing to the wall beside the bed. Looking closer, Margarita saw a faint line and realised there was a door hidden in the panelling. 'But that's been locked for decades. It was meant for the Grand Master to escape if he was in danger.'

'I don't know if I believe in ghosts,' said Margarita, although she could hear the uncertainty in her voice.

'Lots of people have seen her over the years. They say she was a noble lady who was going to be forced to marry a man she disliked,' said Daniela.

'Was she murdered?'

Daniela shook her head. 'Supposedly she jumped out of a window to avoid the marriage. They must have found her body on the terrace below. Can you imagine?'

That night, Margarita dreamed of the Blue Lady, following her as she roamed the halls of the Palace. At last, the woman stopped and turned towards her. Instead of looking distressed or tearful, she looked content.

It was worth it, she said, her voice echoing, and Margarita went closer and the woman's face became Vera's, then she woke up, breathing heavily, her entire body tense and covered with sweat. For a moment she was sure someone was in the room. Fumbling, she lit a lamp. The curtain rustled in the warm breeze, but there was no one there.

*

Wilson thumbed through Pratchett's notes again and leaned back in his chair. 'So no one actually saw Curzon's body? We'd better get in touch with the authorities in Syria. Though after seventeen years I don't know how far we'll get.'

'I've already spoken to the vicar who took the memorial service in London,' said Pratchett. 'He said Curzon's body was never brought back to England, and our chaps say there's no record of a body being repatriated. The vicar didn't like to ask Mrs Curzon, but he assumed it had been buried in Syria.'

'We'd better ask her when we get hold of her,' said Wilson.

'She left on a ship bound for Sydney in 1927, but she may well have moved since then,' said Pratchett.

'No children?'

'Apparently not.'

'Well, that's one less complication,' said Wilson. 'Still, it does look odd – that she emigrated so soon after his death.' He tapped a pencil on the desk, thinking of his own wife, Laura. He would never be able to keep a double life from her. She knew what his work entailed and had the good sense not to ask for details – she was busy enough with her own job – but she would know at once if he was hiding something significant.

'You think Dorothy Curzon knew he was a spy?' asked Pratchett.

'Perhaps. You'd think she'd have suspected something. Of course, she may well have been grieving and wanted a new start.' He looked at the photograph they had been given of Curzon a few years before his death – young, darkly handsome, his eyes sharp. He had presumably needed a loving wife to complete the façade he presented, but Wilson wondered if it had really been a stable marriage. If Curzon's wife didn't know that he was involved in espionage, surely that wasn't the only thing he had kept from her.

'With luck, we can ask her,' said Pratchett. He chewed his lip and looked at the map on the wall, where several pins were stuck in at an angle. 'Vera might be able to shed some light on where Dorothy is. She apparently knew the Curzons fairly well.'

'I hope to God we can find her and get some of this straightened out. I spoke to Morton this morning; he's discovered Vera made an unauthorised trip to Damascus not so long ago.'

'Damascus? What was she doing?' asked Pratchett.

'He doesn't know – not part of her usual beat. We know she spent time in Syria in the past. But I wonder if she went there to meet someone, or to look for someone. God, what a mess.'

Wilson scribbled in his notepad, then looked over at Pratchett. 'There's something else we need to consider. We don't know for sure that it's the same Nero.'

Pratchett stared at him. 'What do you mean?'

'Well, what if Curzon really did die? He was certainly Nero once, that seems certain, but the man we're calling Nero now might just have taken up the old code name.'

'So we could be looking for someone else altogether?'

Wilson shrugged. 'I don't know. It seems unlikely ... but then it's equally unlikely that the same man has evaded the authorities for so long.'

The telephone rang shrilly and Wilson answered it. 'Yes? Oh, hello, Margarita.'

There was a pause, and Pratchett tried to pretend he wasn't listening.

'No, I'm afraid not. Look, you must trust us to get on with it. Can you do that?' Wilson's voice softened. 'I promise I'll let you know if we hear anything. All right?'

He shook his head as he put down the receiver. 'Poor girl. She's anxious about Vera.'

'She wants to help,' said Pratchett. 'Understandable, really...'

'She's a civilian,' said Wilson gruffly. 'I never should have involved her.' He looked sharply at Pratchett over his spectacles. 'I don't want you getting tangled up there.'

'I won't,' said Pratchett, feeling stung. Quite aside from anything else, she was engaged – no chance of being tangled up, he thought gloomily.

'I'll let her know if Vera reappears, but it would be better for her to forget the whole issue.'

Pratchett said nothing. If he knew Margarita at all, she would do no such thing.

*

Late in the afternoon, Wilson returned from a meeting to see Pratchett blinking incredulously at a piece of paper. 'We've had a wire back from Australia already.'

'What does it say?' said Wilson impatiently.

'Dorothy Curzon,' said Pratchett, peering again at the message. 'She's dead.'

'How?'

'Shot dead in a rented house in Melbourne in 1932,' said Pratchett. 'Burglary gone wrong, supposedly. She was living under her maiden name – Dorothy Culpepper.'

Wilson frowned. 'We'd better ask for more details.'

'You think Curzon might have killed his own wife?'

'Seems unlikely. If not him, perhaps his German employers – someone might have got wind that she suspected his identity and decided to tidy up the loose end.'

'Or it might have been a real burglary,' said Pratchett. He scribbled a note on the pad beside him. 'I'll ask for more information.'

He sat down again and returned to the report he had been reading. It had been compiled in London the year before and covered all that was known about the Ahnenerbe, a German research institute that had funded numerous secretive archaeological expeditions during the last decade. Pratchett felt sure that Nero would have been involved – after all, they had evidence that he knew Himmler, and Himmler had founded the Ahnenerbe. After faking his death, perhaps Curzon had offered his services to the Nazis on a full-time basis. Travelling the world in search of Aryan prehistory would have given him an income and a role to fall back on between more serious jobs.

Our agent in Ankara witnessed a meeting between a female German agent, who we believe to be Erika Trautmann, a young member of the Ahnenerbe (not confirmed) and a male agent of middle age, as yet unidentified. There was an exchange of materials at this meeting. The same man is thought to have been spotted in Chungking on a German expedition to the Far East but this has not been confirmed.

Pratchett imagined Curzon working for the Germans under a new name, far away from his Oxford study, at last able to devote his life to the cause he believed in.

*

Late in the afternoon, Wilson put down his pen and looked wearily at the letter he was drafting. For the sake of diplomacy he had decided to write in French to the authorities in Syria, with his request for information on Curzon's burial, but he was regretting it. Since the end of a two-year posting in Paris many years earlier, his French had become very rusty.

The telephone rang again. It was Mrs Gordon, from the RAF plotting room.

'An hour ago, we spotted that boat you were interested in – the motorised fishing boat. We think it's the same one. It's called the *Zafferano*.'

'He's back?' said Wilson.

'Yes. In fact, he tied up at the dock in Sliema, bold as you like. Captain Cunningham's men have taken the skipper into custody on Manoel Island. He told them he wants to speak to someone in authority. I thought you'd want to see him straight away.'

*

In a dimly lit interview room, Isaac Cardona sat chewing anxiously at his fingernails. What was the right thing to do? If he told the British about Leonardi's plan, he and his family would be in danger. On the other hand, if he said nothing, he might be a conspirator in an assassination. An innocent person – or perhaps people – would die. Then he started to worry about whether Leonardi would discover he had come here. Perhaps he was already a dead man.

I will look at the face of whoever is sent to interview me, he decided. If I believe that they are good and decent, I will tell them everything.

The door swung open and a man appeared, carefully carrying two cups of black coffee, one of which he placed on the table in front of Cardona. He was slight, middle-aged, his grey hair tousled, and he looked exhausted. But his face was kind, with deep laughter lines around his eyes.

'Mr Cardona? I'm Roger Wilson. I work for the British government.' He pulled out a chair and sat down opposite, putting a notebook neatly in front of him. 'I've asked for some sandwiches to be sent through, in case you're hungry. Now then. I gather you've got some information you want to share with us?'

Cardona thought of Adelina, their children, and then of his own father, who had always instinctively known the right thing to do. He took a deep breath.

Chapter 47

Syria, 1926

Curzon returned in a plume of dust two days later. Schuster, he said, was staying on in Aleppo. He came to the workroom and surveyed the artefacts they had retrieved from the chamber below the throne room, running a finger over the statues and fragments of vases with something like satisfaction.

'I'd like to start boxing things up.'

Vera blinked. 'Boxing up?'

'I've made arrangements to start sending our finds to Aleppo,' said Curzon.

'Why?' asked Vera.

He looked intently at her, and she felt an air of impatience. 'Because I say so, that's why. What's got into you, Vera?'

She forced herself to sound calm. 'Oh, I'm just excited about the dig, that's all.' She cast around for a change of subject, aware that Matthew and Stanley were nearby. 'Have you seen the new figure we turned up yesterday?'

'I look forward to seeing it,' he said, and she felt his eyes flicker over her body. He still had the power to make her knees weak. It was odd, knowing she could distance herself from what he had done. She knew that he was a traitor, perhaps even a killer, and that he had done terrible things, but she desired him more than ever.

Vera hurried away, disturbed and confused, hoping that he would put her anxiety down to girlish infatuation. There was no reason he should know that she had discovered his secret.

That afternoon, on her way back from the dig, she went for a long walk, striding out into the desert. She knew the landmarks and glanced back often to make sure that she could still see the camp in the distance. It would not do to get lost out here. The sand dunes rose and fell all around, and if she were to lose sight of the camp, it would be difficult to get her bearings again.

It was warm, but the wind blew strongly, tangling her skirt around her ankles. She wondered what Curzon was doing now and pictured him in his tent, writing to his masters in Berlin. He was up to something with the artefacts they had found. Was he going to steal them and sell them, or perhaps send them to Germany? What other betrayals might he be planning?

It was overwhelming, and for a moment Vera wished that she had never come to Syria, that she had never fallen for Curzon, and most of all that she had never discovered his secret. How could she go back to normal life, now, when she knew so much?

She stared out across the honey-coloured sand and wondered what it would be like to just keep walking. It was tempting. Who knew what was out there? But she carried nothing, no water, no provisions, nothing to protect her from the sun or keep her warm at night. Striding into the desert would lead her to an early death.

Vera wondered what Curzon would think if she disappeared. He would be disappointed, but he wouldn't grieve for her. She was just another one of the girls he had seduced. He could go back to his wife and cry crocodile tears and thank his lucky stars that one complication in his life, at least, was gone.

She would not give him that satisfaction, and she turned back to the camp. There was nothing for it but to confront the problem at hand. One way or another, she would have to settle the matter.

*

She behaved as normal that evening over supper, laughing and joking with the boys and eating as much of Azim's food as she could manage.

Curzon, for his part, seemed withdrawn, quieter than usual.

'Everything all right, Professor?' said Christian when Curzon had failed to reply to a direct question.

'Hmm? Oh – I'm fine,' he said, tearing off a piece of bread and dipping it into his stew. 'Just thinking of Dorothy. In her latest letter, she said she'd twisted her ankle getting off the train in Venice.'

Liar, thought Vera. Dorothy might well have twisted her ankle, but she was sure that wasn't what was preoccupying Curzon. He was thinking of something else – something bigger.

'Sorry to hear that,' she said, looking blandly at Curzon. 'I hope she's all right.'

He went to bed before any of them, for once. Later, when Vera was ensconced in her tent, she wondered vaguely if he would come to her, and felt a frisson of fear and excitement. But he stayed away.

Chapter 48

Roger Wilson marched down the corridor at Lascaris, his mind still on the meeting he had just emerged from. It had included a briefing on the war in Asia, where the Allies were being hammered by the Japanese as they attempted to reconquer Burma. He thought of his son Martin, still – as far as he knew – languishing in a prison camp in Malaya. It had been over a year since they had heard from him and Wilson found himself increasingly preoccupied with how the war there was unfolding. One day, he was certain, Malaya would be liberated, but there was no guarantee that it would be in time to save Martin or the thousands of men interned with him.

And that led, as all roads seemed to now, to Nero. He wasn't the only spy, but he was one of the best, and he was responsible for many deaths. He would do more damage unless he was stopped, that was certain. The arrival of the fisherman, Isaac Cardona, had been a huge stroke of luck, and although Wilson was suspicious of the man's motives, they had learned several significant things.

One was that he had transported a woman fitting Vera's description to Sicily, in the company of a man Cardona knew as Leonardi. He had not seen the woman since then, and Wilson guessed that she might be a prisoner at the house in Agrigento.

The second and most important fact was that, according to what Cardona had overheard, Leonardi and his associates were planning an assassination in Malta in a few days' time. Nero's name had been mentioned. Whoever Nero was, he was going to strike soon.

'Captain Wilson – if I might have a moment?' said Miss Edwards, peering out of her office next door to the operations room at Lascaris.

'Of course,' said Wilson, following her.

'I won't keep you long,' said Miss Edwards, now flicking through a pile of paperwork on her desk. 'I just wanted to show you this. It's that missing page – it's turned up.'

After all that had happened, it took Wilson a moment to remember the page that had gone missing from the operations room visitors' book before the disastrous reconnaissance flight to Italy in April. It seemed unimportant now, although it was yet more evidence to suggest that someone, perhaps Nero, was leaking information about British operations.

'Here. It's the page from the fourth of April,' said Miss Edwards, pushing a sheet of paper across the table.

'Where was it?' asked Wilson, picking it up.

'I don't know,' she said, her smile fading. 'It just turned up again – I was looking in the book for something else, and this one just slipped out. But I'm sure it wasn't there before.'

'I'm sure, too,' said Wilson. He scanned down the page. Only six people had been admitted on the fourth of April. The last name, written in a black scrawl, was 'R. Culpepper'.

He paused. He had heard that name recently. Culpepper was Dorothy Curzon's maiden name. She had been living in Australia under that name until her death in 1932. The Australian authorities had confirmed that she was dead and had included a post-mortem report in their last communication.

It was an unusual surname. If someone had used it in place of their own, it didn't seem too much of a stretch to imagine that it was her husband. Ralph Curzon might well have borrowed his dead wife's maiden name when reaching for an alias.

'You don't know who this Culpepper is, do you?'

'Afraid not,' said Miss Edwards. 'It doesn't ring any bells with me.'

'Who signed these people in and out?' he said.

'Miss Darling. She works weekends, so it's her day off today. The fourth of April was a Sunday. Shall I ask her to get in touch with you tomorrow?'

'That would be helpful,' said Wilson. 'I'd like a description of each of them, if she can remember. It's a few weeks ago now.'

'I'll ask her to telephone you,' said Miss Edwards.

An hour later, when Wilson was back in the office, a message arrived from the French authorities in Syria. According to their records, Ralph Curzon had been buried in Aleppo in late 1926, although thus far they had not located the grave. The paperwork had been mislaid. If they found the grave, the message went on, did he want it exhumed? The British government would be expected to cover the cost.

Wilson wired back at once in the affirmative. It wasn't surprising to hear that the grave had not been found, but if a grave claiming to be Curzon's did turn up, then at least they would know one way or the other. He might have arranged for an empty coffin to be buried, or for another corpse to take his place. If, as he suspected, Ralph Curzon was not buried in Aleppo, it seemed almost a certainty that the man had survived and was still out there.

*

After leaning her bicycle against a wall, Margarita marched towards Archbishop Street. She had been preoccupied with her new job at the Palace, but the nagging issue of Nero would not go away, and she was desperate to know if anything further had been discovered.

'You look purposeful,' said a voice, and she swung around to see Pratchett, holding a paper bag that she supposed contained his breakfast.

'I was coming to see you at the office,' she said.

'I wouldn't,' said Pratchett. 'Wilson won't tell you anything. He thinks we've told you too much already.'

Margarita was indignant. 'I was the one who told *him* about Vera and the photograph, and about Ralph Curzon.'

'I know. Don't take it personally. He's probably just annoyed that he didn't discover the connection himself – I know I am. Do you want to sit down for a moment?'

Pratchett glanced down a side street and led her to a bench that stood in a rare patch of shade. Margarita hesitated then sat down, feeling unaccountably irritated. 'I've got to get to work soon.'

'I saw the club was closed. Bomb damage, I gather?'

'Yes. I've got another job.'

'Glad to hear it.' Pratchett looked at her sympathetically. 'I know this must be frustrating, but Wilson wants to keep things as quiet as possible. If our target gets wind of what we're doing, we'll never catch him.'

'I understand,' said Margarita reluctantly, but she couldn't help herself. 'Does that mean you've found out more about him? Is it really Curzon, as Vera said?'

Pratchett looked around and lowered his voice. 'I made some enquiries while I was back in England, and it seems pretty likely. Vera knew him when she was a student. He was thought to have died years ago but it seems he may be alive after all, and we've had other new information too.' He sighed. 'That was the only successful part of my trip. My uncle was dying. That's why I went back.'

'Oh – I'm sorry.'

'He died the day after I left,' said Pratchett. 'Never woke up, so it wasn't much use my being there. But it was good to see my aunt.'

'I'm sure she was grateful to have you there.' Margarita paused. 'What did you mean about other new information?'

Pratchett hesitated. 'It seems that our man may be planning an assassination,' he said at last. 'Don't tell Wilson I told you that.'

'Assassination? Who?'

He shook his head. 'It's better that you stay out of it. I'm sorry.' He looked at her, and Margarita felt herself flush. She knew he was only telling her anything at all because he was attracted to her, and she had encouraged him to assuage her own curiosity. It was wrong, dishonest, and she felt a guilty twinge.

'I ought to go,' said Pratchett, looking at his watch. 'Wilson's expecting me.' He paused. 'We think Nero is going to try to carry out his plan on the twentieth of June.'

'That's this Sunday!' she said, her eyes wide.

He nodded. 'Promise me you'll be careful, all right? Our intention is to catch him before he can try anything, but it's better that you stay out of the way until it's all over. That's the only reason I'm telling you. Stay at home if you can, and don't breathe a word to anyone else.'

He stood up, and Margarita followed. A sense of dread had gripped her. She imagined Nero walking through Valletta, in plain sight, on his way to kill someone.

'You haven't heard anything from Vera?' she said, before they parted. Pratchett looked grave.

'No sign of her.'

'Do you think . . .'

He was shaking his head.

'We'll know soon enough. One way or the other.'

*

Pratchett returned to the office, feeling as always that he had said too much. But Margarita had a personal interest in Nero – after all, he had caused the death of her former lover and might well be putting her fiancé in danger. She was also fond of Vera, he suspected, although she would never admit it.

He thought of Aunt Emma, who had sounded calm when he last spoke to her, although he guessed she was still in shock. He felt dreadfully guilty for having gone away again, but was glad to hear that his cousin Brian had been granted a week's leave.

While I still can, Brian's telegram to Pratchett had said. *All leave cancelled from end of June. Don't tell Mother.*

He had written separately, before his father's death, alluding to the new orders that he knew would be coming soon. Brian had been on active service now for nearly three years, and Pratchett often felt inadequate, cowardly, for having such a comfortable position in Malta while his cousin was fighting in the desert.

Wilson arrived back half an hour later. He looked grim. 'What's that?' he asked, pointing at the notes that Pratchett was scribbling down, having just come off the phone.

'I've been talking to the Swiss about Walter Sommer,' said Pratchett. 'The journalist killed by Nero in 1935.'

'Go on.'

'Sommer was staying in Lausanne on his way back to Zürich from a conference in Lyon. He disappeared from a hotel there and his remains were found in Lake Geneva the following year.

He told the hotel receptionist that he was going to meet an Englishman. His employers in Zürich understood that he was meeting a source of information about human rights abuses in Germany. Perhaps he was worried for his safety, because he told the receptionist the name of the man he was meeting.'

'And?' said Wilson impatiently.

'Richard Culpepper.' There was a silence. 'This means it's Curzon, doesn't it?' said Pratchett. 'It's got to be. That was his wife's surname!'

Wilson remained silent and sank down into a chair.

'Where have you been, anyway?' said Pratchett, noticing at last his colleague's pale face. He wondered suddenly, his stomach lurching, if Wilson had received bad news – perhaps his son had been killed. 'Is everything all right?'

'Not exactly,' said Wilson quietly. 'I've just come from a meeting at the governor's office.'

'Oh?' Pratchett stared at him.

'Apparently we're expecting an official visitor this weekend.'

'A visitor?'

'The king is in North Africa at present, inspecting the troops, and will be making a brief secret visit to Malta on Sunday,' said Wilson carefully.

Pratchett sat down abruptly, feeling as though a heavy weight was pressing against his chest. 'The king? But that means . . .' He stared at Wilson.

'Exactly,' said Wilson. The room suddenly seemed very quiet, even the traffic sounds seemed to fade away. 'That's Nero's target.'

Chapter 49

Wilson looked at his watch. Almost exactly midday. It was Saturday the nineteenth of June. At some point in the next few hours, if what the fisherman had said was correct, Nero would be departing from Sicily and heading for Malta.

He was wary of letting too much hang on the word of a man who had admitted to working for the enemy, and it had crossed his mind more than once that Cardona might be a plant. The man had seemed genuine enough, particularly when he spoke of his family, but that was what made him vulnerable. He would do whatever was necessary to protect them, including lying to the British. But the king was coming to Malta, that was certain, and Cardona's information about an assassination had begun to look compelling.

The navy were on high alert, with orders to intercept every suspicious or unknown vessel. The police would be stationed at every port and airfield, and soldiers were being deployed at strategic points along the coast to capture anyone landing.

All of this was having to be kept as quiet as possible, as was the king's visit, but Nero had already proven he had ears everywhere. It seemed to Wilson that the only advantage they had over him was the information from Cardona – and that advantage wouldn't last long if Nero caught wind of the operation to catch him.

'Is that Captain Wilson?' said a nervous voice on the telephone. 'This is Miss Darling from the RAF Control Room. Miss Edwards asked me to telephone you about the visitors who were signed in on the fourth of April.'

Wilson picked up a pen and dragged his mind back to the matter at hand. 'Thanks for calling, Miss Darling. The name I'm interested in is R. Culpepper. I don't suppose you recall what he looked like?'

'Well, that's the odd thing,' said Miss Darling, sounding apologetic. 'I don't think there *was* an R. Culpepper there that day.'

Wilson paused. 'What are you saying?'

'I saw the missing page from the book,' she said. 'But it's been changed. There were only five visitors that day, not six. I've got a very good memory, Captain Wilson, and I know the page has been altered.'

Running a hand over his forehead, Wilson tried not to sound impatient. 'What about the five who are listed? Do you remember all of them?'

'Oh, yes.' He heard the rustle of paper as she picked up the list. 'Major Davies and Captain Spiteri – they're regulars. Mr Hill is the governor's private secretary. F. Garzia – that's Captain Garzia from Manoel Island. And Arnold Pemberton is his second-in-command. They came in together at about three o'clock, I remember.'

Wilson sighed. 'So definitely no Culpepper? Could anyone have let another guest in after you left?'

'No, Captain Wilson,' said Miss Darling firmly. 'I work until eight in the evening at weekends. After that, visitors aren't permitted. Someone has added the name Culpepper to the list, but I can't imagine why.'

Neither can I, thought Wilson. He cleared his throat. 'Thank you, Miss Darling. I can't go into details, of course, but I'm looking for any unusual visitors around that time. Anyone out of the ordinary. Will you let me know if anything occurs to you?'

He put the phone down and rubbed his forehead. Perhaps all of this meant nothing at all. Perhaps the missing page was unrelated to Nero. Perhaps the reconnaissance mission to Italy had just been unlucky. But in that case, why on earth had someone added the name Culpepper to a list of visitors? If it was Curzon, he was playing an even more complicated game than they had realised.

Shaking his head, Wilson stood up. Curzon was just one man. A clever man, that much was true – he had evaded justice for thirty years, including faking his own death. But at least they now had an idea of who they were looking for.

Curzon had spent a year in Florence as a young man, where he had learned to speak Italian. It was plausible that his new identity was Italian, especially if he had lived under that name for some years. Cardona, the fisherman, had hesitated on being shown the photograph of the younger Curzon. He wasn't sure that this Leonardi and Curzon were one and the same, but he conceded that it was possible, after all this time, particularly if he had taken steps to alter his appearance.

It was common enough, thought Wilson, recalling the case of a spy who had undergone surgery on his face and fingertips to evade detection. Curzon had had many years to change how he looked. It hardly mattered who Nero had once been: all that mattered was who he was now.

*

It was in Palestine, in 1932, that Henry first met Vera Millward, a successful young English archaeologist. He sometimes joked that he had had to ask her to marry him a hundred times before she said yes. Their marriage, often made difficult by distance, was nevertheless a close and enduring partnership, and she supported Henry and his career for many years.

Pratchett rolled his eyes. He was reading an obituary of Henry Dunn from an American newspaper, and he wondered what the writer – and indeed the paper's readership – would say if they knew that Henry had a penchant for girls in their twenties, or that Vera worked for British intelligence. The article made them out to be the perfect couple, but from the little he knew of them, they were hardly conventional.

He thought once again of Margarita and wondered how she had fallen for Henry. He knew his interest was based on envy. Henry might have been old, but he was handsome, successful, clearly very clever and charming. Vera really knew how to pick them, he thought, remembering that people had said similar things about Ralph Curzon.

He read on through a list of Henry's accomplishments and career highlights.

From April to September 1936, he worked at Biskupin, Poland, advising a team from Poznań University (led by Józef Kostrzewski and Zdzisław Rajewski) who were excavating the Bronze Age settlement there, sometimes compared to Pompeii in its historical significance.

Pratchett frowned. Biskupin was the place that Margarita had seen written down in Henry's diary, he recalled, in amongst his theories about Nero and the death of his friend Jan Novotný. Pratchett looked up the date of Novotný's death and found that it was June 1936. He pulled out an atlas and found Biskupin. It was only a couple of hundred miles from Prague, where Novotný had been killed.

It was probably a coincidence, but it seemed odd that Henry had been working nearby when his friend died. Perhaps he had seen Novotný in the weeks before his death. It was a bit far to drive for lunch, but you might go for a weekend. Or perhaps Novotný had had contacts in Poland that had led to Henry's work at Biskupin.

Pratchett scanned the rest of the obituary, but there was little else of interest. Henry had been buried without ceremony in Malta, at Vera's instruction, but a memorial service was to be held in New York. In lieu of flowers, donations were requested for the Red Cross.

'How was the meeting?' he asked, looking up, as Wilson arrived back.

'Unproductive,' said Wilson, throwing down his hat. 'I argued for the king's visit to be cancelled or postponed, but apparently he's insistent that he wants it to go ahead.'

'He does understand there's a threat to his life?'

'Oh, yes. Unfortunately, madmen are always threatening to kill the king, so he probably doesn't grasp how serious this is. It's been explained that this is a credible threat from a man known to be dangerous, but he's determined not to bow to the pressure – he won't "let this fellow win".'

'How the hell did Nero have advance notice of the trip?' said Pratchett.

Wilson shook his head. 'We knew he had friends in high places,' he said wearily. 'Clearly they go higher than we realised. Perhaps someone in the government or even the king's household leaked his movements. An investigation is underway but it's unlikely to yield fast results.'

Pratchett thought of Curzon, the consummate Englishman who had betrayed his country over and over. In a way, there was a perfect poetry to his intention to assassinate the king; it would be the final and most decisive betrayal, a severing of the last threads that held him to England. He had not been Curzon for a long time, and now he would be Nero, completely and forever.

It occurred to Pratchett that Nero was probably close to retirement. He had lived a life in the shadows for over thirty years and must be planning his exit. He was nearly sixty. Perhaps he had been promised a quiet life if he did one last job. What a way to go out – killing the king of England and ensuring his place in history as the Nazi spy who brought down the British establishment.

Chapter 50

In the early hours of Sunday morning, the telephone rang shrilly. Pratchett snatched at it. 'Yes?'

'We've picked up what we think is the *Zafferano*,' said a tinny voice. 'It's about a mile offshore to the north-west, heading for the coast near Manikata. The unit covering that stretch is led by Captain Daws. He'll meet you there.'

'I'm on my way,' said Pratchett.

He had slept for a few hours in the early evening, but from nine he had been back in the office, much too anxious to sleep. He drove as fast as he could across the island. The roads were empty apart from the occasional delivery van, and the sky, unpunctured on this night by bombers, was vast and silent, with only the light of distant stars.

He got out of the car just outside Manikata and immediately smelled salt and seaweed, rolling in on the warm night air. The village was quiet, but soon he saw a tall figure appear from the darkness.

'Evening, Lieutenant,' said Captain Daws, shaking his hand. 'I'm assuming you want to keep this as quiet as possible.'

Pratchett nodded. 'The man we're after is clever, very clever; if he sees anything he doesn't like, he'll probably just disappear.'

'Understood,' said Daws. 'I think we're best off just taking a handful of trusted men.' He gestured to the coast. 'We can leave the cars here and walk – it's rough ground and anyway we don't want him to hear the engines. The others will station themselves along the cliffs and guard any footpaths up from the shore.'

Pratchett nodded, and soon he and four others were crunching along a narrow farm track, navigating by the dim light of the stars. He could hear the low hum of the sea and was aware of its huge, dark expanse. Italy was somewhere over there, only a few hours away. Strange to think that an enemy nation was so close. With luck, it would be the first one in Europe to be liberated, but only if Nero and his masters were thwarted in their plans.

'We think it's this cove,' said Daws, gesturing to a rocky path that led away down the hill. 'There's nowhere else along this stretch you can safely bring a boat in, although we've got people stationed at the other possible landing spots.'

Pratchett followed them down the steep path, grabbing onto shrubs to ease his descent. He felt gravel slide under his feet and leaned against a rock, looking down at the beach below, silent in the darkness.

Waves sighed onto the sand, but the sea was calm. He reached the bottom of the cliff and found Daws and his men huddling behind a large outcrop of rock.

'He hasn't arrived yet, by the look of it,' said Daws. Pratchett peered gingerly around the rocks and saw that the beach was empty. No boats could be seen in the cove. He thought he saw a light out at sea, but then it came again, and he realised that it was just the moon, emerging from behind a cloud and reflected brightly on the water.

He noticed the men glancing uneasily at the sky, and the relief on their faces as the moon was covered again. It would illuminate Nero, if he arrived, but it would also light them up.

They waited for some time, but no boat appeared. Then Daws stiffened and held up a hand. 'Did you hear that?'

They all listened, and faintly in the distance came another sharp crack from the direction of the open sea.

'Could have been a rock falling,' murmured one of the men and Daws nodded slowly.

'Perhaps. It sounded like a shot to me.'

Who the hell would Nero be shooting at, thought Pratchett, but he said nothing and listened intently. No more noises came, and after a few minutes, it seemed unlikely that they had heard anything at all.

He glanced idly down the beach. For a moment, he thought he could see the shape of someone standing on a rock close to the shoreline, only visible because his body was a denser black than the surface of the sea behind.

Pratchett watched the figure and found himself blinking hard. It was like one of those optical illusions where you had to see a shape in a mass of dots that all looked the same. If he shifted slightly, the figure seemed to fade.

'Can you . . .' he began to murmur, glancing up at Daws, but when he looked back and pointed, he could no longer see the figure, just the rocks and, beyond them, the sea.

He told Daws what he thought he had seen, and the captain went to investigate, his rubber-soled boots making almost no sound as he crossed the beach and climbed the rocks.

There were men stationed on the cliffs, but Pratchett knew, with a sinking feeling, that if Nero was really here, he would not be caught by them. From all that he knew of the man, he was quite capable of scaling a cliff and avoiding an ambush.

They stayed on the beach until the first light of dawn began to seep across the horizon, but no boat appeared.

*

Margarita couldn't sleep. At about four, she gave up the attempt and got up. She did some cleaning, trying to stay quiet so as not to disturb her neighbours. Then she made a pot of soup, putting it to one side to cool. She sat for a while on the balcony, watching Valletta sleep.

Shortly before five she went to the wireless and switched it on, hearing a buzz of static as she fiddled with the tuner. All she could hear was jazz, fading in and out, and she glanced up at the clock, wondering if it was fast.

As she did so, the music came to an end, and on the stroke of five, a voice began to speak. 'Good morning. It's five o'clock on Sunday the twentieth of June.' A brief pause, and the sound of rustling paper. 'His Majesty King George VI will be making an unexpected visit to Malta today as part of a tour of North Africa.' The announcer sounded startled, as though he had only just been handed the news.

Margarita stared at the wireless, astonished, hardly hearing the rest of the segment. The king was coming to Malta. He must be the person Nero is intending to kill, she thought, with a feeling of unreality. But it was all too real. Of course Nero would aim for the very top.

'His Majesty will be sailing into Grand Harbour later this morning,' concluded the announcer.

Perhaps they have already caught Nero, thought Margarita hopefully. She saw Curzon's face, hovering as it had so often in her dreams recently, darkly handsome but deadly. Vera had known him, a long time ago. How was it that she had let him go free, knowing what she knew? Could she possibly have been afraid of him?

She remembered Vera's expression as she had looked down at the photograph of herself and Curzon. Vera had been in love with him, Margarita realised with a jolt. He must have hurt her badly. It was all too close to her own experience with Henry. She remembered the rage and distress she had felt on learning that he was married. But she was philosophical by temperament and not given to melancholy. She had moved on quickly and had been happier for it.

Vera was quite different. Curzon was thought to have died, so she must have put aside the hurt and anger and forged ahead. But what if he reappeared in her life? What would she do?

Margarita remembered Vera mentioning, that evening on the roof terrace, an anonymous parcel that had been sent to her. Doubt began to gnaw. What if Curzon hadn't kidnapped Vera at all? There were only two reasons that she might have gone with him willingly, and neither of them were reassuring. She might be planning to kill him – he was a traitor, after all, as well as the man who had slighted her. Or, she thought, with a sense of dread, perhaps she's still in love with him. Love makes people do crazy things. Perhaps she's been helping him all this time.

Looking around her flat, Margarita felt the hairs on her arms prickle. Vera had stood in this room, eaten her food, talked casually of her life as a spy. But she lied as easily as breathing, that much was clear. If a man from her past had reappeared, someone she had once loved passionately, there was no knowing what she might do.

Chapter 51

The streets approaching the harbour were busy and crowds were starting to form, people hurrying to find good vantage points. Flags were jutting out from balconies and portraits of the king were visible in several windows. In one, a child's poster, painted in thick strokes, said 'MALTA WELCOMES KING GEORGE', with a rather unflattering stick figure of the king below.

Even this early in the morning, the sun was powerful, and the people Margarita passed were wearing cotton clothing and wide-brimmed hats. It was amazing, she thought, that they could all be so light-hearted in the circumstances. Couldn't they sense the feeling of impending disaster that seemed to hang in the air?

She took a detour through the city and went down Archbishop Street, stopping to hammer on the door, but no one answered. Perhaps it was for the best. Pratchett had warned her not to interfere. She wondered if they had guessed what she had – that Vera might be in league with Curzon. She waited a while longer, feeling indecisive, then marched towards the sea, which twinkled, bright blue, at the end of the street.

Margarita emerged on the street by the harbour and paused, looking out over the glittering expanse. A few small sailing boats were dotted across the water, but no one was interested in those. All eyes were on the massive stone breakwaters that guarded the entrance to the harbour.

She struggled through the crowds and into the Lower Barrakka Gardens, where more people were waiting to see the king's ship arrive. Alternately pushing and smiling sweetly, she made her way slowly towards the seaward edge of the gardens.

'Like a peep?' said a skinny boy beside her, offering his binoculars.

'Thank you!'

For a moment, all she could see was water, but she swept the binoculars upwards, and suddenly a ship was in view, seemingly very close, between the two breakwaters.

'That's her,' said the boy proudly. 'The *Aurora*. My older brother's on the crew. Wasn't expecting to see him any time soon!'

The long narrow cruiser steamed unhurriedly into the harbour.

'She's much smaller than I expected,' said Margarita as she handed the binoculars back.

'Light and nippy, that's the ticket,' said the boy, adjusting the view as he scanned the harbour eagerly. 'They'll have been dodging U-boats all the way from Tripoli. The ships escorting her are destroyers.'

The fleet grew larger as it moved smoothly towards the city. The atmosphere in the crowd was electric. People chattered and laughed excitedly, waving to the distant ships, and children were held up by their parents to peer over the wall. Bells had started to ring in churches all across the city, and Margarita felt unexpectedly moved.

'There he is,' said the boy, passing his binoculars over again. 'You can see the king on the bridge of the *Aurora*.'

Margarita looked through them, and after a moment she saw a lone figure, dressed all in white. He was tall and thin, standing very erect. Now and then he raised an arm to salute the crowds who lined the harbour, but mostly he stared straight ahead. The Royal Standard blew out behind him in the stiff breeze, its rich colours contrasting with his pale uniform.

The king looked very vulnerable out there alone. She wondered if he knew there was a threat to his life. They must have told him, she thought, and that means he's chosen to come anyway. He must be a brave man. She could see little of his face, but a row of medals gleamed on his jacket, catching the light.

'Here,' she said, and handed back the binoculars. 'Thank you very much.'

'Don't mention it,' said the boy, grinning as he turned to offer them to someone on his left. 'What a day!'

Margarita glanced uneasily around the harbour, taking in the hordes who lined every road and battlement of the old fort. She had one of the best viewpoints, but all around were places with an excellent view of the harbour. An assassin could be waiting anywhere, especially one who apparently had insider knowledge of the workings of government and the armed forces. Curzon would know where the king was most vulnerable. No doubt the police and the army would do their best to protect him, but she saw the king standing alone and imagined a shot ringing out through the morning air, or a mine exploding under his ship.

The king was gazing up at the buildings of Grand Harbour, and all at once Margarita felt very proud of her country. Valletta looked spectacular in the morning sun, despite the bomb damage that was evident on all sides, and it seemed an outrage that someone was even now planning to disrupt the peace of the day by unleashing terror.

She watched the ship slide past and then, with difficulty, extricated herself from the crowd and walked along the road beside the harbour, following the ship's progress. Often crowds blocked her view, but eventually she saw the ship begin to slow. A small launch approached the cruiser to take the king to shore.

Margarita arrived above the quay at Customs House just in time to see the king stepping ashore from the launch. He was greeted by the governor, Lord Gort, as a band played 'God Save the King', and then inspected the troop of soldiers who were standing to attention. Margarita had not seen the governor at Verdala Palace since starting work there, but she felt a little leap of pride by association to see her employer on such good terms with the king. At last, the governor led him towards a waiting motor car. The king turned to wave to the crowd and then was lost to her view.

Chapter 52

Syria, 1926

'Has the post arrived yet?' asked the Professor, peering into the workroom where Vera sat with Matthew. She was making a careful sketch of a bronze amulet they had found in the chamber under the throne room.

Matthew shook his head. 'Are you waiting for something?'

'Oh, various things,' said Curzon offhandedly. Vera glanced up and caught his eye. He had been distracted since returning from Aleppo, and he had not come to her tent, but now he smiled at her, while Matthew was looking away, and she felt the old swoop in her stomach. She bit her lip and looked down at her drawing, feeling her face growing warm.

'Let me know if anything arrives,' said Curzon. 'I'm heading out to the pit.'

Matthew watched him go, frowning. It was on the tip of Vera's tongue to tell him that his suspicions about Curzon were not unfounded, but there was a flurry of movement and Christian arrived, full of excitement about a diadem that had been unearthed, and the moment was gone.

A little later, as she was preparing to go out to the dig site, there was a call and she saw a boy on a donkey clutching a stack of letters, which he brought every day or two from the post office in the nearest village.

Once he was gone, Vera flicked through the letters. There was one for Stanley – from his father, she guessed – two for Laiq, and one for Curzon. It was handwritten, and the writing was unfamiliar. She slipped it into her pocket before delivering the others.

She passed the kitchen hut where Azim was stirring a huge pot of stew.

'Oh – Azim. Could you possibly take a new barrel of water to my tent? It's too heavy for me.'

'I'm making dinner,' he said with a show of indignation, then laughed. 'Of course, miss.'

'I'll stir the stew,' she said quickly. 'Thank you.'

As soon as he was out of sight, she pulled the envelope addressed to Curzon out of her pocket and held it carefully over the cauldron, turning it so the steam would touch the glued flap. She saw the edges begin to lift very slightly and willed it to open.

At last, the glue melted and with trembling hands she pulled at the flap. The steam scalded her hands, and as soon as the envelope was open, she wrenched them back and pulled out the letter inside. She slipped it into her pocket along with the envelope, then returned to stirring the stew.

'I put the barrel just inside your tent,' said Azim as he returned. 'In the shade.'

'Thank you. I'll manage it from there.'

Once back at her tent, Vera tugged the barrel of water further in and then sat on her bed and took out Curzon's letter.

It was not, as she had expected, written in German. Instead, it was a note, handwritten, from the British consul in Aleppo, an old friend of Curzon's she remembered meeting briefly on their way through.

I was thrilled to hear about your discovery. It sounds as though your instincts of last year were spot on. A pity that there wasn't much to be found under the throne room, but the chamber itself is a tremendous find. As soon as I receive those photographs from you, I shall write to the

PM and to Dawson at The Times. *I shouldn't be at all surprised to see your name in next year's Honours List. Very well done, Ralph.*

Vera blinked and read the letter again. It sounded as though Curzon was about to take all the credit for the discovery he himself had said was hers.

She shook her head. She was angry at what the letter seemed to imply, but that wasn't the worst of it. More alarming was the consul's belief that there hadn't been much of significance in the chamber. Why, they had brought up numerous artefacts and more were being discovered all the time. Why would Curzon have told him the room was empty? The only reason she could think of was that Curzon had made arrangements to dispose of the objects in another way. Was he planning to sell them, or to send them as a gift to his masters in Germany?

After reading the letter again, Vera folded it carefully back into the envelope and lit a candle, holding it as near to the flame as she dared to melt the glue again. She pressed it closed and hoped that Curzon would not notice it had been opened.

Going back outside, she walked to Curzon's tent to drop off the letter and hesitated. She remembered the last time she had been here, when she had found the ring with Nero's seal. If only she had never interfered.

A shadow fell across the tent, making her start. She looked around to see Curzon, his shirtsleeves rolled up, with red dust on his broad forearms. 'Hello, Vera. Are you looking for me?'

'Oh – I was just . . .'

Fumbling, she reached into her pocket and pulled out the letter. She handed it to him, wondering if he too felt the warmth of her body on the paper. 'The post boy called.'

'Ah, I must have missed him.'

'I was just delivering them to everyone's tents.'

He raised an eyebrow. 'Vera, I've been meaning to speak with you.'

Vera felt her heart leap into her throat. She looked out of the corner of her eye, but they were well away from the main camp building, and she and Curzon were out of sight between the tents. If she screamed, no one would come running until it was too late.

'I wanted to apologise,' said Curzon with a sigh, and Vera blinked.

'Apologise?'

'I've been distant,' he said, his eyes fixed on hers. He moved closer. 'Since that night. I wanted to reassure you that . . . that my feelings haven't changed.'

'They haven't?' she said, feeling a mixture of hope and confusion.

'No,' said Curzon, running his finger along her wrist, and then his arms were around her and she felt a sharp stab of desire as he kissed her under the hot morning sun. 'I want you, Vera. More than anything.' He cradled her head in his hands, gazing down at her, as she pressed closer. 'I haven't stopped thinking about you. But there are things to consider, I'm sure you under-stand that. Where there's trust involved, betraying that trust is not to be taken lightly.'

Was he talking about his wife, she wondered, trembling as his fingers traced down her throat. Or something else? He wanted her, or so he said. But what did she want? At this moment, she wanted him, and nothing else.

Someone called out nearby, and with a groan Curzon released her and stepped back, breathing heavily, his eyes dark with desire. 'I must go,' he said, and he sounded regretful. 'There are things I have to sort out for tomorrow.'

'Tomorrow?'

'We need to do some work on reinforcing the pit,' he said, jerking his head. 'I'll be starting at dawn with a couple of workmen. I've told the rest to come later, for once.'

'Oh,' said Vera. 'Can I help?'

'No,' he said firmly. 'I want you and the young chaps to stay here. It won't be safe and we'll get on faster.' He looked at her intently. 'Things will be easier after tomorrow, Vera. I promise. This throne room is an astonishing find. We'll tell the world about it.'

'We?'

'Of course,' he said, brushing her hand. 'I want you by my side.'

'Professor Curzon?' Stanley appeared, looking curiously between them. 'I wondered if you might have a look at—'

'Absolutely,' said Curzon, adjusting his clothing almost imperceptibly, and cleared his throat. His eyes flickered towards Vera, then he followed Stanley towards the workroom. Vera watched him go, feeling deeply unsettled. She wondered what Curzon was really planning. The consul's letter had mentioned photographs – perhaps Curzon was going to take them, although Christian was their resident camera expert. Why was the Professor so keen not to have an audience?

She sighed, feeling the mixture of lust and anger that he always incited in her. The weak, flesh-and-blood part of her said that perhaps he wasn't a spy, after all. Perhaps there was an innocent explanation. Perhaps he meant it when he spoke of a future with her, and for a moment she lost herself in fantasies of spending each night with him, being by his side every day. But her mind counselled caution. He was involved in something, that was certain, and she could not forget what she had read. The only thing to do was to demand the truth, once and for all.

Chapter 53

Pratchett marched back into Manikata, his calves aching from a night spent scrambling up and down cliffs and along beaches. He was exhausted and felt the weight of failure bearing down on him. They had searched each tiny cove and inlet and the villages near the coast, but there was no sign of Nero. Pratchett remembered again the shadowy figure he had seen on the beach and felt convinced that the man had already landed and left the area.

'We've found the boat, sir. The *Zafferano*,' called one of the soldiers as he reached the village square. 'They're bringing her in.'

Pratchett followed the man back along the winding path towards the beach where they had first waited for Nero.

'Where was it?' said Pratchett breathlessly.

'Floating half a mile or so out. Seems to have been abandoned.'

They waited on the beach, Pratchett trying to control his impatience. Eventually he saw movement just beyond the mouth of the cove and gradually the shape of Cardona's large fishing boat solidified. The *Zafferano* was being pulled by a much smaller motorboat, fast and powerful.

'They tried to start her but no luck, apparently.'

So either the boat had broken down or someone had sabotaged her engine, thought Pratchett. He would bet a lot of money that it was the latter.

When the two boats were close to the shore, Pratchett was taken across in the motorboat to the *Zafferano*.

'No sign of anyone aboard?'

'No one alive,' said Captain Daws, easing off the throttle.

Pratchett's heart sank. 'A body?'

'Just blood,' Daws said apologetically. The motorboat nudged gently at the side of the *Zafferano* and Pratchett followed the others over the side.

Almost immediately he stepped back, trying not to step in the blood that was smeared across the deck. It was dry and had obviously been there for hours, but he still found himself retching. The strong smell of warm fish blended with the faint, tinny smell of blood.

Evidence of Cardona's trade was neatly piled across the deck: coils of rope, empty lobster cages, and here and there a tray containing a heap of large fish, dead and gleaming under the hot sun. The door of the wheelhouse hung open.

Pratchett could see footprints here and there, and over near the starboard side of the boat was a long dragging mark, as though the wounded man had been hauled across the deck.

Stepping carefully over to it, he saw more blood on the side of the boat. 'He must have been thrown overboard,' said Pratchett, feeling his heart sink as he remembered what Cardona had told them. The fisherman had a wife and family. They would be expecting him to come home.

'There's more blood in the wheelhouse,' said a muffled voice, and he looked over to see Daws peering in.

The dragging mark led that way, and he followed it. At the door of the wheelhouse, he looked down into the well, where a thick pool of blood had gathered in one corner.

'Oh, Christ.'

'He must have tried to hide here,' said Daws. 'There's blood on the inside handle.'

Pratchett pictured the fisherman huddling in a corner, trying to keep the door closed as the man hunting him paced across the deck outside in the darkness of early morning.

'I'm afraid there's a bullet stuck in the wall,' said Daws, who was peering at the panels. 'Looks like the killer finished him off here and then disposed of the body.'

Pratchett knelt to look at the floor and saw the bright red smear across the boards, the fingermarks where hands had scrabbled across the wall.

Blinking, he looked closer. In among the seemingly random marks caused by twitching hands, letters had been written by a fingertip coated in blood.

Pratchett stood, indecisive for a moment. Cardona must have known he was going to die. He had used his last moments on earth to scrawl a message. He must have seen something, overheard something – either way, he had left them a snippet of information.

Pratchett glanced back at the shore. 'I've got to go.'

'What do you want us to do?' said Daws. 'Bring the boat in?'

'Yes,' said Pratchett, looking back at the smear to memorise the letters. 'And start looking for the body.'

*

Returning to where she had left her bicycle, Margarita pedalled slowly into the city. A massive crowd had assembled – the king was to appear on a balcony that looked over the square, someone said behind her – and she didn't even attempt to get close this time.

Several policemen were standing at the entrance to the square, observing the crowd closely, but it was largely good-natured. People were waving flags and cheering and a band was playing somewhere nearby.

Margarita went along Archbishop Street but was unsurprised to find that no one answered the door. Wilson and Pratchett were probably out somewhere, trying to catch Curzon. What if they had already caught him? The idea took her breath away. After all the weeks of worrying, of sleepless nights over Arthur's safety, perhaps it was all over. She thought more about this. The king was out and about, with only a handful of men around him. Surely, if Nero was still on the loose, the king wouldn't be wandering about in the open. But where was Vera?

She heard a clock chime and sped up. She needed to get to work. It was hot already, but the breeze grew stronger as she cycled out of the city towards Żebbuġ. When she had worked at the Phoenix Club, Sundays had been a blur. She was usually tired from a late night, and sometimes her head was muzzy if she had been drinking. She felt fresh now, despite waking early, and it was pleasant to be on the move, seeing the landscape zip by her. Even having to work didn't seem too bad on a day like this. The traffic going back to Valletta was heavy and she guessed that people were hoping to get a glimpse of the king.

Pedalling hard, in half an hour Margarita was in sight of Verdala Palace, where a flag flew high in the stiff breeze. She went in through the back gates, surprised to find that her identification card was checked by the two guards on duty, and put her bicycle out of sight in a shed.

'Oh, thank goodness,' said Daniela, dragging her in as she appeared in the corridor that led to the kitchen. 'Cook's in a terrible state and we've got a list of work as long as my arm.'

'What's happening?' said Margarita, pulling on her apron.

'The king's coming!'

'Here?' said Margarita, feeling her stomach lurch. 'I saw him in Valletta this morning, when his ship arrived. I thought he'd just stay in the city. Why's he coming here?'

'This place has hosted lots of kings and queens,' said Daniela with a shrug as they hurried to the store cupboard. 'They're coming for lunch as part of a tour round the island.'

The old sense of gnawing dread returned as Margarita contemplated the king being taken around Malta to see the sights. He would be terribly vulnerable. She wondered again where Wilson and Pratchett were. Surely Wilson would have things under control.

A little later, she had polished the silver until it gleamed and helped two of the other maids to prepare the dining room for the king's visit. Ornate gravy boats and antique plates had been hauled out from cupboards, the best linen had been ironed to within an inch of its life, and a florist had arrived with new displays to be placed around the room.

In the kitchen, all was chaos, as the cook tearfully insisted that it wasn't enough time, and her helpers hurried to and fro, stoking the range, rolling pastry, and plucking poultry. Someone switched on the wireless and each time Margarita went down to the kitchen, over the clanging and hissing she could hear updates on the king's progress as he travelled out from Valletta to the dockyards at Senglea, beginning the tour that would eventually bring him to the Palace.

Chapter 54

The man on the roof of the Chapel of St Nicholas and St Lucy had been there for some time. He was lying in a small patch of shade beside the wall, but the sun was high overhead and soon there would be no shade left.

He swept the binoculars around. Even from the top of this small chapel, the views were tremendous, although much of the landscape looked dry and dusty. Hardly anything moved except for a pair of skinny cows a few fields away.

He had planned the day carefully, like all professionals. He had arrived early and from the nearby woodland had watched the old priest going into the chapel. He knew that no services took place here anymore. Earlier in the war, the chapel had housed refugees from the bombing, but it seemed that they had moved on.

The assassin sat patiently among the trees beside the chapel, listening to the faint noises coming from inside – the occasional clink, the thud of a dropped book and the priest's exclamation of annoyance. At last, he heard a high, unsteady sound warbling out of the chapel and realised, with a smile, that the old man was singing.

He did not know the song, but the tune sounded vaguely familiar, and he supposed it was a Latin prayer. Soon the sound was followed by the drifting smell of incense. That, at least, was a scent he knew.

Finally, a bell rang within and a little later the old priest shuffled out of the chapel, closing the door carefully behind him. The man noticed that he did not bother to lock it.

The priest stopped to speak to a young boy with a bucket, who made a respectful gesture, and together they walked along the lane and out of sight.

He could not afford to go properly to sleep, but he was able to doze a little, lying on the roof with one hand on his revolver. He could hear faint sounds now and then – the rumbling of cartwheels over uneven ground, the laughter of children, the engine of a car, and a plane going in to land. Otherwise, Malta dozed with him.

The assassin felt himself falling asleep and jerked awake, pulling himself into a seated position. He ran a hand over his gun, checking for the hundredth time that everything was in its place. He had bought it from an acquaintance who smuggled weapons all around the Mediterranean, shipping them from the battle-fields of North Africa to wherever else they might be needed.

The serial number had been carefully filed off, and now there was nothing to link the gun to the German who had carried it for three years before losing it and then his life at the Second Battle of El Alamein, seven months earlier.

The man knew of its provenance and imagined he could smell the desert. It had been many years since he had lived in the desert, but sometimes at night he remembered the flap of the tent and the pale pink sky in the early morning. He recalled kneeling in the sand, running his hands through dirt, feeling it clog under his nails. And Vera – Vera in her white dress, running across the dig site, calling out to him, her dark hair blowing in the wind.

He shook his head. Those days were long gone. In the years since his departure from Syria, he had preferred to live in cities, where the teeming streets made him anonymous. He had followed the news of the battles across North Africa with interest and pitied the soldiers who were living out there in the desert, experiencing the great emptiness that he had tried to leave behind.

He knew his associates found him hard to understand. It wasn't often a man of his background ended up where he had. He had not followed the path laid down for him; in fact, he had deviated sharply away from it. He had chosen rebirth. They had never trusted him completely, he knew, but they trusted him to get the job done.

But this job was different – and it was personal. He measured the weight of the gun in his hands again and thought of what was to come. The king and his entourage would soon be on their way, and the events that had been set in motion would come to their inevitable conclusion.

It was worth the risk, he told himself. It would be the last time, at least with this name; if he survived, he would leave Malta at once and fade back into the shadows. He had changed his identity before and he would do it again.

He had carried his grudge for many years, more than he liked to count, and it was time to lay it to rest. Who knew how many years he had left? He had no wish to waste them. He had wasted enough time already.

He looked at his watch. It was time to get into position. He took the gun and clambered down the iron rivets on the back wall of the chapel, then started walking.

Chapter 55

Pratchett parked in Senglea and followed the sounds of cheering. He knew the king would be surrounded by crowds, and sure enough, the roads near the dockyards were packed. Petals had been thrown and crushed by hundreds of feet.

He saw Wilson in the distance, standing by an expensive car that he recognised as Lord Gort's. He was scanning the crowds and looked anxious.

Pratchett showed his identification and was allowed through to the cordoned-off area where Wilson was waiting. Several other men stood a little way off, including their superior, Major Ede, who was chatting to the governor. An operator was crouched beside a compact radio set, his ear pressed to the receiver.

As Pratchett arrived at Wilson's side, he looked along the street. The king, followed by two soldiers but protected from the crowds only by a rope on each side of the road, was walking slowly through the city, deep in conversation with a clergyman in an extravagant robe. On either side, children called and people cheered as the king passed, and now and then he paused to receive a flower or to shake a hand, looking completely unconcerned.

'He's a brave man,' said Wilson, following his gaze. He shook his head, half admiring, half frustrated. 'And possibly a foolish one.'

Pratchett glanced around uneasily, but no one was close enough to hear. 'You're keeping him updated?'

Wilson shook his head. 'He said he doesn't want to know anything until we've caught the fellow in question.'

Pratchett felt a hot throb of shame. He had failed to catch Nero. He looked around at the crowds again. Most of the people gathered were cheery Maltese, all wearing their Sunday best, their faces bright with happiness and pride as the king visited their city and commiserated with their losses. He could see the king gesturing up at one of the buildings, which was covered in scaffolding, and imagined the concern in his voice. His Majesty was reportedly shy, but there was little sign of it today as he faced the hordes. Pratchett imagined Curzon slipping through the joyful crowd, gun in hand, and felt a lurch of fear.

'What about the boat?' said Wilson. Pratchett shook his head, remembering the blood-soaked deck, and described the scene to Wilson.

'Christ! Cardona was brave in coming to us. We should have realised that Curzon wouldn't leave any witnesses. I wonder if he knew Cardona had squealed on him?' Wilson chewed on his lip, his eyes never leaving the king's back. 'We'll have to contact Cardona's wife at some point. But that's a problem for another time. What were these letters on the wall?'

'VERD,' said Pratchett. 'V – E – R – D. No idea what it means yet, possibly something to do with the Italian for green? He was trying to help us, poor chap, and we let him down. I let him down.'

Wilson glanced at him. 'It happens. Curzon's a professional – older and more experienced men than you have failed to catch him for decades.'

Pratchett nodded, but he could not help recalling that dark figure on the beach. If only he had run over there. If only he had raised the alarm sooner. If only they had had more men on the beach. If only—

'What do you want me to do?' he said, pulling himself sharply away from the introspection that was crowding his thoughts.

'I've got men doing a door-to-door search in the villages near the coast in case anyone saw—'

There was a loud burst of static behind them, then urgent discussion. They both swung around to see the radio operator holding up the receiver. 'Captain Wilson, sir, you ought to take this. They've caught someone!'

'Where?' said Pratchett, as Wilson grabbed the receiver. The soldier looked to Wilson, who exhaled sharply as he heard the voice at the other end, then pulled down the headset for a moment.

'Verdala Palace.'

Pratchett shook his head as he ran to the car. VERD. Verdala Palace. Cardona must have discovered where Nero was heading. Perhaps that was what had got him killed.

*

Margarita was cleaning the guest lavatory for the third time that morning. This certainly wasn't a glamorous job, she thought wearily, as she wiped her forehead with the back of her arm and gave the cistern another flick with a cloth. Mrs Lastra had claimed she could still see dust after the first two cleans and so Margarita had promised to stay until not a speck could be seen.

Verdala Palace had hosted many monarchs over the years and the lavatory was the grandest Margarita had ever seen. Peering out of the small window, which looked over the moat to the garden beyond, she saw a gardener carefully pruning a rose bush, standing on a small set of steps as a boy hurried past with a wheelbarrow full of cuttings for the compost heap.

In the distance, there was a shout. A moment later two soldiers could be seen running along the side of the garden.

Wondering if the king had arrived, Margarita gave one more polish to the cistern, swept a few imaginary specks of lint into her apron pocket, and closed the door to the lavatory, wiping the doorknob carefully.

On her way back to the kitchen she paused in a corner of the entrance hall and peered out of the open doorway. Several soldiers were congregating on the front steps, watching something happening in the yard, and she could hear vehicles crunching their way up the drive.

'Margarita!' hissed a voice, and she jumped as Mrs Lastra appeared from the dining room. 'What are you doing?'

'Sorry – just on my way to the kitchen,' she said hurriedly.

'It's an exciting day,' conceded the housekeeper as Margarita darted across to the staircase. 'But don't let that get in the way of doing your job. We're here to serve, not to be seen.' Mrs Lastra smoothed her apron with a deep sigh and marched off, her heels clicking on the polished floor.

'They've caught someone,' said Daniela breathlessly from the corridor, as Margarita entered the laundry room and threw her pile of dirty cloths into a bucket.

Margarita felt her heart leap. 'Caught someone?'

'The guards found a man breaking in through a first-floor window. He'd already managed to get over the boundary wall, heaven knows how.'

Daniela shook her head, marvelling, as she dashed away, but Margarita was reeling. Surely it could only be Nero? She remembered Curzon's face in the photograph, handsome but arrogant, certain of his own success.

'Oh, and I haven't even had time to tell you . . .' Daniela was back, with a basin full of used kitchen rags in her arms. 'I saw the Blue Lady again! Perhaps she knows there's a king visiting and wants to make his acquaintance!'

'The ghost? When?'

'Oh, half an hour or so ago,' said Daniela. 'A little while before they caught the intruder. I saw her, but she was on the landing this time. She's usually in the Grand Master's bedroom.'

Margarita stared after her. It could not be a coincidence. She thought of the cars she had heard. Was the king already here?

Forgetting the list of jobs she was supposed to be completing, she went out to the cellar passage and followed it to the end, where a small door led out to the moat. It was locked, but the key was kept in the lock during the day.

Looking around, Margarita took a deep breath and unlocked the door, pushing it open carefully. The moat had never been filled with water and the door was all but invisible from ground level. Pushing it closed behind her, she stepped down into the moat, which was carpeted in dry, scrubby grass, and followed it around the corner of the building.

Voices were still echoing across the front yard as she reached the front of the Palace. Ahead, she could see the small chapel that stood close to the Palace wall, surrounded by trees. Peering around the corner, Margarita could see several soldiers standing on the bridge that led to the front door, but none of them were looking into the moat – their attention was focused on the main yard, where, she guessed, the king and his entourage had just arrived.

Darting across the moat, Margarita clambered up the bank and stood panting in the shade of the chapel wall, thankful for the trees that hid this spot from view. She made her way cautiously around the side of the chapel, just in time to see a third gleaming car rumble slowly past. Who else had been invited to lunch with the king and the governor?

She could see another, shabbier car, which had pulled up a few yards from the chapel, under the trees. A man was leaning into the boot, his back towards her, and as he stood and slammed the door, she saw that it was Dennis Pratchett.

'Dennis!' hissed Margarita, before she could change her mind. He looked around, squinting in the broad sunlight, then caught sight of her, peeping from behind the chapel wall, and hurried across, looking around anxiously.

'Margarita, what on earth are you doing here?' For the first time he sounded cross.

'I work here,' she said impatiently, gesturing at the uniform she was wearing. 'Listen—'

'But what are you doing out here? Shouldn't you be inside?'

'Yes, but I need to tell you something.'

Pratchett shook his head. 'I've got to go. The guards have caught Curzon prowling around.'

'Thank God,' said Margarita, feeling a swell of relief. 'But what about Vera? I think she's been helping Curzon.'

Pratchett stared at her. 'Vera? She's disappeared, remember? Curzon has probably killed her. We have it on good authority that she was taken to Sicily by boat and no one's seen her since.'

'You didn't hear the way she spoke about him,' said Margarita, feeling frustrated. 'That night, when I showed her the photograph . . . I think she was in love with him.'

'It hardly matters,' said Pratchett firmly. 'Our priority at this point has to be catching Nero. We can worry about Vera Dunn and her emotions later – if she's even alive.'

'I think she's involved in this,' said Margarita quietly.

'In an attempted assassination?' scoffed Pratchett.

'You underestimate her. You don't know what she's capable of.'

'I've got to go,' said Pratchett sharply, turning towards the yard. 'Go inside, Margarita. I know you want to be helpful, but you're just getting in the way.'

Almost at once she saw a penitent look cross his face, as if he knew he'd gone too far, but it was too late. Without a word, Margarita marched behind the chapel and back the way she'd come.

Chapter 56

Roger Wilson stood beside the governor outside the Palace, participating in the conversation but barely registering it. The governor was answering a question, posed by the king, about Grand Master Verdalle, who had built the place in the sixteenth century.

The king was looking up at the Palace, his uniform still white and crisp, his cap set at a jaunty angle. He must have been tired after a night on board ship and then a busy morning being rushed around the island, but he was chatting pleasantly and appeared bright and interested.

A gong rang somewhere and the royal party began to move towards the front door. The king saluted the soldiers guarding it and disappeared into the gloom of the entrance hall.

Breathing out heavily, Wilson looked up at the Palace. He glimpsed movement at one of the windows on the top floor. It was probably a servant, but he felt unsettled. The most important thing was to ascertain that Curzon was securely locked up.

'Where is he?' said Pratchett eagerly, as he hurried over.

'Locked in the stable,' said Wilson, gesturing across the yard, where two armed soldiers stood outside a heavy wooden door. 'Let's get on with it, then.'

'Captain Wilson?' came a voice.

He swung to see a footman, who looked uncertain. 'There's a telephone call for you, sir. The gentleman said it's urgent.'

'Oh, hell.' He looked at Pratchett. 'I'd better take this. Wait here, all right? I'll just be a few minutes.'

'But Curzon—'

'I said wait.'

Wilson followed the footman in through a side entrance to an anteroom, where a telephone rested on a heavy wooden desk.

'Wilson here,' he said into the receiver.

'Peters at the switchboard, here, sir. You asked me to let you know if anything arrived from Syria.'

'Of course. What is it?'

'They've just sent through a message for you, from Aleppo. It's about Ralph Curzon.'

*

Margarita scampered up the stairs, her footsteps as light as she could manage. The king and his party were mingling over canapés in the drawing room. The guards in the front hall had seen her emerging from the kitchen, but her uniform seemed to make her invisible, and no one had challenged her. She was supposed to be downstairs, helping to load plates into the dumb waiter, and knew that she would be lucky to keep her job after this.

'His Majesty would like to tour the gardens before lunch,' said an echoing voice below her to someone unseen. 'Let Mr Mifsud know, will you?'

Margarita continued briskly up the stairs. The lamps that lit the oval stairwell flickered and she suddenly felt afraid. Pratchett said they had caught Nero, but the sinister feeling was impossible to dispel. Something was going to happen, she was sure of it. She stood still, wondering whether to go back.

Get a grip, she told herself firmly, and climbed the last few steps to the second floor. This was where Daniela thought she had seen the ghost. The door beside the suit of armour was open a crack, she noticed. She was sure it was usually kept locked. A narrow spiral staircase was visible: the route to the roof. Before she could change her mind, Margarita went up it, holding tightly to the central pillar. She couldn't tell how many loops the staircase took, but suddenly she was standing at the top in front of a heavy wooden door.

Perhaps this one's locked, thought Margarita hopefully, but as she prodded it, the door swung open, and she stepped out onto the flat roof of Verdala Palace.

Taking a breath, she looked out in wonder at the view across the island. She had never been this high up before. Crossing to the stone balustrade, she peered down into the yard, feeling slightly dizzy. Two soldiers stood by the door of one of the stables.

Looking around, she noted the squat towers that stood at each corner of the roof. Crossing to the nearest, she peered in through the open doorway and saw a mess of empty sacks, a stack of tiles, and a long section of broken guttering.

She heard voices below and looked down to the yard. Half a dozen people were crossing the stone bridge that led across the moat from the front door. They must have finished mingling. Among them, she could see the gleaming white uniform of the king. He was talking cheerfully, gesturing to the chapel, and betrayed no hint of anxiety.

Turning away, Margarita walked lightly across the rooftop towards the tower on the eastern corner. The door was closed and she turned the handle gently.

Inside were a couple of old chairs and a pile of folded sacks, as well as other items of junk. Then she gasped, feeling her stomach lurch. At the window was a rifle, positioned carefully on a tripod, with a telescopic attachment. It was pointing down into the grounds, where a terrace descended from French windows to a lush and beautiful rose garden. Margarita stared down, her heart almost thudding out of her chest.

There was a faint noise behind her and she turned, but not fast enough. A pair of strong arms encircled her, a hand over her mouth, and she choked, trying to breathe, and smelled the chemical scent of the handkerchief pressed against her mouth and nose. Then Margarita was falling into blackness, her body weightless as she spun and drifted, vaguely aware of someone looking down as the darkness rose up to meet her.

Chapter 57

Syria, 1926

Vera woke abruptly and reached for her watch. It was still an hour before dawn. She lay still, wondering what to do. This feeling of powerlessness was infuriating. Curzon could do whatever he wanted. But she could not go back to sleep, not while he was out there at the dig site, doing something underhand. She had to know.

She lit a candle and dressed quickly, slipping into her riding clothes and sturdy boots, and wrapped a shawl around her shoulders, as the air was cool.

Standing in the entrance to her tent, Vera listened. The camp was silent. She stepped out and looked quickly around. No lights could be seen in any of the tents and nothing moved except the gentle flapping of cotton in the breeze.

Vera walked slowly out of camp, her whole body alert. Several sets of recent footprints were visible on the sand alongside the track, but they might have been from the day before.

A pink flush was spreading across the navy dome of the sky and she felt a quickening of the pulse, that exhilaration that she had first felt in the desert, weeks before, as they travelled out from Aleppo. Walking beneath this sky before dawn made one feel very small, but not insignificant – quite the opposite.

It was cold. Vera flexed her fingers, looking down to see that they had gone white, as they always used to do when she swam in the sea as a little girl.

'Mine do the same,' her mother had said, showing Vera her own hands. 'It's genetic. Bad circulation.'

'Here,' her father had said, kneeling beside them, and he had put his large warm hands over their cold ones and breathed gently on them.

The night on which they had died had been one of the coldest of the winter. January 1920, over five years since their rushed departure from Vienna at the outbreak of war. Vera, away at Oxford, had to piece the details together later, for no one wanted to burden a young woman with information that could only distress her.

Her parents had been in London for the weekend. Her father had met with an old friend from the Foreign Office at his club and had been told once and for all that he would never receive another posting, that he should consider himself retired.

'They don't trust you, Sebastian,' said the friend with a sympathetic shake of the head, tucking into his toasted teacake. 'All that business in Vienna ... well. No one thinks you're a traitor,' he said, and the subtext was clear: *they just think you're a fool.*

After the meeting, they had left London, with Vera's mother, she imagined, trying to comfort her father. There were other jobs he could do. Why, her cousin had been asking him for years to join one of his business ventures—

But Vera could imagine her father's grief, his feeling of loss, as the life he had always known seemed to slip from his grasp.

They said it was an accident, but the policeman who came to see Vera looked unsure, and it did not take much for him to confess that there was some doubt over what had happened. Drinking had been suspected, but the doctor's report had laid that to rest.

Somehow, her father's car had spun off the road and buried itself in a ravine, killing both of them instantly. The final police report decided that an accident was most likely, as nothing else could be proven, and that was what Vera's relatives clung to. A dreadful winter accident.

But Vera knew her parents, knew her father, and it was hard to escape the image of his hands on the wheel, gripping it tightly, then suddenly wrenching it to the left. He was angry, hurt, the emotions of five years erupting like warm breath on the cold air.

At the funeral, Vera shook hands with Sir Edward Grey and Mr Balfour, her father's superiors at the Foreign Office. They expressed sympathy and told her what an excellent diplomat he had been, shaking their heads gravely, and Vera thought: *you did this*.

*

Vera passed the canvas tents where the barrows were kept and the piles of earth that had been removed from the dig. She was nearly at the pit.

It was almost light now. The sun was not yet above the horizon as she clambered up the hillside, but the sky had turned to pale blue, streaked with pink and orange. She came to the mouth of the pit, and looked around, but there was no sign of Curzon.

She could hear a faint hammering somewhere down below. People were working in the tunnel at the bottom of the pit.

'Professor Curzon?' she called cautiously. 'Laiq?'

The noises went on and she could hear the voices of two or three men down there now, all speaking in Arabic. They couldn't hear her up here – her voice was borne away on the wind.

Vera climbed down onto the top level of the wooden scaffolding and felt it lurch. She felt for the next ladder, but it wasn't there. Frowning, she peered into the pit.

'You ought to be careful,' said a voice, and she swung around to see the Professor standing a few yards away. 'That scaffolding isn't safe.'

'What's wrong with it?' she asked, her heart leaping.

'Someone seems to have cut through two of the supports,' said Curzon calmly. He was watching her carefully with that gaze that seemed to go straight through her, but for once she didn't feel excited. She felt afraid.

'Who cut them?' said Vera.

'I've no idea.'

'What are you doing here, Professor?'

'I might ask you the same.'

'I was curious,' she said. 'I just wanted to know what was happening. I heard voices from the pit.'

'They're just making a few adjustments,' he said, still looking intently at her.

'To what?'

Curzon shook his head, looking impatient. 'There's no point in this pretence, Vera. It won't work with me.'

'What do you mean?' she said, trying to stop her voice trembling.

He sighed. 'You're a good actress, my dear, but not good enough. I saw, as soon as I came back last week, that you'd been spying on me. You've been going through my letters, haven't you?'

Vera realised what a fool she'd been coming out here alone. She glanced around, but there was nothing to be seen outside the pit except the desert, glowing golden in the dawn. In the distance, the white canvas tents were visible, but they were too far away.

'You're a thief,' she said. 'And a spy. Nero, isn't that what they call you?' She felt very vulnerable here on the scaffolding, holding tightly to a wooden pole and feeling the boards creak beneath her.

'And what do you plan to do about it?' said Curzon calmly, stepping closer.

'What can I do?' said Vera, licking her dry lips. 'It's my word against yours. Let me go and you'll never hear from me again.'

She glimpsed what looked like regret on his handsome face. 'It doesn't work that way, Vera. On my own account, I'd be willing to trust you – God knows, I meant what I said yesterday. But my employers won't allow it. Nero's identity must remain secret.'

'Your wife knows,' said Vera sharply. 'I heard you arguing with her.'

He shook his head. 'Dorothy thinks I'm caught up in a smuggling scheme with Karl, that's all. They'd kill her if she knew the truth – or make me do it.'

Vera watched him, her heart pounding. 'Are you going to kill me, then?'

Curzon said nothing as he stepped down onto the scaffolding beside her. He rubbed his forehead, looking frustrated, and it occurred to Vera that he was angry. He was used to having things his own way, but she had interfered and thrown everything off course. Now, he would have to choose between his job and his lover. She knew Curzon well enough by now to realise that he would never choose her.

'I thought it was Schuster,' she said, as a delaying tactic. 'I thought he must be the spy.'

'He doesn't know it, but Karl has been a great help to me,' said Curzon with a cold laugh. 'He dabbles in smuggling here and there, a weakness I have exploited. He's too much of a coward to do anything more underhand than that.'

There was a crash somewhere far below, and she heard a male voice shouting, before it was suddenly muffled. There was a low rumbling sound and Vera peered down, but she could see nothing in the darkness.

'What's happening?'

Vera looked back to see Curzon lunging at her. His hand closed on her hair, yanking her towards him, and she cried aloud in pain and fear.

'What have you done?' she exclaimed. 'Down there—'

'An accident,' said Curzon, breathing heavily, still gripping her hair, and she felt him pulling her sideways, towards the edge. There was another crash below. 'A dreadful accident in which several workmen and the lovely Miss Millward were killed. I'm sorry, Vera, I really am – you're the most remarkable woman I've ever met. But I'm afraid you're too clever.'

'Wait!' said Vera, holding tightly to the wooden pole as she thought rapidly. 'I've got Nero's ring in my pocket. I took it from your tent just now. It'll be lost forever if you push me in.'

Curzon paused, looking ruffled for the first time, and she could almost hear him thinking, wondering if she was bluffing. He came closer, still gripping her by the hair.

'Hand it over, Vera.'

The scaffolding shifted sharply, as though something had broken below, and suddenly she was standing on a sloping platform, the splinters in the wood digging into her hands, her heart galloping in her chest. Curzon had let go of her hair and was scrabbling at the planks for a handhold.

'I could have given you everything,' he said, panting slightly, his face flushed in the dawn light. 'We could have been together, if you hadn't interfered. We could have shared the successes – the glory—'

'I work best alone,' said Vera.

She reached for the wooden pole above her, trying to pull herself up and away from him, and felt Curzon's hand close on her wrist. They struggled, and she felt the wind whipping her hair around. She knew they were too close to the edge, that the scaffolding wasn't safe.

'Where's the ring?' he demanded, then he sighed. 'You haven't got it, have you?'

'No. I imagine it's still in your tent.'

Curzon had let go of her wrist and was trying to balance himself on the sloping platform. Vera reached out and held his shoulder, steadying him. The wind stilled, and they stared at one another, as if they were the only two people in the world.

Vera tightened her grip on the Professor's shoulder for a second and then gave him the gentlest of pushes.

He fell quickly, silently, and Vera was aware of the scaffolding collapsing as she scrambled to the steps. Her fingers gripped the edge and she climbed quickly up, feeling the wooden supports giving way.

She hauled herself onto solid ground and moved away from the pit, turning to look back as she gasped for breath. The platform was slipping into the hole, dust billowing up as the dirt walls, no longer shored up, began to crumble. She wondered vaguely what Curzon had done below, and which workmen had been killed by the tunnels as they collapsed.

Vera watched the sun coming up. She must have been sitting there for a long time, although dust kept rising from the pit.

Eventually, she heard shouts and turned to see people running towards her.

'Vera!' said Matthew, and he came and took her hand, holding it tightly. 'Vera, are you all right?'

She looked up at him, feeling numb. 'There's been an accident.'

Chapter 58

'Yes?' said Wilson impatiently into the receiver, as he stood in the anteroom, listening to the echoes of the Palace around him. 'What about Curzon?'

'The message is in French, sir. It says that they carried out an exhumation in Aleppo, followed by a post-mortem yesterday, and are able to confirm that the body in the grave is Professor Ralph Curzon.'

Wilson blinked. 'What?'

'They've also found the relevant records. It seems he was buried in 1926. The neck is broken and the skull fractured, which seems congruent with the circumstances of his death, which were apparently in an accident on an archaeological dig somewhere in northern Syria.'

Curzon was dead.

'Are you there, sir? I wasn't sure whether to disturb you, but you said that . . .'

'It's fine,' said Wilson abruptly. 'I've got to go.'

*

'Wake up, Margarita,' said a gentle voice, and she felt a hand on her cheek. Her eyes felt heavy, but she opened them slowly and saw Vera kneeling beside her.

'Vera?'

She looked just the same as she had done that night at her house in Senglea – her face a little paler, her hair awry, but otherwise she seemed unharmed.

'You're alive.'

'Of course,' said Vera. 'I'm fine.' She frowned, seeing Margarita trying to move, and laid a hand on her arm, the silver ring on her finger cool against Margarita's skin. 'Don't. You'll be woozy for some time.'

The blackness was lapping at the edges of her vision and Margarita put her head back down. There was something soft underneath her. She looked up at Vera.

'You're working with him . . . aren't you?'

'With whom?' said Vera, sitting back on her haunches.

'Curzon.'

'Curzon?' Vera shook her head. 'Ralph Curzon died in Syria seventeen years ago, I'm afraid. I was there.' She held up her hand, the ring glinting on it. 'This was his.'

Margarita, struggling to process this, looked at the ring. It had a familiar shape on it and she craned to see it. It looked like the snake symbol she had seen above Pratchett's desk, crudely scribbled in pencil – a snake which formed a circle.

'Did you kill him? Nero?' She stared up at Vera, feeling her mind working sluggishly, as though steeped in treacle. Her head was throbbing, and all her limbs ached. She longed for sleep.

'No,' said Vera, and now her expression was confident, almost proud. 'I killed Curzon, but I didn't kill Nero.'

Margarita felt a wave of confusion as she struggled to process this. Then realisation began to dawn. How could she not have seen it? She stared up at Vera.

'You *became* Nero.'

'Don't feel too bad, Margarita,' said Vera sardonically. 'The best intelligence operatives in several countries have been trying to catch Nero for thirty years. No reason you should have done any better.'

'What – what happened to Curzon?'

'I pushed him,' said Vera quietly. 'There was a struggle and it was him or me. I'd discovered who he was, you see. I thought of trying to blackmail him, but I knew that as long as he lived, I'd be in danger.'

'Are you going to kill me?'

Vera rolled her eyes. 'Don't be absurd.'

'Then why are you telling me this?'

'You deserve to know the truth.'

Margarita closed her eyes, trying to take it all in. A thought struck her. 'You killed Henry, didn't you?'

'No.'

'I don't believe you.'

'Believe what you want,' said Vera, shrugging. 'I didn't kill him.' She stood up and went to the window, peering down into the gardens.

*

Wilson ran across the yard, passing the parked cars and the huddles of soldiers, to the stable where the intruder was being kept. 'Where's Lieutenant Pratchett?'

'He went in, sir,' said the guard, already starting to unlock the door. 'The prisoner was shouting for someone to speak with him, so the lieutenant said he'd go and . . .'

'Open it!'

Cursing, Wilson crossed the threshold, and immediately saw a prone figure on the floor.

'Oh, Christ!'

Pratchett's head was bleeding heavily where he had been hit by something solid. 'Bloody fool,' said Wilson, once he had established Pratchett was breathing. There was no one else in the stable, but at the back there was a tiny window. He marched quickly to look out of it, and saw that one of the bars that covered it had been loose at one end. The prisoner had evidently forced his way out. He couldn't be Curzon – so who the hell was he?

'Go and raise the alarm,' Wilson said to the guard. 'The prisoner has escaped, and the king is in danger.'

*

There was a faint noise outside on the roof and Margarita felt a wave of relief. Vera was still facing the window and did not appear to have heard it.

Margarita wondered if Wilson or Pratchett might be outside and tried to think of a way of alerting them. Vera's hand was on the rifle and surely the king would soon be in range. Margarita felt sweat pooling under her back and tried to move her legs, but they were still heavy.

The door opened a crack and the man outside stepped over the threshold, a revolver in his hand.

Vera swung sharply around and stared at him in surprise. 'Tariq?'

Chapter 59

Vera had planned everything carefully, as always, but this was something she had not foreseen. Tariq, who she had last seen in Cairo, offering to sell German intelligence, was here, apparently intending to kill her. She glanced at Margarita, who was blinking in confusion and disappointment.

'What are you doing here, Tariq?' said Vera, noting the revolver in his hand.

'Don't you know?' he said, looking intently at her.

'No, I don't,' said Vera. 'You seemed very keen to meet me and share information in Cairo. Why have you suddenly decided to kill me?' He could ruin everything, she thought, clenching her fists.

He laughed, and she was disconcerted. She stared at him and felt a flash of suspicion.

'I knew you hadn't recognised me,' said Tariq with a smile. 'It was a long time ago.'

'I knew you?' She shook her head. 'Who are you?'

'I was the one who found the treasure.'

Vera stared at him, trying to place those eyes, the round face, and suddenly she saw a boy hunched over a bucket of water, crowing triumphantly as a statue emerged from the mud.

'You're Mohammed,' she said, exhaling sharply. 'Mo.'

Tariq bowed his head. 'That is no longer my name. But it is who I was many years ago. I was twelve years old when I went to work on Curzon's dig in 1926.'

'You and I were friends,' said Vera, remembering how they had laughed together. 'Weren't we?'

Tariq laughed. 'Friends? A wealthy Englishwoman and a little Syrian boy?'

'It's not impossible.'

'You were kind to me at times, I suppose.'

'I was more than kind,' said Vera, feeling her anger returning. 'I liked you. I pushed for you and the others to be properly rewarded when you helped us.'

'Helped?' said Tariq bitterly. He shook his head. 'You were as deluded then as now. You put Arab men and boys to work and then claimed any triumphs as your own.'

Vera raised an eyebrow. 'Curzon found that site. Would you have known where to dig if he had not shown you? Did you have the tools, the knowledge? Like it or not, the vast majority of archaeological finds in Arabia have been made by Europeans.'

'Using local labour.'

'Labour fairly bought,' she said.

Tariq shook his head, still looking faintly amused. 'I still remember that throne room. What happened to the artefacts that were found within it? I know where the little gold woman is, of course. I found her for sale in Cairo and knew I had to have her.'

Vera shrugged. 'I imagine the rest found their way to museums or collections. We weren't allowed to be involved. The French took over the site after Curzon was killed.'

'Ah, yes. Curzon. What happened to him?'

'You know what happened.'

'They told us he died in an accident, along with two of our countrymen,' said Tariq. 'The dig was closed, the gold was taken away, and you all left Syria. What do you think happened to us?'

She remembered visiting Laiq Khalil's wife in Damascus and felt a sense of dread. 'Were you among those who were jailed?'

'Ah, you know about that?'

'Only recently.'

He smiled thinly. 'Soon after you left we were called back to receive our final wages. Instead of being paid, we were arrested and taken to Aleppo. They said that we had been negligent and were responsible for Curzon's death. Someone had cut through the supports while digging illegal tunnels – or so we were told. They also blamed us for the theft of several items from the dig. The seven of us who were jailed were those who stayed by the collapsed pit, trying to recover our dead friends.'

'I didn't know,' said Vera quietly.

'We could not afford lawyers. We were found guilty and imprisoned.'

Vera did not like Tariq at all, but she had liked the little boy he had been very much. She imagined him being dragged away by the police, tearful and uncomprehending, and felt a stab of guilt. She had never thought to contact him again after leaving Syria, never once wondered what had become of him.

'When did you get out?' she said at last.

'I was twenty when they freed me,' said Tariq meditatively. 'Can you imagine that, Vera? Nearly half of my young life had been spent in a stinking cell smaller than this room, shared with five others.'

'I'm sorry,' said Vera, cursing herself for not having recognised Tariq before. He had changed a great deal, but she ought to have known. It seemed she had never really seen him properly at all. No wonder he was angry. She glanced at the window, but she could not see the king or his entourage yet. She would have to act fast when the time came.

'It's too late for apologies,' said Tariq. 'When I left prison, I decided to better myself. I went to Damascus and then to Cairo.'

'Why Cairo?'

'It's the centre of the world,' he said with a shrug. 'All life is there. Your politicians in London and Washington think they are making the world turn by their decisions, but Cairo is where the cogs are going round.'

'So you became a criminal.'

'Of sorts, yes,' said Tariq, although he frowned. 'I prefer to think of myself as a diplomat.'

Vera laughed despite herself. 'For what nation?'

'For many nations,' he said. 'I began by working for a man who smuggled drugs and antiquities in and out of the city. I had a knack for recognising pieces that might be valuable – skills I learned from you.'

'And then what?'

'I traded in many things. Gold, opium, artefacts found in the desert. Eventually I realised that the greatest trade of all was in secrets. Governments all over the world pay vast sums of money for information.'

Vera was silent, imagining the young man slipping unnoticed through the streets of Cairo. She had seen his potential the last time they met, but she had been distracted, preoccupied by memories of Curzon and the great task ahead of her. She had gravely underestimated him.

Tariq smiled. 'I have worked hard. I now communicate with spies from over a dozen countries, and employ many men. I'm not the only one in this business in Cairo, of course, but I have carved out a place for myself.'

'You've built quite an empire,' Vera conceded.

'It was around 1938 that I first heard the name Nero,' said Tariq. 'It was whispered here and there in tones of reverence and hatred. One of the most successful spies of the twentieth century. When the war began, it seemed clear that Nero was active again. I became curious about his identity.'

'Why did you care?'

'I wanted to learn,' said Tariq. 'I wanted to discover what he could teach me. I met a German who claimed that Nero was an English academic with aristocratic connections. Soon I realised that he meant Ralph Curzon, the man I had known years before in Syria, and whose death I had been jailed for.'

Vera listened intently. How had she overlooked his potential? He had made connections that no one else had.

'I knew Curzon was dead – I had seen his broken body laid out on a stretcher after they retrieved it from the pit, his skull smashed by rocks. So I kept looking, gathering information where I could. At last I found another German who had grown disillusioned with his Nazi employers. He was easily bought. He told me that Nero was rumoured to be a woman and gave me a description of her. Finally, from a high-ranking source, I extracted her name. Imagine my surprise when I realised that the great Nazi spy Nero was the Englishwoman I had known in Syria all those years before – the pretty young archaeologist.'

'I am the same person as I was then,' said Vera, remembering the skies over the desert and the feeling of freedom. She had been chasing that sensation ever since.

'Yes, you wanted power even then, I saw that,' said Tariq. 'I was an innocent child. I helped you and you discarded me.'

'I had no idea you'd gone to prison,' said Vera firmly. 'I wouldn't have allowed that to happen.' She glanced out of the window. The royal party were coming into view. She could see the governor pointing at a trellis and the bright white of the king's hat as he talked with the head gardener.

'But you did allow it,' Tariq said, shrugging. 'Every year, Curzon and his ilk would turn up in Syria. They had no interest in the men who worked for them, or what happened to us when all the money had gone. You left, just like the rest of them, and never looked back.'

'Have you really spent all these years hating me?' asked Vera. 'It seems rather a waste.'

'I've done a great many other things too,' he said, looking smug. 'I am wealthy. I can have any woman I want. I know secrets that could bring down whole nations. This is just a loose end, you might say.'

'What is? Killing me?'

'Yes.'

Vera remembered that night in Cairo. 'Did you send the car that knocked me down?'

For the first time, Tariq looked sheepish. 'That was a mistake,' he said at last. 'It was not honourable. I was angry after seeing you again. But I knew, when you easily survived it, that it was a sign. If you were to die, it ought to be at my own hands and I would look you in the eye as I did it.' He held his hands out, raising the gun a little. 'And here I am.'

'Why risk everything?' she said.

'I risk nothing.'

'Oh, you'd get out of here, I'm sure. But what about later? Don't you think my masters would be angry that you've killed their greatest asset?'

Tariq looked unsure for a moment, but he shook his head. 'Spies are ruthless and practical. They will regret the loss of Nero, but it won't take long before they find a new agent to replace you. I intend to convince them that I am a suitable candidate.'

Vera stared at him. 'I see. You think you are capable of becoming Nero?'

'Of course,' said Tariq, and she laughed, although she felt anger pulsing through her veins.

'Nero is not just a name,' she said, feeling her nails biting into her palms. 'You can't just pick it up and put it on.'

'You did,' said Tariq mildly.

'I grew into the role as the years went by. But I had certain qualities that were essential.'

'And you don't think I have those qualities?'

'No,' she said. 'The fact that you're here tells me that you don't.'

'How so?'

'Nero never kills in anger,' she said. 'You've come here, holding a grudge for God knows how many years, to kill someone who is no threat to you. I have only ever done what I was contracted to do or when I truly believed it was the only course of action available to me. I have never killed out of pique.'

'What about Curzon?' said Tariq.

'Curzon was different,' said Vera, hating the uncertainty in her voice.

'How?'

'He would have killed me. I was defending myself.'

She could see the king clearly now, his head turning as he laughed at something the gardener had said. He was standing directly in her eyeline, at the top of a flight of steps, looking out across the garden. It was now or never.

*

From her stupor, Margarita heard some of the conversation as she slipped in and out of consciousness. She did not understand what was happening, or who the man Vera was talking to was. All she knew was that Vera was Nero, that she was about to kill the king – and there was nothing she could do to stop her.

Suddenly, things began to happen very fast. Vera swung towards the young man and slammed his arms with one of hers, making him drop the gun with a grunt. As he lunged to pick it up, she kicked him hard in the knee, making him sprawl across the floor, the revolver clattering under a chair.

Vera turned back to the window and leaned to look through the sights of the rifle.

'Don't,' said Margarita weakly.

The young man seized the revolver and fired at Vera, just as she pulled the trigger of the rifle. The two shots rang out over the garden below.

Chapter 60

The streets of Valletta were quiet as Margarita walked briskly through the city. The strings of flags had gone, the posters had been taken down, and there were no crowds to be seen. The only evidence of the king's visit to Malta was the crushed piles of red and white petals that lay rotting in the gutter.

'How are you feeling?' said Pratchett anxiously as Margarita sat down in the office in Archbishop Street. 'Better, I hope?' He looked younger, somehow, less confident, as if some of the stuffing had been knocked out of him.

'Oh, completely,' said Margarita, looking around.

A week had passed since that day at Verdala Palace. She had spent a night in hospital, where she had had to give a statement, but she had insisted on going home once the doctors were sure there was no lasting damage.

The last few hours at the Palace were a blur. After Vera had fired the rifle, there were shouts outside and soon the sound of several pairs of heavy footsteps racing up the stairs and across the roof.

She thought she recalled seeing Vera at the window, smoking and looking down at her, blood seeping through her shirt where the young man had shot her in the shoulder. 'Well done, Margarita,' she had said, her voice echoing. 'You did very well.' The next time she looked, Vera was gone, and there was just a crowd of anxious faces looking down at her.

'Is the king dead?' Margarita asked weakly as she was carried away.

'No,' said a voice by her ear. 'Lie still, now.'

The newspapers the next day were full of the triumphant news that the king had evaded an assassination attempt and that a German spy, hunted for decades, had been captured.

Margarita noted the white cotton dressing on Pratchett's head. 'What about you?'

'Still a bit sore,' he said, lifting a hand sheepishly to touch the bandage. 'No concussion, apparently. I had a couple of days off but thought I should get back to work. Wilson said I could fill you in, given that your statement was vital in understanding what happened in the tower. He's with the governor today.'

Margarita nodded, trying to find the words for the next big question. 'Where's Vera?'

'In custody,' said Pratchett.

She breathed out heavily. 'What happened?'

'Vera's bullet missed the king by about an inch,' said Pratchett. 'It was very close – too close. He moved slightly to brush a fly away and that probably saved his life. Things could have been very different.'

'I see. The papers just said he was unhurt. Has Vera said anything?'

'Enough,' said Pratchett crisply. 'We know she was working for the Germans. Her Abwehr case officer in Sicily came up with this idea to assassinate the king, or perhaps it was her idea. They obviously felt that his visit to Malta was too good an opportunity to miss.'

'But why did she do it?' asked Margarita, still reeling.

'I'm not sure we'll ever know the full story,' said Pratchett, looking down at the notes in front of him, 'but apparently Vera blamed the British government for the death of her parents – her father was a disgraced diplomat who killed himself and her mother in 1920. After that, I suppose it wasn't a huge step to offering her services to those who opposed the British. I doubt she would have become a spy if she hadn't discovered Ralph Curzon's identity in Syria, but somehow the fates aligned.'

'So she began working for the enemy,' said Margarita, almost to herself.

'I don't think she was a natural traitor,' said Pratchett. 'And, of course, she worked for British intelligence even while she was Nero.'

'But all of that's a lie, isn't it?' said Margarita. 'She used her position to steal secrets for the Nazis.'

'So it seems,' he said, 'although I still can't quite believe it. Wilson thinks . . . well. It's a complicated situation.' Pratchett sighed. 'I was so sure Curzon was still alive. We think Vera must have used his name sometimes after he died, in order to muddy the waters. It would have been beneficial for her and her masters to keep up the pretence that Curzon was alive and working for them. And their still referring to Nero as if he was a man helped her fly under the radar. For instance, they often referred to their "old friend", but they used the male term, "Freund", rather than the female term, "Freundin". Anyone reading their communications would have believed they were talking about a man. So simple, but brilliant, really.'

Margarita nodded slowly. 'What about Henry? Vera said she didn't kill him. I suppose she was lying again.'

'Henry must have discovered that she was responsible for the death of Jan Novotný in 1936,' said Pratchett. 'He was a friend of Henry's from university. Henry campaigned for years for the Americans to pursue Novotný's killers but initially they were reluctant to antagonise Hitler, and then later the war came and it was all superseded.'

'But Henry didn't forget.'

'No. He started investigating Nero seriously a few months ago and at some point he must have suspected that it was Vera. In 1936 he was working in Biskupin in Poland when Novotný was killed a couple of hundred miles away – we think Vera was visiting Henry at the time and travelled south to assassinate Novotný. Henry must have confronted her, or perhaps she realised what he was up to. Anyway, he disappeared. The smuggler, Matteo, was keeping him prisoner. Then, of course, they both ended up dead.'

Margarita bit her lip, feeling overwhelmed. 'So Vera must have killed him.'

'Or her German handlers didn't trust her to do it and took matters into their own hands. That's the theory we're working with at the moment.'

Margarita sat back in the chair, her mind whirling. She could not get the image of Vera out of her mind: Vera standing at the window, as the young man behind her dived for the revolver.

'What happened to Tariq?' she said suddenly. 'The man who came to kill Vera?'

Pratchett frowned. 'He got away.'

'Got away? How?'

'We're not sure yet,' he said. 'I suppose he may have had help.'

Margarita shook her head. If they had not caught him yet, they never would. She pictured Tariq walking away down the narrow streets of some eastern city, blending into the crowds until he disappeared.

Something struck her. 'Where was Vera in the week she was missing?'

'Sicily,' said Pratchett. 'At least, that's what we believe. It seems she had a rendezvous planned with her case officer, an Italian called Leonardi, that night. When you showed her the photograph, she made the decision to flee with him to Sicily until the date they'd agreed for the assassination. She must have known we'd bring her in for questioning. We think she posed as a German while she was there – the fisherman, Cardona, suggested as much. It was he who took her there on his boat and brought her back to Malta last week.'

'Can't he identify her or this Leonardi?'

'He's dead,' said Pratchett glumly. 'It seems that Vera killed him on arrival to avoid just such an eventuality.'

Margarita felt as if someone had punched her. She understood, in the abstract, that Vera was a killer, but it was another thing altogether to know that she had done it here, and so recently. She must have killed the poor fisherman just a few hours before drugging Margarita at Verdala Palace. *Why on earth did she allow me to go free?*

'The most important thing,' said Pratchett, leaning back in his chair, 'is that plans for the re-invasion of Europe haven't been jeopardised. Vera seems to have held back that information, for reasons we can only guess at.'

'It's going ahead? When?'

'Even if I knew, I couldn't tell you,' said Pratchett regretfully. 'I'm not privy to that sort of information. But I suspect it will be soon.'

In Arthur's latest letter from Alexandria, he had said that he was thinking about returning to Europe for a long holiday, which Margarita guessed was a coded way of saying he was expecting to leave soon. He had also mentioned collecting his car from the garage as it had a new engine – he had no car, so presumably it was a reference to his submarine, the *Tenacious*, being overhauled. Would he be involved in this new battle, wherever it was to take place?

'I ought to go,' she said, standing up. 'I'm due at the Palace. I thought they'd fire me, but I think Wilson must have put in a good word.'

'Margarita,' said Pratchett quickly, and she felt her heart plummet. He hesitated. 'I wanted to say I'm sorry. For what I said outside the Palace. You were right about Vera, of course, and I was a fool not to listen to you. I just got carried away by my own – well . . .'

'It doesn't matter,' said Margarita. 'Really.' She had almost forgotten their altercation. It seemed like something from another life. After working in a nightclub, she was used to men not taking her seriously. She had hoped that Pratchett was different, that was all.

'There's something else. A permanent job may be coming up here in Malta.'

'Oh,' she said. 'Are you going to apply?'

'I don't know. Originally, I was intending to apply for a transfer to Lisbon. That's where a lot of the really exciting work is happening. But this offer came up and I thought . . .'

He hesitated again. She knew that he would stay in Malta if he believed there might be a chance of something happening between them, however tiny. But I love Arthur, thought Margarita. It was as simple as that. Pratchett had been a friend, but he did not think of her as an equal, and he probably never would.

'You should go to Lisbon,' she said, turning towards the door. He looked downcast when she glanced back. 'I'm sure you'll have a brilliant career,' she said, softening slightly. 'You won't find that here. Good luck, Dennis.'

Chapter 61

Vienna, 1926

In a side street off one of the great thoroughfares of Vienna, a chill wind rattled the sign above the inn, making it creak loudly.

Inside, a thin man known as Walter sat in a corner, drinking sparingly. The inn was busy and hardly anyone looked at him. He had a forgettable face.

Late in the evening, at the appointed time, the door swung open and he looked up, but it was not the middle-aged man he was expecting to see. Instead, a young woman entered, wearing a heavy coat, and looked around the room. Her eyes brushed past and then returned to settle on him.

She went to the bar and spoke to the landlord, shaking snow off her shoulders, and ordered a drink. Then she crossed over to Walter's table and put her hand on the back of the chair opposite.

'May I?'

'I'm waiting for someone, Fräulein.'

She smiled. 'I know. I bring word of the man you're meant to be meeting,' she said. Her accent was strong and she spoke carefully. 'May I sit down?'

'Very well.' He watched her narrowly as she sat and arranged her coat around her. 'Who are you? And what is it you want to tell me?'

'Your associate is Ralph Curzon. You don't have to confirm it if you don't want to, I know what the arrangement is.' She took a sip of wine. 'Unfortunately, Ralph was killed in an accident in Syria two weeks ago.'

Walter stared at her. 'How do you know?'

'I was there.'

He exhaled heavily. 'I see. That is . . . inconvenient.'

She pulled out a thick envelope, which was closed with a wax seal. 'I believe you were expecting this. It's all in order.'

Walter took the folder and examined it carefully. He looked up, running his fingers over the seal. 'You have the ring. May I see it?'

She drew off her gloves, and the heavy ring gleamed. She held it out for inspection, and he took her hand, holding it like a suitor as he peered closely at the ring.

'What do you want, Fräulein? Money?'

'I intend to continue his work,' she said.

He stared at her. 'Well, now. This is an interesting development.' He leaned back in his chair, watching her closely, and a smile flickered at the corner of his mouth. 'You're English, are you not? Why would you want to work with us?'

'I imagine my reasons are similar to Ralph's,' she said calmly. 'I would rather not discuss them here, but of course I'm willing to tell you anything you want to know. For now, I hope it will suffice to say that the country of my birth betrayed someone I loved very much.'

'I see.' Walter observed her again for a long moment. 'Coming here was dangerous, you know.'

'I know.'

'You might have been killed on the spot.'

She shrugged, although she looked uncertain. 'I believe I can be useful to you, as he was. I want to prove myself.'

Walter nodded slowly. 'I will have to discuss the matter with my superiors. I'm sure you understand. There are . . . formalities that we must go through. I can't promise anything yet.'

'Of course,' she said. 'I'm staying at the Krantz-Ambassador. I'll remain in Vienna until I hear from you.'

'How did Curzon die?' asked Walter as she stood up.

'A pit collapsed on the dig.'

'One more thing.' He looked at her curiously. 'Who are you?'

'My name is Vera Millward. As for who I am . . .' She held up the ring.

Once outside, Vera strode briskly away, feeling snowflakes brush her cheeks. Almost half her life had passed since she had last been in Vienna, and the city had changed. It was not the same place she had left as a girl at the outbreak of war. But it seemed appropriate, somehow, that she should return here on the first day of her new life.

Chapter 62

Early one morning, as Margarita was getting ready for work and listening to the wireless, a note arrived from the naval base. Nearly a month had passed since the first Allied paratroopers had landed in Sicily, swiftly followed by thousands of soldiers who arrived by sea: the first step on the long journey to reconquering Europe. The Italians were putting up a spirited defence, reinforced by the Germans, and the fighting was fierce.

The message asked her to contact Captain Langdon as soon as possible. Langdon, she recalled, was a friend of Arthur's. Feeling numb, she walked to the nearest public telephone.

'We've lost contact with the *Tenacious*, I'm afraid,' said Langdon, when she finally got hold of him.

'What does that mean?' asked Margarita faintly. 'Is he dead?'

'I'm afraid we don't know,' said Langdon apologetically. 'The communication link has been broken and, as far as we know, she's failed to surface. Her last known position was somewhere south of Licata in Sicily. I haven't heard any more details than that yet, but Arthur asked me to keep you in the loop if something should happen.'

'Were they torpedoed?'

'It's a distinct possibility. No sign of wreckage, so she may not have been sunk.'

'But how could they survive?' asked Margarita, feeling agitated. 'If the sub hasn't surfaced, they must be dead.'

'People have survived even torpedoed subs,' said Langdon, although she could tell his heart wasn't in it. 'I don't want to give you false hope, Miss Farrugia – it's a very serious situation. But please don't lose heart yet. No news may be good news.'

'Keep me informed, won't you?' she said at last. 'If you hear anything . . .'

'I certainly will. Just – try not to worry.'

Margarita felt a mad urge to laugh, which she suppressed. She felt sorry for Captain Langdon. How often had he had to make these sorts of telephone calls? Conversations with distraught parents and grieving widows, trying to give comfort but knowing it was impossible. She thought of Arthur's mother and father in England, in their cottage in Yorkshire, weeping when they received the telegram.

She had not even had a chance to tell Arthur about what had happened at the Palace, about her part in catching Nero. Putting anything in writing was out of the question, and now she might never see him again to tell him in person.

Abruptly, Margarita remembered Vera. Even now, she sometimes forgot that Vera and Nero were one and the same. Vera had been working with the Nazis all along, and her information was probably being used by Axis troops in Sicily as they attacked Allied forces. That night, Margarita dreamed of Arthur, choking and trying to shout orders as water rushed into his submarine, deep beneath the surface.

*

Margarita walked through the centre of the small town of Paola, passing a whitewashed church. She could see Corradino Prison ahead, its high walls ominous. She had never visited anyone in prison before. She was surprised that her request to visit had been accepted and she suspected that Roger Wilson had pulled a few strings.

At the prison she was kept waiting for a long time in a drab room with a handful of other visitors. Most of the inmates they were visiting were looters, still in prison long after the bombing had eased.

She was called at last and led along a hallway that smelled of damp to the women's section of the prison. There she was taken into a larger room, where six or seven tables were set out as if it was a dining hall. The only light came from a dirty window high above and a few dim bulbs. Pale women in baggy grey uniforms sat with their families, some looking bored, others weeping.

Margarita saw a girl of her own age, or perhaps younger, looking across the table at her two small children, clearly desperate to hold their hands and stroke their hair but afraid to invoke the wrath of the guards.

And suddenly Vera was there, being led in by two guards, a man and a woman. Margarita was startled to see that her hands were shackled and that when she reached the table her handcuffs were fastened by a chain to a bolt on the floor.

'High security,' said Vera, nodding to the guards, who had moved back to stand against the wall but were watching carefully. 'They've got to stick with me, unfortunately. Bit of a drag for them.'

She too wore the ugly uniform of the prisoners, which hung off her slim frame. But her hair and her skin were clean, and she somehow managed to look as chic in a drab shirt and skirt as she had in silk and pearls the first time they met.

'They told me you were coming,' said Vera. She leaned forward, her elbows on the table, her dark eyes serious. 'It's good to see you, Margarita. What brings you here?'

'I just … I wanted to see you. To speak with you,' said Margarita, feeling flustered.

'It's going to be a grave disappointment,' said Vera. 'If you're looking for some sort of closure, that is. I can't tell you anything you haven't already worked out. Sometimes a cigar is, as Dr Freud said, just a cigar.' She brushed a speck of dust from the sleeve of her uniform. 'I do owe you an apology, though.'

'Me?'

'For drugging you. I'm sorry about that. I should never have involved you.' She watched Margarita carefully. 'Why are you really here? What's happened?'

Margarita stared at her for a long moment. She felt, as always, wrongfooted by Vera. It was hard to imagine that this clever, elegant woman could be responsible for so much suffering, and somehow that made her worse: more deceptive, and far more dangerous.

'It's Arthur,' said Margarita at last. 'His submarine is missing. Near Sicily.'

'I'm sorry to hear that.'

'You're sorry?' The anger, bubbling quietly away, rose a little closer to the surface.

'Of course. I've never wanted to hurt you, Margarita, or anyone close to you.'

'And yet you have.'

Vera said nothing. Margarita dropped her head into her hands. 'I feel as though I've dreamed the last few weeks. Everything seems … unreal. Ever since you appeared at the Palace.' She shook her head, looking up at Vera. 'I was so sure it was Curzon.'

'You thought that because it was what I wanted you to think,' said Vera, with a shrug. 'Ralph Curzon has been very useful to me in the years since his death.'

'I thought you were in love with him,' said Margarita. 'The way you looked at that photograph . . .'

'I wasn't in love with him,' said Vera crisply. 'I was obsessed by him. They aren't the same thing – I know that now. I didn't then.'

A gong sounded somewhere. Two of the inmates stood up and were led away by the guards.

'We should have a bit longer,' said Vera. 'Anything else you want to ask?'

'Yes,' said Margarita, feeling her nails biting into her palms. 'Tell me why you did it.'

'Why does anyone do anything?' said Vera, leaning back in her chair. 'Money and power.'

Margarita stared at her and shook her head.

'You look disappointed,' said Vera.

'I thought there must be more to it than that.'

'That's because you can't imagine betraying your country or those you love, and you don't care about power.'

'And you do?'

'Always,' said Vera. 'Power gives you options – freedom.' She smiled thinly. 'And, of course, an opportunity to punish those who have wronged you.'

'Who were you punishing?'

'My father killed himself and my mother because his country had betrayed him,' said Vera. 'It can't be surprising that I felt very little loyalty towards the government who had sent him to his death.'

'So you transferred your allegiance, just like that?' Margarita heard her voice tremble, exhausted by the effort of suppressing her anger and disappointment.

Vera shook her head. 'My first loyalty has always been to myself. I have been utterly alone since I was nineteen – no one else was going to look out for me.'

'What about Henry?'

'He looked after me as well as he could,' said Vera thought-fully. 'But, as you know very well, he was weak. Poor Henry. He could only give me so much.'

'So you killed him.'

'No,' said Vera, and something like pain flashed across her face. 'The people who killed Henry will be brought to justice eventually. I'll make sure of it.'

'From here?' said Margarita scornfully, gesturing to the prison, and Vera was silent. 'Anyway, it's not just Henry, is it? I knew people who were killed in the bombing of Malta. Old women. Children. My friend's husband was shot down by the Italians. And now Arthur . . .'

Vera listened carefully, her face impassive, and Margarita wanted to slap her.

'You betrayed them all.'

'It's more complicated than that,' said Vera coolly. 'War isn't as black and white as you imagine, Margarita. You should read up about the crew of the HMS *Torbay*, who murdered unarmed German sailors when their ship sank off Alexandria. Or the *Arno*, the Italian hospital ship that was sunk last year off Tobruk on the recommendation of British intelligence. That's war for you. Awful things happen.'

Margarita felt her fists clench and a feeling of rage swept over her. She could not recall ever having felt this burning, visceral hatred, and wanted to break something, to wipe the complacent look from Vera's face.

'That's war?' she said, hearing her voice grow louder. 'Is that all you can say? This isn't just war, Vera, this is betrayal – cruelty – cowardice.' She thought again of Arthur, saw fragments of the *Tenacious* still dispersing from the blast of the torpedo, his green face beneath the water, terrified, struggling to breathe, his heart pounding faster and faster.

Vera shook her head. 'Think what you like of me, Margarita, but don't ever think me a coward.'

Hardly aware of her own actions, Margarita lunged forwards, overcome by a powerful urge to hurt, to make Vera suffer as she had made others suffer. For a moment, she wanted to kill her and imagined raining blows down on her elegant head until it was unrecognisable. The guards reacted quickly and before her hands had closed around Vera's neck, they were pulling her away.

Shocked at her loss of control, Margarita stumbled back, feeling another warder gripping her arm. She had never wished to harm anyone before, and that it should be Vera who incited these feelings in her was disconcerting. Vera had been a friend to her – of sorts. But that was just it: she had been betrayed by someone she had begun to care for, and it made the deception all the more painful.

Vera had barely moved, even as Margarita was reaching for her, and she sat now, very still, her eyes fixed on Margarita's. As always, her face gave little away, but there was something unbearably close to pity in her eyes.

'I'm sorry,' she said quietly. That was all.

Margarita stared back at Vera for a long moment, feeling anger and hurt coursing through her veins. The guard next to her was saying something, telling her it was time to go. She felt her breathing begin to calm and straightened her shoulders. She had allowed Vera to make her angry. She would never allow her that satisfaction again.

The guards beside Vera were reaching for her shackles; suddenly she was standing up and they were holding her arms.

'Anyway, it's over,' Margarita said at last, trying to find a parting shot. 'You've lost.'

'Have I?' said Vera, raising an eyebrow, and Margarita felt the fire starting to burn again. But the guards on either side of Vera were pulling her away, leading her out of the room.

For a split second, Vera looked back over her shoulder and caught Margarita's eye for the last time, the sardonic smile back on her face. Then she was gone.

Chapter 63

On the seafront in San Leone, Roger Wilson stood watching two little boys fishing from the end of the jetty. Their shrill shouts made him remember fishing with his own son on the pier at Aberystwyth, many years before, and he felt the familiar tug of regret.

He had arrived in Agrigento a day after it had been liberated by the Americans, but it was already too late. The man known as Leonardi was gone. People in the town spoke of seeing him a few days earlier, driving north, but so far they had not picked up the trail. Leonardi, whoever he was – and he was certainly not Ralph Curzon – had disappeared. By now, he could be in Rome or Berlin.

Wilson knew he wasn't supposed to be here. He had been assured by London that everything was in hand, but they didn't seem in a hurry to send anyone to Sicily to follow up on the information given by Isaac Cardona, the fisherman, whose body had never been found. Vera had refused to reveal anything about Leonardi. Acting more impulsively than he could remember doing for a long time, Wilson had hitched a lift from Malta on a small plane heading for Licata, and from there had been driven in an American jeep to Agrigento.

At the Villa Concordia, two young soldiers were doing a thorough search of the office, but on the back lawn was a blackened circle – Leonardi had evidently burned anything he could find before leaving.

Wilson had come down to San Leone to visit Cardona's family, but no one had answered the door. Returning to the house now, he tapped on the door of Cardona's neighbour. After a few minutes, an elderly woman emerged, looking anxious. A little boy, presumably her grandson, peered around her.

'Afternoon, signora,' said Wilson in his faltering Italian. 'Sorry to bother you.' She nodded and waited for him to speak.

'I'm looking for Signora Cardona – do you know where she is?'

'Adelina? She's gone away,' said the old woman, her voice hoarse. 'Who are you? American?'

'British,' said Wilson. 'I just wanted to make sure that she and her children are safe. Do you know where she went?'

'She didn't say – perhaps to her parents at Sciacca.'

'When was this?'

'Months ago, long before the Americans came. June, perhaps? Her husband died, you know.'

'I know,' said Wilson heavily. So Cardona's wife had fled once he failed to return from Malta, or perhaps she had been threatened by Leonardi and his cronies. He hoped that it was the former, and that she and her children were far away.

'I saw Signor Cardona,' said the little boy, looking up at Wilson. 'In the night.'

'Don't be silly, Gino,' said his grandmother, frowning at him.

'I did!'

'When?' said Wilson.

'I looked out of the window and he was there, helping Signora Cardona to pack the van. They were gone in the morning,' said Gino. He looked up at his grandmother. 'You said he died but he was there. I saw him.'

'He is mixed up,' said the old woman, looking back at Wilson with a shrug. 'We went to Isaac's funeral. He was lost in a storm while fishing. Poor Adelina.'

'I *saw* him,' said the boy stubbornly.

'You must have been dreaming,' said the old woman.

Wilson bade them farewell and walked back along the sea-front, feeling unsettled. The matter of Cardona had been bothering him, and now it seemed that it would never be resolved. He might be able to track Adelina down eventually, but she clearly did not wish to be found, and he was running out of time.

Climbing back into the borrowed car, he drove out of the village and back up the hill towards Agrigento and the Villa Concordia. Inside, he could tell from the banging and scraping that the soldiers had moved upstairs to search the bedrooms.

As he stood in the dining room, there was a tap on the door. Wilson swung around to see the young maid who had let him in when he first arrived.

She was carrying a wooden box, which she placed on the table. Wilson looked curiously at it before lifting the lid off. He sucked in a breath at once, for inside was a stack of papers, and on the top sheet he could see words written in what was unmistakably German.

'Did you take this?' he said, remembering at once that she was deaf. But she grasped the meaning of his question and pointed to Leonardi's study along the hall, then did an impression of someone tearing his hair out.

'I see,' said Wilson. 'You took it while he was rushing around burning things . . . and you hid it?'

She tugged his sleeve and led him through to the kitchen, then into the pantry beyond, where a stack of boxes could be seen. Looking into one, Wilson saw that it was half full of tinned food. She gestured to a gap behind the boxes.

'Very clever,' he said, nodding at her. 'You did this . . . alone?'

'She wasn't alone,' said a voice, and he swung around to see the cook, who put her arm around the maid's shoulder protectively. 'I helped her hide it. She thought it might be useful when the British arrived. Or perhaps we should have given it to the Americans?'

'It's very useful,' said Wilson. 'I'm grateful to you both.'

He went back to the dining room and slowly unpacked the box, making a list in pencil of its contents, and laying each document out on the huge table. They were predominantly in German. Many of them seemed to be decoded copies of reports from Abwehr stations throughout Italy and North Africa. He thought longingly of all the other paperwork that Leonardi had burned or taken with him. All that was left was this little box.

Near the bottom was a thin card folder. Inside were five or six typed reports dealing with Allied activity in the Mediterranean – transcriptions of coded messages, he guessed. One listed divisions that were based in Malta and Cairo, noting identifying insignia, significant personnel, and predicted movements. Another, dated early June, focused on submarines and listed the names of numerous British subs along with their coordinates. Each of these reports had the letter N scribbled in the corner.

Wilson breathed out heavily. There was nothing else to indicate that these reports were from Nero, but it seemed likely. Vera had been the Germans' main operative in Malta and she had had access to a wealth of classified information.

Wilson skimmed over a 1942 report about the delivery of aircraft to Ta' Qali. He paused, frowning. His German was frustratingly rusty, and the words and numbers didn't make much sense. Perhaps he was misreading it.

There was a knock at the front door and Wilson went to answer it. The young American soldier who had been guarding the door held out an envelope. In the yard, a motorcycle messenger was already zipping out between the pillars.

The soldier smiled wryly. 'Looks like we may be headed for trouble, Captain.'

The message was short and to the point. Wilson was ordered not to touch anything at the Villa Concordia. A truck was on its way to take anything important away, presumably to Allied headquarters, and Wilson himself was to return to Malta at once, where – the subtext was clear – he would be expected to explain himself.

'Bureaucracy, eh?' he said with a smile, crumpling up the paper. After asking around among the soldiers, he borrowed a German phrasebook, brought along by its owner with the optimistic belief that it would be only a short push from Sicily to Berlin, with which he returned to the dining room and shut the door.

This would be his last chance to play an active part in the Nero business. From here, it would be handled by higher-ups in London and these documents would disappear into the bowels of the intelligence service. He didn't know what he was looking for, but he couldn't bear to see the work he and Pratchett had done over the last few months be hijacked without knowing something – anything – of the operation they had helped to destroy.

With the assistance of the phrasebook, Wilson worked his way through the report on aircraft deliveries, dated April 1942. He started to wonder if it was still in code, for the numbers did not make sense. The report described how an American vessel, USS *Wasp*, had delivered forty-eight Spitfires to Malta. Wilson remembered the day well. He had been listening to enemy radio activity, which had spiked shortly before the arrival of the first plane. All forty-eight landed successfully, but almost as soon as they had touched down, the Luftwaffe had appeared in huge numbers and began bombing the airfield. The island's defences had been useless. The report implied that information previously sent by Nero had been vital in the Luftwaffe being in the right place at the right time.

As on so many other nights during the siege of Malta, Wilson had not slept that night. The bombing of the airfield had continued for two days, and even the few planes that made it off the ground could not hold off the onslaught. By the third day, the airfield was carpeted with the burning wreckage of dozens of planes. Not a single one of the aircraft, which had been treasured all the way from England, had survived.

But Nero's report, sent to the Abwehr a few days after the bombing, said merely that 'at least half' of the planes had been destroyed, described extensive repairs that were taking place at Ta' Qali and elsewhere, and even noted the arrival of a handful of Spitfires separate from the main batch, which were unscathed and apparently ready for action. This Wilson knew to be fiction, for he had sat in on several meetings that awful week as the island's governing bodies discussed the very real possibility that it would soon be left defenceless. The disaster had led to the removal of the governor, Sir William Dobbie, and the arrival of Lord Gort as his replacement.

Scrabbling through the other papers, Wilson laboriously made notes on their contents, grunting now and then. Much of the information imparted by Nero was based on reality, although without access to his files he couldn't verify much. But there were other statements that he knew to be fabrications. A report by Nero in the summer of 1942 described the construction of a new water pipeline in the desert near El Alamein, which Wilson recalled had been one element of a complex Allied deception campaign against Rommel's troops. Tanks constructed from wood and cardboard had been deployed to give the impression that the Allied forces were stronger than they really were.

Von Thoma, a captured German general now serving in a POW camp in England, had admitted that he and Rommel had believed the Allies had a whole extra division, and that the attack had come weeks sooner than expected. Success at the Second Battle of El Alamein had been the turning point in the Western Desert Campaign.

In short, the deception had worked. Could it really be true that even the great spy Nero had been taken in? Would Vera have passed on such information to her German masters without verifying it?

Wilson breathed out heavily and stared blankly at the papers in front of him. He heard the crunch of tyres on the gravel outside and looked at his watch. He had been reading for hours. The truck must be here to take Leonardi's belongings away. He stood and briskly packed the papers back into the box. There was nothing more he could do.

But the sudden theory, the realisation that had begun to dawn as soon as he read the false report of the Spitfires arriving in Malta, would not leave him alone.

Later, when Wilson was back in Valletta, he stood before the man who had arrived from London and did not listen to a word of the ticking-off that he had fully expected. Instead, he stared into the man's blank, inscrutable face and felt his conviction growing. Vera had been knowingly passing false information to the Germans. If that was true, then everything he had believed was wrong.

Chapter 64

Wilson checked the filing cabinet one more time and then pushed the drawers closed. He looked around the office. The shelves that had once bowed under the weight of accumulated books and paperwork were now empty. Pratchett had left for Lisbon and the important documents and equipment had been carted away to headquarters.

The last message of any importance that had come through concerned a body that had been found floating in the Port of Naples. *Our man in Naples says he fits the description of this Leonardi you were after, but he couldn't get close enough to get a definite ID. The local police have taken the body away.* Wilson suspected Leonardi had been silenced by the Abwehr after the collapse of their operation in Sicily, but it was no longer his concern.

The telephone rang, shattering the silence. Wilson picked it up and heard the voice of a colleague in London, a man he had worked with in Paris many years before.

'Hello, Foster. Any joy?'

'Nothing concrete, I'm afraid,' said Foster. 'I put a watch on the PO Box you mentioned to see if anyone came, but no one did. I made a discreet inquiry to see who the box belongs to. It's registered to a firm of lawyers but the key was sent back in July.'

'Which firm?' said Wilson.

'Well, that's the thing. It's an old family firm based in the East End called Cooper and Sons, but they appear to have gone out of business years ago. I went to the registered address and it doesn't exist. Whoever really held that box didn't want to be found.'

Wilson rubbed his forehead. He had made one last roll of the dice, and it had told him nothing. Vera Dunn had sent multiple letters over the last few years to a PO Box in London, supposedly in relation to her work as an archaeologist. Wilson had asked Foster to poke around and see if that could be substantiated, but the answer was oblique.

'There's one other thing,' said Foster. 'I called the telephone number that was associated with Cooper and Sons in the directory, and it took me to the switchboard at the Cabinet Office. No one there seemed to know anything – they thought it was probably a mistake, said it happens a lot.'

After saying goodbye, Wilson stood motionless beside the telephone. *Enough, now.* On returning from Sicily, he had been instructed, politely but firmly, to submit his resignation. His unauthorised visit to Agrigento had been the tipping point, but he had known for some time that his superiors wanted him gone. He had failed to discover Nero's identity and had only caught Vera after she had attempted to assassinate the king. He would be allowed to retire honourably, to save their embarrassment rather than his own, he assumed.

'You've had a good run, Roger,' the young man in pinstripes had said insincerely. 'Quit while you're ahead.'

But Wilson was sure that something else was going on, something that even his immediate superiors were unaware of. He had learned two significant things on his visit to Sicily: Vera had been lying to her Nazi masters, and Isaac Cardona was still alive. He thought again of the PO Box, and the Cabinet Office, and began to paint a picture in his mind. Suppose the real owner of the box was someone important, someone right at the top of the intelligence service, or perhaps in government? Vera had been writing to the same address for years. Suppose she and this person had cooked up an idea between them, a scheme absurd in its audacity, to infiltrate the Nazi intelligence network? Suppose Nero had been working for the British after all?

Wilson shook his head. It would never have worked. To start with, she would have needed to convince the Germans she was loyal to them. She would have had to live in deep cover for years, constantly risking discovery, putting herself in huge danger. She had killed people – she'd tried to kill the king, for God's sake! The scope of the deception was impossible. No one would have been able to pull it off. But he could not help imagining Vera planning every move, relishing the challenge, putting that mind of hers to good use. Perhaps, in the end, she had grown tired of the risk, or the damage to her moral core, and had decided to blow it all up, doing as much damage as she could to the Nazi cause while she was at it.

And it seemed to have had the desired effect. Over the summer there had been a flurry of panic in the Nazi intelligence networks at the loss of an important operative, and reading between the lines, it was clear that Nero was the agent in question. They knew, based on past experience, that the British would not hesitate to execute a known enemy spy, and Nero was quite a prize to lose. Numerous schemes had been abandoned, agents caught or recalled, plans delayed. Was this the work of the shadowy figures in British intelligence who had presumably benefitted from the information Vera had passed to them over the months and years? Had they been waiting for the right moment?

The most frustrating thing for Wilson was realising that he would never know. If Vera's efforts had gone to plan, only a few people, somewhere at the top of the intelligence service, would ever be aware of it. Her sacrifice, and the work she had done, depended on secrecy. To the world at large, she was a Nazi spy, and she had been caught.

Wilson brushed the dust from his desk and shook his head. He picked up his briefcase and looked at the room once more. It was over.

*

Margarita floated on her back in the warm clear water of the harbour, looking up at the sky. She had spent the last few days trying simply to exist. Pieces of Arthur's submarine, the *Tenacious*, had been found floating in the sea off Sicily. She was beginning to accept that he would not come back, but this did not reduce the pain or the guilt. Over the last few months she had been preoccupied by Nero, swept away by the mystery of it all, when she ought to have been focusing on what really mattered – the man who loved her and the life they were planning together.

'I ought to head home,' said a reluctant voice. Margarita opened her eyes to see Daniela bobbing beside her, looking concerned. 'Are you sure you'll be all right?'

'I'm fine,' said Margarita. 'My father will be here soon. He was catching the lunchtime ferry from Gozo.'

'How long will you stay with him?'

Margarita shrugged. 'A week or two. Perhaps longer. Mrs Lastra said just to let her know when I want to go back to work. She's been very kind.'

Daniela patted her shoulder. 'Take as much time as you need. And enjoy Gozo. It must be beautiful at the moment. Send us a postcard, won't you?'

'Of course.' Margarita smiled wanly at her. She was looking forward to seeing her father and Livia. She wished that there had been an opportunity to introduce them to Arthur. They would have liked him, she thought.

Daniela began paddling towards the shore. 'Oh – Mr Grech said you'd asked him about the job application that was sent on your behalf.'

After all that had happened, Margarita had to wrench her mind back to recall what her friend was talking about. She had mentioned it to the Verdala Palace estate manager some time ago but had not crossed paths with him since. It hardly seemed to matter now.

'He asked me to tell you that he couldn't find the letter, I'm afraid, he thinks he threw it away. All he could remember was that it was postmarked Senglea. Just someone trying to be helpful, I suppose. A family friend, perhaps?'

'Perhaps,' said Margarita. She watched Daniela climb up the steps to the rocks, where she pulled a dress over her bathing suit and waved before ascending the steep steps to the road high above.

Margarita lay back again, her arms and legs outstretched, feeling the water gently rise and fall. It was a beautiful day. Far across the harbour, she could see the tip of Senglea point, and if she squinted, she was sure she could see the blue flash of Vera's shutters.

I should never have involved you. That was what Vera had said when they had last met in Corradino Prison. It had been nagging at her. At the time, Margarita had assumed she meant coming to see her at the Phoenix Club.

Margarita chewed her lip, trying to push away the doubts that were spiralling. She had been so angry, and Vera had just smiled, as if everything had gone to plan. Not for the first time, Margarita felt that she was playing a complicated game in which she only knew half the rules. But she wasn't a player. She was a pawn. She imagined Vera as a puppet master, pulling the strings from above. Margarita thought of the photograph which had been hidden in Henry's flat. Perhaps Vera herself had put the photo there, intending Margarita should find it. Perhaps she had relied on Margarita recognising her.

You've lost.

Have I?

Margarita swam towards the shore and pulled herself up onto the rocks. She dressed slowly, trying to calm her racing mind. A clock chimed somewhere nearby. She ought to hurry back to her flat to get her things packed before her father arrived.

She walked into the city, feeling the heat rising from the paving slabs. After hesitating briefly, she walked up Archbishop Street and knocked at the office door. It was opened by Wilson, a briefcase under his arm. He was wearing an open-necked shirt and no tie.

'Hello, Margarita.' He studied her face. 'Any more news about your young man?'

She shook her head. 'Nothing good.'

'I'm sorry. I wish there was something I could do. Although . . .' He waved the set of keys. 'I'm leaving.' He stepped out, then closed the door behind him before locking it.

'Oh.'

'Retiring,' he added, with a half-smile.

'I wanted to ask,' said Margarita, fumbling for the words, 'about Vera. I've been thinking . . . wondering . . . if we've got it wrong, somehow. If Vera . . .' She looked up at Wilson, and for a long moment their eyes met. Then he shook his head.

'Forget about Vera.'

'But what if she . . .'

'It's over,' said Wilson firmly, putting his keys into his pocket. 'She's going to be executed. You do understand that? She was flown to Cairo a few days ago.'

Margarita sagged. 'Oh. I see.'

'Vera knew what she was doing,' said Wilson. He hesitated. 'You must leave this alone, Margarita. Do you understand? It's over.'

She stared at him numbly, then nodded. He held out his hand and shook hers, holding it tightly. He smiled at her in a fatherly way, as he had done the first time they met.

'I wish you the best of luck.'

Margarita watched Wilson walk away and out of sight. He looked more relaxed than she had ever seen him and she wondered vaguely who was responsible for his abrupt retirement. He didn't look sorry to be leaving.

The clock chimed the quarter. Margarita hurried to the bus stop. Before long, she was alighting in Floriana, where she walked the short distance to her flat between palm trees and beds of bright snapdragons. Her father would be here soon. By nightfall, they would be back at the farm on Gozo with Livia and there would be good food and long walks and lazy days by the sea.

As Margarita went up the stairs to the flat, she could not help thinking of that night when Vera had arrived, her clothes damp, after a trip to Tunis, and they had talked like friends.

She remembered Vera's description of a diplomatic party she had attended in London as a child – the dancing, the candlelight, and the boy, a naval cadet, who had talked and laughed with her. His father was someone important. He had advised Vera to embrace her freedom, as he could not. *A life in the service of others . . .* Margarita stopped abruptly halfway up the stairs.

The king had insisted on continuing his visit to Malta and had requested a tour of the gardens at Verdala Palace. Perhaps he knew Vera, had known her since they were children. Perhaps he was confident because he knew he had nothing to fear.

With a jolt, Margarita remembered the crack of Vera's rifle, then saw her at Corradino Prison, turning to look over her shoulder before she was taken away, a sly smile on her face.

Chapter 65

Rome, 1933

At Roma Termini, Vera stepped down from the train with her small case. She made her way along the platform and out onto the busy concourse where hundreds of people were waiting.

Vera saw a girl with a suitcase, probably in her early twenties, standing alone, fiddling with the ticket in her hand and glancing anxiously up at the departures board. For a moment she felt a powerful sense of déjà vu, as if the last seven years had never happened, and she was waiting in London for the train that would take her to Paris and eventually to Aleppo.

She had been young and very naïve when she had first gone to Syria. Even after Curzon's death, when she felt almost invincible, there had been times of fear and panic as the mantle she had inherited settled on her shoulders.

More than once, in the years that followed, she had thought of giving it up, but she knew they would kill her if she did. And she was good at it, there was no doubt about that. She did the job that was expected of her, absorbed information, filing it away for a day when it might be useful – to whom, she wasn't sure, but knowledge meant power.

When Hitler was appointed chancellor, Vera knew that the day had arrived. Shortly after her honeymoon with Henry, she had travelled to London to see an old friend, who had arranged this meeting in Rome.

She had been given an address, an anonymous office, and they were expecting her. She saw the receptionist's eyes settle on the flower that was pinned to her lapel before she was ushered quickly up the back stairs to a large but almost empty study, where she was left alone. An African mask hung on the wall, but there were no other decorations.

At last, the door opened and a man came in. He was stocky, with a thick head of greying hair and his features were strong but unmemorable.

'Edward Haywood,' he said, shaking her hand and looking her in the eye. She knew it wasn't his real name. 'You must be Mrs Dunn.'

'Vera.'

'You've friends in high places, Mrs Dunn,' he said, ignoring her words as he sat heavily in his chair, watching her closely. 'I agreed to this meeting as a courtesy to the individual who requested it.'

'I gather you don't like using women as agents,' she said. To her satisfaction, he looked put out.

'That's a generalisation,' said Haywood at last. 'It's no slight on your sex.'

'The fact is, Mr Haywood, I am irrevocably involved already,' said Vera. 'If you don't want me, I shall simply try elsewhere. But I understand that you are the best. I don't mean to flatter you. I came to you because our mutual friend sent me here.'

She paused, expecting him to be angry, but he looked thoughtful. 'I know a little about you, Mrs Dunn. You're clever and extremely dangerous.'

'Then you know you can use me.'

'I don't doubt your abilities. But the question is whether I can trust you.'

Vera shrugged. 'I've proven myself before and I'll do it again. I'll do whatever it takes to show that I can be of use.'

'Is that all you want?'

She raised an eyebrow. 'I don't want money, if that's what you mean.'

Haywood shook his head. 'Some people come to us because they want to make amends for things they've done in the past.'

'My soul is beyond saving,' said Vera wryly, but she looked at him seriously. 'I believe, as I'm sure you do, that there will be another war. Not next year, perhaps not for ten years, but it will come eventually. I intend to do everything in my power to stop the fascists from winning it.'

'Very well,' said Haywood suddenly. She caught his eye and saw steel there. 'I'm setting up a new organisation in which you could be very useful. But there can't be any surprises, Mrs Dunn. I'll need you to tell me everything, from the beginning. I need to know all of it.'

'I'll tell you,' said Vera, and she knew it would be the last time she told anyone what she had become. There was no going back once she had shared her past with him – they would be bound for the rest of their lives. 'And what then?'

The spymaster looked up at her and smiled thinly, his eyes flicking to the snowdrop on her lapel. 'Then we get to work.'

Chapter 66

In a military prison close to the Nile, a guard stood outside a cell, listening to the faint noises echoing from around the building.

The prisoner was asleep. Glancing through the observation flap, Fletcher could see her short dark hair on the pillow and the slow rise and fall of her shoulders as she slept. She had bade him goodnight an hour earlier, her manner, as always, cool but mildly flirtatious.

'Oh – that submarine you asked for news of – the *Tenacious*?'

'Yes,' she had said, leaning forward keenly.

'Most of the crew were saved. It was in the paper today. The sub was torpedoed but the survivors were rescued by fishermen somewhere off Sicily. The captain's been tipped for a gallantry medal. He's on his way home.'

'I'm very glad to hear it,' she had said. 'Thank you.'

He knew what she'd done and it was hard to reconcile the whispers about the Nazi spy with the woman before him. But it would all be over soon.

Fletcher heard footsteps in the corridor and saw another guard approaching.

'The Colonel wants to see you,' said Jones. 'Told me to switch with you.'

'Any clue what it's about?'

'No idea,' said Jones, shrugging. He yawned and looked at the cell door. 'Any trouble from her ladyship?'

'All quiet,' said Fletcher. 'She's been asleep for an hour or so.'

Feeling unsettled, he marched briskly through the building, wondering why he was being summoned. He had guarded the prisoner every night since her arrival.

The Colonel looked tired, his face craggy in the flickering lamplight.

'You asked for me, sir?' Fletcher said, saluting.

'At ease, Corporal. I'm sending you home. You've done a lot of overtime recently. Have the rest of the night off and then take a day's leave to recharge.'

'That's good of you, sir. Why?'

'Does it matter? Get your things. You're off duty.'

Fletcher closed the door and trudged away along the corridor. He had expected to be able to say goodbye to the prisoner, but that was out of the question now. He would not see her again. By the time he returned to work, she would be dead.

He sighed. It was best this way. He had pitied her a little, but she was dangerous and her death was inevitable. Perhaps they had disapproved of his conversations with her and suspected that he would not be able to do his job properly when the time came.

There was no fear of that, he thought, as he returned his weapon to the armoury. But still. Perhaps it was for the best. He put her out of his mind and hurried home.

*

Six guards marched through the long corridors of the prison. Two came first, followed by the prisoner, who was manacled and hooded. To her left and right were two more guards, each holding her arms to stop her from tripping.

She had put in a request to be allowed to wear her own clothes for the execution, but it had been denied, and so she wore the shapeless garments that had been issued on arrival.

Her footsteps were silent. They made their way into the depths of the building, until all outside sounds faded away and even the hoots of steamers on the Nile could no longer be heard.

At last, the guards paused outside a door; it was unlocked from within and they proceeded inside.

The journalists who came to the prison each day had not been told the exact date of the execution. They would be told in the morning, when it was certain that everything had gone to plan.

The guards stood back against the wall and the hangman led the prisoner to the gallows.

He wondered if she understood what was happening to her. They said that she had been a brilliant spy, so she must have known, but it was impossible to tell her emotions under the black hood, and she said nothing. As he propelled her by the shoulders, he could feel the slight frame. He never allowed emotion to interfere, although he felt faintly sorry for everyone who came through his chamber, whatever they had done.

She stood very still on the platform as he adjusted the rope. At last he moved away and he could see her tense, listening to the creaking of the boards as he trod on them, and the distant sounds of the prison.

He looked at his watch. It was time. On the stroke of midnight, the lever was pulled, the floor fell away, the rope snapped taut, and Nero died.

Epilogue

A hundred miles away, in the harbour at Alexandria, the *Supreme* readied itself for departure. The steward welcomed the few passengers who were boarding, holding out his hand to a woman in a headscarf.

She smiled graciously and thanked him before making her way to the upper deck. She stood at the rail, looking back at the gently twinkling lights of the city and watching the last few people come aboard.

Eventually, she heard a soft hoot and felt the ship begin to move beneath her. The lights of Alexandria started to recede. She took a last look and then made her way down to her cabin, where a decanter of whisky was waiting. The ship picked up speed and soon nothing could be seen from the portholes except darkness and the occasional gleam of moonlight on the wide, restless sea.

Author's Note

While this story is fictional, some aspects of it are based in reality. King George VI did visit Malta on 20 June 1943, in order to raise morale among the brave citizens of the war-torn island, to which he had awarded the George Cross the year before, and he really did have lunch at Verdala Palace with the governor, Lord Gort. I drew on eyewitness reports of the day when describing his arrival on the *Aurora* and his itinerary as he toured the island.

Throughout the book, I aimed to follow the true timeline of the war as closely as possible, so military events in North Africa, the Middle East, and mainland Europe took place largely as described.

The re-invasion of Europe, specifically how it would begin, was one of the most carefully guarded secrets in British military history. It was feared that enemy agents would discover the plan to invade Sicily – known as Operation Husky – and so various misinformation schemes were launched, including the most famous, Operation Mincemeat, which has featured in numerous books and films.

There was, to my knowledge, no Nazi spy known as Nero, and I have taken enormous liberties in writing Nero's story, although it does occasionally coincide with reality. There are numerous examples of men and women who risked their lives as double or triple agents before and during the Second World War, notably Juan Pujol García, the Spaniard codenamed Garbo who created a web of fictitious agents in order to pass bogus information to German high command. With the aid of his SIS handlers, he invented details of operations, troop movements, and entire ghost armies – peppered with snippets of real information – that successfully befuddled his Nazi employers into wasting time and resources and prevented them from discovering important information until it was too late (not least the date and location of the Normandy landings).

Smuggling between Sicily and Malta was common in this period, as was espionage. In 1942, Carmelo Borg Pisani, a Maltese fascist who had become an Italian citizen, arrived in Malta by boat to gather information for the hoped-for invasion of the island by the Axis. He was caught and interned at Corradino Prison, and was executed by hanging six months later. He was called a martyr by Mussolini and is still commemorated by the far right in Italy and Malta.

There is no suggestion that King George VI was directly involved in espionage activities (although he would have been regularly briefed by the prime minister on what was unfolding, and he and his family were enlisted in 1944 to help conceal the details of the D-Day landings by making misleading troop visits). That element of the story is entirely my fabrication, as is the attempt on his life which takes place in the novel, although there were doubtless many who wished to harm him.

Edward Haywood, the spymaster who brings Vera into the fold in 1933, is loosely based on Claude Dansey, the wartime deputy chief of SIS often known as Colonel Z (he also used the name Haywood as an alias). Dansey is generally credited with the development of spying as we know it today. Until 1936, he worked undercover in Rome as passport control officer, while covertly setting up a Europe-wide network of secret agents known as Z section. During the war he was placed in overall charge of all active espionage operations. It is believed that he had agents embedded in the upper echelons of the Third Reich, but, as his biographers say, 'he and his successors chose to protect them in the best possible way: by denying they ever existed' (Anthony Read and David Fisher, *Colonel Z: The Life and Times of a Master of Spies*, 1984).

Most of the activities of the intelligence operatives in this book are, by necessity, my own invention, but I found a great deal of useful background information in the many available books about the history of the intelligence and security services. To borrow a line from Terry Pratchett, writers generally have to infer from revealed self-evident wisdom (make it up) and extrapolate from associated sources (read a lot of stuff that other people have made up). For all the things I have doubtless got wrong (or deliberately distorted), I can only hold my hands up. Facts are helpful for novel-writing but sometimes they get in the way.

Vera's archaeological experiences in Syria were influenced by the recollections of Agatha Christie, who wrote extensively about her lengthy visits to digs in Syria, Iraq and Egypt. Her second husband, Max Mallowan, was a well-known archaeologist, and Christie herself worked hard – on a voluntary basis – at each dig site, including making drawings of finds and developing photographs. Her memoir of those years – *Come, Tell Me How You Live* – is a delight, hugely funny as well as educational. I hope it will be possible in my lifetime to visit Syria; for sadly obvious reasons, my explorations there were confined to the page, notably the works of Gertrude Bell and Freya Stark.

I made several visits to Malta while writing this book to research the locations and talk to knowledgeable people. I am grateful to Anthony Mifsud, the caretaker at Verdala Palace (these days closed to the public), who kindly gave me a private tour after my hopeful email. He was hugely informative about its history and architecture and allowed me to go up onto the roof so I could see how the towers were accessed and showed me the entrance to the secret passage. References in the book to the layout of the Palace and its gardens broadly follow the reality, but I have filled in the blanks and taken great liberties in imagining the day of the king's visit.

The network of tunnels under Valletta used as bomb shelters still exists, as do the Lascaris War Rooms, sunk deep in the rock beside the harbour, which are open to the public and give a fascinating insight into how the war in the Mediterranean was directed and fought.

Other trips took me around Sicily by train, where I visited Agrigento and San Leone, and to Egypt, to explore Cairo and Alexandria. In both cases I found myself visiting locations long after I had written the relevant scenes, so it was a useful exercise, matching fiction to reality and finding out how accurate my earnest internet research had been.

I am grateful to everyone involved in the publication of this book, in particular my agent Charlotte Colwill, for her ongoing support and commitment to my writing. At Bonnier, thank you to Salma Begum, Claire Johnson-Creek and the rest of the team for their hard work. Getting a book out is a long process that involves a lot of people, and I appreciate all of them.

Thank you to Elaine Harper and Anna Millward, both of whom read the book at various stages and gave me valuable feedback and suggestions (and in Anna's case let me borrow her surname!). I'm grateful for your generous comments and ideas, many of which were implemented. Thank you to Sam Cooper, my Egyptian travelling companion, with whom I stood by the harbour at Alexandria and imagined a secret agent disappearing into the night. Thank you to everyone who has been supportive and said nice things about my first book – it certainly helped when writing the second!

Finally, a huge thank you to my family for their unwavering support and input on the manuscript: my parents, Pete Blench and Felicity Norman, to whom this book is dedicated, my sister Daisy Blench, and my partner Mark Wheeldon, who willingly accompanied me on numerous research expeditions and listened to me plotting aloud. Thank you all for your love and support!

If you enjoyed *Secrets of Malta* don't miss Cecily Blench's debut novel . . .

It's 1941 and Kate is living in Rangoon, Burma. A world away from her traditional English upbringing, she is bewitched by the country and the kindness of the Burmese people. When Edwin, a young teacher from London, starts working in the government office with her, a friendship develops between them. But Kate can sense that Edwin has secrets and is looking for a place to call home – something she shares.

As their bond grows, Kate begins to understand Edwin's past and the tragic events that brought them both to Burma. But war is coming and, when the Japanese invade, Kate and Edwin are forced to flee, along with thousands of others. They begin a perilous journey to India but soon become separated. As Kate continues alone, she can't get the troubled young man she has come to care so deeply for out of her head.

With the fallout of war all around them, in a place far from home, will Kate and Edwin survive their journey and find the new beginning they both seek?

Available now